W9-BCC-727

CHARGE!

Foster grabbed his gun as a trio of helmeted men trotted into sight. They seemed oblivious to the fact that they were all within easy range of the rifled slugs in Foster's riotgun as they jogged forward. His first shot—fired mostly in warning—plowed up dust and stone shards a few feet in front of their muddy boots. But when they started firing back, he decided to stop being civilized and to start playing for keeps.

At his second shot, a mob of at least a dozen of the helmeted men poured from among the outbuildings, shouting and waving long, heavy swords. Foster opened fire carefully, making every slug count. He got five before they broke; the sixth one he shot in the back.

He was relaxing for a minute, feeling for his canteen, when a section of the wall behind him fell away and several pairs of strong hands dragged him down, into blackness. . . .

GREAT SCIENCE FICTION from SIGNET

☐ **SWORDS OF THE HORSECLANS (Horseclans #2)**
   by Robert Adams. (#E9988—$2.50)*

☐ **A CAT OF SILVERY HUE (Horseclans #4) by Robert Adams.**
   (#AE1579—$2.25)*

☐ **THE SAVAGE MOUNTAINS (Horseclans #5)**
   by Robert Adams. (#AJ1589—$1.95)

☐ **THE PATRIMONY (Horseclans #6) by Robert Adams.**
   (#AE1238—$2.25)*

☐ **HORSECLANS ODYSSEY (Horseclans #7) by Robert Adams.**
   (#E9744—$2.75)*

☐ **THE DEATH OF A LEGEND (Horseclans #8)**
   by Robert Adams. (#AE1126—$2.50)*

☐ **KILLBIRD by Zach Hughes.** (#E9263—$1.75)

☐ **PRESSURE MAN by Zach Hughes.** (#J9498—$1.95)*

☐ **TIME GATE by John Jakes.** (#Y7889—$1.25)

☐ **BEYOND THIS HORIZON by Robert A. Heinlein.**
   (#J9833—$1.95)

☐ **PLANET OF THE APES by Pierre Boulle.** (#E8632—$1.25)

☐ **GREYBEARD by Brian Aldiss.** (#E9035—$1.75)

☐ **JACK OF SHADOWS by Roger Zelazny.** (#E9370—$1.75)

*Prices slightly higher in Canada

CASTAWAYS IN TIME

By
Robert Adams

Ⓢ
A SIGNET BOOK
NEW AMERICAN LIBRARY
TIMES MIRROR

Publisher's Note

This novel is a work of fiction. Names, characters, places, and incidents are either the product of the author's imagination or are used fictitiously, and any resemblance to actual persons, living or dead, events, or locales is entirely coincidental.

Copyright © 1979 by Robert Adams

All rights reserved, including the right to reproduce this book in any form whatsoever without permission in writing from the publisher, except for brief passages in connection with a review.

Published by arrangement with Starblaze Editions of The Donning Company/Publishers

 SIGNET TRADEMARK REG. U.S. PAT. OFF. AND FOREIGN COUNTRIES
REGISTERED TRADEMARK—MARCA REGISTRADA
HECHO EN CHICAGO, U.S.A.

SIGNET, SIGNET CLASSICS, MENTOR, PLUME, MERIDIAN AND NAL BOOKS are published by The New American Library, Inc., 1633 Broadway, New York, New York 10019

First Signet Printing, April, 1982

1 2 3 4 5 6 7 8 9

PRINTED IN THE UNITED STATES OF AMERICA

To Robert Bloch

PROLOGUE

Raibert Armstrong sat his fine, tall, long-legged horse—spoils of this extended reaving—atop a low-browed ridge, just above the sleeping camp of his largish band. Every so often, he would take the slowmatch from out the clamp and whirl it around several times in the air before once more securing it back into the serpentine of his clumsy arquebus, for if that scurvy, ill-natured pig of a Seosaidh Scot who had robbed him of his well-earned sleep and set him to this useless, thankless task should come by and find his match unlit, he surely would set about thrashing Raibert. And Raibert would then have to kill the bully and then, even if he were fortunate enough to escape north to Armstrong lands, he would be forever marked as the man who brought back into being the long, costly, bloody feud betwixt the two clans, and it ended but less than a score of years.

Of a sudden, the horse raised its well-formed head and snorted, dancing in place, its small ears twitching forward. Then, faintly, Raibert heard it too—a deep, but blaring, buglelike sound, seemingly coming from somewhere beyond the slightly higher ridge on the other side of the camp of nearly two thousand sleeping Lowlander Scots.

Raibert gave the beast just enough knee to set it to a distance-eating trot, loath to gallop so marvelous a prize when he could see but dimly the way ahead. He took time to blow upon that slowmatch, but then, as he harbored scant faith in the ability of the ancient, ill-balanced and woefully inaccurate firelock to accomplish anything more of value than a loud noise to alert the camp, he reined up long enough to check by a vagrant beam of moonlight that the priming had not shaken from out the pan of his new wheellock pistol. He also made certain that the falchion was loose in the sheath—the broad, thick, heavy blade was centuries older than the elderly arquebus, but cold steel was at least always dependable, if well-honed and hard-swung.

At the foot of the higher ridge, the Armstrong clansman blew one last time upon the smoldering match, then snapped the metal ring of the shoulder strap to the similar ring in the weapon's wooden stock so that when its single charge had been fired he could drop it to dangle, leaving both hands free for horse-handling and bladework.

All preparations for alarm and battle complete, he set his prize horse to the heather-thick ridge, a sudden gust of night wind, blowing down cold from off the distant highlands and the icy seas beyond, whipping his *breacan-feile* about his shoulders and tugging at the flat bonnet he wore over his rusty mail coif.

But at the ridge crest, Raibert Armstrong reined up with such suddenness and force that the horse almost reared. Up the opposite slope, headed directly for him, was a monster, an eldritch demon surely loosed by none other than Auld Clootie, Himself, and straight from a deeper pit of Hell!

No less than six eyes had the demon—four glaring a blinding, soulless white, the lowest-set pair a feral, beastly yellow-amber. Of the rest of the demon, Raibert could descry but little, save a dense, dark mass, low to the ground, wheezing and whining, snorting and bellowing its bloodlust as it eassayed the steep slope. The hornlike bellowing was constant, as if the creature had no need to pause and take fresh breath.

Perhaps it did not need to breathe air at all? What man, priest or lay, truly knew aught of the bodily working of a Fiend from Hell? Certainly not Calum Armstrong's son, Raibert. Nor did he intend to learn more, not at any close proximity.

Moaning with his terror of the Unearthly, he had reined the skittish horse half about when the monster changed its course, bearing off to Raibert's left. Seeking the gentler slope of the ridge, was it? Or was the diabolical Thing seeking rather to flank him, to place its awesomeness twixt him and the camp?

At the new angle, whereat the glaring eyes did not so blind

him, Raibert could discern more of this foul Thing—long as a good-sized wain, it was, but far lower. He could see no part of the legs for the high-grown heather, but he suspected it to possess at least a score, to move it so fast across the rising, uneven ground.

But most sinister of all, he could now see that a dozen or more warlocks—or were they manshaped fiends?—were borne upon the thrice-damned Beast's back, all bearing blue-black Rods of Power.

Whimpering, Raibert Armstrong still set himself to do his sworn duty, despite his quite-justifiable horror. He presented the heavy shoulder gun and, taking dead aim downward into the thick of the knot of manlike creatures, he drew back the pan cover, his fingers so tremulous that they almost spilled out the priming powder. Once again, he checked his aim at the Beast lumbering below his position, shut his eyes tight, then drew back the lower arm of the serpentine, thrusting the match end clamped to the tip of the upper arm into the pow-der-filled priming pan. He braced himself for the powerful kick of the piece.

But that kick never came; the match had smoldered out. And still the glaring, blaring Thing lumbered across the low saddle, leaving smoking heather wherever its demon feet had trod, excreting fire and roils of noxious gases from some-where beneath its awful bulk.

Dropping the useless arquebus, Raibert sensed that his only chance now lay in escape—for who ever heard of a lone, common man trying to fight a Monster out of Hell with only a pistol and an old *chlaidhimh*?—and while he could go back the way he had come, the Monster seemed headed that way too . . . and Raibert felt that that was just what the hellish Thing wanted him to do.

There seemed but one thing for it, in Raibert Armstrong's mind; he must try—with Christ's help—to outfox the eldritch Beast. Reining about, he trotted the frightened, but still obedient, horse a few yards back along the ridge crest, as if he were blindly falling into the Monster's coils. Then, sud-denly, he drew his antique *chlaidhimh*—for, if die he must, far better to do so with a yard of steel in his freckled fist; and besides, touch of iron or steel was held by some to be inimi-cal to the Auld Evil—wheeled that hot-bred hunter about and spurraked a full gallop, leaning low on the animal's neck to lessen wind resistance.

Where the hill abruptly dropped away, the horse hesitated

but the briefest instant, then launched itself in a long jump which sent ridden and rider soaring overtop the still-soaring six-eyed monster.

The horse alit on the slope below and to the right flank of the unheeding Hellspawn, then Raibert Armstrong was spurring northward, toward the ill-defined border, toward Scotland and his ancestral home. Forgot were the near two thousand reavers, forgot was the raid upon the interdicted Sassenachs, forgot was Sir David Scott and all. But Raibert Armstrong knew that never, until the very hour of his death, would he, could he forget the sight and the sound and the hot, oily, evil stench of the Devilspawn Horror he had faced on the Northumbrian Moors on that dark and windswept night.

put the hristian instant, they launched itself in a slow pitch which sent everything and rider... convulsive cast all revolving

CHAPTER 1

Bass Foster sat directly under the ceiling vent, bathed in the cool flow from the air conditioner, watching the Collier woman swill straight vodka and trying to think of a tactful way to cut her off—his modest supply of potables would not last long under her inroads; she had guzzled the last of the gin hours ago.

The professor, her husband, seemed to have barely touched his own weak highball, but he had used the last of the tobacco in his own pouch and now was stuffing his pipe out of one of Bass's cans of Borkum Riff. Mid-fiftyish—which made him some ten years Bass's senior—he seemed as quiet and courteous as his wife was loud and snotty. His liver-spotted hands moving slowly, he frowned in concentration over the pipe, his bushy salt-and-pepper eyebrows bunched into a single line.

Across the width of the oversized cocktail table from the couple, Krystal Kent sat with one long leg tucked beneath her, doing yeoman work on a half-gallon jug of Gallo burgundy, and taking hesitant drags at one of her last three cigarettes. Bass shifted his eyes to her; she was far nicer to look at, with the sunlight delineating bluish highlights in her long, lustrous black hair.

Bass and the other three carefully avoided looking out the big window at the impossiblity that commenced beyond the manicured lawn. Each time Bass's thoughts even wandered in that direction he felt his mind reel, start to slip, and he assumed the others suffered the same, for all the five people who now shared his house had seemed in one degree or another of shock when first they had arrived at his doors—the Colliers at the front, the other three at the back, first Krystal Kent, then Dave Atkins and the grubby little teenager who went by the name of Susan Sunshine.

Eschewing chairs, the two were lying side by side on the wall-to-wall carpet before Bass's stereo. One of his very few tapes of acid rock was in place and both Dave and Susan had fitted padded earphones on their heads. They, at least, were not slopping up their host's booze; Dave had rolled a double-thick joint—of the diameter of an ordinary cigarette and almost as long—and, smilingly, they were passing it back and forth. Despite the efforts of the air conditioner, the room already contained an acrid reek of burning rope.

According to the story given by Collier when first he and his wife had arrived, yesterday noon—both of them soaking wet and he slimed all over with reddish-brown mud, his hands and shirtfront smudged as well with greasy black grime—they had been driving from Chapel Hill, North Carolina, to Washington, D.C., had gone off at the incorrect beltway exit, become lost and spent seeming hours driving the backroads and byways of rural Maryland. Finally, a blowout of their right rear tire had forced a stop on a muddy shoulder under the driving rain of the approaching storm.

While Arbor Collier sat and fumed in the car, nipping at one of the several pints of gin she had hidden in various locations for the long trip, Collier had jacked up the aging Ford and gotten the wheel off with much effort and was kneeling in the slippery mud, putting the spare in place, when he felt the shoulder under him seem to become fluid . . . and Arbor had chosen that moment to open the passenger-side door and make to step out. Collier had tried to shout a warning, then he was falling. . . .

Seconds later, or eons, Collier had found himself lying—still muddy, still gripping his lug wrench—near the base of a stone wall. Arbor was sitting, dazed, a few feet away, in her sensible traveling suit and with her huge purse still slung from her shoulder. The grass directly under Collier was wet, but that surrounding him was dry as a bone under the bright, hot sun.

"*William!*" Arbor had shrieked. "Where *are* we? How . . . how did we get here and . . . where's our . . . car? All my clothes are in the car, William, my medicine and my vitamins, everything. You've got to find the car!"

She had continued the same selfish, shrewish litany all the way to Bass's trilevel—maybe a hundred feet. But when she discovered that Bass stocked a fair amount of the "medicine" she required, in varying proof and flavors, she had set about dosing herself, even taking a bottle of gin up to bed with her.

This morning, she had mechanically eaten the breakfast Bass and Krystal had together cooked, then had sought out the liquor cabinet. She had nagged her husband for a short while about Bass's lack of any more gin, but had soon settled on one of the couches with a water glass and a bottle of 100-proof vodka.

With his eyes on Krystal Kent's slender loveliness, Bass had allowed his mind to slip back to pleasurable thoughts of last night with her—two frightened people, taking solace and comfort in each other.

". . . ster Foster, I'm speaking to you!" The nasal, strident, supercilious voice was Arbor Collier's.

Bass turned his head to face her. "Uh, sorry, I was . . . was thinking, Mrs. Collier. What is it?"

Arbor smiled a nasty, knowing smirk. "Yes, I know the way you dirty men all think when you're looking at women the way you were looking at Miss Kent," she sniggered.

Bass felt his face going hot. Forcing calm, he inquired coldly, "If that was all you had on your pickled brain, Mrs. Collier, it could have been left unsaid. I don't like you any better than you apparently like me. If we continue to ignore each other, maybe we can make it through the day without coming to blows."

"*Mr.* Foster," hissed Arbor, clenching her half-glassful of vodka until her bony knuckles shone white, "you are a rude, crude lout, ill-bred and uneducated; I knew that the minute I met you. You are the type one thinks of whenever one speaks of 'dirty old men'—a lewd, low, lascivious, middle-aged Lothario. I think—"

"I don't know how you *can* think, Mrs. Collier, with all the booze you've been slopping down since breakfast," said Bass in frigid tones, adding, "And I warn you, ma'am, if you don't just shut up, I'm going to heave you out that door on your damned ear!"

Arbor raised her plucked brows, then nodded. "The final argument of barbarians, force. But let me warn you, Mr.

Foster, my husband served with the OSS, during the war. They were taught how to kill with their bare hands."

"Now Arbor," Professor Collier began. "You know that I never left Wash—"

"Shut up, William!" she snarled. "*I'm* talking to this male chauvinist pig!"

Then she returned her attention to Bass. "I *insist*, Mr. Foster, that you make those two, filthy, disgusting hippies stop using narcotics in this house."

Before Bass could frame an answer not obscene and physically impossible, Krystal Kent spoke up.

"Mrs. Collier, they're smoking pot . . . marijuana. It's not a narcotic, it's a hallucinogen, and—"

"Miss Kent," Arbor snapped coldly, "I was addressing Mr. Foster, if you please. I, for one, do not care to have my friends hear that my husband and I were arrested at a house where a dope orgy was going on."

Krystal threw back her head and laughed throatily. "*Orgy?* Two kids smoking a joint? You call that an orgy? I've heard of prudes, in my time, but you—"

Arbor pursed thin lips. "Prudence, *Miss* Kent, is not prudery. Though I suppose a woman of your kind would call anyone less licentious than herself a prude."

"And just what," snapped Krystal brittlely, "is that remark supposed to mean, *Mrs.* Collier? What kind of woman do you type me as? Or, need I really ask?"

The older woman picked up the half-full glass, drained it effortlessly, and smirked. "Oh, Miss Kent, do you really think my husband and I didn't *hear* you sneaking up the hall and into Mr. Foster's room, last night? Think we didn't have to endure the sounds of the unhallowed filth you two committed together?"

"What the hell business of yours is it," Krystal grated from between clenched teeth, "whether or not Bass and I sexed last night . . . or any other time, for that matter?"

Arbor's death's-head face assumed the look of a martyr. "*Mr.* Foster would not allow my husband—and my husband is a full professor, *with tenure,* and he holds no less than six doctorates!—and me the use of his big, airy room and a *private* bath, no, he showed us into that squalid little guest room, with that old, musty bed." Abruptly, the martyred look disappeared, to be replaced with a cold anger.

Professor Collier had again snapped out of his study. "Now Arbor, dear," he said slowly and tiredly, "this is Mr.

Foster's house, and who but he has better right to the master bedroom? He wasn't in any degree obligated to afford us accommodations, you know. I feel—"

"You feel?" snarled his wife. "You feel? Why, you bumbling, overeducated jackass! You, William Willingham Collier, never had a feeling, an emotion, in your life! You're so weak, so passive-natured that anyone can manipulate you . . . and generally they do, too. That's why you weren't even really considered for department head when that old queer Dr. Ellison died.

"If I played dutiful little wife and left it to you, I'd be nothing but a doormat for all the world to walk on. God knows, in the twenty-two years I've been married to you, I've *tried* to make something of you, make you something I could be proud of, but . . ."

Stonefaced, Krystal picked up her glass and the winejug and padded into the kitchen. Foster, too, felt embarrassment at being unavoidably privy to what should have been a private matter.

Muttering, "My ice is all melted," to no one in particular, he followed the young woman.

But even with the door to the dining room firmly shut, still the pudgy woman's strident tones penetrated.

". . . in one ear and out the other. You've *never* heeded any advice I've ever given you, *never* stood up to people the way you should, the way a *real* man would. You're always off in a fog somewhere, like you just were; allowing your own wife—a good, decent, Christian woman—to be compelled to be around degenerate dope addicts and fornicators and, for all we know, adulterers and perverts, and you didn't open your mouth once. No, as usual, *I* had to be the one to protest these outrages against decency and God's Law. You always, you *have* always . . ."

In unvoiced concord, both Foster and Krystal descended the three steps to the laundryroom-workshop and thence to the spacious den. The addition of two more closed doors finally made the noise emanating from the living room almost inaudible.

Krystal sank into the fake-fur double lounge, shaking her head. "Oh, that dear, sweet, gentle man. Bass, just think of it! Twenty-two *years* in hell! Christ, I'm ready to kill the bitch after only twenty-odd *hours*."

Foster shrugged. "Human beings have a bad habit of manufacturing their own hells, Krys. I'm sure Collier didn't

9

marry her at gunpoint." He grinned. "He doesn't strike me as the type.

"I just hope," he went on as he seated himself beside her and placed a hand on her bare knee, "that your father doesn't have a shotgun."

She almost smiled. "Poor Poppa doesn't know one end of any gun from the other."

"Big, mean, nasty brothers, then?" he probed.

"I only have one brother, Bass, and he ran off to Canada to keep from getting drafted. He's still there . . . living on the money Momma sneaks out of what Poppa gives her."

"Oh, your brother was an anti-war activist?"

She barked a short, humorless laugh. "Baby Brother Seymour *said* that he opposed 'the unjust, illegal war,' of course, but that's not really the reason he cut out. He was just afraid somebody might force an honest day's work out of him, for the first time in his pampered, sheltered life, that's all. The snotty little leech! If he wasn't so goddamned lazy, he wouldn't have flunked out of dental school and been liable to the draft to start out."

"Not much love lost on your little brother, is there?" Foster chuckled. "Don't you ever feel guilty about hating your own flesh and blood, Krys?"

Her short, softly waving dark-brown hair rippled to the shake of her head. "Brother Seymour's not worth a hate, or a shit, for that matter. I don't hate him, Bass, I despise him. He's never ever tried to do one damned thing to please Poppa and Momma, while I've always broken my ass to make them happy, to make myself into a person they could take pride in . . . that's why I thought it so unjust, so unfair, that he should be fat and spoiled and utterly useless and alive up in Canada, while I . . ." She trailed off into silence, a sudden fear darkening her eyes.

"While you what, Krys?" There was all at once an almost-desperate intensity in Foster's voice. "While your brother was alive in Canada and you *what*? What were you about to say?"

But Krystal maintained her silence. Arising, she took glass and jug with her when she strode over to the sliding glass door, opened it and took a step onto the concrete patio, then she half turned. Her voice low but as intense as his own, she said, "Please, Bass, let it go . . . let it go, for now. If things keep going as good for you and me as they promise to, I'll

10

tell you . . . I promise. But, please, just let me alone for a while; I have to think."

Alone for almost the first time in the last full day, Foster faced the fact that he, himself, had some thinking to do.

Just what in hell *had* happened?

He remembered the big, beefy state trooper, soaking wet in the driving rain and shouting to make himself heard above the storm, the rushing of the near-floodstage river and the roaring of the 'copter.

"A'right, Foster, I ain' got no right to force you to abandon yore prop'ty, but I done tol' you the way she's stacked. The river's goin' to crest ten, fifteen foot higher'n it is right now, and way yore house's sitchated, it'll be at leas' two foot of water in the top level, even if you don' get undermined an' come all apart.

"An' thishere's the las' roun' the choppuh's gonna make, an' yore friggin' lil boat won' las' two hoots in hell in thet river, iffen you change your min' later. So, you sure you ain' comin' with us?"

Foster shook his head forcefully. "No. No thank you, officer, I appreciate it, but no."

The trooper blew at the water cascading off his nose. "A'right, citizen, it's yore funeral . . . iffen we evuh fin' yore body, thet is."

And he remembered sitting in that same living room now filled with the bitchy sounds of Arbor Collier. He remembered watching the rampant river tear away his small runabout, then his dock, sweeping both downstream along with its other booty—animal, vegetable and mineral.

He remembered thinking that that trooper had been right, he had been a fool to remain, but then he had sunk everything he owned into this, his home, the only real property he had ever been able to call his. And he was damned if he would leave it to the ravages of wind and water or to the unwelcome attentions of the packs of looters sure to follow. Besides, he trusted less the dire pronouncements of "authorities" and "experts" than he did his own unexplainable dead certainty that both he and his house would, somehow, survive the oncoming disaster.

Not that that certainty had not been shaken a bit when, hearing odd noises from above, during a brief lull in the storm, he had discovered all three of his cats in the low attic, clinging tightly to the rafters and mewling feline moans of terror. All three—the huge, rangy black tom, the older, spayed queen, and the younger, silver Persian tom, which had been Carol's last gift to him—were good hunters, merciless killers, yet they shared the rafters with several flying squirrels plus a couple of small brown house mice . . . peaceably. That had been when he started getting worried and started calling himself a fool, aloud.

That was when he had decided to phone Herb Highgate, who lived a half mile upriver and who had, like Foster, vowed to stay with his house and property; but the phone proved dead. Then the lights went out, so he had dragged a chair over to the picture window, fetched a bottle, and sat, watching the inexorable rise of the angry gray water, reflecting upon the joys and sorrows, the victories and defeats, the wins and losses, which had marked his forty-five years of living. And, as the water level got higher and the bottle level got lower, he thought of Carol, grieved again, briefly, then began to feel that she was very near to him.

The hot, bright sun on his face had awakened him, had blinded him when first he opened his bleary eyes.

"Well, what the hell, I was right after all. *Christ*, my mouth tastes like used kitty litter. *Ugh!*"

Stumbling into the kitchen, he had flicked the wall switch from force of habit. And the light came on!

"Well, good God, those utilities boys are on the ball, for a change . . . either that or I slept a hell of a lot longer than usual. Well, since it's miracle time, let's have a go at the phone."

But the telephone had remained dead. With the coffee merrily perking, Foster had decided to walk out and see just how much damage his property had sustained.

He took two steps outside, looked about him in wondering disbelief, then reeled back inside. Slammed the door, locked it, threw the massive barrel bolt, sank down into the familiar chair, and cradled his head in his shaking hands. Drawing upon his last reserves of courage, he had, at some length, found the guts to look out the window, to see . . . to see . . .

It could not be called a castle, not in the accepted sense, although one corner of the U-shaped house incorporated a sixty-foot-tall stone tower, and the entire complex of buildings and grounds was girded by a high and thick wall of dressed stones, pierced with one large and two smaller ironbound gates.

A creepy-crawliness still gnawed at Foster whenever he looked across his well-tended lawn to behold, where the river used to be, the windows of that huge, archaic house, staring back at him like the empty eye sockets of a grinning death's-head.

House and tower and two stretches of wall were clearly visible, now, through the front window of the paneled den, and Foster forced down his repugnance in order to really study the view, this time. Compared to the wall, the house looked new, the stones of the house walls not only dressed, but polished and carved, as well. A wide stairway mounted up to a broad stoop—actually, rather more a terrace—on a level with the second story of the house, where was what was apparently the entrance door, recessed within a stone archway.

Shifting his gave to the walls, Foster could see that they were crenellated and wide enough for a couple of men to walk their tops abreast. But, in several places, the merlons were askew and at last one of the huge, square stones had fallen completely off its setting, back onto the top of the wall.

On sudden impulse, he arose and crossed to his guncase. Kneeling, he unlocked the bottom drawer and took out the pair of bulky 7x50 binoculars that had departed the army with him, years back. Then he dragged a chair closer to the window and set the optics to his eyes.

The details leapt out at him then . . . and some were more than a little sinister. The askew merlons all showed cracks and chips— recent, unweathered ones. There were cracks and scars, as well, on the rough masonry of the square, brownish-gray tower—obviously, on closer scrutiny, far older than either house or walls. But there was no visible damage to the house, nor could Foster detect any sign of life or movement anywhere within or about it.

Absorbed, he nearly jumped out of his skin when Krystal laid a hand on his shoulder. "Oh, God, you're a Peeping Tom! Why is it that every man I like turns out to be a kook?"

"Just trying to see what my new neighbors are like." He forced a grin and a light, bantering tone. "But nobody seems to be home."

Setting down the half empty wine jug, she sank onto her haunches beside the chair and reached for the binoculars. "May I?"

Wordlessly, he handed them over.

After adjusting the lenses, the young woman swiveled from left to right and back, slowly, studying details of the view. At length, she stiffened, then said in a low voice, "Bass, I . . . I could have sworn I saw some . . . something *move*. It was inside those windows just above the door to that . . . that *place*. Do you think . . . ?"

He shook his head and stood up. "Krys, I don't know what to think or imagine about any of the happenings of the last day, and I gave up trying several hours ago. The time's come to find a way to get into that building, for I've got a . . . a *feeling* that there's a lot of answers in there."

Opening again the drawer from which he had taken the binoculars, he removed a web pistol belt, two small web pouches, and a leather holster.

"Krys, if you can take a few seconds of that old biddy's yapping, I wonder if you'd go up to my bedroom and look in the closet. There's a brown canvas shell vest up there. You know what a shell vest looks like?"

She nodded.

"Okay, bring it down to me, huh? And the pair of army boots, too."

With only her long-suffering spouse for audience and sounding board, Arbor Collier had wound down and was lapping up alcohol in silence until Krystal came through the room. Then she smirked nastily.

"I'll bet I know what you two have been doing down there!" she crowed.

Krystal's smile was icily contemptuous. "A woman like you could read pornography into *Pilgrim's Progress*, but"—deviltry shone from her eyes and a hint of mockery entered her voice—"this time is so happens you're right. Bass and I spent all the time we were gone in mutual analingus. You should try it sometime."

Arobr Collier appeared to be still in shock when Krystal came back down the stairs with Foster's boots and vest. Glass clenched tightly in her hand, her jaw hanging slackly, she just stared at the younger woman in mute horror. The grin of triumph on Krystal's face abruptly dissipated, however, when she reentered the den to see Foster feeding shells into the loading gate of a short-barreled pump shotgun. The web belt was now clasped around his waist, and the holster clipped to it now contained a big automatic pistol, and as well as the two pouches, there was also a nasty-looking knife sheathed over his right hip, a coil of nylon rope and a canteen over his left, and an angled flashlight clipped opposite the holstered pistol.

"Good God, Bass! You said you were going to try to get into that house, but you look as if you're getting ready to go to war. A shotgun? A knife, I can see, but *two* guns?"

He kicked off his short Wellingtons and, sitting down, pulled on the jumpboots and began to lace them as he spoke.

"Krystal, I'm going to say some of this again, upstairs, but I'll say it to you first. We—none of us—really have the slightest idea *where* we are, *how* we got here, or *what* our situation actually is, now or in the future. The forty-odd years I've lived, my dear, have taught me at least one thing: when faced with the unknown, always expect and prepare for the worst; that way, you'll not be disappointed or taken by surprise."

Standing again, he shrugged his arms into the vest and crossed to the cabinet to begin slipping gun shells into the elastic loops, while continuing his monologue. "I really hope to God I am being overcautious, Krys, but I get bad vibes, as Dave would say, every time I look at that tower, even from this distance. And I'm going to be a helluva lot closer to it before long.

"Now, you haven't told me that awfully much about yourself, your background, I mean, but I get the impression sometimes that you're into psychology or psychiatry or medicine. Under the circumstances, just consider the Winchester"—he tapped the gleaming buttstock of the shotgun—"and my Colt as security blankets. Believe me, I'd feel damned insecure if I had to go closer to that tower without them. Damned insecure!"

She smiled then. "I'm sorry, Bass, you're right, of course. It's just that I was raised in a home where there were no guns—they're illegal to own in New York City, you know, and my father is a very law-abiding man. I got that feeling of . . . of lurking menace, of something so far beyond the ordinary as to be unnatural, supernatural, even, when I viewed the tower with your glasses, so you're most likely right to go prepared."

She stepped closer and swiftly kissed his lips. "Please be careful, Bass. Take care of yourself, huh? I've become very fond of you in a very short time."

Taking her head in his free hand, he returned her kiss, with interest. "You're a sweet gal, Krys, I'll do my best. Believe me. Now, please do me another favor. See if you can snap Dave out of his fog long enough to get him down here . . . and the Professor, too, I guess."

But only she and Collier came back into the den.

"Where's Dave?"

She shook her head disgustedly. "I suppose those two are into something other than, stronger than, grass; they're practically comatose up there. I did everything but kick him and he never even twitched."

"Okay." Foster nodded shortly, then asked, "Professor, have you ever fired a shotgun?" He proffered the Winchester Model 21 double twelve which had been his father's pride.

The older man took the fine weapon gingerly, touching only the wood surfaces. There was a hint of almost reverence in his voice when he said, "This piece is truly beautiful, Mr. Foster, a work of art, nothing less. But in answer, yes, I am conversant with most categories of firearms, though I do not hunt and have not owned a weapon since my marriage." With a note of apology, he added, "My wife, you see, considers the acquisition of firearms to be a dangerous waste of one's resources."

Foster ascended the broad stairs, feeling, as he had since the door of his home had closed behind him, the weight of unseen eyes upon him, feeling some sentience marking his progress from within the brooding pile he was reluctantly approaching.

The doors, when he got up to them, proved to be fabricated in some dark, dense-grained wood and liberally studded with nailheads each an inch or more in diameter. Nor was a knob or handle of any sort in evidence. The doors yielded as much to the shove of his shoulder as would have the high stone walls, so he made for the nearer row of windows. But only a cursory glance was necessary to dash his hopes of a quick and easy entry. The small, diamond-shaped panes were set in lead and could have been easily removed; however, a few inches behind them were heavy shutters, appearing to be of the same dense wood as the doors and looking every bit as resistant to penetration.

"Well," he muttered to himself, "we've only seen one side of this place, so far. Maybe . . ." Slowly, he set off to his right, walking well away from the house walls, but going nearer to examine each set of windows, only to find that all were as thoroughly secured as the first. The flagstones under his feet were, he noticed, fancifully carved, though rather worn-down in places. But no plant of any description sprouted between them, and this fact, added to that of the well-kept formal garden below, reinforced the feeling that, for all its lack of apparent life, this fine house was no deserted one.

As he turned the corner and started down the side he began to realize just how big this house was. "House, hell," he mumbled, "this is the size of a palace!"

But it was not until Foster had rounded to the rear that the awesome size of the structure became truly apparent. The paving of the side terrace blended into the plainer paving of a wide, deep courtyard stretching away from where he stood to lap about the base of that brooding tower, nearly a hundred feet away. Off to his right was a cluster of smaller buildings, most of stone but one or two of timber, the larger ones with roofs of slate, the smaller looking to be thatch or turf. The nearest of these buildings was pierced, just under the eave line, with rows of small, round holes, and Foster tried vainly to recall just where he had once seen a similar building.

It was then, however, that he noticed several birds fluttering and hopping about a darkish bundle lying near the foot of that grim tower. Resisting an impulse to cross the open courtyard, he set himself back to his original task, but every rear window as well as the two smaller doors he found were shuttered or tightly bolted from within.

The tower was certainly very much older than the mansion and outbuildings; its base was fabricated of massive, cyclopean stones, but the stonework was crude, primitive, and the only window he could see on this side—if "window" the foot-wide aperture could truly be called—was a good thirty feet above his head. Before he examined it in more detail, he decided to check out that object about which the birds still were congregating.

Foster gagged, his stomach heaving, as the interrupted crows and starlings circled, cawing vehement protests, above and around him. He stood over the huddled body of a man. The eyes of the corpse were both gone, the lips and tongue and most of the flesh of the face shredded away from white bone by the sharp beaks of the carrion birds.

The means of the man's death was obvious—standing out from the bridge of what was left of the nose was the leather-fletched butt end of the shortest, thickest arrow Foster had ever seen. When he was once again master of his stomach, he was able to take note of the singularly strange clothing and equipment of the body.

The close-fitting steel helmet had certainly been of no protection this time, though old nicks and dents evidenced that it had served its function in times past. Nicked and dented too was the steel breastplate. Heavy, clumsy-looking leather boots encased most of both legs, their tops being tightly buckled high on the thighs, well under the skirts of a stiff jerkin of dun-colored leather. The hands were hidden in gloves reaching almost to the elbows, patterns of tiny steel rings sewn to the backs and cuffs. The stretch of shirtsleeves visible between those cuffs and the areas just below the shoulders seemed to Foster of the consistency of tent canvas, horizontally striped off-white and faded red-brown.

A handspan-wide belt, mounting the biggest brass buckle Foster had ever seen, rested on the right shoulder and bisected the breastplate, a cased sword attached to its lower ends. Laying the shotgun near to hand, Foster drew the weapon and hefted it. The straight blade was at least a yard long, wide and thick and heavy, double-edged and basket-hilted. Foster had fenced, in prep school and college, but he had never before handled a sword like this. The only one he remembered even seeing at all like it had been a Highland broadsword. There was no balance to the dead man's weapon, all the weight being in the blade. Even so, its condition testified to lengthy and hard service.

He was trying to pull a leather pouch of some kind from under the dead weight of its former owner when the shrill scream of an infuriated horse came from among the outbuildings and he glanced up just in time to see a man garbed exactly like the dead one level what looked to be a sawed-off shotgun and fire in his direction. Something *spannngged* on the corpse's breastplate and caromed off, leaving a smear of silvery lead on the steel.

But Foster did not see it. He had grabbed his own gun and was frantically rolling across the bare flagstones toward the tower, an angle of which offered the only nearby cover. He heard two more of the booming reports before he gained the partial protection of the rough-hewn stones, but arrived there unharmed, save for bruises and abrasions.

A cautious peek around the angle of the tower revealed only the outbuildings; the man or men who had been shooting at him were nowhere in sight, though he could hear a voice shouting something or other from that area.

Abruptly, a trio of helmeted men trotted into sight from behind the largest of the buildings, each armed with two of

18

the thick, stubby firearms. They seemed oblivious to the fact that they were all within easy range of the rifled slugs in Foster's riot gun as they jogged forward, silent but for the jingle of their equipment and the clump of their boots, their stubbled faces grim.

The man in the center had a good start of a reddish beard and he showed a gapped set of yellow-and-brown teeth in a wolfish grin when Foster's first shot—fired mostly in warning—plowed up dust and stone shards a few feet in front of his muddy boots, crackling something that sounded like "Unduhsharshed!" before bringing one of his own weapons to bear on Foster's hiding place.

As he shook the bits of rock and moss from his hair, Foster decided to stop being civilized and to start playing for keeps, as the approaching trio so obviously were. Jacking another shell into the chamber, he put the twelve-gauge slug into redbeard's unprotected face. The force of the lead lifted the man clear off his feet, throwing him backward so hard that his armored shoulders clanged onto the paving fully eight feet from where he had stood.

At this second shot, a mob of at least a dozen of the helmeted men poured from among the outbuildings, shouting and waving those long, heavy swords. With only four rounds left in the shotgun, Foster dropped the two gunmen first. As the two closest men tumbled, the mob stopped, wavered for a moment, then came on again, but more slowly this time, clearly no longer so sure of themselves.

Hurriedly, Foster jerked shells from the shell vest and fed four into the gun. Snapping his lanyard to the ring of his pistol, he drew it, jacked a round into the chamber, then removed the clip and replaced it with a full one.

"Six shells in the Winchester, eight in the .45," he mused to himself, aloud. "I may not get all the bastards, but they'll damn well know they've been in a firefight!" He loosened the trench knife in its scabbard.

"I'd forgotten, after all these years," he thought. "Forgotten how exhilarating this kind of thing can be. I wonder why I didn't stay in the army after Korea?"

When the vanguard of the enemy—now grown to more than a score, as more men trickled out from among the outbuildings—had gotten to the bodies of the three gunmen, Foster opened fire, carefully, making every lead slug count. He got five before they broke; a sixth one he shot in the back.

Slipping an arm through the sling of his hot-barreled weapon, gasping with the exertion, he was feeling for his canteen when a section of the wall behind him fell away and several pairs of strong hands dragged him down, into blackness.

Shortly after Foster left his house, Arbor Collier passed out and her husband carried her up to the guest room, where she snored loudly enough for Krystal to hear above the sounds of the water in the sink and the rattling of the glasses and dishes she was washing.

Collier himself sat at the kitchen table, sipping at cold coffee. The shotgun lay on the tabletop, and thrust under his belt was a pistol he had found in the back of the gun cabinet.

As she let out the water and turned from the sink, wiping her hands, just about to speak her mind about how silly this entire gun business seemed to her, there was a booming report from somewhere beyond the big, stone building, followed, almost immediately, by two more.

Collier carefully set down his mug and grasped the ornate two-barreled gun, his jaws clenched, and Krystal thought he no longer looked at all gentle.

"Was . . . is that Bass's gun, Professor? Do you think it was?"

He shook his gray head. "No way of telling, my dear. I can only say that it was definitely a smooth bore, not a rifle or a pistol."

Before she could think of anything to say, a fourth boom reached them, then a brief pause and another, another pause and a sixth. At that, she started for the door, but the seated man closed a powerful hand around her arm.

"Where do you think *you're* going, young lady?"

"To help Bass. To see what's going on, anyway."

But he shook his head again. "No, I'm sorry. Mr. Foster is well armed and he seems quite a capable man, in all ways. He said that we were all to remain here and that is precisely what we are going to do."

She jerked savagely against his grip. "Damn you! Let me go. Who the hell are you to tell me what to do?"

Though he smiled, his grasp never slackened. "For one thing, Mr. Foster left me in charge, in his absence. For another, I'm easily old enough to give you fatherly advice. And for a third, I've had far more training than I care to recall in combat and general mankilling. You're unarmed; what good could you do him if I did let you go to wherever he now is?"

While he spoke, they had heard the shouts of many men, dim with distance, then two more booms, in quick succession.

"Dammit! Then *you* go find him!"

"Who's going to take care of those two in the parlor, and my wife?" He elevated his shaggy brows.

"Hell, I will. Give me the pistol." She held out her free hand.

Smiling, he pulled the weapon from his belt and extended it, butt first. "Do you know how to use it, my dear?"

"I . . . well, I *think* so. That is, I've seen people shoot them," she stuttered.

"All right." He let her arm go. "Stand at the head of the stairs, there, and fire a round into that stack of logs in the fireplace. That's a nine-millimeter; those logs are sufficiently thick to stop the slug."

"All right." Her lips tight, she raised the pistol, held it wobbling at arm's length, shut both eyes, and jerked the trigger. Nothing happened. Opening her eyes, she tried it again; still nothing. She looked, felt with her thumb, for the hammer they cocked on television shows, but this weapon had no such thing. At the sound of a dry chuckle behind her, she reddened, spun about, and thrust the pistol back at Professor Collier, saying angrily, "It doesn't work. What's wrong, did you take the bullets all out?"

"No," he answered gently. "The Luger is fully loaded and armed, it simply has the safety engaged. Miss Kent, you clearly know nothing whatsoever concerning firearms. Until you learn a modicum of their usage, you'll be far safer to let them entirely alone."

Before she could answer, there were six more booms, evenly spaced, at least one scream, then total silence for a moment . . . before the clop-clop of horses' hooves sounded from the front yard and something metallic began to pound against the front door.

And Krystal found herself rooted where she stood, unable to move an inch, as Collier snapped the shotgun closed and headed for the door.

The hands which had grabbed Foster quickly dragged him several yards along a stone passageway, then a man-shape stepped over him and, with a grating noise, closed out the last trace of daylight. Then he was pulled to his feet, turned about, and hustled up a flight of narrow, stone stairs, aware that there were persons both before and behind. His unseen captors were not exactly gentle, but neither did it seem that they were trying to hurt him. No word was spoken, only occasional grunts and one wheezing gasp.

After at least two dozen stairs, the hands halted him, then a low, narrow door opened and the two men ahead of him stooped and went through it. As he was being firmly pushed from behind, Foster, too, stooped low enough to negotiate the constricted opening. He straightened, to find himself in a high-ceilinged, if smallish, chamber, stone-walled and floored and windowless. It was completely devoid of furnishings, unless three long-bladed spears and a clumsy-looking gun could be considered furniture.

Foster would have liked to examine the gun more closely, but he was hurried through the small room so fast that his only impressions were of a trigger guard large enough to put the whole hand in, action too close to the buttplate for comfort in handling, and a bore that seemed at least ten-gauge and possibly eight-gauge, with a brass-tipped wooden ramrod slotted into the handguard. One other point: overall, the piece was close to five feet long!

As for the men who had dragged him through the wall, all were at least a head less than his own six feet, a couple even shorter, but without exception they were wiry and muscular, with broad, thick shoulders and arms and big, callused hands. Their clothing was rough—brogans of half-cured hide, trousers and shirts of what looked very much like homespun broadcloth—but skillfully patched, where worn, and clean, though showing multitudinous old stains. Clothing color was uniform, looking to be that of unbleached wool.

In personal appearance, they might have been the twins of those same men who had charged toward him outside—hair and facial stubble of varying shades of brown or dark blond, fair though tanned skin, here a splash of freckles, there a hint of auburn in wavy and coarsely trimmed hair, eyes brown or blue or hazel—in short, they might have been any group of workmen encountered on any street. Might have been, save for the fact that, in most places, men who strolled down the street bearing such an assortment of lethal-looking cutlery as these bore on or in their belts would quickly have been collected and taken away to explain.

Another thick, nail-studded door was opened and Foster was thrust into a larger room, this one carpeted, wood-paneled, and furnished with a refectory table, a couple of high-backed chairs, and several stools. The table was set before the tight-shuttered windows, and behind it sat a man considerably older than Foster's captors.

One of those accompanying him crossed the room and laid the Winchester and the trench knife on the tabletop, rendered a bobbing bow while tugging at the hair over his right eye, then stepped back to his place beside the door.

The oldster tested the point of the knife, then ran a thumb along the honed edge, grunted, and laid it aside. He picked up the pumpgun and turned it round and about in his hands, then shook his balding head and laid it beside the knife. When he looked up and crooked a finger, Foster was led forward.

Pushing back from the table, the older man smoothed down the long skirts of his leather coat, thrust out his booted legs, and leaned back in the chair, clasping his long-fingered hands on the lower part of his steel breastplate.

Fixing his faded-blue eyes on Foster, he snapped something that sounded to his listener like, "H'b'y? Hwah'b'y'ahboot, mahn?"

Foster just looked at his questioner blankly. The words sounded almost familiar, maddeningly so, but for a moment he could not make rhyme or reason of them. Then, suddenly, as the old man began to converse with one of those who had brought him there, the words and phrases began to take on meaning. Foster decided that the language was certainly English, of a sort—Shakespearean-like English spoken with a thick, Gaelic brogue.

He spoke. "I am Sebastian Foster, sir."

The oldster's eyes snapped back to him. "Forster, be y'?" He ran a finger under his wide lace collar and moved his lips in the hint of a smile. "An' come t' help Sir Francis, en? Belike, y'll only die w' us a', but f'r a', y're well come." Standing, he extended his hand and, automatically, Foster took and gripped it. "I be Geoffrey Musgrave, Squire Forster, steward o' a' Sir Francis' lands. But set y'doon."

Foster felt a chair being pressed against the backs of his legs and sank onto it, as Musgrave picked up a big leather pitcher and poured measures of a pale-yellow liquid into leather mugs, then pushed one across the table and seated himself with the others. But when Foster picked up his mug, the old man rose again, holding his cup aloft, saying, "Squire

Forster, let us drink the health of our King, God bless him, and damnation t' a' rebels."

A sip. The stuff was sour and watery, with an aftertaste that hinted of herbs, but Foster found its thirst-quenching properties sovereign, so took several long drafts before setting the mug down. "Thank you very much, Mr. Musgrave. It's delicious, but what is it?"

The old man looked at him oddly and raised one eyebrow. "Why it be Sir Francis' famous ale, o' course. Y' looked t' need a stoup, Squire Forster, an' the best be ne'er too good f'r a mon as would fight his way in t' die w' us."

Foster had no intention of dying, with these people or without, not if he could do anything about it. There had been a time—was it only a couple of days ago? It now seemed like far longer than that—as he had sat, watching the raging Potomac lap further and further beyond its highest previous floodpoint, when he had felt very close to Carol, when he had been ready to leave a world that had become all but unbearable since her untimely death. He had deliberately drunk himself into a stupor, expecting never to waken again, but the events of the past hours, the mysteries presented for unraveling, and especially the short, vicious little gunfight down in the courtyard had brought about a fierce resurgence of his will to live.

He took another swallow of the ale. "How many men have you here, Mr. Musgrave?"

The oldster sighed gustily. "Only seven and twenty be left, alas. Mony died on the walls when first yon host come on us, more fell when young Sir Cuthbert led that braw sallyforth wha' gie him his death's-wound, God harbor safely his gallant soul. These lads still wi' us be braw an' bonny a lot, but nae sojers, ye ken, for a' that their sires an' grandsires were reavers a'. Still they love Sir Francis—as do mesel' an' ye, eh?—an' they an' the sairvin' gels an' me an' ye, Squire Forster, an' the Lady Arabella, we'll cost the whoresons dear, ere Whyffler Ha' fa's!

"When Sir Francis took to his bed—an' would ye see him, y' maun see him soon, for I dinna think he's lang tae live, more's the pity—an' command fell tae meself, I drew a' intae the north wing, here, sealed us off frae the bulk o' the hoose. We'll hold here sae lang as we can, then tae the Towerkeep."

"But," said Foster, "if you've got twenty-seven men, why in hell don't you go out and drive those few bastards out of the outbuildings? I don't think there were more than twenty-five, to start out, and I shot six of those."

"I could nae take a' the lads oot agin yon poodle-fakers; besides, they hae gonnes an' a braw plenitood a' poudre."

"Don't *you* have guns?" demanded Foster. "You've got one, anyhow—I saw it in the other room there."

"Och, aye, Squire Forster, gonnes in plenty, but almost nae poudre, nor ane left as can mix it. An' I wot Sir David—forsworn rebel, he be bot a canny sojer, for a' that—spiered oot our lack an' so stationed only Redhand Ramsay an' thirty launces tae hold us here until he an' his rebel reavers maun fetch back a great gonne, for he wot he cannae tek the auld tower wi'oot ane. That ane he drug here wi' him burst a' the secon' firin'." The old man showed every remaining yellow tooth in a wolfish grin. "Aye, Squire Forster, that were suthin tae see, it were! Blew the great gonne tae flinders, it did, sent a' the gonners tae meet Auld Clootie, fired a' the timbers alang wi' fu' mickle caskets a' poudre!"

"Why can't someone here make powder?" asked Foster. "It's simple enough to do."

"Why surely ye ken, Squire Forster, Sir Francis be a King's man, an' what wi' a' the bad blude twixt the Kirk an' the King, none wi' sell Sir Francis the sacred poudre. Och, aye, charcoal an' bernstane we hae in plenty, but wha' gude be they wi'oot priests' poudre, eh?"

The old man could be referring only to niter, Foster thought, something simple enough to obtain, especially where there was livestock. So why all this mumbo-jumbo about sacred powder, priests' powder?

"Mr. Musgrave, you show me an old dungheap and I'll make you all the powder you can use," he declared flatly.

The steward's jaw plopped open, his eyes goggled. "Do I ken y'r meaning? You can make sacred poudre? Frae *muck*?"

"Not exactly *from* dung, itself," grinned Foster. "Let's see if I can explain."

Musgrave stood up quickly, took a broad baldric from a hook on the wall, slipped it over his head, and positioned the long sword for easy walking.

"Not tae me, Squire Forster, I be but a poor, iggernant wight. But Sir Francis, for a' I fear me he's dyin', be a well-readed gentleman, like y'sel'. 'Tis past time y' presented y'sel tae him, enyhoo. Tell y' him o' this wonder o' poudre wrought by a laymon."

He waved a liver-spotted hand at the shotgun and knife.

"Tak oop y'r weepons, Squire Forster. *Willy*," he turned to one of the men by the door, "wher be the gentlemon's sword?"

Again Foster saw the man pull at his forelock and bob a bow. "He dinnae hae sich, an' it please y' Captain Musgrave."

Foster anticipated the question and, recalling the Civil War saber hanging over the hearth in his den, decided to say, "Your man's telling the truth, captain; my sword is heavy and it's a hot day and—"

"And," Musgrave said as he rounded the table and clapped a hand to Foster's shoulder in comradely fashion, "any mon wha' can reload sae fast and shoot straight an' mek his ane poudre oons scant need o' a sword, I be thinkin'. But Sir Francis be summat old-fashioned, y' ken? We'll find y' a sword an' a' in the armory."

Dave and Susan still lay side by side on the floor before the stereo, the headphones still clamped over their ears, only the steady movement of their chests showing them to be not dead. Arbor Collier still lay asleep in the guest bedroom, snoring with the sound and volume of an unmuffled lawnmower engine. Foster had been gone for something over two hours.

Professor Collier sat in the chair his wife had previously occupied, a long sword lying across his knees and a huge muzzle-loading pistol in his hands. Krystal Kent was curled up in the chair that had been Foster's, watching the two newcomers on the couch pour beer down their throats almost as fast as they could pop the tops of the cans.

She watched the prominent Adam's apple of the smaller and younger of the two, Carey Carr, bob jerkily as he chugged down his fifth or sixth brew, and thought that the black-haired, sharp-featured little man seemed to be teetering on the edge of hysteria.

The other man was big, bigger even than Foster, broad at both shoulder and hip, thick-bodied with the hint of a beer-gut. His bare arms were both heavily tatooed and bulging with round, rolling muscles, ending in hands like hams. The light-brown hair on his head was cropped so short that Krystal could see the scalp, his eyes were a bright blue and set well apart over wide cheekbones. He had given the name of Buddy Webster and he smiled often. Also, he had done almost all the talking since they had arrived.

Krystal could see that he was as mystified and excited as the other man, but his almost bovine placidity of nature acted as a shock absorber, protecting him from emotional extreme.

"We was driving," he had begun, "down Innastate eighty-three, fum Harrisburg, headin' for Richmond, V'ginya, me 'n' Pete Fairley, in ouwuh rig, an' good-buddy Carey, heanh, an' Harry Kallin, ovuh my shoulduh, in theirn. We all knowed it'uz a hurr'cain perdicted, but hell, I done drove in all kinda weather. But long about the four-oh-one turnoff to Butluh, Merluhn, it'd got so gadhawful bad awn the road you couldn' see more'n ten foot ahead an' the wipers won't no good at-tall.

"So I got awn the See-Bee an' tol' ol' Harry—he'uz a-drivin' t'othuh rig—he 'n' Carey could do everythin' they wawnted, but iffen it didn't git no better time we come to Cockeysville, I'uz gone turn off 'n' lay ovuh till it did."

He had then grinned, slugged down a can of beer and continued. "Well, when I told him bout this lil ol' gal I knows is a waitress at thishere big ol' motel in Cockeysville, he allowed he'd lay ovuh, too.

"Well, enyhow, we'uz almost to Cockeysville an' the rain was a-comin' down fit to bust an' jest as my front wheels lit ontuh thishere ovuhpass, it . . . it jest felt like the road wuz movin' like, you know. So I slowed down—couldna been doing moren thirty, thirty-five to start out, but I geared 'er down. An' then I felt like I's in a elevatuh goin' down, an' I figgered the foundashuns of thet ol' ovuhpass had done washed out an' the ovuhpass had done caved in an' I *knowed* this ol' boy wuz dead meat. So I closed my eyes an' said, *Sweet Jesus, I loves You, tek me home.*

"An' then they was this bad bump, an' then anothern, and ol' Pete starts accusin' me from in the sleepuh. An' I opened my eyes, an' they won't no road *nowhere* in sight! The rig uz jest rolling along, real slow, in the middle of this here great big pretty pasture-like. An' I looked in the mirrer an' ol' Harry 'uz still ovuh my shoulduh."

Another grin, another can of beer. Krystal rubbed her arms hard, then, to lay the gooseflesh, recalling with terrifying clarity the hideous indescribable agony as the berserk patient's improvised knife tore through her tender breast and remembered the horrible awareness of inchs of icy, razor-edged steel slicing the throbbing heart deep in her chest. As she now recollected, she, too, had closed her eyes, had felt a thump which she had then assumed was that of her body

27

falling to the floor of the psychiatric ward. Every bit as frightening was the memory of what she first had seen when again she had opened her eyes—a stark, gray stone tower, battlemented, and rising above the roofline of Bass Foster's house!

Long and strict self-discipline had imparted to her the ability to quickly will a return of composure, and she now exercised it and glanced at the Professor in time to glimpse a hint of remembered horror in his eyes, too. Then the trucker recommenced his narrative.

"Well, enyhow, I braked up hard an' fas', an' Harry did too. An' Pete come a-rollin' out an-yellin' an' cussin' an I don' know whatall, an' I'uz a-tryin' to tell him what done gone down, when thesehere two fellers come a-ridin' hosses ovuh thishere lil hill an' intuh thishere pasture where we wuz. They wuz all dolled up like thet feller in thet movie this ol' gal took me to oncet, thet feller Don Kwixoat, 'cept they didn' have them no shields, jest spears an' steel hardhats-like an' thesehere swords an' all.

"Well, enyhow, we hadn't got moren twenny yards from the rig, when them bastards come a-ridin' straight for us. C'n you b'lieve thet? Then they split up, thet's awl whut saved this ol' boy, I tell you. Pete had done got down from the truck an' one of them maniacs headed for him an' the othern kep awn at me an oll Harry, an' thet bastard got to us afore his pal got to where Pete was, natcherly, 'cause we wuz closer to where they started from.

"Well, enyhow, thet sonuvabitch—pard'n me, ma'am, I'm sorry." The big man flushed and dropped his eyes in embarrassment. "But, enyhow, thet feller took his spear an' *stuck it clear through pore ol' Harry! I mean it, clear through 'im!*

"Well, I'm a peaceable ol' boy, but when I seed what been done to ol' Harry, I'uz scared, damn raht, but I come to git so mad I couldn' see straight, hardly. I jes' jumped ovuh an' grabbed me thet ol' spear whut thet bastard had jest done pullted outen ol' Harry, an' I jerkted it an' he hung awnta it and I pulled him raht awfen his hoss an' his hardhat come awf when he hit the groun' an' he let go thet ol' spear too an' I took an bashted his damn haid with it so dang hard it busted, but"—he grinned again—"it busted his haid too, caved 'er raht awn in, it did."

Another beer followed the grin, then, "Well, enyhow, when ol' Pete seed whut the feller I kilt done to ol' Harry, he 'uz back awn an' back in the rig fore you could say 'Jack Christufuh.' He'd alluz carr'ed him a ol' thutty-eight pistol in the sleepuh an' I done razzed him moren one time bout it, but I shorelawd won't no more.

"Well, enyhow, he took thet ol' pistol an' shot thet othuh murderin' bastard raht awfen his dang hoss! An' it served him raht, too, cause we hadn't done nuthin' to neithuh one of 'em, an' jest drivin' crosst a feller's pasture ain't no call to *kill* 'em, is it?"

"It may well be, here," commented Collier.

"Well, where's 'here,' enyhow?" pled the big, square-faced man.

Collier sighed. "I sincerely wish I could tell you, sir. My wife and I arrived here quite as suddenly, if, thank God, less violently, as did you and your friends. I believe that all the others now here, as well as Mr. Foster, who is presently absent, found themselves here every bit as suddenly and inexplicably.

"But come, tell us the remainder of the tale."

As there had been but the two horses, it had been decided that Pete, who had never in his life been astride a horse, would remain with the trucks and Harry's body, while Carey and Buddy rode to find a telephone, a law officer, or both. For, strangely enough, they could raise not a living soul on either of the CBs. Before the two men had ridden off, they had both received a crash course in the basics of charging and firing the huge horsepistols—a pair of which were holstered on the pommel of each saddle—from Pete, who once had belonged to a muzzle-loading club. He had persuaded them to take along the swords and big knives, as well, retaining his revolver for his own protection.

CHAPTER 2

Immediately after Sir Francis Whyffler was mounted, he called for the stirrup cup and, before drinking, raised the ancient, silver-mounted horn in a health to the King. When he had downed the horn of ale, he drew his broadsword, brought his prancing stallion into a sustained rear, and flourished an elaborate salute to the ladies—his widowed sister, Mary, his daughter, Arabella, Dr. Krystal Kent, Arbor Collier, and Catherine Musgrave, widowed daughter-in-law of the steward—then brought the animal back down, sheathed his blade, and kneed the mount over to have a few last words with Geoffrey Musgrave and the newly appointed chamberlain, Henry Turnbull.

Keeping his fettlesome bay gelding in check with some difficulty, Foster was frankly amazed at the miraculous recuperative powers of the elderly nobleman. Even granting the excellent care of Krystal and the administration of massive dosages of the penicillin tablets from Foster's medicine cabinet, it still seemed astounding that a man who had, when Foster first had seen him two weeks ago, been on his virtual deathbed, should be today not only up and in the saddle in three-quarter armor but preparing to take to the road and lead his party the leagues of hard riding to York, whereat the King was most recently reported.

Glancing to right and left, Foster thought that both Professor Collier and Buddy Webster could easily pass a casual inspection as born residents of this time and place, albeit somewhat larger than the average of their peers. As for himself, though he had been fitted out in lobstertail helmet, leather buffcoat and steel cuirass, vambraces, cuishes and gauntlets, and had a broadsword—somewhat altered—depending from a wide leather baldric, the clothing beneath was anachronistic—his old GI coveralls and a handsome pair of hand-tooled Western boots.

At fast walk, the little column headed down the dusty track toward the main gate, Sir Francis in the lead, sitting erect, head high, shoulders squared, smiling and nodding acknowledgment of the cheers of the crowd which had gathered to render their homage and wish their loved lord Godspeed. As soon as it had been bruited about that Sir Francis again had powder, that his forces had broken the siege of Whyffler Hall, and that Sir David the Scot had been slain—he being one of the two men who had so savagely attacked the truckers—refugees from about the ravaged countryside, King's men and friends and supporters of Sir Francis and of his house had flocked to his side. Indeed, so many had come that food was running low and many had had to be lodged in tents and makeshift lean-tos, but the walls were fully manned by determined men.

Nor were the restrengthened defenses lacking firearms and artillery wherein to use the new plentitude of gunpowder, for immediately old Geoffrey Musgrave found himself in command of a score of experienced fighters rather than the scratch force of servants and farmhands with which he had so stoutly defended the wing of the hall, he had ridden forth with Sir David's head impaled on his lance point, gathering more fighters as he rode. His raiders, by purest chance, came upon the baggage-and-booty train of the late Sir David, ambushed it, coldly butchered the guards and drivers, and brought it in triumph back to Whyffler Hall.

As for the unlamented Sir David's main force of nearly two thousand border Scots, other foreigners, and assorted outlaws and broken men from both sides of the border, Foster still laughed when he thought of that rout. A night attack, led by the Jeep pickup—its muffler removed, its lights glaring, and its hornbutton taped down—expertly driven by Carey Carr with Foster literally "riding shotgun," the jouncing bed containing Bill Collier, Buddy Webster, Pete Fairley, Dave Atkins, and Henry Turnbull and his eldest son (these being the only two contemporary men other than Geoff Musgrave, who was needed to lead the main force,

31

with the courage to undertake a ride in this devilish contrivance) and every firearm in Foster's modest collection.

Terror-stricken, the highly superstitious marauders had fled the roaring, blaring, fire-spitting demon without any hint of a stand. Only the rare foeman remained long enough to snatch up more than his filthy *breacan-feile*—the "belted tartan" which was dress during the day and blanket at night—and fewer still stopped by the picket line. Most left barefoot and unarmed, and headed north for the border, as fast as their hairy shanks would carry them. Hundreds were ridden down to be lanced, shot, hacked, or simply trampled before Musgrave could recall his small troop and point out to them the dangers of a night pursuit. He had not needed to add that, afoot and weaponless, few would make it back to Scotland, not through the countryside they themselves had ravaged so short a time agone.

Just outside the gate stood the emptied trailer trucks. After the superhuman labor of getting them to Whyffler Hall, it had been discovered that they were too high to pass through the gate, so they had been emptied, stripped of everything that looked usable, and were presently being used to house some of the villager refugees.

It was the load of one of the trucks that had impelled Sir Francis to ride and seek the sovereign. Careful experiments on the parts of Professor Collier, Foster, Pete Fairley, and Musgrave had determined that a superior gunpowder could be fabricated through substitution of the chemical fertilizer the truck had borne for raw niter. Now several tons of this powder reposed in a newly dug powderhouse, but supplies of charcoal and sulfur had been expended, while nearly eighty tons of fertilizer remained.

Too, there was the immense horse herd that their military actions had amassed. There was little enough grain to feed the folk, much less several hundred animals. The canny Musgrave had chosen the best of the unclaimed stock to add to Sir Francis' stable and to mount the troop of lances he was recruiting, but the large remainder could only be turned out to find their own forage in park and lea.

Sir Francis set a fast pace, cross-country, but straight as an arrow was his route. Shortly before dusk, they forded the Rede and, just as the moon was arising, reined up at the challenge of a knot of well-armed riders. When Sir Francis answered in a clear, ringing voice, a squat, broad man on a tall, powerful destrier separated from the group and kneed his mount forward.

"Be it truly ye, Francis? We'd heard the thrice-domned Scots had slain ye an' young Cuthbert an' razed y'r hall. Ye got away, did ye, then?"

Chuckling, Sir Francis signaled Foster and Collier to follow and rode to meet the speaker, saying, "Better than that, Johnny, far better than that. We'll tell an' that, soon. But we've rode hard, this day, we're drier nor Satan's backside and of a hunger to boil up our boots. Where be y'r famous hospitality, John Heron?"

Loud and wild was the rejoicing of Squire John and his folk at the news of the death of Sir David and the unqualified rout of his reavers. Before they went into the hall to dine, Sir Francis gifted their host several casks of the gunpowder captured from the Scots, but none of the fertilizer powder. And his brief introductions of Foster, Collier and Webster noted only that they were King's men who had fought in the defense of Whyffler Hall.

Squire John welcomed them all and fed them the best meal Foster had enjoyed since his arrival. Heron's lands had not been ravaged, and, though his hall was neither so large nor so fine as Whyffler Hall, he set a fine table—pork, veal, mutton, pigeon, goose, and chicken, fish of several kinds, and eels, a hare pastry, and a whole, roasted badger, cabbage, lambs-quarters, and three kinds of beans, everything well seasoned with onions, garlic, and assorted herbs. There were pitchers of the inevitable ale, but also wines and some fiery cordials. And all the while they sat gorging themselves, their host profusely apologized for the plainness and paucity of the fare, blaming the chaotic conditions of countryside and roads, about which armed bands of every stripe and persuasion rode or marched hither and yon, commanding stores and impressing likely men and boys where they did not burn, rob, rape and kill.

Then Foster had all he could do to not spew up that fine dinner when, as a special fillip, Sir Francis had the pickle cask brought in, the top hoop sprung, and did himself reach into the strong vinegar to haul forth—ghastly, fishbelly-white, and dripping—the head of Sir David the Scot, much to the expressed delight of the assembled company.

With the first cockcrow, they were back in the saddle, and on their way with the earliest light. But not until John Heron's hall was well behind them did Sir Francis sign Foster, Collier, and Webster to leave their places in the column of twos and ride beside him.

Foster thought that, if anything, the nearly twelve hours of extreme exertion the day before had improved the old nobleman's appearance. His face was sun-darkened and the high-bridged nose was peeling a little, but there was immense vitality in his every movement and his sea-green eyes sparkled under their yellowish-white brows.

"I'd not be having ye think that I mistrust my old comrade, Squire John," he began. "Ye all ken that I gi'e him nane of the new powder, nor telled aught of the miracles as brought ye here in the time of the King's need. But I know ye that I would willingly trust Squire John wi' all I hold dear, eek my ain honor.

"We twa soldiered together years agone, in France under the young King's grandsire and during the Crusade agin the Empire, near twenty year agone, and agin the domned Scots near a' our lives. He be a forthright and honorable gentleman, but, much as he'd like tae, he canna speak for a' his folk. His wife be ten years dead, but her uncle lives yet and he be the Bishop o' Preston. And the less the bludey Kirk knows o' ye and a' ye've wrought, ere we reach the King, the better, I be thinking."

That was all he said at the time, but he ruined the appetites of both Foster and Collier, during the late-morning dinner halt. "Whate'er transpires, gentlemen, dinna allow y'r living bodies tae be delivered up tae the Kirk. When the Empire Crusade was won, those as had made unhallowed powder—mostly alchemists and renegade clerics—first were tortured for weeks by the Holy Office, then their broken bodies were carted or dragged, for nane could walk or e'en crawl by that time, tae the place o' their doom. There, before the princes o' the domned Kirk and a' o' us Crusaders as hadna gane hame, they gelded the poor bastards, gutted them and rammed them fu' o' their ane powder, then burnt them at stakes, an' wi' the domned fires slow, so it was lang ere they were blown intae gobbets."

Their second night on the journey was wakeful and wary, in a well-concealed, cold camp on the north bank of the Tyne, just upstream from Overwarden Town. The campfires of a sizable force flickered on the south bank, and the travelers were glad to have heeded Sir Francis' warnings to keep low and silent through the night, when with the gray false-dawn came the sound of chanting, and the first rays of the sun revealed some four thousand foot and at least half a thousand horse, all bearing Church pennons or wearing the white surcoat of Crusaders.

As the enemy host broke camp and prepared to take up their journey, Sir Francis scrutinized them through Foster's big 7x50 binoculars, of which he had become quite fond.

"They be French, the bastards," he announced, at length, though never taking the optics from his eyes.

"You can hear that well?" queried Collier. "It all sounds just a confused babble to me."

The old nobleman's pointed vandyke—not quite pure white, being shot through with errant strands of light auburn—bobbed as he silently laughed. "Och, nae, my gude magister, I can but tell from the moving o' the whoresons' lips wha' whords they be speaking. Aye, they be mostly French, wi' at least a few Savoyards . . . wait noo, some Flemishers, too. Och, 'tis a fine kettle o' tainted fish the thrice-domned Pope has sent intae our lands."

They stayed close until the enemy rear guard was nearly an hour over the horizon, then hurriedly crossed the ford and rode hard to the southeast. It was not until they were bare miles from York that they were forced to fight for their passage, and this not with foreign Crusaders, but with a band of common brigands. In a morning's misty rain, the highwaymen must have mistaken the party with its long packtrain for merchants, rather than armed, alert and bellicose gentlemen and their retainers; few of them lived to reflect on their hasty follies. Briskly, Sir Francis' men stripped the dead and dying robbers of their arms and anything else that looked to be usable or of value, loaded the booty onto such horses as could be easily caught, and resumed their ride.

In midafternoon, they came within sight of York.

The town was filled to more than overflowing, what with the King and his retinue, gathering supporters and their armed bands, hordes of humbler folk from smaller towns and villages and the countryside seeking the protection of the strong walls and trained fighters afforded by this temporary capital—all in addition to the usual inhabitants. The provost was allowed to believe that they were but another trooplet of King's men from the northern marches, whereupon he assigned them an area in which to pitch their tents. When all was in order in his camp, Sir Francis rode to seek the King.

Seated on the groundcloth of his pyramid-tent, his disassembled firearms spread on an improvised table made of a piece of planking atop his tight-rolled sleeping bag, Foster was absorbed in carefully cleaning and oiling his Colt, his Winchester pumpgun, and his two new horsepistols. In the rear of the tent lay Webster, snoring resoundingly on his blankets, his leather buffcoat rolled up for a pillow. Collier was out roaming the camps, fascinatedly.

When he had reassembled the automatic and the shotgun, he broke the two Stevens Model 94s—only the pistol grip and fore-end remaining of the stock, and with barrels shortened to thirteen inches—and held them up to the light of the doorway. The black-powder-reloaded shells had left an unbelievable amount of fouling in the smooth bore. He set himself to the task of removing it.

"Amazing." Collier wandered in, still armored and helmeted, his filthy, muddy jackboots leaving broad stains on the groundcloth.

"What's going to be amazing," Foster grinned, "is the size of the hole I'm going to blast through you if you don't remember to take off those cobbler's nightmares or at least clean them before you come into this tent. God knows how long we're going to have to live in it, and my standards of cleanliness are somewhat higher than those of our British friends here."

Hanging his ugly head sheepishly, Collier sat down and began to struggle out of the ungainly footwear, speaking all the while. "This place, those camps, ugh . . . philologist's dream, Bass. I've just been in the camp of a squadron from Dartmoor, and they speak Cornish. Can you believe it, Bass, *Cornish*!" At last, big boots shed, he slid on his rump over to Foster's "table," unholstering his long-barreled Luger.

"I'd best clean this, too, I suppose. I fired four or five rounds from it, back on the road, there."

Foster shook his head and said, "You should've used the horsepistols, Bill. Save the Luger for dire emergencies; I told you and Webster that."

"Well, you used your .45, Bass. Dammit, what's the difference?" demanded the Professor peevedly.

"The difference is that I have over two hundred rounds for the Colt, but only fifty—less than that, now—for your pistol or for Buddy's, and once they're fired, there'll be no more."

The older man delved a hand into one of the pouches at his belt—his contemporary clothing had no pockets—then extended the open palm containing a trio of 9mm cases to Foster. "Reload them, as you reload your shot shells. I'm reasonably certain that I can devise a means of fabricating primers."

Foster shook his head slowly. "You, your many accomplishments, never cease to amaze me, Bill. You're not at all the sort of man I assumed you to be during the first day I knew you. You're the best pistol or rifle or wing shot I've ever seen, and I've seen a lot. You can fence me into the ground, and I wasn't all that bad a fencer, once. You're a better horseman than anyone at Whyffler Hall . . . except, maybe, Sir Francis and Geoff Musgrave.

"It was you that remembered Webster saying that he was hauling a load of chemical fertilizer, and you that worked out a way to use it in place of niter crystals. It was your mind and Pete Fairley's hands that also worked out a quick and simple method for converting matchlocks to flintlocks. And it was you who thought up the bit with my Jeep pickup." He couldn't repress a grin and a chuckle. "Christ, I'll bet some of those barefoot bastards are *still* running.

"No doubt you'll have other surprises in store for us, in time, and I don't doubt for a minute that you can and will make primers when the couple of thousand I have with my reloading set are gone.

"But, Bill, there are one or two gaps in your knowledge. First off, my Colt and Luger and Buddy's .380 are all three automatics; that is to say, they're operated by their recoil and the gases from their charges. Black powder just isn't a powerful enough propellant to make them work."

"Then put in more powder, Bass."

He grimaced. "The cases aren't big enough to put in that much powder, Bill—as much as we'd need, I mean. Besides which, there's more to reloading cases than simply knocking out the old primer, fitting in a new one, and adding powder. You need the proper dies for each caliber, and the only dies I own are for three shotgun gauges. You start playing around with reloaded ammo, you'll soon wind up missing fingers or a whole hand or with a big chunk of steel in your head. I stick to the rules and the load tables, and I'm not about to do any experimenting . . . not unless somebody else is going to do the test firing. Unless you want that job, you'd better just forget about reloading 9mm or .45 hulls, Bill, and hoard the few you have for a real emergency.

"Use the horsepistols, and thank God Carey's load included a case of those single-shots. You may think they're slow-firing, but believe me you've got one helluva edge over these muzzleloaders."

Sir Francis stamped in, his fine-boned face a study in disgust, frustration, and rage. "Och, the black-hirted, self-sairvin', meacock wretch of a whoreson carpet-knicht! Wi' the domned French and Flemings landed ain the east, the wild Irish ain the west, Spanishers and Portagees a-gnawing at the southerly coasts and the domned Scots massing their domned army on the north bank o' the Tweed, still the bull's pizzle pandar be oot tae line his purse, and me wi'oot gold enow tae sate his base demands! I fear me we'll nae see the King, alas."

"Bureaucrats are always the same, eh, Bill." Foster smiled. "My late father used to say that 'crooked politician' was a gross redundancy." To Sir Francis, "How much does the thieving bastard want?"

The old man sighed. "Ten shilling tae see the King late next week, twenty tae see him arily next week, but it maun be in gold, nae siller."

"And how much to see him tomorrow?" Bass asked, while unzipping his coveralls and pulling up his T-shirt, glad now that he'd heeded the hunch and brought part of Carol's coin collection along.

"A fu' Spanish onza o' gold." Sir Francis shook his white head in weary resignation. "More hard money than mony see in a' the year. And a' I brocht be siller."

Foster fumbled for a moment in the nylon money belt, then handed the old nobleman a South African krugerrand. "Will that do it?"

CHAPTER 3

Dear Krystal,

I am sending this letter by way of the trooper who was my orderly, Olly Shaftoe. The poor fellow lost his forearm and hand when an arquebus ball took him just at the elbow and so ended his soldiering days. The miracle is that he failed to bleed to death or die of infection. He's a bright fellow and learns quickly, so tell Pete to find a job for him.

Bill Collier is also sending a letter to his wife, and Sir Francis one to his daughter, a second to his sister, and two shorter ones to Geoff Musgrave and Henry Turnbull.

Buddy Webster and I are well, if overworked and somewhat underfed all too often, and not because we cannot buy food—I still have quite a bit of the coin collection I brought along—but because there is damn-all food to buy hereabouts. We did eat pretty well for a couple of weeks after the battle near Haltwhistle, where we virtually annihilated about five thousand of these so-called Crusaders, most of them from France and Belgium. My troop—I bought commissions for Buddy and myself, early on; you simply would not believe the purchasing power of gold and silver coin, Krystal—was in the thick of things. We were part of that squadron (commanded by Sir Francis, who else) that rolled up their left flank.

We see very little of Bill anymore. He made a deep impression on the King at first meeting, quickly was appointed to His Majesty's personal retinue, and is, we understand, planning most of the royal strategy now.

We break camp in the morning to march south. There is a larger French force advancing from the east along the Welland valley, but we'll probably have to fight the Irish, first, as they are encamped near Manchester. Granting we overcome both the Irish and the French, there still is an even larger Spanish-Portuguese-Italian force to the far south, last reported somewhere west of Chichester. And we can only hope and pray that King Alexander's internal problems not only continue but multiply, else we'll have his Scots on our backs before we can drive off the other three armies.

Re the letter you sent me with the last powder train: No, stay where you are! The only women with the army, "ladies" and commoners alike, are out-and-out whores. True, they do aid the surgeons in caring for the sick and wounded, but their status is definitely inferior. They share all the filth and hardships of camp life, so they are mostly in poor health and their death rate is high.

With autumn coming in, it is beginning to get downright cold; therefore, I'd appreciate it if you could send me a few things with the next powder train. In the attic of my house you'll find an old footlocker with my name stenciled on the lid; it's heavy as lead, but damned strong. Put the biggest padlock you can find in my shop on it and give the key to Pete; tell him to pack it in with a box of five hundred twelve-gauge shells (all slugs) for Webster and me.

Put the following in the footlocker: my other two coveralls, all the wool sox you can find, the two sets of insulated underwear, all my undershorts and T-shirts, the two replacement liners for my sleeping bag, the large can of foot powder, the big pasteboard box labeled "motel soap," all the razorblades you can locate, the green parka, any bottles of aftershave you can find, and the prescription bottle of Lomotil (also in the medicine cabinet).

I don't ask for food because I know how short you are of it there; however, a couple of fifths would be nice (if you have room for them and if Arbor hasn't guzzled them all by now), also some vitamin tabs and perhaps a few bouillon cubes. There are a couple of chapsticks around the house somewhere, and I can certainly use them, along with the big jar of petroleum jelly and one of the hundred tab bottles of aspirin.

Put in all my handkerchiefs, four bath towels, a big pair of scissors, two ballpoint pens, a couple of the black market pens, and a pack of the 8 x 11 bond. There is a brass police whistle and chain in the bottom drawer of my gun cabinet; that too.

If I said that I love you, Krystal, I'd be lying, but I do miss you and I wish I could be with you. However, we—all of us—are irrevocably committed to His Majesty and his cause, like it or not, so it is sure to be some time before I can return to Whyffler Hall . . . and to you.

As for the BIG QUESTION, *where* we are is assuredly England, *when* is a little trickier as these people (those to whom I've spoken, at least) reckon time according to the individual kings or popes. This is the ninth year since the crowning of Arthur III of England and Wales, the fourth year since the ascension of Pope Boniface XI. I don't know all that much history, but I never heard of an English king named Arthur III.

The present King is a Tudor, and his great-grandfather was Henry VII, but the only reference I can find to the Henry VIII of our history is the memory of the King's great-uncle, Henry, who was killed on some European field more than eighty years ago. Arthur III was preceded by his elder brother, Richard IV, who died suddenly and mysteriously (it is widely believed that he was poisoned at the instigation of the Archbishop of Canterbury, but that may well be just anti-clerical propaganda). His wife bore a son seven months later, but by then Arthur had already been crowned.

Richard's widow, Angela, is the niece of the previous Pope. As such, her son is the favorite of the Church and Rome has turned all the screws they can to force Arthur to abdicate in his nephew's favor; everything else failing, they excommunicated him. But a wave of anticlerical feeling has been building up in England for generations so that now Arthur has the full support of at least sixty percent of his nobles and closer to eighty percent of the common people. And the more foreign armies and raiders the Church sends into England, the wider and stronger becomes the open, public support.

The center of pro-Church sentiment is in and around London. When the King marched his army north at the news of the then-imminent invasion of the Scots, a strong force of Crusaders sailed over from the Continent and garrisoned the capital. The Archbishop of Canterbury and certain pro-Church nobles acclaimed and crowned Angela's son as Richard V, proclaiming his mother his regent.

So that's how matters stand.

As for Arthur, from the little I've seen of him, he seems a personable man of thirty years. He seems intelligent; they say he speaks seven or eight languages fluently. He's strong as the proverbial ox and has been a soldier since his early teens (but that's par for the course among noblemen); he has a build that probably will run to fat as he gets older, but now he's all big bones and sinew.

He had a wife (a daughter of Lothair III, Emperor of what I surmise is the Holy Roman Empire, although its boundaries seem different from what I can recall of my European history), two young sons, and an infant daughter, but they were butchered at the order of the Regent, Angela, soon after her son was crowned.

I think, all things considered, we're definitely on the right side in this conflict, Krystal. For all that the King's people can be rather crude and barbaric, the Church people strike me as mercilessly savage, not my kind at all.

There was more, additional little items Bass requested for his health or comfort, instructions for turning on the heating system in his house—he clearly assumed that she still was living in his trilevel, but she had long ago moved into Whyffler Hall, to be near her many patients, and turned the anachronistic house nestled among Sir Francis' specimen shrubs over to Pete Fairley and Carey Carr. Dave Atkins moved in with them whenever he and Susan had a tiff, which was why Krystal had dumped everything resembling a drug into a cardboard box and locked it into the big, heavy antique safe, along with the rest of the coin collection, the silverware, Bass's jewelry, and the remainder of the liquor.

Dave had proved a good worker, innovative and knowledgeable of weapons . . . when he wasn't tripping on drugs. He would swallow any pill or capsule he came across, however, as too would Susan.

Krystal broke the seals of Professor Collier's letter next, knowing that Arbor would be in no condition even to hold the missive, much less read it. The months here had not been kind to her; she was a mere shadow of her former self, thanks to the rough food to which her digestive tract could not seem to adapt, and to the constant intestinal irritation produced by the gallons of ale she swilled each day.

My Dear,

Please forgive me for leaving you, for much good has come

of it. I have been able to help a very fine young man, whom I have come to love almost as a son; his name is Arthur Tudor and he is the King. It is truly amazing, but he and I bear a marked physical resemblance, one to the other. He it was who first noticed and remarked upon it and that remark was the inception of our present intimate friendship. I have become one of his three principal and most trusted advisers, nor has he been unappreciative; not only has he maintained me as lavishly as present conditions allow, he has ennobled me as well. You may now style yourself "Countess of Sussex," as I have been appointed Earl of that holding (the present Earl is a traitor and rebel and, when once this rebellion is quashed and the invaders driven out of our realm, he stands to forfeit not only his lands and all other holdings but his head as well).

I know that you have always disapproved my consuming interest in the military aspects of history, thought my fascination with games involving strategy and tactics childish in the extreme, but it has been this very knowledge and expertise in the proper techniques of marshaling and movement of troops that has proven of such aid to young Arthur and to his hard-pressed army.

He is a very intelligent young man and possessed of personal courage, but he was as ignorant of the skillful conduct of maneuver warfare as are still our opponents.

When once I had explained the value and necessity of disciplined units of uniform sizes to Arthur, he quickly ordered that my suggestions be carried out. Within the short space of a month, Mr. Webster and Mr. Foster and I had trained a cadre of open-minded noblemen and set them, under our supervision, to imparting of their new knowledge to selected units, both horse and foot. Then I set myself to the organization of the artillery, such as it was.

There was little I or anyone could do to make the larger pieces maneuverable for field service. That was when I suggested to Arthur that they had best be permanently emplaced and their large field crews and draft animals put to better use.

The heaviest guns I kept in the field are classed as demiculverins, are about ten feet long, and weigh over two and one half tons, exclusive of carriage. Depending upon type, the shot they throw weighs from eight to eleven pounds, and their effective range is somewhat less than six hundred meters. A good crew can fire all of six shots, the hour.

My experiments with light artillery, fashioned along the lines of what I can remember of King Gustavus Adolphus' leather guns, have been dismal failure, deadly to many of the brave men who volunteered to man them. Mr. Foster has persuaded me to desist of these experiments, although young Arthur would have backed me, had I considered it worthwhile to continue.

Mr. Webster is no more nor less than what he has seemed from the beginning. Mr. Foster, however, is proving disappointing in many ways. He cannot seem to observe the broad picture of events as they occur; his perspective is invariably narrow, shallow, ascientific, and disgustingly individual-oriented, and he becomes emotional to the point of total immaturity if others fail to agree with him.

In the above-mentioned matter of the leather guns, for instance, he refused to consider the necessity for my experiments; rather, he insisted upon morbidly dwelling on the inconsequential fact that some ten or twelve volunteer gunners had been killed or injured in the course of the project. When I told him that I had already decided to discontinue the test, he was briefly jovial. However, when I added that the project was only being suspended due to the imminent departure of the army on the southern campaign and that I fully intended further testing when again the circumstances were favorable, he threatened me. He promised to kill me himself if I did not personally apply the linstock to the next trial gun I had constructed.

When I then attempted to reason with him, to make it clear to him how infinitely much more valuable my genius is to the king, to England, to all this backward world, he not only interrupted me (most profanely, I might add), he struck me, three times, in the face and with his clenched fist. Had my own bodyguards and two of his officers not restrained him, I fear that he would have beaten me senseless.

Dear Arthur, when he heard of the incident, offered to have Mr. Foster summarily hanged, but, recalling the modest contributions he has made to all our welfares since our arrivals here, I chose rather to allow one of the King's champions to represent me in a duel; Mr. Foster killed my proxy, one Sir Herbert something-or-other, in about ten minutes' swordplay, but he lost part of his right ear, which will possibly serve as a reminder to him that neither young Arthur nor I will brook future interference from him in matters affecting the furtherance of the welfare of our kingdom.

Shuddering, Krystal laid the letter aside unfinished. How like Bass not to have even mentioned any of the events related with such relish by the new-made Earl of Sussex, Professor William Collier, lest the news worry her. As for the Professor, he obviously had become unbalanced and in his present position of power would be highly dangerous; she resolved to send Bass a letter warning him to be very cautious around Collier when he could not avoid him altogether.

CHAPTER 4

Foster sagged in the saddle of his worn-out, foam-flecked warhorse. Behind the three widespread bars of his visor, his face was black with the residue of fired gunpowder, and copious outpourings of sweat had carved a crisscross of canyons through the dirt. His Winchester was empty, along with both horsepistols and all three magazines for his Colt, nor were there any shells remaining in his bandolier. His broadsword hung by its knot from his wrist, its long blade hacked and nicked and dulled from point to quillions with clotting red-brown stains.

Strung out on his flanks and to his rear was what was left of his command—all the horses as done-in as his own, the men gasping and wheezing, many of them bleeding as well, their swords dull and edgeless, their pistols and powder flasks empty.

Arctic wind, straight down from the frigid ocean wastes of Ultima Thule, lashed them with icy salt spray each time another wave came crashing in on the strand before them, driving the limp bodies of the slower Crusaders farther up onto sand littered with the debris of their faster companions' sudden departure.

Far, far out to the west, Foster could see, now and again, one or more of the long boats lifted high on the apex of a wave, before abruptly dropping from sight in the trough. Even farther out, beyond the range of any but the heaviest cannon, were anchored five or six of the High King's ships, more than ample to take off the pitiful remnant of the Irish army.

The first battle—was it only three days ago? It seemed at least a week—had been little short of a massacre of the invading Crusaders, who had been less an army than a huge raiding party—a bastard concoction composed of jailbirds and gutter scrapings and gentleman-adventurers, cutthroats and sneakthieves and pirates, leavened by a horde of religious fanatics, with a thin streaking of regular soldiers of the Irish Royal Army, and a sprinkling of Continental mercenaries.

A good half of the heterogeneous mob had broken and ridden or run away as the first rounds of barshot had come howling from the heights whereon King Arthur's artillery was positioned to batter sanguineous gaps in the Irish lines. More had scattered to the winds when ordered units of dragoons had ridden in and poured two deadly pistol volleys against the straggling, vulnerable flanks, then regrouped and reloaded out of arquebus range.

With even the few western Crusaders in understandable confusion amid the turmoil of their fleeing countrymen, the opposing ranks of English foot suddenly turned to left and right and trotted aside to reveal the grinning mouths of two dozen minions and sakers—four-pounder and six-pounder cannon—and the grapeshot, caseshot, and shovelfuls of coarse gravel that they spewed into the close-packed ranks of gunmen and pikemen and halberdiers and swordsmen turned a partial rout into a general one.

The battle—if battle it could be called, thought Foster—had taken place a few miles east of Blackburn. The cavalry had been dispatched to prevent any large number of the fleeing Irish from reaching the Mersey, wherein lay their fleet.

"And we've been in the saddle damned near every hour since," ruminated Foster.

He realized that he and his men should have long since dismounted and begun walking their mounts, but he knew that to do so would be, for him at least, to fall flat on his face. Pulling listlessly at yellowed wisps of dune grass, Prideful, his bay gelding, appeared anything but, his pride and his spirit run out, like Foster's, in three grueling days of hack and slash and shoot and stab, of a few brief moments of sleep snatched fully clothed and armed on wet ground, too tired to heed the icy drizzle or the pains of a stomach wrestling with wolfed-down hunks of hard, stale bread, moldy cheese, and stinking stockfish, the whole washed down with mouthfuls of muddy ditchwater.

Foster licked his parched tongue over his cracked lips, dropped the reins on the neck of the played-out horse, and fumbled for his canteen. Found the empty cover.

"Foster, you dumb shit!" he muttered. "Now where in hell did you drop it?"

Then his dulled, fuzzy mind dredged up the memory. The memory of throwing back his head to suck greedily at the glorious water, only to have it ripped from his hand with a deafening clang, sent spinning through the air, to bounce crazily along the rocky ground, observed for but the split second before he and his men spurred for the copse from whence had come the shot, to hack the two mercenary musquetiers hiding there into bloody bundles of flesh and rags that steamed as the hot life fluids met the cold air.

Locating the brass chain and pulling the police whistle from the pocket of the chamois cloth shirt under his buffcoat, he blew a long, loud blast, followed by two short ones, a pause, then another long—his signal to dismount.

He kicked his right leg free of the offside stirrup and painfully swung it over the pommel and the drooping head of Prideful. But when he slid to the ground, his legs buckled beneath him. Kneeling on the damp sand, he knew that he had reached the very end of his strength, knew that in another eyeblink he would be stretched full-length, sleeping the sleep of utter exhaustion. He could already feel the waves sweeping over him, covering all thought, all sensation, nestling him, cuddling his weary body, soothing his aches and worries and cares. The soft, warm waves crooned a lullaby.

"*Sleep,*" they whispered, "*sleep. Forget the cold, the pain, the world. Forget all and sleep.*"

"Dammit, the men . . . *my* men, the horses! Got to find powder . . . find the army."

He took his lower lip between his teeth and bit it, bit harder, furiously. The hot, salt blood oozed over his coated teeth, wetted his parched tongue. He found himself gulping his own blood, avidly.

Grasping the stirrup leathers, he slowly hauled himself onto his clumsy, unfeeling feet, found the broadsword still hanging from his wrist and sheathed it, bloody or no. But it took him three tries to get the point of the blade between the lips of the scabbard, so tremulous were his hands.

He took hold of the cheekpiece of Prideful's bridle and began to walk the weakly resisting animal in a slow, erratic circle, wincing and mumbling curses as each new ache and agony made itself known. Gradually, one or two at a time, the troopers and officers up and down the strand commenced to emulate him . . . most of them, anyway. Some still sat on their horses or had fallen off and lay huddled beside them. Up to Foster's left, a horse had fallen and both horse and rider lay motionless.

Trudging up the shallow beachfront because the sand was there firmer and did not drag so heavily against his still-unsteady legs, he consciously focused his red-rimmed eyes on each man he passed, croaking a greeting to those he knew. Not all were his; other units from Sir Francis' Horse were intermixed, as well as strays from the North Wales Dragoons, the Glamorgan Lancers, slant-eyed mercenaries of the Totenkopf Schwadron of Reichsherzog Wolfgang—King Arthur's brother-in-law, furious with grief at the murder of his youngest sister—and even a few King's Own Heavy Horse—their gilded armor nicked and dented and spotted with rust, now, their showy finery tattered and sodden and as filthy as Foster's own clothing.

A hundred yards from his starting point, he heard, from somewhere far ahead, the unmistakable bass bellow of Sir Francis' aurochs horn, calling his officers to him. At almost the same instant, he spotted familiar trappings on a fallen horse.

The big, black mare was dead and Foster first thought the rider dead as well, until he noticed the shaking of the man's shoulders, the tight clasp of the arms about that stiffening neck—until he heard the gut-wrenching sobs.

Leaving Prideful where the gelding stood, he leaned over and gently shook the man, sucking enough blood from his tooth-torn lip to prime his throat for speech. "Guy, *Guy*, are you wounded? It's me, Bass, Bass Foster."

After a moment, the long-bodied man humped up his flat buttocks, got his short, slightly bowed legs under him, and came to his knees. He had thrown off his helmet, and the wind-driven spray had quickly plastered his dull hair to his dirty nape. Black blood was crusted over and beneath a shallow cut under one bleary, teary brown eye.

Gulping back a sob, he answered, "Nae, Bass, I be wi'oot wound. But m' puir, baw Bess be dead." Fresh tears trickled down his black-stubbled cheeks, his gaze wandering back to the dead warhorse, from the flank of which the spray and persistent drizzle were slowly laving away the wide streaks of foam.

Grabbing the shoulder of the buffcoat, Foster shook the man again, harder. "I'm sorry about your mare, Guy, but she's not the only dead thing on this beach; there's more dead horses, and dead or dying men, too. You're the first officer I've come across. You have to take command of our troop, rally them. And see if anyone has some powder; the scrub brush back yonder could be hiding a hundred Irishmen. I have to report to Sir Francis, immediately."

If the grieving man heard him, he gave no indication of the fact. Tenderly brushing grains of sand from off the glazing eye of the carcass, he sobbed, "Puir, gude beastie, faithful tae the last, y' were. Y' run y'r noble hairt oot, y' did. An' a' for me. Fie, braw lassie, ne'er wi' it be ane other like tae y'."

As the grief-stricken man's body inclined forward again, Foster took firm hold of the other shoulder as well and hauled him back onto his knees.

"Goddammitall, Squire Guy Dodd, you've got to take over command until I get back! Snap out of it, man. D'you hear me? I said, snap out of it!"

Still getting no reaction, Foster drew back his gauntleted right hand and dealt Dodd's gashed left cheek a stinging slap, followed by a backhand buffet to the right one, then again, with back and palm, and yet again. His blows reopened the clotted cut and fresh, bright-red blood poured over the old to drip from the square chin.

Then the brown eyes sparked with rage and, powered with a rush of adrenaline, the Northumbrian lieutenant stumbled to his feet, his hand fumbling for the hilt of his broadsword.

"Y' whoreson! I'll hae oot y'r wormy lights!"

Stepping over the outstretched neck of the dead mare, Foster again grabbed both the wide-spreading shoulders and shook the stocky little man, while lifting him from off his feet with a strength he would have doubted he could summon up.

"Now damn you, Guy, *listen to me!* I'm called to Sir Francis, to the south, there. The men have got to be rallied and you've got to do it; we could be attacked by hidden stragglers any minute. There's not another officer or sergeant in sight, so you're volunteered. Take over, *now!*"

Continuing up the beach, toward the sound of the rally-horn, Foster took the time to cursorily examine each corpse he came across, seeking potable water and gunpowder. That was how he happened upon the strange body.

It was the unusual pair of boots that first drew his attention to the particular corpse, lying well above the surf line among a huddle of other dead Irishmen, apparently a group that had made a suicidal stand, perhaps to allow some high-ranking notables to gain the safety of the sea.

Dazed with exhaustion, thirst, and hunger as he was, it took him a minute or so to comprehend just what was so odd about the boots on that one man. Then it came to him: in this world, every pair of indigenously fashioned boots or brogans he had seen were straight-sided; that is, each boot would fit either right or left foot . . . but not those of this dead man; like Foster's own, they were properly curved—one for only right, one for only left.

Trudging closer, he noted other unique features. For one thing, the boots were almost new; for another, stitched to the outside of each calf was a holster and each holster contained a miniature wheellock horsepistol—light, beautiful, and richly decorated they were, with bores looking to be about .50 caliber, smallbore for this time and place. Furthermore, the boots appeared to be about Foster's own size.

Deciding to take boots and pistols as well—the stripping of useful equipment or valuables from enemy slain was here commonplace and, indeed, part of a soldier's reward for winning battles—he had knelt to unbuckle the high straps when the gilded sword hilt attracted him. He drew the weapon and hefted it, then whistled soundlessly. The long, bluish blade bore blood streaks, so it certainly had been in use during these hellish three days, yet it still retained a razor edge and a sharp point. It looked about as long and as wide as any average broadsword, but it was so finely balanced as to feel feather-light even to his tired, aching muscles. On impulse, he worked the baldric of Kelly-green leather off the stiff corpse, slid the exceptional sword into its case, set it aside, and started to turn back to his original purpose.

But something drew his eyes back to the Irishman's torso. The dagger? He pulled it far enough out to see that it was of the same steel as the sword; he added it and its belt to his trophies. No, not the dagger, the hand. The cold, gray hand, its callused fingers splayed upon the hacked and dented breastplate. No, not the hand, either, the ring. Something about the ring.

At first, Foster involuntarily recoiled at the feel of the cold, clammy, dead flesh, but he set himself to the task. At last he managed to wrench off the gold ring.

So poor was the light and so worn down the lettering that at first it seemed indecipherable. Then he painfully picked out the words *MASSACHUSETTS INSTITUTE OF TECHNOLOGY CLASS OF 1998!*

Foster sank back onto his haunches, stunned, his head awhirl of inchoate, half-formed thoughts. *How? When? Where? Who?* Impossible, yet the proof of possibility was clenched in his hand.

"But how can I call anything impossible," he silently mused, "after all that happened last spring? I was born the fifth of January, 1930, which makes me almost forty-three years old. This man is . . . was . . . at least my age, and that tallies with the wear and tear of the ring; hell, it's almost smooth, in places.

"But 1998? Did I read it wrong? No, that's a nine, all right, one, nine, nine, eight. Most guys finish college at twenty-two, twenty-three. Christalmightydamn! This guy isn't . . . wasn't . . . hasn't been even *born* yet.

"I wonder . . . could he have had anything to do with what happened to me, to us, all of us? Alive, God, think of the answers he might have given me. But, hell, all he does dead is just complicate the problem."

The aurochs horn bellowed its summons yet again, closer this time. He shook his head, rose again to his knees, and finished unbuckling the dead man's boot tops, worked them off the rigid legs, rose, and fastened them together. When they were slung over Prideful's withers, he added his sword and baldric, replacing them with the mysterious man's finer, richer equipage. Attached to the dagger belt were a silver powder flask and a lacquered-leather box fitted for and containing a wad of greased-cloth patches, a dozen bullets, a brass mold for casting them, and the spanner for winding the pistols' mechanisms, as well as a small flask of fine priming powder. Once two loaded and primed pistols were thrust under his belt and a keen, finely balanced sword hung at his side, he felt a good deal more confident that he could deal with whatever might lie ahead.

Among the pile of dead men, he found two almost full waterbottles. Jerking out the cork, he raised one of them, greedily gulped down about half of it. The cold water was liberally laced with strong whiskey, and soon the warmth in his belly was spreading out into his chilled limbs, soothing the multitudinous pains, replacing his almost-sapped stores of energy, dispelling a measure of his mental fogginess.

Thus refreshed, he expanded his searching, hauling aside a couple of the stiff, cold foemen. When at last he led Prideful on toward the sound of the horn, he had added to the gelding's load three full water bottles, a half-dozen powder flasks of varying degrees of fullness, and three pairs of big wheel-lock pistols—valuable, because many horsemen of King Arthur's army still were armed with matchlock weapons—and his new jackboots were stuffed with cased broadswords and daggers, none of them so ornate as the set he had appropriated, but all of the same superb steel and balance.

And under his stinking, soaked clothing, the moneybelt about his waist sagged, bulging with an assortment of golden coins. Tightly buttoned into his shirt pockets under his corselet were two little doeskin bags filled with scintillating gemstones. He recognized that the treasure was most probably loot, but rationalized that the original owners were likely dead.

Several of the squadron's captains were already gathered under the tattered, sodden banner bearing the Whyffler arms, all looking wrung-out, spent, haggard. Buddy Webster sat propped against a dead horse with the hornblower beside him; the massive man's chin was sunk onto his chest and his snores rivaled the intermittent bellows of the horn.

Sir Francis, at least ten years the senior of the eldest of his captains, was the freshest-looking of the lot, though his armor and clothing showed that he had been in the thick of more than one engagement. His face was as clean as cold seawater could make it, his cheeks were shaven, and his beard trimmed.

He strode briskly through the deep sand, threw his arms about Foster, and hugged him with fierce affection. "Ah, Bash, Bash . . . *fagh!*" He spat out the pebble he had been rolling on his tongue to dampen his mouth.

"Bass, lad, I'd afeered ye slain, for a' I ken ye Forsters be a mickle hard lot tae put paid tae."

Long ago, Foster had given up trying to convince Sir Francis that he was not a member of that famous and ferocious borderer house, and, in consequence, he was now Captain Squire Forster to all the army, save only Collier and Webster.

Stepping back, the old man noticed the laden horse, and the skin at the corners of his bright eyes crinkled. "*Ha!* Been a-looting, have ye? The mark o' the old sojer, that be. Did ye chance on a stoup o' water, lad?"

When Foster had led Prideful—looking fitter and more

mettlesome after the long, slow walk and a helmetful of whiskey-and-water—over to the group of officers, he first passed around the three canteens, then shared enough of his looted gunpowder for each man to recharge his weapons. Then, noting the empty scabbard still buckled to the squadron commander's baldric, he pulled the best-looking sword from the bundle of captured weapons and presented it.

Sir Francis drew the long blade and, shedding his gauntlet, tested edge and point, then flexed and weighed it, ending with a look of reverent awe on his well-bred features. But then he sheathed the blade slowly and shaking his head said, "Och, nae, Bass, lad. 'Twas a noble gesture an' a', an' I'll e'er remember ye for 't. But yon blade's a rich trophy, nae doot ata' but ye'll get twenty pound or more, an' ye be fool enough tae sell it. It be o' the renowed Tara steel, sich as the High King's royal smith alane can fashion. They be rare e'en in Ireland, rarer still here. They ne'er break, ne'er rust, an' ne'er lose edge. 'Tis ever sojer's dream tae c'n touch ane."

But Foster insistently pushed the weapon back into his leader's hands. "No, Sir Francis; this fight may not be over, and you need a sword. I didn't know these blades to be anything special when I gathered them, and I'd intended them for such of my men as had lost or broken their own. So take it, sir. Please do. Why not consider the sword payment for Prideful, here?"

"Would ye sae shame me then, Bass? The geldin' were a puir, partial payment tae ye for a' ye done in service tae the Hoose o' Whyffler. An' for a' he be the get of a fine *eich* what I lifted outen the Merse, back in me reavin' days, yet this fine blade will easy buy four o' his like."

But he finally accepted the weapon, thanking Foster humbly. And Foster, seeing tears in the old man's eyes, swallowed hard through a suddenly tight throat, unable to just then sort out or name the emotions he was feeling.

He came back from hobbling Prideful with the other officers' horses, in a sheltered spot thick with rank dune-grass, leading a richly caparisoned stallion.

Sir Francis, who had been speaking to the captains while absently fondling his precious new sword, suddenly fell silent, his mouth agape.

"Someone," grinned Foster, "forgot to hobble his mount, and this is too fine an animal to chance losing." He chuckled. "Bastard tried to bite me, before we came to an agreement."

Captain Sir Herbert Little took a couple of paces toward

Foster, his beady black eyes scrutinizing the stallion and his equipage. "Saints of Heaven!" he exclaimed. "It canna be nought but a *Bhreac Mhoir Ech*, by a' what's holy!"

"It couldnae be," stated Sir Francis flatly. "Sich be unheard o', *Hisel'* on a reavin', *fagh*."

"What in hell is a . . . a whatchicallit? What's so special about the bruiser here, aside from the facts that he's damned big and he tries to take chunks out of people he doesn't know?" To Foster, the phrase Sir Herbert had first used to describe the stallion had sounded less like any language than like the clearing of a congested throat.

As always, Sir Francis' perception was keen. "*Bhreac Mhoir Ech?* That be wha' the domned Irishers ca' horses o' the strain o' yon beastie, Bass. First, Tara steel blades, an' noo a spackley stallion. Och, aye, nae doot but it were ane o' the Seven Cantin' Kinglets on this reavin', mayhap, e'en ane o' oors. He was left ahint o' the domned Irishers, an' nae mistake."

As he trotted back down the beach toward where he had left the survivors of his troop, Foster found Bruiser responsive, tractable, and easy-gaited, and he thought it just as well for his hide, for, powerful as the uncut animal was, he could have been deadly, if unruly.

He had tried to present one of the Tara swords to Buddy Webster, but the huge man had declined, even when apprised of the worth of the weapon. "Naw, Bass, thanks enyhow, but thet lil ole thing's just too light for me; sides, the handle's too lil-bit for my hand. I'll stick to what I got, she done done me right, so far."

What he had and preferred was an ancient bastard-sword dug out of the armory of Whyffler Hall, fitted out with a basket guard by the hall smith. It was longer, wider, thicker, and far heavier than a broadsword and, combined with Webster's massive thews and overlong arms, made the trucker-cum-cavalryman a truly fearsome opponent. He and it had become a veritable legend in the army.

The other three captains, however, had eagerly traded their broadswords for the beautiful treasures, and even Webster had accepted one of the fine daggers. Sir Francis took also two of the last three sets.

"T'were best, Bass, that these twain gae tae the King an' Earl William, methinks. Alsae, the sooner ye get that golden hilt o' yer ane hid under honest leather, the better for ye."

Certain privately spoken words to Sir Francis brought the

old nobleman and three trusted retainers along with him as far as that spot whereon the Irish royal guardsmen had made their last stand. While the troopers lashed the two small, heavy caskets onto a powder mule's empty packsaddle, draping the bloodstained woolen cloak of one of the Irishmen over them, the commander paced over to Foster. He jumped back barely in time to avoid the teeth of the stallion.

But, to Foster's surprise, he smiled. "Ye've a gude mount there, lad. He be fu' war-trained an' not tae mony are, these days. But he be a true, auld-fashion destrier, an' he'll sairve ye weel, but keep ye a tight reain tae him, till he lairns the smell o' yer retainers.

"As tae this matter"—he jerked a thumb back over his steel-clad shoulder—"breathe ye nae world o' it tae any mon, for some would allow it be the King's, by rights. Ne'er ye fear, I'll be gie'in' ye a proper accountin', ere I send it oot o' camp for safekeepin'.

"Noo, y know wha' maun be done, Bass. Rally a' ye can find and coom back."

Guy Dodd, ably assisted by a tall, blond, hawknosed young ensign of the Totenkoph Schwadron, had assembled some twoscore troopers, few of them seriously hurt, but all of them thirsty, hungry, worn-out, and grumbling.

With a click of boot heels and a stiff, formal bow, the strange officer introduced himself. *Herr Hauptmann, ich bin Egon von Hirschburg, Fahnrich zu dem Schwadron Totenkopf.*"

"The lad doesnae speak verra mooch Engish, Bass," Guy said, "but he do talk the tongue o' them slit-eyed de'ils o' his'n." He waved at a quartet of short, squat, bandy-legged orientals who had laid aside their crossbows and were rubbing down their smallish, big-headed horses with handfuls of dead grass.

Foster had never seen them fight but, he thought, if they were as mean as they looked, he was glad they were on his side. They had shed their chainmail hauberks and quilted gambesons, and even their shirts—bare to the waist and seemingly immune to the cold drizzle and icy winds. They grinned and chattered constantly in a language at once singsong and guttural.

Two more of the orientals squatted close by, on either side a heap of broken pike and lance shafts. With flashing knives and nimble yellow-brown fingers, they were transforming the battle debris into quarrel-sized dowels for the waiting cross-

56

bows. Foster reflected that there were some plus points for the more primitive weapons.

Aside from a few brushes with isolated stragglers of the Irish force, the squadron regained the camp nearby the original field of battle in slow, easy stages, and only nine days after they had left it; since many troopers and even a few officers were afoot, this was fast indeed.

When all of his troopers were fed and bedded down, with those of their comrades who had come back to camp a few days earlier seeing to the surviving horses, when he had personally seen the men of other units who had made the long march back with him delivered over to their respective commanders along with compliments on their bravery, training and discipline; only then did Foster seek his tent, his arrival simultaneous with that of Buddy Webster and Sir Francis, along with an arrogant young officer of the Sussex Legion, William Collier's personal troops. Save for a modicum of camp mud along soles and heels, his jackboots were as shiny as his polished cuirass and helmet, his rich clothing clean and whole, and he made no attempt to mask his distaste at the filthy, rusty, tatterdemalion aspects of the three other officers.

Sketching the very briefest bow and salute that courtesy would permit, he snapped in a high-pitched, nasal voice, "The Lord William, Earl of Sussex and Grand Marshal of the Armies of His Majesty, Arthur, King of England and Wales, commands that Captain of Dragoons Sebastian Forster and Captain of Dragoons Buddy Webster immediately report to his pavilion."

This said, he sniffed haughtily and added, "However, I am certain that my lord did not know just how disreputable would be your appearances. You will don clean clothing, wash, and shave before you accompany me to my lord."

Foster's eyes flashed fire, everything about the supercilious young noncombatant grating on his sensibilities. Sir Francis noticed and tried vainly to catch his eye, but he was too late.

"So," he growled from between clenched teeth, "Bill Collier *commands* that I report to him, does he? And you, you arrogant young puppy, *command* me to wash and shave and change clothing, do you? Well, boyo, Bill Collier will see me as I stand this minute or not at all! As for you, were I not so damned tired, I'd have your guts for garters, here and now; however, my late father used to say that dogs and damn fools deserved one free mistake. You've now had yours, remember that, in future!"

In a few moments inside his tent, however, he removed his weighty, bulging moneybelt, entrusting it to Sir Francis, along with the little gold-chased wheellock pistols, his silver-buckled daggerbelt, and his rich new sword, taking Sir Francis' plainer one in exchange. He then slipped a full magazine into his Colt and another into his pocket. He no longer liked Collier or trusted him in any regard. On inexplicable impulse, he took the worn finger ring from the moneybelt and slipped it over his middle finger—the only one it would fit snugly, as the dead Irishman had had larger hands.

Because neither Foster nor Webster would consider riding their tired horses, Collier's errand boy had no choice but to walk as well; the three officers trailed by a trooper leading the sleek, shiny, high-stepping horse, and by a second carrying the two sets of Tara-steel cutlery intended for the King and his marshal. In tacit agreement, Foster and Webster maneuvered the flashy young officer between them and deliberately made their way through the wettest and foulest quagmires of the camp streets. Twice, Webster's long sword "accidentally" found its way between the now mud-coated legs of the once dapper Sussexer. The first time, he sat down forcefully and with a mighty splash; the second, his arms flailing futilely, he measured his length, face first, in a soft ooze of fecal-smelling muck.

The pavillion proved to be quite near to the royal complex. Arrived, the muddy and foul-odored Sussexer turned Foster and Webster over to a dried-up wisp of a little man who led them into a lamp-lit anteroom, instructed a pair of servitors to sponge the worst of the soil from their boots, then danced about them, chattering while his orders were performed.

"Goodness me, young Edwin takes orders too literally, yes he does. His Grace said immediately, but you gentlemen should have been allowed time to array yourself decently, indeed yes.

"And young Edwin, himself, tchtch, haste makes waste, oh yes; the lad looks as if he'd ottered here on his belly, goodness gracious, but he does."

When their footwear met the oldster's critical taste, he ushered them through several more canvas-walled chambers, fetching up in a larger one which obviously was a guardroom. Two captains, one of the Sussex Legion and one of the King's Own Heavy Horse, sat on either side of a brazier, sipping ale and conversing in hushed tones. They arose when they spied the newcomers, and the King's Own officer strode over to them, spurs jingling, boots creaking.

"These be the gentlemen-officers summoned by Earl William, Corwin?" At the oldster's nod, he bespoke Foster, "We twain ne'er have met, Squire Forster, but I know ye by repute, and all know of the mighty Captain Webster. Welcome, gentlemen. I fear I must request that you leave your swords in this room, your dirks as well, none save guardsmen are allowed to go armed beyond this point."

When Foster set down the bundle, in order to remove his baldric, one of the Irish daggers clattered out.

"What's this? What's this?" The Sussex captain half-drew his broadsword.

"They're two broadswords and two daggers of Tara steel," said Foster. "I captured them on the beach and we have brought them to present to His Majesty and to Earl William. The cloak in which they're wrapped came off the corpse of an Irish nobleman."

The first captain drew one of the trophies and fingered the blade, flexed it, and returned it to its case. "A princely gift, sirs, a princely gift indeed, but you cannot bear them into His Grace's presence. I will do it, however."

"God, you sthink, Mr. Foster." Collier wrinkled his nose, waving a pomander of spices under it.

Foster snapped coldly, "You would, too, had you spent the last two weeks in the saddle, *Professor* Collier. Now, what's so urgent? What d'you want with us? We're tired and hungry and thirsty and very dirty, as you just noted. Spit it out, man, I want a bath and a feed. You've got it too damned hot in here, too. And what the hell are you burning in those braziers? The place smells like a Hindu whorehouse."

Thick layers of carpets lay underfoot in the tent chamber, and others hung in place to conceal the canvas walls. Collier sat behind a long, heavy table, and, for all the sweltering heat cast by three huge braziers of polished bronze, he was wrapped in a full length cassock of thick, rich samite, with a velvet cap on his head and a *gairbhe* or thick shawl of shepherd plaid across his round shoulders. One gloved hand held a white linen cloth with which he intermittently dabbed at a dripping nose.

"I am afflicted with a virus, Mr. Foster. I have been for ten days and I need medical attention. You are to ride up to Whyffler Hall and fetch back Miss . . . ah, Dr. Kent, along with any anticongestants and antibiotics she has left."

"You've got to be kidding." Foster shook his head slowly. "I just told you, we've spent the bulk of the last fortnight in the saddle; now you want me to undertake a round trip of better than a hundred and fifty miles, simply because you've got a cold? Doesn't King Arthur have a doctor or two about?"

"They're all ignorant quacks," croaked Collier. "All they know is bleeding and purging and compounding foul, witch's-brew concoctions of unmentionable ingredients. I need a *real* doctor, some penicillin, some vitamins. I seem to recall you having a big jar of vitamins somewhere in the kitchen of your house? Well, I want them. I command you to bring them back to me. My continued health and well-being is of vast importance to the kingdom."

"You don't just have a cold, Collier, you've come down with severe megalomania, d'you know that? You've gone nutty as a frigging fruitcake, and hell will freeze over solid before I saddle-pound my tired ass up to the Cheviots and back, just to pump your overinflated ego up a little more. Have you got that?"

The armchair crashed over backward as Collier sprang to his feet, empurpled with outrage. "*No* one addresses the Earl of Sussex in that tone, Foster! The well-deserved loss of half your ear apparently taught you nothing. I think you need a bodkin through your insubordinate tongue. Perhaps a flogging would teach you how to speak to and behave in the presence of your betters. You'd best get started for Whyffler Hall, before I call my Legion and—"

"Go fuck yourself, Collier," snarled Foster. "You want a doctor, go to one of these you call 'quacks'; as full of shit as you've become, a purge would do you good."

He had spun on his heel and started out of the chamber when Collier struck a small gong and shouted, "*Guards!* Guards, to me!"

A dozen Sussex Legionnaires poured into the chamber, blocking Foster's exit, led by the Legionary captain, his long sword bared.

"Seize Captain Foster! Take him outside and flog him, thirty . . . no, *fifty* lashes. Put a blunt brass pin through his tongue. Let—"

"Nowl you jest hol' on there, Perfesser," put in Webster. "I don't give a gol'-plated fuck if you play-ack big dog all you wants to, but when you gets to where you gonna *whip* folks and stick pins in 'em 'cause they won' do crazy things 'long with you, this ole boy's done had hisself enough."

"Stay out of this affair, Webster," warned Collier, smiling cruelly. "This is between Foster and me. You already know your place; he must learn his own."

Webster said no more; he acted, instead. His long, powerful arm shot out and the huge hand closed with the fingers under the backplate of the soldier who held Foster's right arm. He jerked the man off his feet and flung him full into the Sussex captain; both men went down in a heap.

"Help! Guards! Mutiny! Murder!" Collier had time to scream but the four words before the soldier who had had Foster's left arm came flying, to crash onto the tabletop and skid full into his master, his helmeted head taking the Earl in the pit of the stomach, both crashing back onto the overturned chair.

Shaking with laughter, the captain of the King's Own, who had accompanied them and heard everything, partially unwrapped the bundle of weapons and extended them toward Foster. "You can keep your hands off me, Captain Webster; I've no part in this sorry affair. I shall say as much at your trial, but if you're to live to have one, you'd best take these swords and defend yourselves ere the damned Sussex pigs chop you into gobbets."

But it was not to be. With Foster and Webster backed against the wall, their blue-shimmering Irish swords and daggers confronting a triple rank of Collier's guardmen, the chamber was suddenly filled with royal-liveried infantry, their knife-bladed pikes threatening every man in the tent. Then Arthur, himself, strode in, flanked by Reichsherzog Wolfgang and Harold, Archbishop of York.

When the King had heard Captain Cromwell's terse report, dismissed the Sussexers, and had his pikemen right the overturned chair and place the wheezing, gasping, red-faced Earl of Sussex into it, he spoke to him sternly.

"Uncle William, you have overstepped your authority. These brave officers are but just come in from half a month of riding and fighting in this bitter weather, and right was with them to refuse your unreasonable commands. And our own physicians' pills and nostrums are enough; you need not send north for more.

"All the camp knows that bad blood runs twixt you and Squire Forster here, as all know that you've not the stomach to meet him, man to man, at swordpoints, as gentlemen should, to settle their differences. You'll not abuse the power *we* gave you to torture a fine captain into humility. Do you ken us, Uncle?"

He turned to Foster and Webster. "Those blades are Tara? How came you by them?"

But Collier refused to let things ride. His speech slurred due to a bitten tongue, he rose to lean against the heavy table, needing the support.

"Your Majethy should not have humiliated me before theeth lowborn pigth." He waved a hand toward Foster and Webster. "I have given you power and victorieth, Arthur; perhapth my geniuth had been better uthed by Holy Mother, the Church."

Growling guttural German curses, his big, hairy hand grasping the hilt of a *cinquedea dagger*—its two-foot blade so wide as to be reminiscent of a Roman short sword—the Reichsherzog started forward, but Arthur's arm barred his path.

"No, Cousin Wolf." Then, to Collier, "Do our ears deceive us, or did you threaten us with desertion to our enemies, Earl William? For, if you did so, why, we shall be most happy to speed you on your way. There be at least a hundred spies and agents of the Usurper in this camp. We know them all. Several are on your staff or among your guards, and we are certain that they would be easily enticed to help you to journey to London, where some very inventive torturers and, in time, a stake await you. The Church does not forgive, nor do Her servants trust turncoat traitors."

Suddenly realizing what his precipitate words had wrought, Collier had paled, his hands gripping the edge of the table so hard that his big knuckles stood out stark white against its dark wood. "But . . . but, I gave Your Majethty victorieth. It wath I who ethtablithed the powder manufactory at Whyffler Hall. I gave dithipline to your army and formed it into ordered, uniform unith and brought thanity to your thythtem of military rankth. I—"

The King left the chamber, trailed by the Archbishop and the Reichsherzog, the pikemen politely escorting Foster and Webster in the King's wake.

CHAPTER 5

The snow lay deep on ancient Eboracum as the long, well-guarded column of wagons and wains, heavy-laden with the component parts and the raw materials of Pete Fairley's gunpowder-manufacturing operation, neared. With William Collier across the border to Scotland and Whyffler Hall situated but a few miles from that same border, a hastily called conference—King Arthur, Archbishop Harold, Reichsherzog Wolfgang, Sir Francis Whyffler, and Foster—had agreed that the vital operation would be safer and more centrally located in eastern Yorkshire.

As the ice-sheathed spires of York topped the horizon before him, Foster reflected that he would not care to be beginning rather than ending this hellish trek. He now knew exactly why folk of this kingdom seldom tried to travel far in winter and why their various armies almost never fought then.

The distance was not great, less than seventy-five miles, measured on the map in his atlas. But such few roads, he soon discovered, as existed were hardly worthy of being called such at even the best of times, which this time decidedly was not. Where the deep-rutted, potholed tracks did lie, they wandered up hill and down dale, curved back upon themselves, and ran every way but straight, so that his huge, ungainly "command" averaged no more than three miles progress on good days. In the foothills of the Pennines, that figure was halved.

Tight security had had to be constantly maintained, as well, whether on the march or encamped, for survivors of the French-led Crusaders smashed last summer were wandering, starving, about the countryside they needs must traverse, huge aggregations of well-armed robbers prowled by day and by night; and Scot reavers were not left behind until the column had crossed the Tees and were into Swaledale itself.

Too, the weather had been bitter—there had been three- and four-day stretches of time when they could move not at all and had sat, shivering and cursing, within the ring of their transport while knife-sharp winds howled, and driven snow reduced visibility to mere inches.

Tempers frayed and flared, axles split and broke, and the beds had to be emptied and jacked up so that axles or wheels could be replaced. Horses stepped into snow-concealed ruts or holes and broke legs. The delicate beasts died of cold and exposure or slipped on icy rocks and fell, killing themselves and sometimes their riders, as well. Supplies brought from the north were expended and the column needs must camp for an entire week, while dragoons roved the surrounding countryside, foraging—buying from those few who would sell, seizing at swordpoints from those who would not.

He knew that he could not possibly have accomplished the herculean task alone. Had he not been blessed with the inventive and innovative talents of Pete Fairley and Carey Carr, the stolid strength of Buddy Webster, and the cool, calm rationality of Krystal Kent, he would have become a raving lunatic before the journey had hardly commenced. And Collier had banked on the fact that a winter transfer of the powder industry from north to south was a physical impossibility; he had told Foster as much just before his departure.

The weather having turned entirely too foul for any attempt at large-scale raiding, much less campaigning, King Arthur's army had gone into winter bivouac, in and around Manchester. Harold, Archbishop of York, had retired to his seat for the winter, and Arthur, himself, would have preferred the more familiar comforts of that staunchly loyal city. But the marshaling of his troops had sorely tried the supply capabilities of all the North and East Ridings, nor had the situation been in any manner helped by the incursion of the Crusader army from France.

Foster and Buddy Webster had ridden north with Sir Francis and the survivors of their original armed band to celebrate Christmas and see in the New Year at Whyffler

Hall. It was a long ride, in the face of bitter winds howling down off the distant highlands of Scotland, cold as a hound's tooth and sharp as the edge of a dirk. For all that the journey was accomplished in slow, easy stages, both men and animals suffered, so much so that the sight of Heron Hall was a welcome one indeed.

For all his mixed and ambiguous loyalties, Squire John Heron was as jolly and hospitable as ever, though Foster's war-sharpened eye noted that his host had added several medium-sized cannon—sakers and small minions, they looked to be—and a dozen or more swivel-guns to his defenses, while a dry ditch, six feet deep and ten or more wide, now circuited the walls of his bailey. He had added to his garrison, too, but for all that he still entertained them royally, setting before them the best meal Foster had downed since last he had sat to table under the roof of Heron Hall. It was all that he could do, however, to keep his heavy-lidded eyes open and maintain his place in the armchair, for the warmth and the tasty, hot food had the effect of a powerful soporific on his body, so long now accustomed to endless cold and ill-prepared, tasteless camp fare.

He allowed Sir Francis and Squire Heron to carry the conversation, and as soon as courtesy permitted he sought his bed. He slept the most of the next day, as well, a fierce storm having blown down from the north overnight, and Sir Francis, for all his eagerness to be again at his seat—now so tantalizingly near—was unwilling to put tired horses and men on the march in such weather.

John Heron's larder seemed to be bottomless, for if anything the second night's repast—which commenced in late afternoon and continued unabated until the host finally arose to weave his staggering way up to his bedchamber, leaving many a guest and retainer snoring in drunken stupor under the trestletables or on the benches—was several cuts above that of the first night. Pork there was, both wild and domestic, and venison, for such of the King's foresters as were not with the royal army were understandably loath to ride against a nobleman who kept so large and well armed a band. There was goose and duck and chicken and pigeon and even a swan, roasted whole and stuffed with a mixture of breadcrumbs, mashed apples, herbs, pepper, and tiny sausages.

Foster found the swan's flesh tough and unpleasantly fishy-tasting, but Squire Heron seemed so proud to serve the dish, and Sir Francis made so much of being served it, that he forced himself to give the appearance of enjoying the portion allotted to him, although when he saw his chance he surreptitiously slipped most of it under the table to the waiting boarhounds. But he did yeoman work on the well-larded venison, rich goose, and highly spiced pasties of chicken, veal, and mutton, washing them down with long drafts of Rhenish wine and Heron's fine brown ale.

The meal finally done, Squire John courteously but firmly pressed Webster and Foster for their accounts of the recent campaigns. True, he had had Sir Francis' recountal on the previous evening, but never a Borderer born, English or Scots, who was not warrior bred, and Foster noted that even the ladies at the high table and the women at the low seemed to both understand and relish the necessarily sanguineous recitals of crashing charges and merciless pursuits.

Once the three ladies—Heron's second wife, Emma (at least thirty years younger than her lord, Foster figured, but seemingly quite happy, nonetheless), her unmarried younger sister, Anne Taylor, and the girls' widowed aunt, Mary Noble —had bade their goodnights and retired abovestairs, the women and common servants quickly departed to their straw-tick beds or their night duties, leaving the gentlemen and the soldiers to get down to the serious drinking.

Although their host and Sir Francis commenced to pour down quantities of brandies and raw Scots spirits, Webster continued on ale only and Foster confined himself to the pale wine. He had never really cared much for brandy and had, during the past months, made the sad discovery that the only thing the Scots *uisgebeatha* shared in common with the smooth Scotch whiskies of his own world was their place of origin. But he did as well by the wine as he had by the food, putting down at least three pints of it before Dan Smith rose to sing.

A great bear of a man, big as Buddy Webster, which made him huge indeed as compared to the average man of this time, Smith was the master smith of Heron Hall, and blessed with a fine, deep bass singing voice, plus a good memory and the gift to improvisation.

His first few selections were ballads dealing with incidents of the bloody warfare that had seesawed back and forth across the English-Scots border for centuries. Foster knew the antiquity of some of them, as he had heard troopers sing them many times. Then, with a twinkle in his brown eyes, the smith sang a ditty that had most of his listeners alternately grinning broadly or gasping with laughter. It was a Scots song delivered in a broad brogue and interspersed with much Gaelic as well as idioms with which Foster was not familiar, but what little he did comprehend was of a degree of bawdiness to toast the ears of a camp whore.

When the song was done and the listeners had given over pounding the tables and gasping with laughter, the smith made a suggestion, whereupon the men-at-arms commenced to bellow for some songs from the high table. John Heron arose to oblige them and, standing at his place and tapping out his rhythm on the table with the hilt of his knife, sang the tale of a young girl who wed the richest man in the town to find only too late that he totally lacked some essential physiological appendages.

Sir Francis followed with the first vaguely familiar song Foster had heard in this time. In that clear tenor that had risen above the din of so many battles, the white haired knight sang some twenty verses:

> "Then Bob, he were ca'ed tae answer the Session,
> An' they a cried, Mon, ye maun mek a confession.
> But braw Bob ne'er said him a word ava',
> Save, The win' blew the lassie's plaidie awa'."

And then all the men bawled out the chorus:

> "Her plaidie's awa', tis awa' wi' the win',
> Her plaidie's awa' an' it cannae be foun'.
> Och, wha' wi' the auld uns say ava'
> She cannae say the win' blew her plaidie awa'."

As Sir Francis resumed his seat, Heron turned to Foster. "An' noo, Squire Forster, wi' ye oblige us a' wi' a ditty?"

Foster did not think he could expect his audience to understand "The Fighter Pilot's Lament," so he launched into what he could remember of the infamous "Ball of Kerriemuir" and soon had loud assistance on the chorus: "Wha' screw ye las' nicht, wha' screw ye noo? The mon wha' screw ye last nicht, he cannae screw ye noo."

When he had exhausted his store of verses, Webster stood to contribute several more and followed the contribution with an indescribably filthy Marine Corps song, couched in an English so basic that there was no one but could understand it.

Thereafter, things became livelier. Dan Smith cheerfully

wrestled three of the bigger men-at-arms, before Webster shucked jerkin, shirt, and boots and jumped from off the dais to confront the metalworker in the wide, shallow U formed by the lower tables. Webster at length was declared winner, but it was not a quick or easy victory for all his knowledge of oriental martial skills. Next two pairs of tipsy men fought with quarter-staves, and two more pairs with blunted, edgeless, and padded swords, while the drinking went on . . . and on and on.

The next day proved clear, though cold as a whore's heart, and they were a-horse for Whyffler Hall, hangovers be damned. The horses, if not fully recovered of their ordeal, at least seemed refreshed, for all that many of the riders swayed in their saddles, looking to be at death's door, with drawn faces and red, bleary eyes.

For all their own imbiding, however, neither Sir Francis nor Squire John showed more than traces of overindulgence. Webster did, though. He, at the insistence of his new friend, Dan Smith, had switched in the latter part of the evening to bastard concoctions of brandy, hard cider, and burned—distilled, that is—ale. It had taken the brute strength of five men to help him onto his horse, and Foster thought he looked as if he should have been buried days ago.

Sir Francis drained off the stirrup cup and reached across the black stallion's withers to take Heron's hand. "Johnny, ye be nae Pope's man, an' ye ken it. Wha' wi' it tek tae see ye declare for young King Arthur, God keep him?"

Heron's lips set in a grim line. "Ane thrice-domnt Scot 'pon me lands, that be wha, Fran Whyffler! Noo, I've been given assurances, boot I've scant faith in them, for a'. Sae dinnae be surprised tae spy me an' me braw launces come a-clatterin' intae y'r camp, ane day."

Sir Francis looked deep into the eyes of his old friend and spoke solemnly. "Ye be a stark fighter, Johnny Heron. Come tae me soon. Our King needs a' sich he can find. God keep ye."

They had been told that the Rede was frozen, and this proved accurate, allowing them to take a more direct route and shorten their journey by the miles the track meandered to the ford; even so, the distance they had ridden in a bare fifteen hours last summer took the best part of two days to complete in the dead of winter. The only good thing any of them could say about the weather was that, such was its severity, it had driven even the brigands to den up.

Three days after the first day of the New Year of 1640 (Foster had finally been able to get the *anno domini* date from the Archbishop of York), Foster was entertaining in the den of his trilevel. Carey Carr and Pete Fairley sat in rapt attendance to Buddy Webster's enthusiastic account of his troop's role in the three days' butchery of the Irish Crusaders. A log fire crackled on the hearth and the howling winds had driven the past week's snowfall into eaves-high drifts on the north and west sides of the house. Pete had been ready to get a levy to clear the house, but Foster dissuaded him, for the power still—and inexplicably!—was working, so they did not need the light from the covered windows, and the snow served as excellent insulation from the cold and the winds.

With the front door behind five feet or more of snow and ice, they all had been using the patio door to effect entrance, and it was through that door that a booted, spurred, and heavily cloaked figure strode. Before they could say a word, the newcomer was across the room and facing the fire, holding open his cloak to warm his body. He threw back the cloak's hood and took off a lobstertail helmet, placed it on the mantel, then unwound a long strip of wool from about his face, head, and neck. Then William Collier turned to face them.

Carey and Pete smiled greeting, but Foster did not, nor did either Webster or Krystal. Clad in slacks and chamois-cloth shirt, shod only in slippers, Foster was unarmed, and Collier was between him and the gun cabinet, as well as being fully armed with broadsword, Luger, and dirk.

Foster arose and strolled—casually, he hoped—past the uninvited guest to the gun cabinet, his spine tingling, opened the wooden door, and took out the big Colt Peacemaker, quickly made certain that it was loaded, then brought the hammer to full cock and spun about to level the long barrel at Collier.

"You're not welcome under my roof, my lord Earl," he grated, rendering the title mockingly. "I strongly advise you to leave, *now*. Or have you forgotten the way to the door?"

"You're acting childish, Foster." Collier's tone was superciliously reproving. "But then, ordering someone you consider to be an enemy from your property at gunpoint is just the sort of flamboyant, swashbuckling action I should have expected from a perpetual adolescent such as you.

"But, gun or no gun, I shall not leave until I have said

what I came to say, and shooting me would be most unwise, as I travel under the King's protection."

Webster snorted. "And this ole boy says you lyin', Perfesser. I hear tell the King done took back damn near everythin' he give you, so you shore lawd ain't no fav'rite of his no more, and it jest don't stand to reason he'd stend you no kinda perteckshun."

"Although parts of what you say are true, Webster, you are substantially wrong; I am not lying. Yes, that arrogant young puppy who calls himself 'King' stripped me of my lands and title, disregarding all that I and I alone had done for him and his ragtag army, simply because of a few intemperate words I spoke in a moment of frustrated anger, when I was suffering both illness and injury.

"Were I a vindictive man, I might blame Foster for all my reverses. I—"

"Me?" exploded Foster. "What the hell did I do?" He then spoke to Carey, Pete and Krystal. "This yoyo here went a little crazy, I think, when Arthur ennobled him. No sooner had Buddy and I ridden in dog-tired from that Irish business than Earl William sends an arrogant ape to order us to his tent. Then he demands that I immediately ride clear up here to fetch some antibiotics for the goddam head cold he had."

"And," Webster took up the sorry tale, "when Bass tole him he won't gonna do it, the ole bastid tried to have Bass tied up and *whipped*. You ever hear tell of suthin' like thet, Pete? And now he ain't a earl no more, he wants us to treat him like he's still a frind. Shit!"

The smiles had departed the faces of Carr and Fairley, and they now regarded Collier with plain hostility. Fairley arose and stretched with a crackling of his joints. "You wawnt we should chuck the muthuh out, Bass?" he asked, taking a slow step toward Collier.

Hurriedly, Collier held up both hands, palms outward, looking at Foster. "Wait, dammit. Before you eject me, hear me out. I advise you all to forget the past and think of the future. As you'll shortly be aware, Arthur has no future and you'll be wise to come with me, to Scotland."

"So, that's it, is it?" snapped Foster. "You're deserting the King."

"Why not? He deserted me," replied Collier coldly. "But it's not really desertion, you know; he is fully aware of my intended destination. Indeed, his own guards are escorting me to the border, under command of Captain William ap Owen and the godson of the prince of boors, Reichsherzog Wolfgang, with some of his Tartar Cossacks. Arthur guaranteed my safety as far as the border, but he warned me that to set foot back across it would be death; apparently he means to declare me outlaw, the thankless young swine. But come back I will, with the victorious Scots, as a conqueror."

Fairley shook his head. "No you won't, feller. You won't cawse you won't git to Edinburgh."

"The King's guarantee and his escort—" began Collier.

"Goes only far as the borduh," nodded Fairley. "And I hear tell it's a good seventy, eighty miles from there to Edinburgh, and the most of it smack through the stompin' groun's of somma the meanest, orneriest, nastiest, bloodthirstiest folks this side o' hell. If they ketches you alive, they'll tek you apart a lil bit at a time, jest so's they kin hear you screech. These ole boys 'roun' here done tol' me all 'bout the thrice-damned Scots."

Collier just smiled. "Oh, never fear, Fairley, I shall reach Edinburgh whole, unharmed, and with some style. It developed that two of my Sussex officers were, in reality, agents of the Regent and the Church. Arthur and that damned renegade Archbishop, Harold, had known about their duplicity all along, yet had told me nothing of it, damned ingrates. Both are English, of course, but Captain Michael Glede has close blood ties with two very powerful families of southern Scotland, the Humes and the Kerrs. No, I shall reach Edinburgh."

"Where," commented Foster, "there's at least one Papal Legate, not to mention assorted archbishops, and other clerics who'll no doubt be very anxious to make an example of you for the edification of laymen who might scheme to make their own niter. You've heard what happened to the poor bastards they caught after the Empire lost to Crusaders. You've got to be nuts to put yourself into the bloody hands of churchmen, Collier." Then he added, "What ever happened to the teachings of that gentle man called Jesus?"

"In our world, Foster, there is doubt, among sophisticated scholars at least, that such a person ever lived. That matter aside, if you please, because we are not in our world, we are in this backward and savage one.

"During the weeks the army was at York and since, at Manchester, I've engaged in considerable research. Of course, almost all the available books are written in Latin, but that's no problem for a man of my erudition; and I speak the lan-

71

guage as well, but I'll get to that shortly. For a long while, I thought that we had gone backward in time, something which *is* theoretically possible, for all that frightened scientists assure the general public to the contrary. But I have changed my mind on the basis of what facts I have uncovered.

"Foster, similar in so many ways as this world is to our own, still it is not ours at any era in our world's history. Can't you see what this means? I, William Collier, have *proven* the theory of parallel worlds! We are on one of them."

"So? Well how in hell'd we gitchere, Perfesser?" demanded Webster pugnaciously.

Collier waved a hand impatiently. "Later, Webster, later, but I do have a reasonable theory.

"The first thing I determined was that the Holy Roman Catholic Church of this world is most radically different from the Church of our own world. There are three Popes—the Pope of the West in Rome, the Pope of the East in Constantinople, and the Pope of the South whose seat is called *Roma Africana* and is somewhere on the east coast of Africa, but the few maps are so inexact that that city could be anywhere between Durban and Mogishu."

"What do the Moslems have to say about this Pope of the South, Collier? As I recall, East Africa—hell, most of Africa—was their private preserve for one heck of a long time," asked Foster dubiously.

Collier rested his elbows on the mantel and leaned back, his long cloak steaming in the heat from the fire. "There are no Moslems, Foster, not here and now."

"Oh, come on, Professor, they have Templars here, too."

Collier smiled again. "Quite so, Foster, and if you'll but check you'll find that their main Consistory is located, even now, in Jerusalem and has been for five hundred years within Palestine."

"But, dammit, there have to be Moslems! Sir Francis' family's patents of noblity date from an ancestor who was with Richard I on the Third Crusade. I know, he told me."

Collier smiled at Krystal. "Miss Kent, that mulled wine smells delicious. May I have some?"

Krystal wordlessly filled a ceramic beer mug, arose, and served Collier, then resumed her seat, still unspeaking.

Collier sipped, then took a long draught and, still holding the mug, continued. "Oh, yes, Foster, there were Moslems here, as on our own world, but they . . . but let me backtrack a bit. In our world, the Church suffered a schism in the fifth century which weakened both resulting churches and made the Moslem conquests easier and quicker—*divide et vincit*. That never happened on this world; rather, it was amicably decided to split the papacy into two separate but equal sees, East and West. The Moslems enjoyed some successes, as too did the Seljuk Turks, and the same number of Crusades were launched against them as were in our own history, but with about equal results.

"The difference occurred in the middle of the thirteenth century, here, when hordes of Mongols began to pour in from the east, sacking Samarkand and overrunning most of the expanse of the old Parthia before a Moslem army of Seljuks, Swarizmi, Kurds, Ortuquids, Zangids, Abbasids, and Azerbaijans met them on the banks of the Tigris and were soundly trounced. The same thing happened to them twice more, and in the third defeat the Seljuk Sultan was killed.

"At that juncture, Alexius VII of Byzantium offered the new young Sultan, Kilji Arslan III, the aid of a huge Christian army—in return for certain concessions, of course; trust a Greek to make a profit, they're as bad as Jews—to stiffen his own, which I imagine was by that time a battered, draggle-tailed lot. An agreement was reached and the combined armies had their first meeting with the Mongols near Mosu, and, while the Mongols did not lose, they did not win, either, but their khan fell at that battle and they retired to Bagdad to choose a new one.

"They spent most of the next year assassinating claimants and fighting out the succession among rival clans, and all the while both Popes were preaching a Crusade against them, so that when they had patched together enough cohesiveness to again take the field, they were faced by a host nearly as large as their own, even including the fresh fighters who had ridden in from the east during that year, better armed and mounted for the most part and with a knowledge of the terrain which allowed them to choose advantageous battle sites.

"It is chronicled that one hundred and fifty thousand Mongols were slain at the Battle of Samarra." He smiled another of those infuriatingly superior smiles. "Naturally, the figures are open to question; but, be that as it may, the Mongol migration into the Middle East did not here succeed, as it did in our own world. And when, some thirty years later, the infamous Golden Horde swept across Russia, one arm of it was stopped and generally extirpated at Tula, another arm at

73

Novgorod, and both battles were won by combined armies of Christians and Moslems, drawn from almost every principality of Europe, Africa, and the Middle East. Those Mongols who were not killed or did not return to the east settled in various enclaves from southern Finland to the Caucasus and as far west as portions of Poland and Transylvania. It is their descendants who are Wolfgang's mercenaries.

"I've no time to go into all the details, but suffice it to say that as time went on the two faiths—widely disparate, at their respective inceptions—began imperceptibly to merge, to adapt certain of each others' usages and formulae. Now, Christianity of a sort extends from Cape Finisterre to Kashmir and from the Arctic Circle to the Cape of Good Hope."

Krystal wrinkled her high forehead. "But was there no Reformation here?"

Collier took another pull at the wine. "No. First, the Church here is, due to Her amalgamated composition, less hidebound, dogmatic, intolerant of variations and shadings of belief and practice in religious matters, and less corrupt than the Church of our world was at the time of our Reformation; also, this Church is far more powerful, in large measure because of her monopoly of niter."

Foster had taken a seat, although the Peacemaker still was cocked and still was pointed in Collier's direction. "How in hell did that come about, anyway, Collier?"

"The Church chronicles attribute the invention to two English monks-alchemists," replied the broken Earl. "Roger Bacon, here, and Berthold Black—also called *die Englander*—living in a monastery in the Empire, they were in correspondence and made their discoveries virtually simultaneously. The then Pope, Alexander IV, was a highly intelligent, enlightened man, and when he was apprised of the unusual discoveries, he had Bacon and Black summoned to Rome and set them up under ideal conditions to pursue their experiments. The upshot was that by the middle of the fourteenth century, the use of bombards or large cannon was widespread through all three papal dominions and the innovation of hand-held firearms was beginning.

"Throughout the ensuing centuries, the Church has kept a very tight rein on this, her most valuable asset, and through judicious use of her power has been able to keep wars small and prevent them being waged against the best interests of the Church as a whole, through the simple and effective means of placing a ban on the sale of sacred powder—

niter—to one or both sides. Whenever some renegade church-men or inventive laymen start making their own, it is considered rebellion; they are excommunicated and a Crusade is preached against them.

"There have been any number of smaller rebellions, but the first one of any note or enduring consequence took place in North Africa near the end of the fifteenth century; fifty or sixty years later, there was another in the Crimea. Then, thirty-odd years back, when a duke of Bavaria died without issue, an aggregation of commoners and petty nobles tried to set up a confederation along the lines of that of the Swiss.

"The Church might have let them alone, stayed out of the issue entirely, had the fools not started producing unhallowed niter. A Crusade was preached, of course. The Bavarians fought long and hard, but they had no chance of victory against the tens of thousands, and when they were at last crushed, the Church made a savage example of the ringlead-ers and made quite certain that a maximum number of Crusaders witnessed the example."

"So why was a Crusade launched against England, hey?" asked Foster. "No powder was manufactured by the loyal forces until our arrival, and the invading troops were already here then, most of them."

"Arthur," replied Collier, "defied the temporal authority of Rome in another way. The Treaty of Tordesillas, in 1494, di-vided all the Western Hemisphere between Spain and Portu-gal, excepting those northerly portions long settled by the Norse and the Irish. Since then, the French have established fur-trading stations at points too far north to be challenged by either Spain or Portugal and too far south to interest the Norse; the Irish are constantly carping on French trespassing but—though, of course, the chronicles record no such thing—I would say that the French have been greasing choice churchly palms and, since only small numbers of Frenchmen and a mere handful of tiny settlements are involved, Rome has cast a blind eye on the incursions, thus far.

"The deposed English King, on the other hand, has de-clared that while the Norse and the Irish claims are legal, the Spanish, Portuguese and French are all interlopers and that the rightful owners of all the northerly landmass are the En-glish—or, more precisely, the Welsh—by right of first settle-ment. This tenuous claim is based upon certain questionable records reposing in the Abbey of Strata Florida in South Wales. They detail a certain Prince Madoc ap Owen who is said to have settled with ten shiploads of his adherents somewhere in the interior during the latter half of the twelfth century.

"When first he ascended the throne, Arthur put forward this bizarre claim, documented with copies of the Strata Florida manuscripts into which had been inserted a map—which map Vatican scholars quickly determined to be a clever forgery—and this discovery clouded the whole issue to the point that Rome refused even to consider an English claim. Arthur, naturally, disavowed any knowledge of the map or of how it might have become bound in with the authentic records, but the damage was done and the then Pope forbade any English encroachment in the West."

"Well, dammit, it stands to reason, doesn't it," demanded Foster with some heat, "that anti-English people could easily have doctored the King's proofs?"

"Tchtchtch." Collier again smiled that ultra-superior smile. "We have become a fanatic royalist, have we not? But do not allow Arthur to deceive you as, for so long, he deceived me. He is an exceedingly devious young man, Foster, and not above exploiting anyone or utilizing any means to justify his actions or bring about his desired ends. But I disgress.

"With rank insubordination of the Church and her definite authority, Arthur planted three colonies—fortified colonies—on the mainland at various points between Spanish and Irish lands. The Irish quickly eliminated the northernmost colony, leaving no single survivor. The Spanish were not so thorough, however, and a few settlers got back to England to tell of the butchery of colonists who had honorably surrendered to the Spaniards.

"Now, both the previous and the present Popes and Queen Angela, the Regent, all were born in Spain. When Arthur added insult to injury, petulantly ordering his brother's widow and his own nephew incarcerated as enemies of the state until he made up his mind whether to execute them or simply exile them, the present civil war commenced. When word of his transgressions reached Rome, moreover, he was excommunicated and Rome expected that his nobles and people would then either depose him or force him to bow to the just dictates of the Church."

Foster shook his head in disgust. "Talk about theocratic despotism! Well, it must have really toasted the goddam Pope's balls when the most of Arthur's subjects stood with him against everything the meddling bastards could do."

"You still don't or can't or, more likely, refuse to understand, Foster," Collier sighed, then went on as if addressing a retarded pupil. "Arthur *is* in the wrong, Foster. Rightfully, he is not even King. His illegal actions have brought destruction and immense suffering upon his lands and people, death to his wife and family and, no doubt, ramifications more widespread and long-lasting than any of us can now imagine. This rebellion is the largest and most stubborn that the Church ever has faced, involving not just a province or two and a few tens of thousands of peasants, burghers and minor nobles, but an entire kingdom, its ruler, and a large proportion of its total population, *including* one of its highest clergymen.

"Two months ago, Rome finally got around to excommunicating Harold, the Archbishop of York, and declaring his see vacant. But all churchly functions he performed prior to that are valid, including his sanctification of the Whyffler Hall powder mill. So, you see, I—and all of you—have nothing to fear from Church authorities, on this ground, at least. Furthermore, if we go over to the side of the right, devote our future energies and talents to furtherance of the Holy Cause of the Church, we will be forgiven our earlier efforts on the side of Arthur and his rebels."

"Says who?" barked Foster.

"No less a personage than Cardinal Ramón de Mandojana, and Papal Legate now in Edinburgh," announced Collier with a satisfied smirk.

Webster lifted a buttock and broke wind, loudly.

Foster chuckled. "I echo and endorse Buddy's sentiments, Collier. In the first place, I do not and will not share your newfound belief that King Arthur is wrong, not on what obviously biased evidence you've given us tonight. In the second place, I value my neck and I've got no intention of risking it to prove whether this Mandapajamas is a man of his word. You're more than welcome, as far as I'm concerned, to jump out of the frying pan, but don't expect me to join you in the fire, fella; I ignite easily."

Collier talked and argued on for some hours, but made no converts. As dawn paled the sky, he pulled his gauntlets back on with stiff, jerky movements. Only Foster and Krystal were left in the den, the other three having retired long since.

"I'll say but one thing more, Foster," the former Earl began coolly.

Foster was infinitely weary of listening to his uninvited

guest. His muscles were stiff and his eyelids heavy and gummy-feeling. He realized that his temper was frayed to the point of sudden murder. "I wish you wouldn't, Collier, not if it's some more of your damned preachments. You've foresworn King Arthur, we haven't, it's that simple, and nothing you can say is going to change our feelings about the King, the Church, or the rightnesses or wrongnesses of the causes."

"Professor Collier," put in Krystal, "when first you arrived tonight, and told us you were leaving England, I thought that you might have come here for your wife, but you've not even mentioned her in all the hours you've been talking. Do you intend deserting her, too?"

Collier shrugged. "Perhaps you would call it 'desertion,' Doctor, but I feel Arbor will be better off here until I come with the Scottish army in the spring. The last encumbrance I expect to need would be an ailing, alcoholic wife."

Krystal's eyes glittered like ice. "Yes, Professor, I would say that you're deserting your wife. You know, it's funny now, but during that first day we were here I felt sorry for you in your marital situation; then I came to truly respect you, as you proved so versatile and commanding a figure. Now, however, you've betrayed your friends, the King that favored you, and now you're about to betray and desert your wife, and you disgust me, Professor."

The former Earl shrugged again, then ignored the woman, addressing himself to Foster. "If there is anything in this house you want to save, I would strongly advise that you move it and yourself well south before the spring, my dear Captain. Whyffler Hall and the Royal Gunpowder Manufactory herein contained will be one of the earliest and foremost objectives of the Scottish Crusaders. Sir Francis is certain to make an effort to hold the hall with whatever troops he can beg or borrow from the Usurper or enlist hereabouts, so it will most likely be reduced from a distance with bombards, and a few sixty-pound stone balls will quickly render your twentieth-century home into matchwood."

"Before you leave," said Foster, "I'll have my father's Luger back, if you please, and the pair of breech-loading pistols on your pommel, as well. They were yours while you remained a King's man, but I'll be damned if I'll see them used against the King by a turncoat traitor."

And as soon as there was enough pale light to indicate that, somewhere behind the storm clouds, the sun had risen,

Foster and Pete Fairley were at the hall and in conference with Sir Francis and Geoffrey Musgrave.

The old nobleman's cap and voluminous robe were both of the same thick, rusty-black velvet. Foster recalled the garments clearly; they were those Sir Francis had been wearing when first they had met. But the pale, trembling, dim-eyed old man who had greeted and thanked him for his support in a quavering voice, then, was now replaced by a soldier who, though admittedly elderly, was possessed of keen faculties and intuitive judgment.

"Nay, lad," he answered Foster's suggestion. "Dinnae ye ride tae the King. Anely God kens where His Majesty be noo. Och, aye, mayhap he bides wi' the army, but too he could be wi' his ane folk in Wales.

"Nay, let Captain Webster ride in sairrch o' the King; he be known tae His Highness as well as yersel', an' he'll be bearing letters both frae ye an' me. Geoffrey can gi' him some dozen launces tae ride at his back and there still be horses a-plenty aboot ma' park."

Properly gauging their temperatures through dint of long experience, Musgrave leaned forward, drew four loggerheads from the fire, and plunged them hissing and steaming into four tankards, then passed a heated cup to first his lord, then the other two.

Sir Francis sipped, then took a long draught. "Nay, Bass, ye maun ride tae York, tae Harold Kenmore, the Archbishop. York be for certain sure the anely place our manufactory will be safe and, too, if ye bring wagons frae York empty, nae doot ye'll be mindfu' o' the best routes o'er which ye'll lead them fu'."

But Francis Whyffler's assurance had not been shared by Harold of York. "I much fear me, Squire Forster, that you cannot do it, nor could I, nor could the King himself, not at this wretched time of the year. Even so, 'twere better than the powder and wherewithal to fashion it should lie a-rotting in the Pennines than that they should fall to the thrice-damned Scots; therefore, I shall warrant you to fetch back all you can. You'll have *carte blanche* of garrison, city and country men, horses, wagons, provisions—take whatever you feel needful to our purpose. My secretary here will see to the necessary papers. God be with you."

Then the armored and padded clergyman had hidden his head in an old-fashioned casque and resumed his practice bout with blunted broadsword and *main gauche* dagger, stamping and grunting and swearing like any trooper.

He found Sir Francis had been correct, too. The trip north with empty wagons had helped mightily in planning the trip south with full ones, although the sufferings and difficulties of that northbound preview in no way mitigated the waking nightmare that the southbound main show proved to be.

Arrived finally at Whyffler Hall, having lost only eleven wagons out of the sixty with which he had left York, Foster was pleasantly surprised to find Buddy Webster, several companies of Welsh pikemen, the Royal Artificiers Corps and Riechsherzog Wolfgang.

The snow had been cleared or tramped away from the environs of the hall's circuit of walls, and under direction of the European and the artificiers, levies of countryfolk and soldiers were feverishly strengthening the ancient walls, fronting them with deep ditches, and constructing artillery emplacements. Drawn by lowing, steaming oxen on log sledges, or huge, creaking wains, bombards captured from the French Crusaders were arriving at the average rate of three per day, each escorted by mounted artillerists and dragoons.

Every couple of days, Duke Wolfgang would have the five or six new pieces loaded and fired a few times. Then he would confer with their gunners, make a few calculations, and decide just where each gun was to be mounted on the walls.

"Each gonne an individual iss," he told Foster and Sir Francis, one night after dinner. "If a man a goot rider iss, ve poot him on a horse; if not, ve teach him to pike. So why not each gonne place vhere even its flaws goot are?"

By the time Foster's caravan was ready to leave, Whyffler Hall was well on the way to becoming a stout fortress, and more royal troops were arriving to man the defenses. The walls were become stronger than ever they had been, and they and the newmade outworks now guarding them were bristling with bombards and swivels, and the powder manufactory had worked ceaselessly to fill each cask and gunbox to overflowing.

When a last, long powder train had departed, bound southwest toward the camp of the Royal Force, Pete Fairley supervised the loading of all his equipment and supplies into wooden crates bearing misleading markings; then, previously hidden replicas of his devices were put in place of the originals, and empty fertilizer bags were each filled with a hundredweight of earth and carefully resewn before being stacked in the storage area. Whyffler Hall was to maintain as long as possible the appearance of still housing the manufactory and would, it was hoped, bog down sizable elements of the Scots army, whenever they organized sufficiently to cross the border.

Sir Francis' sixteen-year-old daughter, Arabella, flatly refused to join the exodus of noncombatants, and neither cooed importunings nor heated shoutings would move her. A dimpled smile on her heart-shaped face, she gave that same answer to any who pressed her.

"Och, nay, I be chatelaine o' Whyffler Ha', by war or reavin' or nae. My place be here. I maun care for Fither, an' I cannae do sich in York. And I *shall* stay!"

But her expressed filial sentiments were not her sole reason for remaining . . . and all knew it. There was also the only remaining patient in the hall, who still was too ill to be waggoned south.

Several times each week, mounted patrols composed of royal dragoons and local lancers swung north into the Cheviot Hills, keeping watch on the likeliest routes of invasion, and one day Foster, beginning to feel a sort of cabin fever, joined the unit as a supernumerary. At midday they had paused on a prominence overlooking the very border itself, or so the cairns proclaimed. Staying below the ridge as they munched their rations, they posted a brace of Musgrave's troopers to keep watch on the narrow gap below.

The patrol leader, one Lieutenant Edgar Lloyd, had just put foot to stirrup when one of the sentries slid down the precipitous slope with word of approaching horsemen. Both officers returned to the man's vantage point and witnessed the unfolding of the drama.

First one, then a second horse careened down a wooded hillside, slipping and sliding on icy rocks and patches of old snow, but somehow retaining their balance. Once safely on the more level surface leading to the gap, the two riders spurred the obviously tired mounts to the best speed they could maintain, but would have stood little chance of keeping their lead had the party pursuing been as fortunate in negotiating the hillside.

There was not room for the score or so of heavily armed riders to descend abreast on the narrow, winding track—even four would have been too many, and the canny Scots should have known as much—nonetheless, six essayed the trail, with disastrous results. Almost at once, a horse and a rider went off the righthand side and out of sight of the English watchers, followed very shortly by one, then another on the left. The shrill screams of the injured animals were clearly audible to Foster and Lloyd, as were the guttural shouts and war cries of the Scots.

Fourteen of the pursuers managed to reach the bottom of the slope mounted and unhurt, to take up their hot chase afresh. A couple of shots were loosed off at the escaping prey, but, now more than halfway to the gap, they were well beyond the range of horsepistols. But the flight of arrows that followed was a much more successful and deadly ploy.

The second horse shrieked and surged ahead, briefly, then fell all in a heap, quivering all over, legs churning the snow, while gouts of steaming blood poured from mouth and distended nostrils. The rider sailed from the saddle, bounced once, and rolled to a stop, then lay still . . . terribly still, his head at an impossible angle.

The leading rider and his horse both seemed to suddenly sprout jouncing, jiggling slivers of wood—the horse, in his straining offside haunch, the rider, in his right arm, just below the shoulder. But the now-wounded man retained his seat and firm control of the pain-maddened horse.

There was something tantalizingly familiar about that rider's bearing, and Foster sharpened the focus of his binoculars in an attempt to discern more. But the man's head and upper torso were wrapped in a faded, dirty length of tartan and his face was obscured by the long, whipping mane of his shaggy mount.

The Scots formed up and resumed the hunt, lancepoints and broadswords glittering in the sun. Scots they certainly were, but Foster could see nothing in their clothing, armaments, or appearance to differentiate them from a like number of the armed retainers of Sir Francis or John Heron—jackboots, rough trousers, buffcoats, most wearing some model of helmet, several in cuirasses and a couple in three-quarter armor.

Beside him, the Musgrave lancer grunted, "Robsons, Jaysus domn 'em! 'Twill be ane gude an' holy killin', we'll be doin', fer a' I pitty the puir De'il an' Him havin' tae tek on sae scurfy a pack."

Foster was just about to remark that they were here to observe only, not to become embroiled in border feuds, when the wounded horse, which had been slowing as bright-red arterial blood continued to geyser up the shaft of the arrow, stumbled once, twice, then simply stood, swaying, head sunk low. The rider turned in the saddle, looked at the oncoming Scots, then half slid, half fell from his dying mount. Hobbling, decidedly favoring his left leg, he came on toward the gap, and it was then that Foster first saw his face.

"Edgar!" He gripped the junior officer's arm so hard that the Welshman winced. "Mount the patrol. At once! That man the Scots are after. That's Egon von Hirschburg, the Reichsherzog's godson!"

Even when faced with a far superior force, the Scots declined to forsake their quarry and died to the last man, most of them shot from their saddles long before they came close enough to have made use of their lances or steel.

The young ensign lay unconscious in the snow by the time Foster got to him. In addition to the arrow in his right arm, the broken shaft of another stuck out from his left hip, and the wound it had made was oozing pus through folds of the stiff, smelly bandage wrapped around it. The evil stench of the wound filled Foster with a chill foreboding.

"Who put the tourniquet on his arm, Bass, you?" Krystal bent over the still, fair-skinned body of Egon von Hirschburg, mercifully unconscious again. At his nod, she added, "Damned good thing you did, too. The arrow nicked an artery and he'd've been dead long before you got him here, otherwise."

She straightened and brushed back her hair with her wrist, carefully keeping her bloody fingers out of contact with it. "Bass, this boy means something to you, doesn't he? I mean, more than just because he's the godson of your big German friend?"

"Yes, Krys, he does," answered Foster soberly. "Egon served under me during the closing segments of that hellish extermination of the Irish Crusaders. He's . . . well, he's what I'd have wanted my own son to be, if ever I'd had one, pure guts from breakfast to sundown and a mile wide, energetic, nervy, and knowledgeable, proud to the point of seeming stiffnecked, but withal very conscious of the responsibilities as well as the privileges of his station.

"And now this." He shook his head in wonderment. "Can you imagine what it must have taken, what it must have cost in terms of determination for Egon to have ridden up hill and down dale for God knows how many hours with a damned iron arrowhead grating on his hipbone? But, Krys, he sat that scrubby horse so naturally that we never even noticed the old wound."

"It is old, Bass, perhaps as much as three days old. And," she announced grimly, choosing to not meet his eyes, "he may very well die of it. I'm sorry. The surrounding area is terribly infected, verging very close to gangrenous, so the arrowhead must come out at once, along with a good bit of tissue.

"But he's weak, Bass. There's precious little vitality left in him. I don't think he would survive the type of procedure indicated, even in a modern O.R. with sterile surroundings, anesthetics, whole blood, and antibiotic I.V.s. Here and now, with my make-do equipment, nothing but brandy to ease his pain and the pitifully few penicillin tablets to retard the infection . . ." Her voice trailed off into a long sigh and her shoulders slumped in defeat. "Perhaps we should let his godfather decide?"

"No, Krys, poor old Wolf has enough to weigh him down just now, and there's really no choice. The young man is all whipcord and sinew, so it's possible he can live through the operation, but he certainly can't survive gangrene. So go ahead, sweetheart, tell me everything you need."

The surgery was performed in the kitchen of Foster's home, on the heavy butcherblock table. Dr. Kent was ably assisted by Carey Carr (who had had army medical training and had worked several years with a rescue squad), the hall-village midwife, and Arabella Whyffler, with Foster and Webster on hand to hold the patient down, should such become necessary.

For all the brandy poured down his throat before and during the bloody business, the boy's agony must have been indescribably obscene, but only once, at the very beginning, did he courteously ask that Webster restrain his arms. With deft fingers carefully flying, Krystal Kent performed as rapidly as she could, steeling herself to not flinch at the screams.

But, miraculously, the screams never came. Egon's body ran with sweat, his face with tears, his high-bridged nose gushed mucus, and his even white teeth met in the half-inch-thick strip of leather between his working jaws. His rectal sphincter failed him and his urethral, his nails sliced deep gashes in his callused palms, but no single sound louder than a gasp did Egon von Hirschburg emit, from start to finish. Foster could have wept his pride in the boy.

Since, Arabella Whyffler had virtually lived with Egon, and

all concerned considered the young nobleman the primary reason she refused to leave Whyffler Hall.

Foster sought out the Reichsherzog on the day before his departure with the York-bound wagons, offering to delay that departure for a few days on the chance that the young convalescent might regain strength enough to accompany him out of danger.

"Nein, danke, gut mein Herr Hauptmann Forster," the Emperor's brother had replied. "Enough for my house you have already done and repaid in time you vill be. But the vinter mild hass been, und the whoreson Scots anytime could march. Important it iss that your train reach York.

"As for Egon, if vell enough he iss ven I ride south, mit me he vill come . . . und the scharming Mistress Arabella, as vell." His big yellow teeth flashed. "If not, he vill a fine *leutnant* to Sir Francis make. Conduct of a siege goot seasoning for the boy vill be. *Nicht wahr?*"

Foster left the bulk of his furniture behind, some in Whyffler Hall, some in his house. He had given up trying to reason out the whys and hows of the myriad impossibilities which confronted him whenever he considered that not only were all his electrical appliances and devices still functioning normally—heat, lights, air conditioning, refrigerator/freezer, washer/dryer, power tools, everything—but the taps still poured forth unlimited quantites of clear, fresh, *chlorinated* water.

Sir Francis and the Reichsherzog, however, did not question the source of the tap flow. " 'Tis but God's mysterious will, Bass, wha' ither? Aye, glad be I tae hae sich, I trow, for ne'er did ony fort or castle or burgh hae tae much potable water. An' this be ane soorce the thrice-domned Scots cannae sully or stop."

"Ach, ja," the hulking German had nodded vigorous assent. "Vhen gone iss the food, rats roasted can be and boots boiled, but when *wasser* gone iss, surrender or die vun must."

Jack-of-all-trades Pete Fairley had taken apart the two truck trailers and worked the thin, light, strong sheet metal into six watertight, capacious, and relatively comfortable wagon bodies. He had then had three dozen sets of running gear reduced to component parts, had had a pair of master wagonmakers scrutinize and test every wheelrim spoke, axletree, singletree, doubletree, bolster, pole, and hub. The six sets of running gear assembled from these parts were the best that the hand of man could fashion, and the leather springs on which the bodies were mounted were a wonder to all who beheld them.

One of these masterpieces was packed with the clothing and other possessions Foster was taking to York, one each was assigned as a trekhome to Foster and Krystal, Dave and Webster, Pete and the lusty young wench with whom he had been living for some months, Carey Carr and Susan.

Foster had first thought of taking Arbor Collier along, but Krystal had demurred, saying, "No, Bass, she'd never survive the trip. She's a very sick woman and has shown little improvement in response to anything I've tried to do for her. I think she hasn't got long to live, even here, but the kind of trip you say this is going to be would kill her in less than a week."

The trek started well—clear, if bitingly cold. During the first night out, the temperature rose amazingly, and though the dawn brought a fine, misty drizzle, all the men and women felt the unexpected warmth to be worth a little wetness. But as the day wore on, the rain became heavier, and soon feet and hooves and wheels were squishing into and dragging out of deep mud. The rain still poured as the soaked and bedraggled party went into the second night's camp, and in that night the temperature dropped, plunged at least—Foster figured—thirty-odd degrees. By morning, the rain had become pelting sleet and the wheels of heavy-laden wagons and wains were fast-frozen into the rock-hard earth the mud was become. Many had to be completely unloaded before straining teams could drag them free. It was almost noon before they were moving again.

And it got progressively worse . . . but arrive at their destination they did, most of them.

CHAPTER 6

Harold of York leaned both elbows on the gaming table as he studied the chessboard separating him from Foster; suddenly, the strong, slender fingers of his right hand swooped down to bring a tall, beautifully carved knight into position.

"Check," he smiled triumphantly.

After a brief moment, Foster's queen was moved out and the ivory knight joined the small host of captures, leaving the Archbishop only two pawns and a rook with which to defend the beleaguered king. Shortly, that king was boxed into an inescapable *cul-de-sac*. With a gusty sign, Harold tipped the six-inch-high, gold-crowned sovereignty onto its side. *"Le roi est mort."* At a wave of his hand, a silent, catfooted servant stepped up to refill the goblets of his master and guest, then just as silently returned to his place near the door.

After savoring the rich Canary, the churchman remarked, "Your mind assuredly be on weightier matters, my son. You won but five of this night's seven encounters. Or doth my skill so wax, eh?"

Foster sipped politely, then set the silver goblet down. He would have preferred ale or even water to the sweet, sweet wine. He nodded. "Your game is definitely improving, Your Eminence. But you're right, I am thinking about something else."

He leaned forward and lowered his voice. "The Lady Krystal and I, we . . . well, we must be married, and *soon*."

The Archbishop leaned back against the tall, canopied

backrest of his heavy chair, his bushy-white eyebrows arching up. Smiling gently, he said, "May I ask the reason for this precipitate haste . . . or must I guess?" But when Foster would have replied, he waved his hand. "No, my son, that question was rhetorical. Of course you two shall be wed, by me, and this very night, and you so wish it."

But the wedding—a simple, beautiful ceremony—took place three nights later in one of the smaller chapels of the cathedral complex.

And at noon the following day, Reichsherzog Wolfgang arrived from the north.

Foster heard of the arrival long before the newcomers reached the Archbishop's commodious stone residence, and so was in the courtyard to greet the big, gruff German. For all that increasing numbers of Scot reavers had begun to roam the Northumbrian Marches, making life chancy and increasingly hazardous for natives and travelers alike, the Emperor's brother had, it developed, ridden that deadly gauntlet with but eight of his Mongol troopers.

Six of the flat-faced, bowlegged little men still rode at his back, though Foster noted that at least one was tied into his saddle, his jaws clenched and his black eyes dulled with pain. To two other saddles were lashed the frozen bodies of dead Mongols, while a rough, largish bundle covered with tartan was packed upon another riderless horse.

Wolfgang handled the reins of his tired charger with his right hand; his left arm was wrapped in dirty, blood-crusty bandages and tucked under his baldric, but his blue eyes lit with pleasure when he espied Foster in the doorway, and, tossing his reins to a waiting groom, he slid from the saddle and strode over, smiling.

"Ach, *Herr Hauptmann* Forster, to see again old friends iss *gut, ja? Ach, ja!* Gut hunting had *mein jungen* and me, sree-und-tventy heads of Scots, ve bring to decorate the gates. You vell are? Und the scharming Mistress Krystal von Kent?"

For all the royal duke's bluff heartiness, however, Foster saw him stumble twice as he ascended the steps, and the gauntleted hand that gripped his own was weak, devoid of the famous crushing grip.

Foster turned to the young pageboy assigned him. "Oliver, my compliments to my lady wife. Please tell her that I will be shortly arriving with Reichsherzog Wolfgang. Tell her as well that the Reichsherzog be wounded."

"Nonsense," snapped Wolfgang as the little page scuttled off. He gestured at the immobilized left arm. "This but a trifle be, the bones in the forearm broke, but the edge from my flesh my gut mail gauntlets kept; the other a clean vound iss, through muscle the ball vent und out und the bone unscathed iss."

Then belatedly, comprehension of what he had heard manifested itself in a yellow-toothed grin. "Lady vife? You? Und Mistress Krystal? Ach, goot, goot. My congratulations."

The two men proceeded toward Foster's quarters, Foster himself moving far more deliberately than usual, in order to spare Wolfgang's obviously failing strength. "And your godson, my lord? Egon, what of him? He was still too infirm to ride down with you?"

The big man vented a gasping chuckle. "Sound as a suit of proof iss the *jung,* but stubborn, like all his House, hah! Mit me he rode into Schottlandt, to the hall of those *schweinhunden* who hiss troopers killed und to take him for ransom tried. Efery man ve slew, their spawn into the snow ve drove out und their women too . . . vhen done mit them ve vere." He grinned wolfishly, then went on. "Goot looting vas that hall und a fine fire it made, after.

"But Egon, hah! Mit reavers ahorse over most of the Northumbria, Sir Francis to let hiss daughter now ride south vill not allow, und of rightness he iss. But Egon romantic iss as the *jungen* so often are, und he insists that to remain by his chosen lady he vill. So, mit him I left my faithful Amadeo und most of my goot Tartars. Most potent and solemn oaths did they svear to protect him and hiss lady, so fear not for our Egon."

Recalling the silent and immensely powerful Savoyard called Amadeo, who had been Wolfgang's personal servant and bodyguard for many years, not to mention the several dozens of Mongol horsearchers who virtually worshiped their German commanders, Foster had not the slightest doubt that Egon von Hirschburg and Arabella Whyffler would be as safe as human flesh could wreak.

The snow melted, the streams rose over their banks, the rivers became boiling torrents of frigid water, laden with a flotsam of ice chunks and uprooted trees. Very gradually, a few bare degrees each succeeding week, the winds from off the far highlands shed their biting teeth and, here and there, tiny flowers began to show a bit of color.

As soon as the gaps were passable and the streams fordable, King Alexander led his host across the ancient boundary and into England. Thirty thousand fighting men followed his banner. There were a vast host of Highlanders, lean as winter wolves, unshod and barelegged in the cold mud, dirty, disheveled, usually bearded and armed only with dirks, cowhide targets, and a miscellany of archaic polearms. The most of them owned no single piece of armor; indeed, few owned even a rough shirt. Flat, feathered bonnets and the long, pleated, filthy tartans which were clothing and cloak by day and blanket by night were their sole attire.

The Lowland troops were mostly better clothed and armed, but there were far fewer of them. Since Alexander had yet to settle his multitudinous differences with certain powerful and influential lairds, they had flatly refused to either march with his invasion army or to allow their folk to do so. For that reason, the personal troops of the Papal Legate—two thousand Genovese crossbowmen and four thousand mercenary *landesknechten*—were a welcome addition, in the Scottish king's mind.

So, too, were the multitude of Crusader-noblemen of assorted nationalities—renegade Englishmen, Irish, French, Flemings, Burgundians, Scandinavians, Portuguese and Spaniards, Savoyards, Italians, Dalmatians, Croatians, Greeks and Bulgars, even a few Turkish and Egyptian knights—and the handful of tightly disciplined, ebon-skinned, Ghanaian mercenaries whom Papal agents had found for him to hire.

Withal, he was vastly deficient in cavalry—only a little over ten percentum of his army was mounted—and such artillery as he possessed was hardly worthy of the name. Nor could he safely get any of the heavy, clumsy, unwieldy bombards close enough to the well-designed defenses of Whyffler Hall to effectively reduce it. The two mass assaults launched against the place accomplished nothing save a couple of thousand dead and wounded Scots and a distinct plunge in the morale of the generally courageous but always volatile Highlanders.

Deciding Whyffler Hall too tough a nut to crack, Alexander left a contingent of his less dependable troops to invest the fort and marched on southeast with his reduced host. The English army met them just south of Hexham.

Foster lay propped against his rolled sleeping bag, heedlessly dripping blood on the floor of his tattered pyramid tent, and wishing he had something more effective than a jug of captured whiskey to dull the waves of pain.

Nugai, the bodyguard-batman assigned to him by the Reichsherzog, had pulled off his master's left boot, unbuckled and removed the cuishe-plate and the knee-cop, and carefully cut away the blood-stiff trouser leg. Lacking water, he had sloshed a measure of the raw whiskey onto the cloth adhering to the long slash in Foster's leg—at which point only Foster's pride kept him from shrieking like a banshee and blasting headfirst through the roof like a rocket—then gently worried the fabric from the flesh. Ignoring the gush of fresh blood brought by his ministrations, the impassive little man had scooped a handful of a stinking brownish paste from an earthenware bowl. With strong yellow fingers, he had stretched open the mouth of the wound and stuffed it full of the concoction, then smeared more of it over the gash before bandaging the injured leg.

Foster had been afraid to ask the oriental what went to make up the paste, but within a few minutes after the treatment, his leg not only no longer pained him but was almost numb from foot to crotch.

He thought, lying there alone, that he would never again hear a bagpipe without recalling the grim horror and chaos of the two-day battle against the Scots. And he did not even know who—if anyone!—had won, yet.

Camped on the marshy moor, the outnumbered English army had watched the flicker of fires in and about what was left of the town of Hexham through the hours of a drizzly night. And through all that night, those damned pipes had droned and wailed, while the wild, wardancing Highlanders yelped and howled.

As the new day's sun peeked above the horizon, Arthur's army stood to arms and moved in disciplined ranks across the mile of slick, spongy earth toward the forming Scots.

Holding the fractious Bruiser tight-reined, Foster felt that his bladder would surely burst, and his mouth was dry as sand. He drew and balanced his blade, made certain his dirk was loose enough, checked the priming and the springs of his Irish wheellocks, made certain that his horsepistols were loaded. Then he checked the Luger which had been Collier's and with which he had replaced the Colt, since the .45 ACP ammo was exhausted. These things done, he half-turned in the saddle and considered the alignment of his squadron, noted that they had trailed a bit behind the center and so gave Bruiser a bit more rein.

Looking forward, Foster wished he had his binoculars—they were on loan to King Arthur—for he could make out no details of the wing his squadron was advancing upon; his vision registered only a roiling mass of multihued tartans. But white steel flashed above and among the mob of shaggy men in soggy wool and the warcries in guttural Gaelic rang more clearly with every passing moment.

King Alexander's center was formed well before his wings had achieved anything approaching stability, and a galloper pounded up to Foster only a moment after he had brought his Squadron to a halt.

Walk. Draw pistols. Trot. Gallop! Present pistols. *FIRE!* Right wheel. Right wheel. Right wheel. Walk. Replace pistols. Draw pistols. Trot. Gallop! Present pistols. *FIRE!*

The two ordered volleys produced vast confusion in the "ranks" of the Highlanders who composed King Alexander's left wing. Numbers of the barbaric, ill-armed men ran out in pursuit of the withdrawing dragoons, waving glaives and bills and halberds, two-handed swords and war hammers. The various chiefs ran or rode out to belabor and curse their clansmen back into some sort of order, but some of those clansmen were gone berserk with battlelust, and it was a slow and dangerous undertaking.

Blessed with a spine of the steadier Lowland axmen, the right wing held a bit better under the volleys of Webster's squadron. Both squadrons of dragoons had retired behind the infantry of their respective wings to reload their pistols when, with a horrific wailing of pipes and clamor of drums, the Scots commenced an advance along their entire front. At a distance still well beyond accurate musket range, the center halted long enough for the Genovese to pace forward and release their deadly quarrels.

But before the Scottish center could resume the advance, the front ranks of the English center opened and two dozen small field guns on odd-looking carriages were wheeled out and fired, their grape and chainshot tearing sanguineous gaps in the ranks of the best Scottish troops upon the field. Then, smoothly, the guns were withdrawn from view of the battered and bemused enemy.

The right wing had halted when did the center, but the left had either not received, or—more likely, considering the self-willed and independent Highland chiefs—chosen to ignore the command. Screaming theats and taunts, roaring their slogans and warcries, they rolled down upon the English right wing in a formless mob.

When the charging horde was a bit over a hundred yards away, fifty pairs of men paced deliberately forward of the formations of pikemen. When their partners had placed the rests firmly, the gunners rested the long barrels of their strangely shaped arquebuses in the forks, blew on their matches, aimed, and fired a ragged volley. Here and there, a Scot fell, but the chiefs had expected such a volley.

After their volley, the gunners were supposed to rapidly retire behind the pikewall to reload, if they had time, but these remained in place. If the Scots had been observing at close range, they would have seen each gunner draw back his serpentine, carefully turn the big, heavy iron cylinder affixed within the breech of his weapon, and shove it forward to fit tightly into the tapered rear of the barrel. After thumbing back the cover of a small pan at the rear of the cylinder and glancing down to make sure that it still was filled with priming powder, each gunner blew on his match, took aim, and fired.

By the time the seventh volley had been fired, and gunners and assistants were cooperating in fitting another iron cylinder to each arquebus, hundreds of clansmen were down, still or kicking and screaming, and most of the initial impetus of the advance had been lost. Justly renowned for their courage and tenacity, the Highlanders did continue the advance, but considerably more slowly. And this gave the gunners time to pour seven more withering volleys into the oncoming foe.

Even with their losses, however, the Scots still were far more numerous than the English right and, when it was obvious that they would vastly overlap and be able to flank the English formation, Foster's dragoons, reinforced with three troops of lancers, were ordered to charge.

Holding the lances back for the nonce, Foster led his dragoons against the left flank of the yelling mob. They poured in a single pistol volley, then retired, reformed with the lancers, and charged in a triangular, spearpoint formation that cleaved through the motley throng like a hot knife through butter. Then they turned, regrouped and rode through again . . . and again, and yet again.

For the extent of those long, busy minutes, Foster could never after recall much more than a terrible, jumbled kaleidoscope of faces twisted in bloodlust or agony; hairy, sinewy arms; and a vast assortment of weapons, their points and edges all seeking his flesh and blood.

He rode with Bruiser's loose reins clenched between his teeth, his superposed two-barreled horsepistol (cut down by Pete Fletcher from one of the two Browning over-under shotguns which had been part of Webster's load) in his left hand, his long, flashing Tara-steel sword in his right. A superbly trained destrier, the big, spotted horse was perfectly tractable when the smells of powder and blood were in his wide-flared nostrils and acres of manflesh awaited his square, yellow teeth and steel-shod hooves.

Foster remembered confronting a tall, slender man, probably a chief, as he was mounted on a bay cobby and wore a rust-spotted chain-mail hauberk. The foeman's head and face were hidden from view by a flat-topped barrel-helm that probably dated from the thirteenth century. Both horses reared, and Foster fenced briefly with the Scot around and over Bruiser's muscle-bulging neck, until the stallion's savage ferocity and superior weight brought the small, ponylike horse crashing onto its back, the mailed rider beneath it.

Another mounted man loomed over the press of infantry ahead. His mount was bigger but his armor was just as ancient and sketchy—jazeran and dogfaced basinet with a two-hand *claidheamh*, five feet in the blade. Instantly aware that he could never effectively parry a full-force blow from that twenty-pound sword, Foster used his last pistol charge to shoot the huge, stocky man out of his old saddle, then had to hack and slash his way through the press of berserk clansmen.

A wolf spear was thrust at him; he grasped the crossbar and jerked the wielder close enough to drive his dripping swordpoint into a bulging, red-rimmed eye, while Bruiser's lashing hooves caved in chests and cracked skulls. The sharp-edged Tara sword cut through pikeshafts and the arms that powered them, sliced through straining muscles and took hirsute heads from off hunched shoulders. The arm that impelled that sword was become a single, whitehot agony with the unceasing impacts, but when he sensed his battered command once more clear, he hastily grouped them after a fashion and once more hurled them and himself at the foe.

But this time opposition was scant and sketchy. Those front-rank Scots still able to crawl or hobble were in full retreat from the serried formation of red-dripping Welsh pikes. A few of the clansmen behind pressed forward, but most—

bereft by Foster's squadron of a large proportion of their chiefs—milled in aimless confusion, the berserkers striking out blindly at anyone who moved, and frequently being cut down by fellow clansmen simply as a matter of self-protection.

Then, when Foster expected his force to be in the clear, the point was suddenly driving into the exposed flank of a formation of morioned and buffcoated Lowlander infantry. Had the ordered troops been prepared and expecting the calvary, their *langues de boeuf* and poleaxes could have wrought gory havoc on Foster's squadron, but struck by surprise at flank and rear, they panicked and broke. Heedless of their lairds' commands and verbal abuse, they fled in any direction that took them from the path of those dripping broadswords and the soot-blackened men who bore them. Some fled to the rear areas to spread a measure of their mindless terror among the troops not yet committed, some careened into the rear of units already engaging the English line, but the bulk of the two thousand Lowlanders pelted to their right, straight into the flank of the Papal *landesknechten,* already hard-pressed at their van by Northumbrian infantry.

Confused by the buffcoats and morions—which also happened to be the attire of the troops they faced—the European mercenaries faced about and had already cut down several hundred of the Lowlanders before their officers and the surviving lairds could bring the butchery to an end and form the flanks and rear to repel Foster's squadron.

That squadron was, however, down to a little more than half its initial strength, and even had they been at full, reinforced strength, it would have required a royal order for Foster to put them at that glittering hedge of fifteen-foot pikes and the hard-eyed professional soldiers behind it. Rather, he halted his command long enough for pistols to be hastily recharged, then wheeled them into pursuit of the now fully broken Highlanders, with the Welsh pikewall moving forward in his wake.

Ruthlessly, the horsemen cut down or pistoled the slower Scots and the few brave enough or stupid enough to turn and make a stand. The rest they chased all the way back to where the baggage wagons had been drawn up into a fortified square, and drew off only when musketfire had emptied several saddles.

Finding the way back blocked by a hastily formed line of pikemen, Foster led his troopers far over to his left and onto a heath-grown hillock to survey the best means of extricating his remaining force, only to find that he could see little, due to a thickening fog that had commenced to settle over the battlefield. But what glimpses he could espy convinced him that something was wrong, terribly wrong.

The English lines had been drawn up at the beginning of the battle with their backs to a small rill which bisected the plain; but in the raging battle below, the opposing lines appeared to be drawn up at right angles to that stream, the Scottish right and the English left engaged almost at the very site on which the English had camped the night previous.

A bigger shock came when he noted that the pale, cloud-enshrouded glow of the sun was westering. What had happened to the day?

The pikemen who had barred his return to his own lines were abruptly faced about and led trotting off into the fog, but he did not remount this much-reduced command. The troopers were as exhausted as the foam-streaked horses, many were wounded, and few had enough remaining powder to recharge their pistols. He could think of no way in which two hundred-odd tired and pain-racked men on as many plodding horses and with only use-dulled broadswords for armament could effect any favorable outcome in the hellishness beneath the swirling opacity of the fog.

The remaining hours of light were spent in rest and repair of weapons and equipment, bandaging wounds and sharing out water and powder, rubbing down the trembling horses with handfuls of vegetation and slow walking of the animals to cool them gradually. With the fall of darkness, he remounted them and led them a long, circuitous swing among the hillocks, then over the plain to where he thought the baggage train and camp lay.

When they appeared among the scattered tents before the stout wagon fort, muskets were leveled and swivel-guns brought to bear before his spotted horse was recognized. A Welsh officer of foot Foster vaguely remembered as Howard ap Somethingorother hobbled from among the wagons, leaning heavily on a broken pikestaff, his face drawn and wan under the dirty, bloody bandages swathing his head.

"Captain Forster, as I live and breathe! 'Tis dead you were thought, sir, and all your men, as well, when ye rode into the very maw of the Scots. Ye impressed the King mightily, then, they say."

Foster paced Bruiser forward slowly. "Who won the battle?"

The Welshman cackled. "No one, last I heard, b'God."

Foster was amazed; full battles—as opposed to raids, skirmishes and patrol-actions—were *never* fought at night, here and now, due to the lack of effective communications as much as custom.

"I heard no shots?" he said skeptically.

"No powder left, mostly," answered the wounded officer. "An' what little be likely wetted. But the center and right was both rock-steady when I lefted. And the left had been reinforced and was firming up."

Foster thought he could catch a glimmering of how the lines had taken that ninety-degree turn. "The left broke, then?"

The officer unconsciously nodded, then gasped and grimaced with pain. Weakly, he answered, "Oh, aye, they were flanked. The dragoons tried to do what you and your'n did, but they run onto a bit of swamp and ere they could get free, the barbarians were all over them. Captain Webster and several of his officers were slain and—"

"Webster? Bud Webster? Dead?" Foster felt numb.

"Shot from off his horse, or so I heard, God rest him." The Welshman crossed himself solemnly. "He were a gallant sojer."

Foster thought that the long-bodied, short-legged man was beginning to look faint. "Is there room for my animals and men inside the wagon fort?"

The wounded officer nodded, unthinkingly once more, staggered and almost fell. Leaning most of his weight on his staff, he croaked, "More than enough, good sir, and well come ye be. The quartermaster captain and all his war-trained men were thrown into the battle with every other unattached man to bolster the left, and I was brought here to command when I took a quarrel through me thigh. But all it be to defend the baggage and stores be wounded sojers and wagoners what hadden' been shot oe'r, ere this. An' each time the battleline shifts a bit an' we end a-hint the Scots lines, them Satan's-spawn Highlanders make to o'errun us again. Twice now, it's happened, and a chancy thing each time."

Three more times during that long confused night the wagon fort was attacked by roaring, blood-mad, loot-hungry Highlanders. Each time the battle line turned a few degrees, the hordes of tartaned irregulars swept against the embattled wooden walls. Lieutenant Squire Howard ap Harry stumbled and fell into a blazing watch fire during the first attack and died in unspeakable agony an hour later, leaving Foster—as senior officer present—in reluctant command of the vulnerable, valuable, and seriously undermanned position.

Since the King had wisely left most of the trains in Durham, there were but about a hundred and fifty wagons arranged—at Reichsherzog Wolfgang's orders—in a perfect square, fronted by chest-high ramparts of peat. Not a bad arrangement, Foster thought, had there but been enough men to adequately defend it. There were his own two hundred-odd troopers on whom he could depend. For the rest, perhaps two hundred wagoners were left, armed with a miscellany of pole-arms, hangers, and elderly matchlock muskets. Every third wagon was mounted with a breech-loading brass swivel-gun, averaging an inch and a half in the bore and each furnished with four to six brass breechjacks, which arrangement should have made for easy defense of the wagon fort, as the swivels required little or no training and experience to employ and were nothing short of murderous in their effect on targets at three hundred yards or less—being simply huge shotguns.

However, Foster was quickly aware of some glaring snafus, somewhere along the line. There was plenty of powder, of all grades, but all of the stuff was packed in casks, there was no paper to make cartridges, and but a limited number of flasks, roughly one flask for every three and a half muskets. Moreover, no one had been able to locate the grape and canister loads for the swivels, and for want of anything better they had been loaded with handfuls of musket balls, scrap metal, short lengths of light chain, and even dried-out knuckle-bones from last night's stewpots.

In garrison or fort, powder stores were usually kept partially or totally below ground in a heavily timbered pit, but so high was the water table here that this could not be done without serious risk of spoilage, so the volatile stuff had been stacked in the center of the compound and covered against the mist and rain with waxed—and consequently highly inflammable—canvas sheeting. Foster shuddered every time he looked at the incipient disaster, but there was no other way to handle the situation.

In the two hours between the first attack and the second, Foster sent a hundred of his cavalrymen out to strike the tents ranged about that had not already been burned or shot down, aware that they would dispatch any wounded Scots without orders from him. The wounded, those capable of the task, he set to casting pistol and musket balls and refilling powder flasks. Then, with the wagoners and his remaining troopers, he set about emptying every wagon and opening every sack, box, chest, cask, and bale.

After an hour, they chanced across the loads for the swivels, the containers bearing markings clearly indicating that the contents were for 6-pdr. sakers.

First, there was the distant but fast-closing wail of the chaunters, backed by the incessant, nerve-fraying droning; then, boiling up out of the fog, seemingly impervious to the wet chill of the night, the numberless rabble of Highlanders bore down upon them from all sides, heralded by their deep-voiced shouts and curses and, as they neared, by the slap-slap of their bare feet on the wet peat.

Foster had solemnly promised to personally shoot any man who fired prematurely, and such was his reputation with the Royal Army that no single weapon was discharged until his little Irish wheellock spat. By then, the bunches of clansmen were close, deadly close, some only fifty yards distant, and the double-charged swivels wrought pure horror in their tight ranks. While the guns were reloaded, the best musketeers loosed at the Scots still charging, being handed fresh, primed muskets by those poorer shots assigned to load for the shooters.

The swivels roared double death again, canister this time as the Scots were closer, and then the horsepistols joined the muskets in covering the reloading. Once more did the swivels bark, before the mob of Highlanders faded back into the mists that had spawned them. Not one attacker had come closer than twenty yards.

But they tried once more, only a half hour later, and with equally disastrous results. But that was enough for even the stubborn Scots. Foster and his little command were unmolested for the remainder of the night, while, dim with distance, the clash of steel, the shouts and screams, an occasional drumroll or bugle blare, and the ceaseless caterwauling of the bagpipes testified to the ongoing battle.

Under the bright, morning sun, the wagon fort lay secure. But for hundreds of yards in every direction from it the earth was thickly scattered with corpses clad in stained and rent tartan. Closer in, the dead lay in windrows and, closer still, in mangled heaps of gray flesh. Exhausted pikemen stumbled about among them, blinking to keep red-rimmed eyes open, driving their leaf-shaped points down with a grunt in the mercy stroke wherever there was sign of remaining life.

Reichsherzog Wolfgang—his fine armor dented, his boots and clothing slashed and stained—leaned against a wagon wheel, chewing salt bacon and taking in the scene. Foster stood beside him, feeling sick.

"*Gross Gott,* Bass, such a battle never before have I to see. Fighters those Schottlanders be, by the Virgin's toenails, but no brains have they got, ja. Lost vas the day for them ven your squadron their right ving routed. Lost most certainly vas the day for them ven you disrupted at a crucial moment for their central attack the reinforcing. Und vhile your *jungen* behind them galumped, that fool of a king held back his reserves until far too late it vas to anything save mit them.

"Und now, *this!*" He waved one bare, bruised hand at the carnage. "Vasted are your talents, mein freund, vasted. Such a *Soldner* vould you make, *ja!* Consider it you must vonce these vars vun be."

Finally, exhaustion and alcohol overcame Foster's pains enough for him to sleep until he was awakened by the straining sextet of troopers who bore Webster's massive weight into the tent. The big man's body was covered from head to foot with slimy, brown mud, and he was dripping foul-smelling water and fouler curses.

"Goddamm it, Bud Webster, I thought you were finally out of my hair for good. Somebody told me you were dead. Now you come roaring in here and wake me out of the best, and only, sleep I've had in—"

Webster almost screamed when the troopers placed him on the ground, and Foster abruptly ordered, "You, there, Allison, isn't it? Fetch my man, Nugai, in here. At the double, trooper!"

Between grunts and groans, between wheezes of choked-backed cries as Nugai and the troopers stripped his armor and boots and clothing from off the fair-skinned body that looked to have become a single blue-black-and-red bruise, Webster told Foster, "Well, thishere galloper brung word from Ole Wolfie to swing round wide an' hit the lef' and front o' them half-nekkid, screechin' devuls."

"That was your left, but the Scots' right, Bud," corrected Foster gently.

"It don' matter a good diddlysquat, do it? Enyhow, we swung wide, a'right, and come back hell-fer-leather and we'uz ackshuly close enough to of pistoled the damn bastids and nex thing I knowed ole Trixie my mare come to rear up and I could feel she's gonna fall and 'fore I could pull leather, she'uz down top o' the mosta me and the onlies' reason this ole boy's still a-kickin' is a-cause the groun' was so fuckin' soft.

"Then a whole passel of them friggin' Scots come a-runnin' and a-roarin' at us and I think I yelled at the boys to pull back, enyhow, they did, them as still could, leastways. I jest played possum. Them thievin' cocksuckers! They took my pistols offen Trixie's saddle and my good sword and even my fuckin' helmet.

"Well, ole buddy, I tell you! I laid in thet friggin' swamp all day and all fuckin' night, too. It'uz purely all I could do jest to keep my face outen the dang water and ever' time I seed or heared somma them damn Scots a pokin' round, I jest tuck me a deep breath and let my haid go under. Ever' time I tried a-pullin' out from under pore ole Trixie, it'uz all I could do to keep from howlin' like a dang coyote, the way my dang leg hurt me. And I—

"GAWDAMNIRECKON! Bass, you git yore tame slope-head offen me or I'll flat tear him in two. You heah?"

Nugai had probed the bared, terribly discolored right leg of the big man with gentle, sensitive fingers; now he turned to Foster. "Herr Hauptman, zee zhigh bone breaken iss undt zee grosser bone ahv zee leg. Set must zhey be undt tight-tied mit boards."

Foster had to listen carefully to the thick, singsong accent to decipher its meaning, then he shook his head. "Allison, you'd better fetch back some more men, a dozen anyway. Captain Webster is going to take a lot of holding down."

But Nugai caught his eye. "To pardon pliss, Herr Hauptmann Forster, better vay iss." Rummaging in his leather bag, the Tartar brought out a small brass cup and a leather flask. He poured the cup half full of a thick, viscous, dark-brown liquid, then added an equal measure of Foster's "liberated" whiskey, stirred it with a yellow finger, then proffered it to Webster.

"To drink all, pliss, noble Herr Hauptmann Vebster. Sleep vill undt no pain feel, ja."

"What the fuck is that goddam witchbrew?" demanded Webster, making no move to accept the cup.

"Do what he says, Bud, drink it," said Foster. "Nugai knows what he's about."

"GOODGAWDIRECKON!" Grimacing, Webster flung the emptied cup from him. "Thet fuckin' stuff tastes like a swig of liquid manure, I swan. If you done let that slant pizen me, Bass, I swear to God, I'm gon' haint you till you dies."

Within bare minutes, Webster lay unconscious, and when Nugai returned with the needed materials, he, Foster and Allison were able to easily accomplish a setting and rough splinting of the breaks, with never a voluntary movement or a sound from the recumbent patient.

The Royal Army was two days in reorganizing, then immediately took up the pursuit of the shattered Scottish host, this time unencumbered by wagons or by any but the lightest of field guns, the necessities on pack animals, and the trains and the wounded well on the way to Durham. Arthur and Wolfgang pressed them hard, marching from before dawn until well after dusk.

Arthur's beloved cousin, the Duke of Northumbria, had fought at the King's side throughout the long battle, and only when the battle was done and won did he suddenly turn purple in the face and fall, clawing feebly at his breastplate. He was dead before many noticed he was down. He had been Lord Commander of the Royal Horse—overall commander of cavalry. Before the pursuit had commenced, Wolfgang, conferring with Arthur, had recommended Foster to fill, for the nonce, the vacant post.

The King slanted his head to one side, wrinkling his brows. "Squire Forster be a valiant man, a doughty sojer and all, Brother Wolf, but he cannot become Lord Commander. He be not a lord . . . and I be not even certain of his patents of nobility. No other Forsters seem to have heard of him ere now, and such a man as he be would surely have been renowned in his youth."

"*Pah!* Brother King, a trifle, that be."

Foster had been readying what was left of his squadron for the road, selecting remounts from captured chargers and from the herd driven up from Durham, when the blank-faced pikemen of the King's Foot Guards found him and hustled him away.

Arthur sat in his canopied armchair at the head of the council table. Several of his noble military commanders sat grouped about the table, and Reichsherzog Wolfgang stood before it, the shimmering Tara-steel broadsword in his hand.

Foster could see no softness or humor on any face in the pavilion, they all looked deadly serious. When he had been maneuvered to a place directly before the big German, Wolfgang spoke but one word.

"Kneel!"

His head spinning, his mind a chaotic jumble of thoughts, Foster just stood, looking from one grim face to another, until two pikemen grabbed his shoulders and forced him to his knees on the carpet, then jerked off his helmet.

The Reichsherzog advanced a single pace, raised his bared blade, and slapped the two shoulders of Foster's well-worn buffcoat with the flat of the steel. Then he sheathed his weapon, bent, and took Foster's hands and clasped them, palm to palm, between his own, all the while intoning what sounded to be a formula in German. Finally, he spoke directly to Foster.

"Sir Bass, ven the speaking I each time stop und mein head I nod, answer you must, *'Ich vill es tun, mein Herr.'* Understood? *Ja,* so."

When at last, the long business was completed, Wolfgang, his eyes now twinkling merrily, grasped Foster's shoulders and set him upon his feet, then embraced him and slapped his back soundly before kissing him on his cheek. Threading his arm through Foster's, he turned and addressed the King.

"So, Brother Arthur, months haf I vanted this jewel of a *soldat* for the Empire, und now he ours iss. Royal Sir, schentlemen, my great pleasure it now iss to present to your graces, mein vassal, Freiherr Hauptmann Sebastianus Forster, Margraf von Velegrad, ja! Your tchance you lost haf, Brother Arthur, now the Empire's he iss!"

The King smiled, shrugging languidly. "Perhaps, Brother Wolf, but mayhap not. Nevertheless, His Lordship now is in all ways qualified for the vacant post. Our thanks to you for that. There can be no questioning the patents of a Marquis of the Holy Roman Empire."

CHAPTER 7

King Alexander rode north in cold fury. Retirement from the blood-soaked peat of Hexham had not been in any part his doing or desire. Had it been up to him, he would have willed that the army fight until either victory was won or not one man of any class stood on his two feet. Cooler and wiser heads had, however, prevailed, most notable among them: Andrew, Earl of Moray; the King's brother, James, Lord Marshal of the Army of Scotland; and the Papal Legate, Ramón de Mandojana.

The retreat was in no way a rout. The trains, the guns and all the noble wounded were in column with the battered troops . . . for a while. That they did not remain so was in no way the doing of the victorious English. Rather was it the English weather.

The bright, warm sunlight under which the withdrawal had begun did not last long. By noon, the sky had become a uniform, dull gray, and the first big drops of cold rain splattered down shortly thereafter. With scant pauses, the rain fell for nearly a week, and a truly deadly rain it was for full many a Scot.

The very lightest of the siege guns weighed, with its massive carriage, in excess of four tons, and the huge, bulky, clumsy weapons were difficult to transport under optimum conditions. By the evening of the third day of rainfall, Alexander had been forced to abandon every big bombard he had taken south and several field guns, as well. There was no way to reckon how many tons of supplies and powder had been surreptitiously cast by the way by wagoners trying to lighten their loads, or how many draft horses and mules had been killed or crippled in heaving to drag mired wagons and gun carriages out of the slimy, sucking mud. While fording some nameless stream, a wagon had lost a wheel, tilted and been overturned by the force of the current, hurling its load of screaming wounded into the racing, icy waters. Alexander had refused to countenance any rescue attempt, for by then English dragoons and lancers were nibbling at the rear and flanks of what was left of the Scottish Army. For all any knew, the entire English army was massing just over the closest southerly hill, and the area surrounding the ford was no place on which to try to make a stand.

Alexander had the place at which he and the army would—regardless of the maunderings of Legate, Lovat, Moray, Ayr or any of the rest of that craven pack—make a stand. He had managed to convince himself that Whyffler Hall must certainly have fallen to Scottish arms by now, conveniently forgetting the poor quality of the troops he had left behind to invest it. It was within those masterfully wrought works that he would mass his remaining force, thundering defiance at the excommunicated and disenfranchised wretch of an Arthur from the mouths of the Sassenachs' own guns.

But when at last he came within view of his objective, cold reality—in the form of the English royal banner, King Arthur's personal banner, and a third bearing the arms of the House of Whyffler, as well as a fourth which was not familiar to him, still snapping proudly upon the apex of the ancient tower—brought his self-delusions crashing about his head. Disregarding the "advices" of his advisers, he ordered the army to take up the positions they had occupied when first he had essayed the fort and, the next dawn, ordered and personally led a full-scale assault against the heavily defended works.

The assault was repulsed, sanguineously repulsed. The Scottish King himself had no less than three horses killed under him, and one of every six Scots and mercenaries was killed or wounded. But immediately after he had reluctantly ordered the recalls sounded, the valiant but impossibly stubborn sovereign was discussing the dispositions of the next morning's assault.

In the night, numerous Continental Crusaders cast off their white surcoats and, after tying rags of them to their lanceshafts, rode silently out of camp . . . headed south. Bearing their wounded and such supplies as they could quickly and easily steal, the surviving mercenaries were not long in following.

At dawn, the bloodied Scots formed for another suicidal effort, awaiting only the King to lead them. Then, just before the hour of tierce, the great lairds—Moray, Lovat, Ayr, Midlothian, Aberdeen, Ross, Angus, Banff, Argyll and Berwick—appeared in company with the Lord Marshal, James Stewart, to announce that King Alexander had died of his wounds in the night, as, too, had Cardinal de Mandojana. The late monarch had not thus far produced a legal heir, and as bastards could not inherit a crown, they had decided upon James to henceforth rein as Fifth of that name.

When the new king's decision to break off the feckless fight and march back into Scotland ere the bulk of English arms caught up to them was bruited about, there was a roar of general acclamation for the newmade sovereign. Only a few of the lesser lairds and chiefs thought to wonder *when* King Alexander had been seriously enough wounded to die, as he had led the actions in full-plate and had shown no signs of having suffered hurt . . . and of how the Legate, who had not fought at all, had suffered fatal wounds. But for all their private doubts and questions as to just precisely how James V had won the throne—for fratricide, patricide, and regicide were neither new nor novel in the violent and volatile Royal House of Scotland—they gladly followed him north, into the relative safety of the hills of home.

Foster sat his spotted stallion on the hill just southeast of Whyffler Hall and watched the Scottish army break camp and head north into the Cheviots, leaving their hundreds of dead heaped about the unbreached defenses of Whyffler Hall. After dispatching a galloper to seek out King Arthur, he toed Bruiser forward to slowly descend the hillslope, his escort of dragoons following him and the foreign nobleman who rode at his side.

Reichsbaron Manfried von Aachen had but recently landed at Hull, paused briefly in York, then ridden on to find the army, pressing his escort hard every mile of the way. Arrived, he had immediately met long and privily with Reichsherzog Wolfgang and the King. Then Wolfgang had summoned Foster.

Throughout the introductions, Foster could detect the

grief and sorrow in the voice and bearing of his friend and new overlord; when at last the rote was done, he was informed of the reason.

"The Emperor is dead," said Baron Manfried, flatly, his English far better and less accented than Wolfgang's. "Killed he was by an aurochs bull during a late-winter hunt in the Osterwald. The Electors met hurriedly and decided upon Otto's eldest son, Karl, but before their messengers could reach him, the Furst was slain in battle with the heathen Kalmyks. The Electors then decreed that Karl's younger brother should succeed their father, but, if he too be dead, that the Purple should pass to his uncle, Reichsherzog Wolfgang."

Wolfgang had sat throughout with his chin on his breastplate, sunk in his private sadness. Now he raised his head. "Zo, good *mein freund* Bass, ride you must, if necessary through all the Schottlandter host, und soon to reach Egon's side. The Empire at var mit neither Church nor Schottlandt iss, zo safe you und your men vill be mit the Imperial Herald, Baron Manfried . . . or zo vould you be mit any civilized monarch, let us to hope that these *verdammt* Schottlandters better know the usages of diplomacy than the practice of var."

"You mean," demanded Foster incredulously, "that Egon von Hirschburg is, has been all along, a royal prince? But you always said . . ."

Wolfgang shrugged his heavy shoulders. "I said that His Imperial Majesty a young noble of the Empire vas und mein godson. These true vere. For the rest . . . vell, better vas it thought that no vun know that a son of mein bruder mit an excommunicant fought, better for Egon, better for the Empire und her relations mit the Church.

"Of course," he zighed deeply, "nefer did any of us to think that efer Egon vould to rule be schosen. But a goot Emperor vill he make, *ja,* far better than vould I. Gott grant he safe still be!"

The track of the Scots had been easy to follow, a blind man could not have missed it in a snowstorm—crates and bales of stores, casks of gunpowder, dead men and dead horses, discarded weapons and bits of armor, a wide track of mud churned up by countless hooves and feet and cut deeply through with the ruts left by the wheels of laden wagons—though twice they had swung wide of that track to avoid contact with bodies of southward-marching troops, first a couple of hundred armored horsemen, then three or four thousand pikemen and crossbowmen quickmarching to the beat of muffled drums. On each occasion, Foster had detached and sent back a galloper to alert the King and Reichsherzog of these units proceeding to meet the English army.

Her Grace, Lady Krystal, the Markgrafin von Velegrad, was experiencing great difficulty in becoming accustomed to the incessant bows and curtsies with which she was greeted wherever she might choose to go in the Archbishop's huge palace. No whit less hard to bear for the gregarious young woman was the constant deference with which former friends and acquaintances now treated her. Aside from Pete, Bud Webster—convalescing in York while his broken leg knitted, and fretting that he could not be with the army as it retraced its way south to deal with the Spaniards on the south coast— Carey and Susan Carr, the only person with whom she found she could have a normal, give-and-take discussion was Archbishop Harold.

On a misty April day, she found the white-haired churchman immured in the extensive alchemical laboratory-workshop that he maintained.

After a few moments of polite chatter, she suddenly said, "Oh, dear Father Hal, why can't things be as they were? I had so many good friends, back at Whyffler Hall and when I first came to York, too. Now there's only Pete and Bud and Carey and Susan and you; all the rest either seem scared to death of me or are so clearly sycophantic that it's sickening. I don't begrudge Bass his rewards, you know that, he earned them. But . . . but my life was so much simpler and happier when I was just the lady-wife of a captain of dragoons."

Harold scribbled a few words on the vellum before him, then turned his craggy face to her. "My dear, deference to one's superiors is the hallmark of good breeding, and it is deference your friends show you now, not fear; they rejoice with you in your deserving husband's elevation. As regards sycophants, self-seeking persons are oft in attendance upon the noble and the mighty; that you can quickly and easily scry them out be a Gift of God. Too many of your peers lack that perception and so are victimized or deluded.

"I was aware that you had not the benefit of gentle upbringing and so understood very little of your present and future privileges and responsibilities; that is why I assigned noble maids and ladies to attend you."

"Dammit, I'm pregnant, but I'm not helpless, Hal," Krystal snapped. "I don't need a gaggle of girls and women to wake me and bathe me and dress me and follow me around all day and finally tuck me into bed at night like some idiot child."

He shook his head slowly. "No, my dear, you do not need such care, but you had best learn to live with it, all the same."

"But, why?" demanded Krystal.

Harold sighed then patiently explained, "For the nonce, my palace is beome the King's court, though His Majesty and most of his nobles be in the field with his army. You represent your husband at court and must comport yourself accordingly. The war will not last forever, and many a man's fortunes are made or dashed by his and his kin's conduct at court.

"Already are you considered rather odd by some folk, since you so abruptly dismissed your attendants, but I and your other friends have bruited it about that your condition has rendered you capricious as is common to gravid women. But such is a shallow untruth and will not bear long scrutiny. You must conform, my dear, must do and act and say what is expected of you here, at King Arthur's court."

"But what does it matter what people here think of me, or of Bass, for that matter?" queried Krystal, adding, "After all, we won't be in England once the war is done. Bass wrote me that the lands he holds for Wolfgang are, as best he can reckon, somewhere in the area that people of our time called Czechoslovakia."

"The fortified city of Velegrad guards an important pass through the Carpathian Mountains, Krystal," Harold informed her, but then admonished, "Not that you ever will see it, I suspect."

"What do you mean, Hal? Wolfgang struck me as definitely a man of his word, and he really likes Bass, too."

Harold smiled. "Oh, I have no doubt that the esteemed Reichsherzog would like nothing better than to install you and your husband as nobles of his seigneury, for the Empire is eternally at war with some nation or some people, and Bass is a superlative cavalry officer. But for that very reason, Arthur will never allow him to leave England to serve another monarch, even the Emperor."

"You have had word from the King, then, Hal?"

"No, Krystal, not concerning this matter, but there be no need. You see, I well know our Arthur. Why he allowed his brother-in-law to knight and enfeoff Bass with foreign lands, I cannot say that I comprehend, but you may rest in assurance that Arthur had, and has, a reason." The old man smiled and, steepling his fingers—blotched and stained now with chemicals—gazed over them into the flame of a beeswax candle.

"Arthur is come of a devious stock. John of Gaunt was a conniver of Machiavellian talents, and most of his descendants have been at least his sly equal in that respect, these Tudors in particular. I recall his grandfather, Arthur II, used to say—"

Krystal felt the hairs rise on her nape. "You . . . you *knew* the King's grandfather?" She shuddered, suddenly feeling herself in the presence of something unnatural. "He reigned a very long time; you can't be *that* old. Can you?" she whispered, fearfully.

The old man chuckled. "I suppose that now and here is a good time to tell you, especially you, since you seem the most rational of your lot. When were you born, Krystal—in what year *anno domini?*"

"Wh . . . what? When? In 1942. But what . . .?"

"Then," he smiled cryptically, "you are actually older than am I, chronologically. I was not born until 1968."

The May morn dawned bright and clear over Salisbury Plain, whereon stood the army of King Arthur, almost thirty thousand strong, in battle array. The battleline faced southeasterly, center and wings strong and deep even in extension, rear and flanks well-guarded by squadrons of horsemen. Well-protected batteries lay emplaced in positions from which they could inflict a deadly crossfire upon the ranks of an advancing enemy, while twos and threes of light cannon were interspersed among and between the *tercios* of pikemen and musketeers, all along the front.

The army of the Crusaders had come up the Avon from Bournemouth by barges and were forming a mile distant across the undulating plain. Fifteen thousand Spaniards, beneath the banner of *Principe* Alberto, bastard half-brother of King Fernando VII. Eighteen thousand Italian troops—though half the horse and nine-tenths of the foot were Slavic and Swiss mercenaries, rather than sons of Italy—under the Papal banner, but really commanded by Wenceslaus, Count Horeszko, a famous but aging *condottiere*. The Portuguese contingent was small—less than five thousand, all told—and were under the banner of Duque Henrique de Oporto. There were also a sprinkling of crusading nobles and knights from widely scattered areas . . . though less than half of what there had been before some of the paroled Crusaders who had survived the Scottish disaster had passed through Bournemouth ere they took ship for their various homelands to scrape up their ransoms.

With the permission of the Imperial Electors, Reichsregent Herzog Wolfgang had been allowed to remain with the English army, so long as he took no personal part in the fighting. This proviso chafed at the vital, active nobleman, but he had sworn a solemn vow to see his sister, nieces, and infant nephew avenged within the walls of London and forced himself to abide by the onerous condition in order to see the end of the war.

Foster, guided by local loyalists, had led a sweeping reconnaissance-raid into the very outskirts of Bournemouth, bringing back a score of prisoners, one a Portuguese noble, Melchoro Salazar, Barón de São Gilberto. The plump, pink-cheeked, jolly little man had made it abundantly clear from the very outset of his capture that no one event could have more pleased him, and immediately upon ascertaining that his captor was indeed a nobleman also, he was quick to give his parole. And he swung his ornate broadsword to some definite effect during a brush with a large band of brigands—not surprising in itself, as such scum were a sore affliction to both armies, but an indication that, for all his effete appearance, the Barón was certainly no mere carpet-knight.

University-educated and extensively traveled, Melchoro possessed fluency in English, German, Italian, Greek, Arabic, French, and basic Slavic, not to mention Latin, Spanish, and his mother tongue. He had a fine tenor singing voice and a seemingly inexhaustible store of humorous and bawdy songs in several languages; his expert transliterations of lewd ditties had his erstwhile captors wheezing and gasping in their saddles many times during the long ride back to the royal camp.

His contempt for the Crusade in general and the leaders of this southerly contingent in particular was abysmal, nor did he seem to hold the Church and her clergy in especially high regard.

"My good Marqués Sebastián, I have almost forty years and I have good use of them made—five universities in as many countries, as well as my other travels. My father had the goodness to live long and to be generous of stipends to his wandering heir, when he could not sell his sword for his keep."

"You have been a mercenary, then, Barón Melchoro?" asked Foster.

The Portuguese smiled. "Not really, no. But in some parts of this huge world men must swing sword in order to survive, so why not get paid for it, I always held. I have fought yellow Kalmyks in the plains of Russland, brown idolators on the borders of Persia, black, pagan maneaters in Africa, and red *Indios* in New Spain. I have slain or maimed many men, but only because they would have done the like to me, not through any love of bringing about suffering and death, nor yet to advance the spread of a Church I have come to feel is as thoroughly rotten as a week-old summer corpse."

"Then why are you here, in England, as a Crusader?" demanded Foster.

"Duty to my overlord." Melchoro shrugged languidly. "Duque Henrique would only excuse Conde João on the condition that he provide two hundred men-at-arms and at least four noble vassals. He, being a sporting man, called us all to his seat, told us of the Duque's commands, and then we diced." He shook his head ruefully. "Gambling, alas, is not my forte."

"And so, you are a Crusader," stated Foster.

"*Was* a Crusader, and a grudging one, at that. But now, thanks to you, my good friend, I am a paroled captive of war, and my thanks to you will be a goodly sum of ransom." He smiled broadly, his bright eyes dancing.

Turning in his saddle, the Barón addressed Nugai, who rode silently behind, never far from Foster's side, day or night, march or battle or camp. "*Vahdah, pahzhahloostah.*"

Wordlessly, the Tartar unslung his waterbottle and passed it forward.

When he had slaked his thirst and returned the canteen, the Barón commented, "Khazans like yours make the very best of bodyguard-servants; your overlord must esteem you most highly to give you such a treasure. Many of them are better at treating wounds and sicknesses than the most noted of our leeches and they are equally adept at compounding poisons, so they make fine assassins, as well. Would that I could afford to import a skilled Khazan, but what with sons to arm and fit out, daughters to dower and lands to maintain ..." He ended with a deep sigh.

"Well, look here, man," Foster began, "I don't want to beggar you. I can wait for the ransom or—"

Melchoro's merry laughter rang out. "Ho, ho, none of *my* gold will go for my ransom, good sir, not a bit of it. I be an old fox, and sly, ho, ho. The esteemed Conde João agreed ere I sailed—in writing, mind you, and legally witnessed—to pay my ransom if I was captured or to settle a largish sum on my family if I was slain.

"Nonetheless"—his tone took on a solemnity and he reached over to squeeze Foster's gauntleted hand resting on his pommel—"your charity is much appreciated, *mein Herr Markgraf*. Had I entertained any doubts of your nobility, they were dispelled; you are a gentleman born, and I shall ever be proud to call you friend."

Later, in camp, Wolfgang questioned the Barón for several hours, but they conversed in German and Foster understood very little of it. Later still, however, with the King present, all spoke English.

Melchoro sat at his ease at the long table, obviously un-abashed by the royal presence. When called upon, after Wolfgang's longish introduction, he sipped delicately from the winecup, then arose and began. He gave first the numbers of the various contingents and their nationalities.

"As regards the great captains, Your Majesty, Principe Alberto is a stiff-necked, supercilious fool, more fanatically religious then even the Cardinal, and his concepts of troopmarshaling and battle are impossibly archaic. Personally, he is brave to the point of stupidity, but no one has ever been able, apparently, to disabuse him of the notion that modes of warfare have not changed at all in the last five hundred years. In his closed mind, the crowning glory of any battle is the all-or-nothing charge of heavy cavalry in full-armor. And on more than one occasion, he has led his *hidalgos* in riding down his own infantry to get more quickly at the enemy ... which makes his pikemen and musketeers very nervous when they know he is behind them.

"My own Duque, Henrique, is here for the good of his

soul, too. But what he knows of *materia militaris* would not fill a mouse's codpiece."

Arthur chuckled at the allusion. He was clearly as taken with their captive as had been both Foster and Wolfgang.

"The Duque is certainly a man of some renown," agreed the King, in a humorous tone. "Frankly, I was surprised to hear that he had been chosen to lead a Crusade. How much does he weigh, these days?"

Melchoro grinned. "As you reckon it, sire, something in excess of twenty stone."

Wolfgang roared with laughter. His sides still shaking, he gasped, *"Lieber Gott! Drei hundert pfunden? Und in armor?* An elephant he must ride."

"No, *mein Herr Reichsregent,* he has a small coach, plated with proof, and drawn by six big geldings of the Boulonnais stock." He grinned. "It is a most singular spectacle, sire—the Duque's silken banner flying from a staff atop the coach, the horses all hung with chainmail and the coachmen and postillons in full plate. Yes, to see the Duque go to war is a rare experience. The Cardinal has taken to sharing his coach, recently."

Arthur nodded. "What of this Cardinal Ahmed? Does he command? What sort of soldier is he? Moorish, is he not?"

"He be a Berber, Sire, but albeit little skilled in war. Such orders as he gives are the 'suggestions' of *Conde* Wenceslaus, the famous *condottiere.* Such a charade is necessary to mollify the few hundred Italian knights and their retainers who value themselves too highly to accept orders from a Slav, even a noble Slav."

Wolfgang's brow wrinkled and he shook his shaven head slowly. "Wenceslaus, Landgraf Horeszko, ach, more battles that man has fought *und vun,* then hairs I haf on my arse. That he commanded only the Papal *condottas,* I had hoped. But if he the vord behind the Cardinal iss, then to lose this battle ve very vell may."

"How many cannon have the Crusaders?" asked King Arthur. "And what weights do they throw?"

"The siege train, Your Majesty, is large and complete. However, most of them are far too large and clumsy for field-of-battle work. Of lighter pieces, well . . . let me see. Each of the three Papal legions has a battery of four guns, nine-pounders, I believe. The Duque has four six-pounders and four fifteen-pounders."

"Und the Spanishers?" probed Wolfgang.

"A good part of the siege train is Spanish, but they own no lighter pieces," replied the Barón, adding, at the looks of utter consternation, "No, it is true. Principe Alberto often avers that while gunpowder is superior to siege engines for knocking down walls, battles are always won by sharp steel, bravery and faith. The Spanish ships offloaded no piece lighter than a full cannon."

The army of the Church advanced across the sunlit plain in battle order, to halt a little over a half-mile from the English. There was a confused wavering and rippling all along the lines of the center, then through the hastily widened intervals trotted thousands of armor-clad gentry and mercenary lancers. At the trot, they spread to form a jagged line, three horsemen deep. Then, with a pealing of trumpets, the leading line broke from trot to gallop, their long lances leveled, shouting their battle cries, their target the glittering pikepoints of the English *tercios*.

They were still a good quarter-mile from that target when the crossfire of the fieldguns almost obliterated them; neither chain nor plate proved any protection against grapeshot. But almost before they had gone down, the second line was at the gallop, secure in the knowledge that the cannon could never be swabbed, reloaded, and relaid in time to do them like damage. There would be a single volley from the contemptible musketeers, then their steel would be hacking at the pike-hedge.

There was a volley from the muskets. But then there was a second, and a third. And then the few survivors lost count of the rolling volleys. But old Count Wenceslaus, watching this idiotic waste of the valuable cavalry, did not lose count. In the silence—if the hideous din compounded of every sound suffering men and horses can make could be deemed silence—following the seventh volley, he solemnly crossed himself, something he had not done in many years.

The third and final line, led by Principe Alberto himself, was virtually annihilated, suffering the cannon fire at long range and the reloaded, multi-shot muskets closer in. Pete Fletcher's new shops at York had been laboring hard, day and night, and now almost every musketeer of the Royal Army bore one of the deadly weapons.

Through his long Venetian spyglass the aging *condottiere*

had the immense satisfaction of watching helmet and head torn off the Principe by, presumably, a piece of grape. Even while his brain spun busily with alternatives that might give him some bare chance of a victory, despite the loss of almost all his cavalry, he grimly reflected that the army was already the better off for the loss of that arrogant, ranting pig of a Spaniard.

Cardinal Ahmed did not see the death of Alberto; he had kept his own glass trained upon the English lines, though little could be seen save black, flame-shot smoke eddying about and among the *tercios* on a gentle breeze. Ahmed was not and had never been a soldier, but his father and brothers had been, so he was as keenly aware as any of the calamity that had here befallen the Crusaders. Cavalry were the very eyes and ears of any army—he recalled his hawknosed, blue-eyed father saying that many times over—and there, thanks to a stubborn and headstrong Spaniard, lay the cavalry of the Church, become little save bloody flesh and scrap metal. While the recall sounded for the pitiful remnant of those thousands of armored horsemen, he ordered the steel carriage drawn to the small knoll whereon stood the grim-faced Wenceslaus, Count Horeszko, his bald, scar-furrowed head glinting in the sun.

Laying aside his dignity of rank in the press of the moment, the thin, wiry churchman dismounted from the coach and paced up to stand beside his employee. "Are then the English foot all musketeers, my son?"

"No, Your Eminence," answered the old soldier gravely. "It would appear that they possess a new musket that fires seven times without reloading. From what little I noticed before the smoke got too thick, I would say that the charges are contained in big iron cylinders affixed under the breeches of their weapons, but I could not tell you more without examining one."

The Cardinal shook his head. "Scant chance of that, my son. I suppose that our *tercios* would fare as poorly as the horse, were we to attack. What would you advise our movement be?"

"The *tercios* would be ground up just like the cavalry, Your Eminence, ground more finely, mayhap. We could try to maneuver, but with no horse to screen our movements . . ." He shrugged and grunted. "The only thing on which we could depend would be that those fast-firing muskets would be waiting to receive our attack, from whatever angle. Damn that Spanish whoreson! God's eyes, if only—"

The Cardinal laid a fine-boned, parchment-skinned hand upon the steel-plated shoulder. "Blaspheme not, my son. What has transpired is assuredly done. You then would advise . . .?"

"That we break off the action and withdraw, Your Eminence. We have the siege train at Bournemouth, some fortifications already are dug and prepared, and we can throw up more. Muskets are heavy enough, and with those clumsylooking devices added to them, I doubt me they'd be much good on the attack. Entrenched, lack of cavalry will be no detriment to us."

The Cardinal sighed and nodded. "So be it. I shall give the order."

So the ranks formed into column and retraced their way to the river, harassed and menaced every step of the way by English horse—dragoons, lancers and irregulars. Many a Crusader prayed for sight of the river and the waiting barges that would bear them back downstream to safety.

But such salvation was not to be. The van arrived to find the riverside camp sacked, the barges either awash with great holes knocked in their hulls or missing entirely from their moorings, presumably set adrift. Most of the bargemen were dead and the draft teams had all been herded off. There was nothing for it but to try to march down the river edge to Bournemouth.

Lacking either food or tents or even blankets, the Spaniards—most of them from dry, sunny, Mediterranean provinces—shivered through the long nights of damp cold, their searches for the blessings of sleep unaided by the piteous moans and cries of the wounded. And despite the attrition of death, there were proportionately more wounded at each succeeding night's encampment, due to the ceaseless and pitiless incursions and ambuscades of the flitting bands of horsemen.

Seemingly from out of empty air, three-quarter-armored dragoons would charge in on flank or rear, huge horsepistols booming, each launching a deadly ball or a dozen small-shot on a yard of flame. Then, before muskets could be presented or pikes lowered, the attackers would have faded back into the nothingness that had spawned them, only to strike again, as suddenly and devastatingly, at another integument of the trudging column.

117

Most of the field guns were lost on the first day's march, and none remained by nightfall of the second day. The few hundred horsemen manfully set themselves to pursuit of the attackers. In the beginning, so few of them ever returned that the Count forbade such heroics . . . but by that time he was numbering his remaining cavalry in mere scores.

The snail's pace of the starving army became slower each day, as the continued lack of sustenance and dearth of sleep took their inevitable toll of the men's strength and vitality. Now, infantry menaced them along with the ruthless cavalry, and even the humble comfort of an evening campfire was denied them, as the tiniest hint of a flame was certain to bring the crashing of a musket or the booming of a pistol or the deadly humming of a quarrel from the merciless foemen who ringed them about.

Every night, somewhere or other, sentries fell silently under knife or garrote, and with a pounding of steel-shod hooves, lines of yelling English horsemen were upon and among the recumbent, fatigue-drugged Crusaders, broadswords and pistols, lances and axes taking a bloody toll.

For four nights the carnage continued, but they were left in an uneasy peace for all of the fifth night, though the sounds of horses and the rattling clinking of equipment told that the English enemy still lurked out there in the darkness.

Near noon of the sixth day, the tattered, battered, weary, and demoralized Crusaders emerged from the marshy forest through which they had been marching since dawn to find the English army drawn up in battle array across a riverside lea.

Count Wenceslaus kneed his drooping destrier forward and took stock of the situation. The English flanks were secured by the river on the one side and by a continuation of the swampy forest on the other. Sunrays sparked on the points of a deep pikehedge, while lazy spirals of smoke rose into the balmy air over the long lines of musketeers blowing upon their slowmatches. Batteries—some of them his own, he noted ruefully through this glass—reinforced the line at obviously well-calculated intervals. He could spy no cavalry, but he had no doubt that they would manifest themselves at a time and place inconvenient to him. There, he thought, stands a first-rate army and well-led.

Turning, he set eyes upon his tatterdemalions, slowly debouching from the swamp and forest to stand gaping in stunned disbelief at the serried ranks blocking their only road to Bournemouth. He shook his head sadly, closed and cased his precious long-glass, set his helmet back over his coif, reined about and set off at a plodding walk toward the steel coach, heedless of the tears coursing down his lined cheeks into his scraggly beard. Surrender was foreign to his nature ... but so, too, was suicide.

CHAPTER 8

With the capitulation of the last and largest force of foreign Crusaders, the counties of the south and the east were a-ripple with the sound of turning coats. Those few men too honest or too stubborn to decide that Arthur was lawful king after all spurred lathered horses for the safety of the walls of London. Some made it. Some did not, and full many a tree and gate lintel and gibbet throughout the realm was decorated with the bird-pecked corpses of churchmen and Church's men, swaying and rotting and stinking under the hot summer sun.

With no less than three captured siege trains, the Royal Army invested London—last remaining stronghold of Church and Pretender—late in May. They still were ringed about the city in December, warm and dry and adequately supplied in well-built encampments, patiently awaiting the order to attack but, meanwhile, seeing to it that no living creature left the city and that no supplies of any sort reached it.

Of scant value to the besiegers, the Royal Cavalry had spent the summer and the autumn riding hither and yon, putting down brigandage, hunting down stragglers from the various foreign armies, and flushing out Church's men and other traitors. But as autumn merged into winter, the Lord Commander of Horse recalled the wide-ranging units to the old campground near Manchester, and after issuing orders that all be ready for instant summons but in any case report to the present encampment no later than the first day of April, he dismissed them to their homes. Then, accompanied by his faithful attendant and along with a score of Borderers, he set out to the northeast, where old friends, wife, and infant son awaited him.

The little party clove to the coast as far north as Kendal, then northwestward up the valley of the Eden River, due west over the northern foothills of the Pennine chain, over the ancient Roman Wall, and so into Tynedale, being welcomed at every hall and hamlet they passed. But there was no welcome for the travelers at Heron Hall.

The smashed gate hung drunkenly on but one hinge, swaying and creaking dolefully to the strong, frigid gusts howling down from Scotland. Most of the outbuildings were but heaps of old ash and tumbled, sooty stones, and the hall itself, wherein had been dispensed so much cheer from year to year, was a smoke-blackened ruin. The windows gaped like the empty eyesockets of some ancient skull, while the soaring chimneys and charred roofbeams now gave roost to a flock of cawing crows which rose in an ebon cloud, loudly shrieking protest, when a trio of dragoons clambered through a front window and drew the rusty bolts so that their officer might enter.

Foster saw that half of the stone stairway still stood, mounting upward from the desolation below to end abruptly in the empty space above. Small vermin scuttered squeaking before his advance, and his boot struck a roundish object that rolled over in the cold, wet ashes to grin up at him with broken teeth—a human skull, a wide, jagged crack running from just above the brow to the crown.

His troopers poked about here and there, but between the Scots and the fire, nothing worth the looting remained in the empty shell of Heron Hall. They soon mounted and rode on northward, a good bit more somber than before, until the banner-crowned keep of Whyffler Hall came into view.

The silken banners snapped taut in a stiff wind from the northwest, and Foster reined up on a knoll to study them through his battered binoculars, with the now-instinctive caution born of the long months of war.

There was the royal banner, of course, as the hall still was reckoned a fort and still housed a reduced garrison; there was Sir Francis' family arms, and Foster's own. But there were several other banners as well. One of them he was dead certain was that of Harold of York, though he could not imagine for what purpose the Archbishop had left his comfortable

121

palace for the long, rugged journey to the northern marches. Beside the episcopal banner floated what could be none but that of Reichsregent Wolfgang, and there were two others, one of which bore a striking resemblance to the arms of the Kingdom of *Scotland*; as to the last, Foster knew that he had seen it before but could not say where or name it.

The alert sentries spotted the mounted party long before they reached the ring of outer fortifications, and they were greeted at the south gate by a well-armed quarterguard and there halted until their identities had been established to the satisfaction of the guard officer. Only then were they escorted to the hall, wherein Sir Francis and his guests sat at meat.

Foster stood before the mirror in the master bathroom of his home, bare to the waist, removing the stubble from his cheeks with slow, even strokes of the rotary razor. Through the connecting closet space, he could see Krystal, still sleeping on their big bed, her fine, exciting body concealed now by the blanket, her raven hair still in the wild disarray in which their early-morning bout of love had left it. Beyond the bed, in an intricately carved and richly inlaid cradle, slept his son, Joseph Sebastian Foster.

He had always been of the opinion that all babies looked alike . . . but that was before he had first held little Joe, gazed into the dark-blue eyes under the already thick shock of blue-black hair, felt the surprising strength of the grip of that tiny pink fist. My *son*, he had thought with fierce pride, *my* son; it all has been worth it—the pain, the cold, the heat, the privation, even the death—you, my son, have made it worthwhile for me, simply by *being*.

The two marriages of his salad days had never been happy or secure enough for him to even consider children. He and Carol had often discussed having a few, as they often had discussed formalizing their relationship with marriage, but they had continually put off both projects . . . and then, one day, Carol was dead.

As he stood beneath the scalding spray of the shower, he thought, "Arthur must find a way to mollify Church and Pope, if I'm to see this son of mine a man. Only a handful of my original troop are left alive, and if more Crusaders come in the spring, if the war drags on for another year, it can only be a matter of time until a swordswipe or an ounce of lead makes me one of the majority, for all that I don't see as much hand-to-hand anymore as I did when I led only a troop or a squadron.

"Of course, I could say 'to hell with it, I've done my bit' and take my sword and my family and my stallion to Europe with Wolfie after London falls, and no man would think any less of me for it; after all, I am a nobleman of the Empire and Wolfie's vassal, and I'm as safe from the Church there as I would be here, at least as long as Egon is Emperor.

"That Egon is quite a boy, but then I always thought highly of him. Took a leaf from Arthur's book, they say, declared his Empire was no longer a Papal feoff and flatly refused to go to Rome to be crowned by the Pope . . . and the Electors backed him up too, to a man. Crowned himself, he did! Then sent Cardinal Eugenio de Lucca back to Rome with a message that it's said sent the Pope into screaming fits. Emperor Egon I solemnly promises that when he can win the support of a majority of the Imperial Electors, he means to enter into a formal alliance with the Kingdom of England and Wales and, if any Crusade is preached against him or the first foreign Crusader sets foot over his boundrics, he will make peace with the heathen hordes on his eastern borders and grant them free passage over his lands that they may descend upon Italy, France, Iberia, and Scandinavia. Obviously, Rome believes him, for they now are playing a very tight game, where Egon is concerned.

"And the buggers should take him seriously, too, because he already has a big minority of those Electors on the hip. When he informed them that he meant to not only pick his own empress but that she'd be the daughter of a simple country *Freiherr*, and English to boot, he got majority approval on the first *vote*.

"So now, dear old Sir Francis and Arabella are enroute to the King's camp, and the escort who came to deliver Arthur's summons and bear them back was already fawning over the old man and addressing him as 'Your Grace' and 'My Lord Duke,' and the ladies of the party were all a-flutter over 'Her Imperial Highness.' Sir Francis seemed to be bearing up well enough—I can't think of any possible circumstance that would rattle that stout old soldier—but poor little Arabella looked dazed. I guess she thought she'd never see Egon again."

He turned, then, to let the steaming water play over his back and shoulders now thickly callused from bearing the weight of a cuirass. He silently mused on.

123

"Well, at least our northern marches are secure—anyway, secure as they've ever been, considering the temper and endless feuds of the Borderers. James of Scotland not only doesn't want any more war with us, he's willing to send unsecured hostages for his continued good conduct. Too, Hal of York says that in addition to offering Arthur his only child as a wife, James' emissary keeps obliquely inquiring whether Arthur might be willing to send part of his army to Scotland to help put down a covey of rebellious lairds.

"And I doubt we'll see much of the Irish, for a while, what with the hot little civil war—five-sided, last I heard!—the High King's got on his bloody hands. If we can put stock in our chubby Barón Melchoro, no Portuguese will be back. But there are still the French and the Spanish, and you can bet that Rome will be hiring another army and another captain, come campaigning weather. Old Count Hereszko will be passing the word among his colleagues that we're a tough nut to crack, but that won't faze the *condottieri*, of course; each one of them thinks he's a better captain than any other, so they'll just put his defeat down to his senility . . . and jack up the price to whatever the Church is willing to pay.

"But the Church dislikes spending money on wars and soldiers to fight them and Wolfie says that, if it appears that the English Crusade is going to continue to drain the Papal treasury at the rate last year's campaignings did, it's more than likely that the Pope will call off the Crusade and try to normalize relations with Arthur. If London falls, he says, and the Pretender and his harridan of a mother should happen to meet with fatal . . . ahh, 'accidents' before a new war season can get under way, it's a near certainty that Rome will try to negotiate. God, I sure hope he's right!"

The sound of the rushing water wakened Krystal Foster, slowly. She stretched once, deliciously, then snuggled back under the blanket, purring like a cat, her mind filled with thoughts of her husband.

There had been many times in the not-too-distant past (or was it future?) when she had thought she would never have either husband or child, as she trod the fine line between the insensate demands of mother, aunts and other relatives—"marry a nice, Jewish boy and settle down and start having babies; that's what a girl is supposed to do with her life, Rebecca, that's what makes life worthwhile"—and the gut knowledge that her baby brother would never willingly amount to a damn and so only *her* accomplishments would be available to salvage her beloved father's pride.

In the eight years of pre-med and medical school, she had done her share of sleeping around, of course, and had soon come to the conclusion that damned few of the young men of her peer group were free of some sort of sexual hangup. She had started to wonder if the religious nuts were not correct in their vociferous assertions that American society was rotten to the core, hopelessly decadent and bound irrevocably for hell in a handcart, until she met Dan.

That was in her junior year of med school and, within two months of meeting, she and Dan Dershkowitz were sharing a tiny off-campus apartment. In the beginning, he seemed the man of her dreams—tall, handsome, trim and athletic, highly intelligent and well-educated, urbane and charming, abrim with humanism. A native of Chicago, he was a psychiatric social worker in Baltimore and also taught a couple of evening classes each week at Krystal's university.

It lasted for five glorious months and ended terribly, traumatically, one lovely spring afternoon. Her last class of the day having been canceled in the unexpected absence of the professor, she had returned to the apartment two hours earlier than usual. As she climbed the stairs, she was already planning to call Dan at his office, cook him a fine meal, and have a wonderful early evening before again hitting the books.

She turned the key in the lock and swung open the door. The air was thick and bluish with hash smoke, but this was not unusual; she and Dan often relaxed with grass or hash, which both of them considered pleasant and innocuous substances. She reeled against the doorframe in sick horror at what she saw upon the Murphy bed.

Dan. Wonderful Dan. Her Dan. Dan, nude but for T-shirt and sox, doing *things* to the wholly nude body of Ricky Pérez, the super's retarded teenaged son!

Her second fiasco started almost a year later, in the person of Harley Fist. Harley was a couple of years older than she, though only an undergraduate senior, due to the fact that he had done two hitches in the army between high school and college. He was not above average in height—only five-nine or so—but was solid and powerful, with long arms and such superb coordination that he was a shining light of the varsity hockey team, though he invariably spent a good bit of each game in the penalty box.

125

Harley's pugnacity on the ice was infamous; he had assaulted opponents with butting head, flailing fists, knees, elbows, forearms, stick, feet and skates and, on occasion, had downed his man by way of a flying body-block. Nor were his attacks limited to sport—his fraternity brothers trod most warily around him, especially on the frequent times he was found in his cups. But he was unquestionably masculine and Krystal needed that super-maleness, after Dan.

As his date of graduation neared, Harley was recipient of several attractive offers from many professional hockey clubs who recognized the box-office potential of his brand of savagery. Immediately he accepted the most promising and lucrative of the commitments, and asked Krystal to marry him in June and accompany him to Canada.

Even had she not already been accepted as an intern at a large, Baltimore hospital, Krystal could not see herself legally bound to Harley Fist. Too many things about him were unsettling. He was crude, and not even four years in a top fraternity had been able to impart sufficient polish to his rough edges to make him more than marginally acceptable in most social situations. Another thing that bothered her was his obvious relish in recountals of thoroughly sickening atrocities he had perpetrated or taken part in during his tours in Southeast Asia. But the most disturbing factor was the fact that, when he was not in strict training, he was never cold sober and, when drunk, he posed a deadly threat to everyone within reach.

As gently as possible, Krystal refused him, citing her past eight years of preparation and her coming internship. Reaching across the table, she took his big, scarred hand in both of hers and sincerely thanked him for the offer, then she finished her coffee and excused herself to go to her next class.

On the evening of the second day after her graduation, her mother and her father were helping her pack her furniture and personal possessions for the storage company to collect the following morning, since she would be required to reside in the hospital during her internship. In the window, the air-conditioning unit fought valiantly against the muggy heat. While her mother boiled eggs and brewed tea in the minuscule kitchenette, she and her father sat carefully wrapping breakables in newspaper before stowing them in the china barrels.

The wall clock showed twenty minutes of midnight when there came the pounding on the apartment door.

"People don't know what a bell is for?" asked her father as she arose and stepped over to open the latch. Leaving the burglar chain engaged, she peered out to see Harley Fist, swaying on his feet, his eyes red-rimmed, his face sullen and stubbled, a livid bruise discoloring one side of his chin and jaw.

Squinting, he peered at her. "Open up the gawdam door, Krystal. I came to give you another chance, 'fore I leave for Canada."

"My answer is still the same, Harley. Thank you so very, very much, but no."

He leaned against the door and leered nastily. "Well, open up, anyhow, sweet chips. We can crawl inna bed and say bye-bye right." He shoved his hips forward, adding, "Stick your hand down here and take a feel of what I got for you."

She shook her head. "Just go home, Harley, please. What we had is over and . . . and I have—"

At that moment, her father called, "Who is it, honey? What do they want?"

Harley took a half-step back and lunged. Krystal barely had time to get out of the way of the wood splinters and brass screws as the chain was ripped from the jamb and the door crashed open.

Harley stalked into the room, snarling, "You gawdam sheenie bitch, you! Couldn't wait till I was gone, 'fore you was slidin' your slimy, fuckin' cooze onta a cock old enough to be your friggin' *father*. Well, I'll just fix his fuckin' apples, and 'fore I'm done with the two of you, tonight, you gone need a fuckin' doctor . . . or a friggin' undertaker!"

Recognizing the clear signs of his killer rage, Krystal grasped his arm, placing herself between him and his intended prey. "Harley, *Harley*, this *is* my father! Harley, listen to me! This is my *father*."

Mr. Kent had stood up. Frowning disapproval, he took the telephone from atop a sealed crate. "Krystal, the young man is obviously drunk. Don't try to argue with him. Tell him to leave. If he won't, call the police. That's the only way to handle people in his condition."

He held the set out. Harley grabbed it, ripped the cord from the wall, and heaved everything through the window above the air conditioner. Followed by a shower of glass and pieces of sash frame, the telephone fell three stories to narrowly miss an open convertible parked in front of the building, and the indignant shouts of the five young men occupying it could be clearly heard through the shattered window.

In his day, Joseph Kent had been a fair boxer, and though his YMHA boxing days were twenty-five years behind him, he still had no fear of the bigger, younger man. Tucking his double chin, he advanced in a weaving crouch, fists cocked and ready.

"No!" screamed Krystal, frantically. *"No, he'll kill you!"*

Harley dealt Krystal a leisurely, backhand cuff that sent her reeling and stumbling, her mouth suddenly flooded with blood from a split lip. Then he turned his attention to her father.

"C'mon, you broadhoppin' old cocksucker. I'm gonna tear your fuckin' head off and jam it up your fuckin' ass!"

But Harley's first roundhouse swing entirely missed its target and he had to struggle to maintain his balance. While he was doing so, Joseph Kent—five-five, paunchy, and balding—danced in and drove one fist into the big man's belly, bringing a wheezing grunt, followed with a hard jab just below the heart.

But before the little man could retreat out of range, Harley had him. Gripping both of Joseph Kent's meaty biceps, he slammed his knee up into the older man's crotch, then threw the helpless, agonized man at Krystal and moved after them, screaming, "GAWDAM NO-GOOD HEBES! YOU KILLED JESUS AND GAWDAM IF I AIN'T GONNA KILL YOU!"

It all had happened in a split second, just as long as it took for Esther Kent to cast about for a weapon . . . and find one. Harley was not even aware that a third person was in the apartment until, as he neared the kitchenette, a saucepan of boiling water was thrown into his face.

Harley Fist screamed in agony. As he staggered about, blindly, Esther dragged both her husband and daughter into the narrow kitchenette and slammed the door, wedging one end of the ironing board under the knob and the other against the baseboard, then taking her place in defense of her battered, bleeding family with a bone-handled carving knife.

A reflexive blink had saved Harley's eyes, but the killer had other problems. The three topmost buttons of his shirt were unfastened and a brace of the eggs had found their way under the shirt to sear his upper abdomen. Instinctively slapping one big hand to the place that hurt, he managed to mash one of the eggs, causing the runny, boiling-hot food to spread the pain over a wider area of sensitive belly skin.

Roaring and stamping with the pain, Harley shredded off his shirt, using the rags of it to wipe the sticky, burning mess from his hairy epidermis. Then he threw himself against the kitchen door. It groaned mightily, but held. Harley screamed again, but this time in frustration. He crashed his bony knuckles into a panel, once, twice. The wood splintered, and he thrust his bare arm through the opening, feeling downward for the lock.

As the fingers of the intruder's hand fumbled at the knob, then began to pull at the ironing board, Esther Kent lunged, skewering the muscular, hirsute hand just behind the knuckles.

Harley screamed once more, jerked his blood-spouting paw back out of the door, and recommenced attacking the portal with his shoulder. With both hinges almost torn loose and the various cracks and bulges showing that the very fabric of the door was about to sunder, Esther began to scream, as well.

Then, suddenly, the assault on the door ceased.

Harley had already downed three of his fraternity brothers and was doing damage to the remaining pair when the police arrived. He broke the arm of one officer, the jaw of a second, and the teeth of a third, before the other three and the two college boys could hold him down long enough to cuff him. Even chained, he fought his captors all the way to the second-floor landing. When, at that point, he smashed the bridge of one policeman's nose with his butting forehead, the injured man's partner released his grip on Harley's arm and gave him a shove.

Harley, his hands fastened behind his back, tumbled the length of the flight of stairs to slam, face first, onto the marble floor of the foyer. After that, he proved much easier to manage.

Lying with her eyes almost closed, Krystal watched her husband through the open doors as he toweled himself dry, then began to dress. She shuddered with delight, recalling the last few moments they had been together.

"Bass Foster," she thought, "is all man, no one could ever doubt that fact; but he's gentle, not brutal, caring, not callous. No doubt he's shot many men or killed them with that lovely, deadly Irish sword, but he did it only to live himself and he's certainly not proud of having killed them. God, if you're really there, somewhere, let our little Joe grow up to be the same, splendid kind of man as his father is."

On the day before his departure, Sir Francis had closeted himself with Foster. "Bass, all mine own sons be mony years dead. Had the elder, Dick, nae been slain, he'd be aboot of an age wi' y'. Forgive an auld mon's folly, but I've come tae think of y' as a son, these last years, for y'r what a' I'd hae a son o'mine tae be, ye ken?"

Foster had only been able to nod, so tight had been his throat. It then came into his conscious mind that he truly loved this bluff, kindly, unassuming old man as he had loved his own father.

"Nae mon can say what-a' may pass on the lang rood tae London, an' me folk maun hae ane o'erlord in these troubled times. Beside," he grinned, "sich will gi' y' saltin' for the lordin' o' y'r ain demesne. There be little work ata', lad, oor good Geoffrey sees tae a' that, but wi' a' these imporrrtant guests, he'd be a mickle-mite uneasy wioot a lord tae make decisions or approve his ain.

"An' so, Bass, wi'y' ease an auld mon's mind an' take this feoff an' fealty tae me until I be back?"

And so, every morning since Sir Francis' departure had found Foster leaving his own, snug home to trudge up to the draughty, chilly hall and there spend the day and early evening serving the functions of master to the servants and host to the guests. Nor was this day different. Bundled in his thickest cloak, he floundered through knee-high snow, his boot-soles slipping on the ice beneath, as far as the broad, stone steps leading up from the formal garden.

Supervised by Olly Shaftoe, who stood just within the recessed doorway, stamping and blowing on the fingers of his single hand, a brace of men were shoveling and sweeping the steps and veranda clear of the night's accumulation of snow. At Foster's approach, both men smiled and bobbed respectful greeting, while Olly fingered his forelock in military fashion.

At the high-table in the dining hall sat Wolfgang, Harold of York, and the Scottish ambassador, Parlan Stewart, Duke of Lennox, King James' first cousin. The Archbishop and the Reichsregent were chatting amiably in German, while breaking their fast on hard bread, strong cheese and hot brandy punch. The Scot, on the other hand, looked to be near death, showed a greenish tinge whenever he caught a whiff of the cheese, and sat in silence, taking cautious sips from a jack of steaming, spiced Spanish *chocolát,* said to be a sovereign remedy for a hangover.

As Foster, relieved of cloak, hat and sword by the servants, strode into the big room—hung with antique tapestries, old banners and weapons, and the trophies of ancient chases—Wolfgang raised his silver mug in greeting, roaring, *"Ach, Bass, guten morgen."*

At the deep bellow, Duke Parlan started, almost dropped his jack and groaned, audibly, carefully setting the *chocolát* by to take his head in both trembling hands.

Taking his place in the cathedral-backed armchair, Foster first gave his desires to the waiting servitors, then turned to the Scottish guest. "You are unwell, my lord Parlan?" he inquired solicitously, though suspecting crapulence.

The Scot's answer was a piteous moan. Wolfgang chuckled, took a long pull at his punch, and said, "Ach, Bass, after you to your home left, last night, our good Duke Parlan to outdrink me set himself. The third time he from out of his chair fell, I had summoned his men to bear him abovestairs." He rumbled another gust of laughter, emptied his cup and began to spread the soft cheese onto another chunk of bread.

Not until he was full of fresh, warm milk and hot oaten porridge did the temporary master of Whyffler Hall accept a mug of mulled wine. He had never gotten accustomed to breakfasting on spirits and wished to keep his wits about him, especially since the invaluable Geoffrey Musgrave was gone to make his rounds of the demesne and consequently Foster would have to perform many of the steward's hall duties himself, during the eight short hours before the serving of the day's meal.

Invaluable and indispensable on campaign, Nugai had proved a well-intentioned nuisance to his master at Whyffler Hall. For the first few days he seldom left Foster's side, day or night, and never withdrew farther than he could accurately throw a knife, taking his sleep on the floor before the door of the master bedroom. Most of the menservants of the hall staff were terrified of the strange, silent, bandy-legged man, who glared grimly and fingered the worn hilt of his big *kindjal*—long as a Scot's dirk, but broader, single-edged and razor-sharp—whenever one of them approached Foster on any errand.

Finally, Foster had ordered him to remain in the trilevel, pointing out to the unprepossessing but highly intelligent little man that Krystal and the wet nurse needed protection from roaming soldiers and Scots of the Duke of Lennox's train far more than did he, since most of his days were spent within the precincts of the Hall, surrounded at all times by servants, many of whom were old soldiers.

For two days, Krystal remained unimpressed by the Khazan or the arrangement; then a trio of drunken kilted gillies—the Scots camped in the outer bailey seemed to have brought along an inexhaustible supply of whiskey and stayed drunk most of the time—wandered by, spied the wet nurse and immediately decided to amuse themselves with a lighthearted gang rape. Nugai shot one, opened a second from crotch to brisket, then threw the dripping *kindjal* with such force that the blade sheared through vertebra and ribs, its point piercing clear through the unfortunate Scot's breastbone. And all this occurred before Krystal, alerted by the nurse's first scream, had time to hurry down to the den from the bedroom.

Thenceforth, the Marchioness of Velegrad found Sergeant Nugai much more acceptable. Too, she soon found, as had her husband, that the taciturn Kalmyk was multi-talented; he could cook, sew, do carpentry and intricate woodcarvings and brew evil-smelling and tasting herbal concoctions that worked medical wonders in alleviating or easing minor ailments of man or beast, and she was pleased by the alacrity with which the little nomad mastered the uses of the various items of plumbing and the electrical fixtures, appliances and gadgets. Soon she had turned over the kitchen and all cooking to her bodyguard.

On the morning of Duke Parlan's monumental hangover, Nugai waited until the wet nurse had removed her charge from his cradle and departed, then he padded up the stairs, down the hallway and into the bedroom, bearing the bedtray on which reposed Krystal's breakfast—boiled eggs, cheese toast, and herb tea . . . enough tea for two, as he customarily sat, sipped, and chatted with his mistress as she breakfasted.

CHAPTER 9

With the Scottish ambassador in his chambers nursing his head and with the Reichsregent and three of the gentlemen-officers of the garrison ahorse in company with the gamekeeper and in pursuit of a small pack of wolves lately seen nearby the hall, Foster had sought out the Lord Archbishop and had been sipping and chatting with him for the last hour. The fire crackled on the hearth and a half-dozen iron loggerheads nestled in the coals, ready to rewarm the two men's drinks.

"And," continued Harold of York, "Mr. Fairley's armorers are hard at work, this winter. He finally has perfected the new ignition system and is having it fitted onto every matchlock and serpentine they can lay hands upon; by spring, all the Royal Army musketeers and horsemen should be equipped either with wheellocks or these new locks, and he has even devised a means to apply his system to cannon."

Foster asked, "How about his lightweight field guns? Has he gotten anywhere with them?"

The old man smiled. "Oh, yes, a score have already gone down to the army. Cast of fine bell bronze, they throw over nine full pounds of canister or grape, for all that the tube is a bare three feet long and weighs only a bit over fifteen stone. Mr. Carey, moreover, has outdone himself on design of the carriages for this new cannon. They are unlike any gun mount ever before seen, here. All the component parts are interchangeable, the carriages are amazingly strong when their

133

lightness—between four and five hundredweight—be considered, and they even incorporate a spoked iron wheel with which the angle of the gun can be raised or lowered without those clumsy wedges gunners now use."

"And Bud Webster?" asked Foster. "What of him?"

"I turned my archepiscopal estates over to him for as long as he wishes," replied the churchman, while thrusting a glowing loggerhead into his cooling ale. "He is selectively breeding swine and kine and promises that within a few years, my herd will produce bigger, stronger oxen, more productive milch cows and larger, meatier porkers. He seems very happy, very content, though he still talks on occasion of returning to the army when his leg improves. But"—he slowly shook his white head—"I fear me that Captain Webster is crippled for life."

"He was a good soldier, a good officer, and is missed by those who served with him," nodded Foster. "But for all his prowess, he's probably doing this kingdom, this world, more good on your farms, improving sources of food and draft animals, than he would be forking a horse and swinging a broadsword. *I* do those things, it's all I seem to be any good at—killing and marshaling troops to do more killing. You didn't get much of a bargain in me, did you?"

Harold's smile abruptly became a frown. "Do not undervalue yourself and your very real accomplishments, Bass. Only overly civilized cultures, decadent and rotting, denigrate the master warrior, and you are such. You know what was the sole function of the royal horse of old, in battle—shock troops, pure and simple. You, as Lord Commander, have made of the heavy horse a tactical force, and thanks to the officers you have trained, the intelligent men you have inspired, even were you to depart tomorrow and never to return, the King's Cavalry still would remain the very envy of other monarchs."

Foster shook his head. "No, Hal, it was Collier who reorganized the army into units of manageable size, taught them drill—"

"Fagh!" snorted the churchman. "I was there, then, Bass. Did Collier ever do aught of the work? Nay, it was you and Webster drilled and redrilled day after day until you'd trained officers to do it for you. Oh, I grant you, the man was useful for some short while, but after Arthur and Wolfgang and I had picked his brain . . . now, do not misunderstand me, Bass, some of his huge store of knowledge *was* helpful, most definitely, and he was amply rewarded, I saw to that matter, since by then Arthur considered him a coward because he had refused to meet you at swordpoints.

"He'd have been allowed to keep those rewards, too, had he not tried to bully you, then so lost his wits as to *publicly* threaten the King. He could have had a good life—those lands he was granted are good ones—instead of howling away his remaining years in a monastery cell near Edinburgh."

"What's this?" snapped Foster. "When he stopped here, he told us that he was to be well received at the Scottish Court."

"And so he probably would have been," nodded Harold soberly, "had he arrived at Alexander's court. But as you know, Alexander had many enemies, more even than his brother and successor, James. Just north of Selkirk Mr. Collier's party was taken by the Earl of Errol and a strong force of his retainers. By the time royal and episcopal pressures forced that noble-born bandit to give up his captives, only Collier remained alive . . . but he had lost his mind."

"Then he was not, after all, with Alexander's army, last year? And it was just happenstance that they besieged this hall?" inquired Foster.

"Oh, no, Bass," said Harold. "For all that Collier was by then in his monastery cell, Alexander was certain that Whyffler Hall still was the site of the manufactory of unhallowed niter, his information derived of his spies with the English army, whose information was, of course, out of date, thanks to you.

"Frankly, Bass, I doubted it could be done, doubted that anyone could shepherd all those folk and heavy wagons from here down to York in the dead of winter. When you rode north, I did not expect to see you and what remained of your train before spring. It was Arthur had faith in your abilities and determination, he and the Reichsregent.

"I am told that when the late Duke of Shrewsbury informed His Highness that what you were about to attempt was impossible, Arthur replied: 'Cousin, *I* know that and *you* know that. Squire Foster obviously does not and let us pray that no one tells him until after he has accomplished it . . . as he will.'"

The Archbishop sipped at his steaming drink, then sighed, "Ahhh, this ale is fine, truly fine. You know, old King Hal often remarked that Northcountry ale was the finest in his realm." His old eyes misted, then, "Good old Hal, bless his noble soul, I miss him right often."

Foster slowly shook his head, saying, "I still find it hard to seriously think that you're as old as you told Krys you are."

Harold smiled fleetingly. "I was three weeks shy of my fortieth birthday when I received the initial longevity treatment, Bass. All those of us scientists who had had even a slight part in its development were given the full treatment, at the direction of the director of the project, before he turned it over to the government. Since that time, I have physically aged one year for every four point sixty-eight years I have lived, and that rate could be doubled or tripled, had I but access to the necessary chemicals and a modern laboratory in which to process them . . . which, friend Bass, is why your house is in the here-and-now intact, with all systems functioning."

Foster sat in silence. He had heard it all from Krystal, but still he wanted to hear the original version of the story.

Harold extended his legs, so that the fire's heat could beat up under his cassock. "It was fifteen . . . no, sixteen years after longevity had become a reality—for a few, and those carefully chosen by a dictatorial government, but that's another tale—that I became involved in the Gamebird Project. A hundred years after the prime of Einstein and still no one was certain as to the exact nature of time, and now, more than a century later and after all I have seen and undergone in that span, I can give no hard and fast answer or definition.

"Gamebird and its dozens of related sub-projects went on and on, lavishly funded by the government, which saw in the project a possible way to rob the past of the raw materials which were in such short supply—thanks in no small part to the greed and inefficiency of that very government and its predecessors, I might add. Most of our facilities were located in a complex built upon riverside land that once had been used for the purpose of raising small feathered and furred game for the restocking of designated wilderness areas. From what occurred, I would assume that the main chemistry laboratory was on the same coordinates as was your house.

"To make a long and tedious story short, Bass, after almost twenty years of trial and error, success and failure, in which a veritable host of experimental animals either disappeared completely or met singularly messy deaths, an apparently effective process was developed. I won't try to explain it to you, because I don't think you'd understand even the basics of it. The government put a great deal of hope in the Project and, as time wore on, brought much pressure to bear upon Dr. Fox, the director, to adapt the process to humans. Finally, Fox acquiesced.

"The first volunteer came back dead and mutilated, but analysis of the clothing in which his returned body was clad showed that he had lived—and had died—in western France during the middle years of the thirteenth century. Adjustments were made in the process and a second volunteer, one who spoke medieval French, was projected. He, too, was dead upon his return, with a stiff parchment placard nailed to his forehead. The language was a corrupt dialect of Low Latin and, when translated, read: 'I am a dead spy.'

"The third volunteer was a young man but recently assigned to Gamebird. Lenny Vincenzo had been a prodigy of sorts, and at only twenty-five years of age already held several doctorates in widely diverse fields. Dr. Fox did not want to use and possibly lose him, but government pressure was intense, the fates of the first two subjects had scared off most prospective volunteers, and, above all, Lenny was eminently qualified, being steeped in late-medieval and Renaissance cultures and speaking early variants of French, Italian, Latin, and Greek.

"So, Lenny was dressed in recreations of fifteenth-century attire, entrusted with a few pounds of gold, and projected."

Harold paused to take a long draft of ale. "Lenny never came back. The device which had been implanted under his skin to allow the projector to home in on and retrieve him did return, tucked just in the proper place under the sloughing skin of a decomposing cadaver, which lacked head, hands, and feet."

"Then how could you say it wasn't your boy?" asked Foster.

"The blood type was wrong," answered the old man. "As were many other factors. At the government's order, the whole affair was hushed up, but the director knew, and so too did some of the senior staffers, of which, by that time, I was one. And it was then that Dr. Emmett O'Malley and I decided to do as Lenny had done."

"But, why, Hal? You have relative immortality, you've just said you were some kind of big mucketymuck in a project that was being supported by your government. So why would you want to run off to another time? Romanticism?" Foster was honestly puzzled.

"Romanticism? Hardly that." The Archbishop smiled fleetingly. "Not in my case, at any rate. Though," he added thoughtfully, "there may well have been an element of romanticism in Emmett's behavior. But then the Celts always have been the master dreamers of Western civilization, the inveterate champions of lost causes.

"Bass, the America from which you were snatched was still a democracy governed by popularly elected men and women, was it not?"

"Yes," said Foster.

"It did not long stay such, Bass; had you and the others remained you would most likely have witnessed the beginning of the change. In 1988, the brother of an earlier President was elected for his second term, for all that the vast majority of the electorate actively hated him. There were long, loud cries of foul play and fixes, but on every level those whose voices were the loudest and most influential met, invariably, with singularly unpleasant and usually fatal 'accidents.' In 1991, our dictator-in-all-but-name was successfully assassinated, only to be succeeded, not by the Vice President, but by his own nephew.

"Thereafter, there were no more popular elections, on any level. Governors were chosen by the President, and they, in turn, appointed the rulers of the cities and counties. Senators chose their successors and the House of Representatives was dissolved as superfluous."

"Well, Jesus Christ," demanded Foster, "what in hell were the American people doing? They'd never sit still for that kind of takeover."

The old man shrugged, saying, "The American people of the first half of the twentieth century would not have, certainly, but by the waning years of that century, they were, if no more placid in basic nature, at least far easier to manage and to delude with distortions of facts and outright lies. Almost all the information-disseminating agencies had by then become nothing more or less than mouthpieces of government; very few really privately owned corporations were left, so nearly everyone worked for some level of government—federal, state or municipal. But I am not a true historian, Bass, and I must admit to having ignored current events, except in those instances which touched upon my several specialities, as did far too many of us until it was far too late.

"Anyway, O'Malley and I surreptitiously studied archaic languages, customs, and skills, late-medieval and Renaissance histories of Europe, horsemanship, and weapons skills; those

138

pursuits we could not conceal from the rest of the staff we passed off as hobbies or physical exercise.

"From the past experiences, O'Malley and I fully expected to wind up in Italy or France of the Renaissance, so we hypnotaped ourselves full of Latin, several dialects of French and Italian, Spanish, Catalonian, and Basque. In addition, I added Old Middle German and Flemish, while O'Malley assimilated Erse, Gaelic, and what little was by then known of such tongues as Frisian and Breton.

"With the announced purpose of taking up jewelry-making, I began to purchase cut gemstones and gold, then spent many an evening casting golden disks of ounce and half-ounce weights. Since Emmett's work at Gamebird was involved with various aspects of metallurgy, he could and did get away with doing much of his private experimentation on the job until, at length, he had mastered a formula for producing a really fine stainless steel that would hold a keen edge indefinitely and that, moreover, could be wrought from raw ores or cast iron with abysmally primitive facilities."

"So that's how Tara steel originated," Foster guessed aloud, tapping the hilt of his dirk.

The churchman nodded. "Yes, true enough, but that's getting a bit ahead of my tale, Bass.

"Emmett and I laid our plans with exceeding care, Bass, for although the Dictator's government could and did treat favored persons such as ourselves infinitely better than the vast bulk of the population, no one—from the highest to the lowest—was really deemed trustworthy; secret police agents and informers swarmed everywhere and the treatment of suspects when arrested was harsh to the point of savagery. Both of us had, unfortunately, had some close exposure to both the cult of the informer and the atrocious handling of those informed upon, you see. It had been those episodes that first had drawn us two together and had placed us in the proper frame of mind to plan our ultimate defection from a world we had begun to find unbearable. But I'll go into no details; even after all these long years, it still hurts to talk of it.

"Emmett had only been in his mid-twenties when he first received the longevity treatment and was still a very handsome, very personable, young-looking man, so he found it quite easy to cultivate a close, very personal relationship with one of the upper-echelon staff members, Jane Stone. Within a few months, she was regularly inviting him to observe testing of the projector and actively encouraging him to study its proper utilization. At the end of twelve months of this, he felt that he knew enough to enable us to use the projector as we had planned. There was no thought of including Dr. Stone in our escape, for all that Emmett had become somewhat attached to her, since we both knew that in addition to her scientific function, she also was a colonel in the secret police and in charge of the entire secret network at Gamebird.

"Obtaining period clothing would have been impossible, but the styles of that day called for trousers to be skin-tight, which we thought might look enough like trunk hose to suffice. Emmett had, in pursuing his 'hobby,' manufactured two broadswords and two long daggers and had openly presented me with a set upon the occasion of the Dictator's last birthday. We had practiced in their use until we both were highly proficient swordsmen.

"I had needed to cultivate no other person to obtain access to the longevity drug, since I had been one of the pioneers in the research and by then had advanced to assistant director of the chemistry complex. The original formula had required injection, and initial treatments still did, but boosters had been so refined that they might be administered orally, a dosage being required at least every five years. I secretly prepared enough to fill six hundred capsules and placed it in capsules color-coded as headache remedy. I stored the big bottle in my private office and took a handful at a time back to my quarters.

"Emmett and I finally decided that our defection should occur during the five-day celebration of the Dictator's birthday, when most of the staff would be either drunk or absent and security most lax. The projector complex was situated on the north side of the river and connected to the main complex and the living quarters by a tunnel running beneath the bed of the river from bank to bank. There were always guards stationed at both ends of the tunnel and usually one or more at the entrance to the projection chamber, as well. Normally, no one would be allowed even to traverse the tunnel without written authorization, much less enter a subcomplex to which he or she was not assigned, but we thought we might be able to get to the projector during the Birthday Days."

Harold again plunged a glowing loggerhead into his drink, sending up a hissing cloud of pungent steam.

"You must understand, Bass, people had changed from your time and so had the customs, even the calendar. It had

140

been juggled into months of an even thirty days; the five or six leftover days were designated Birthday Days, and during those days everyone went a little mad. The government distributed free alcohol, hallucinogens, and food to all the people in almost unlimited quantities. Very few persons worked during the Days and then only in skeleton crews; there was dancing and fornication in the very streets by day and by night. Staff members who were confined to the complex all year long were allowed to leave and visit family or friends during the Days, and those who remained behaved no more sanely than the general populace.

"Emmett and I chose the third night of the Days. We stuffed our pockets with booster capsules, gold discs, little bags of gems, and food concentrates and put even more into the big cargo pockets of the thigh-length parkas we were issued for outside work in bad weather, then we belted our daggers and slipped into our baldrics, thoroughly rinsed our mouths with raw alcohol, and splashed the rest of the bottle over each other's clothing.

"We drew little notice as we staggered through the complex, since many persons dressed oddly during the Days and most of those we encountered were drunk or drugged, in any case. The guard cubicle at our end of the tunnel was empty, so we activated a car and rode to the other side. One of the guards there was lying on his back snoring and the other just stared at us glassy-eyed, obviously all but insensible from drink or drugs or both. We left the car and took the lift up to the level of the projector room. And that was when we ran into our first spot of trouble."

Silently, one of the Archbishop's servants entered, poked at the fire, then heaped two more logs upon it. That done, he took away the near-empty ewer, replacing it with a brimming one, then departing whence he had come.

The old man sipped at his mug, then asked, "Where was I in my tale, Bass?"

"You were approaching this projector-room, and said that there was trouble." Bass sounded and was impatient.

Harold of York nodded. "The guard before the door of the projector-chamber was neither drunk, nor drugged, nor absent, but wide-awake and alert though, fortunately for us, not immediately suspicious of our motives. He was fully armed with a heat-stun weapon hung from his shoulder, a smaller, shorter-range one at his belt, and a truncheon."

"Heat-stun weapons?" queried Bass. "I've never heard of anything like that. Sounds like Buck Rogers stuff to me."

Harold took another sip. "Buck Rogers? No, Bass, the inventor was a man named James Rednick, and the weapons came in a number of sizes and potential intensities, from tiny, handheld, purely defensive units up to big, wide-angle weapons used for crowd control and requiring three or four men to operate properly. I cannot, I fear, tell you too much about the mechanics of them; sonics is not my field. But, when set on 'heat' and within the optimum range of the individual weapon, they could melt plastics, set cloth aflame, and render metal objects too hot to hold; on 'stun,' they brought unconsciousness if set properly for distance, death, if not. Both Emmett and I had small, personal heat-stunners, but they were of very short range and we hoped we'd not have to try to use them until we were within arm's length of the guard, if at all.

"Although feigning the ill-coordination of drunkenness, we narrowly observed the guard for the first signs of tenseness, but he remained relaxed after the first few seconds, recognizing Emmett and speaking to him in the amused patronizing tones one uses to the drunkenly bemused.

"Emmett averred that he had promised to show me certain aspects of the projector and, as he stumbled closer, commenced to fumble for the key card with which his paramour had provided him weeks before. But the guard frowned and said that he would first have to clear through complex Center, whereupon Emmett brought out his heat-stunner, rather than the card, and dropped the man before he could more than reach for the communications button.

"At that point, Bass, the die was irrevocably cast for us—we had committed the inexcusable, and neither our caste, ranks, nor the supposedly altered conditions of our consciousness would mitigate our punishments, this we knew. We had no choice save to proceed. Emmett took the guard's heavy-duty heat-stunner and gave me the belt unit and the pouch of spare charges for both. Then we entered the projector chambers and secured the door behind us.

"While Emmett went from place to place in the main chamber, throwing levers and depressing keys and doing the various things that would bring the projector to full operational life, there was nothing for me to do save stay where he had told me, for I had never before been within the room and knew nothing helpful of it. Finally, he wheeled a console about four feet high and two broad and deep onto the six-foot silver disc sunk into a section of the floor, connected various cables depending from the console and motioned me to join him . . ."

As the old Archbishop painted his word-picture, Bass, despite his impatience, almost felt himself to be within that chamber far in the past/future . . .

Emmett O'Malley had studied hard, so now his big, freckled hands moved surely upon the face of the console, minutely adjusting this, switching on that, slowly setting the other. As the vast, gray bulks of the gigantic computer banks heated up, the soft whirring noises that had greeted their entrance gradually rose in volume, lights began to flicker on here and there, a deep humming commenced, and there seemed to be a smell of power in the very air.

At last he made the final adjustment and stepped back to stand beside Harold Kenmore at the center of the silver disc. "It won't be long now, Ken. I've set the projector to trigger immediately as sufficient power is attained. And—"

"*You fools!*" The low-pitched voice came from the shadows behind the gray metal housing of a computer bank. Then into the light stepped Colonel Jane Stone. She held a heavy-duty heat-stunner leveled at them, and her face was twisted with a mixture of contempt and rage.

"Did you really think me so stupid, Emmett? Think our security so lax and inefficient? Your childish, asinine little conspiracy has been the joke of the security network for months. I was just waiting to see if you two had the guts to go through with it. Will you deactivate that console, Emmett, or shall I simply switch to 'heat' and melt the cables a bit?"

While speaking, the angry woman had been slowly advancing. Harold Kenmore was speechless, his throat dry and constricted with fear, but he saw Emmett open his mouth to speak and—

Doctor Stone was gone! The bank of computers was gone! The console remained, but it and they were surrounded by walls of dark, roughly dressed stones and at their feet lay a decomposing corpse clad in dirty woolens and ill-tanned hide. With a quick bound, Emmett O'Malley was before the console and had thrown a lever and turned two knobs as far to the left as they would go, then he sighed gustily and wiped the back of his hairy hand across his damp forehead.

"Whew, that was far too close, Ken. Sweet Jane would

have had us, had I not put the device on automatic. . . ."
He shuddered, then said, "You've been hypnoing more history than I. Does that . . . that *thing's* clothing tell you anything?"

Harold advanced as closely as his churning stomach would
permit to the stinking cadaver. "Probably Northern European, dead three, maybe four, days. Skull crushed and neck
broken, likely in a fall from up there, somewhere." He gestured at the flight of unrailed stone steps that mounted upward along two of the four walls.

"But his clothing, the way he's dressed?" said O'Malley.
"Can you tell what period, what area?"

Harold shook his head. "Emmett, this kind of rough clothing was normal cold-weather wear for peasants from Scandinavia to Sicily, Poland to England, for close to two
millennia. As for the architecture of this place . . ." He
glanced around the rectangle of stone walls, finding the stones
really massive—some of them looked to be four or five feet
long and at least half that measure in thickness, and nowhere
was there a trace of mortar in their interstices. Here and
there a few iron bolts had been sunk into the stonework, and
thick, handwrought iron rings were affixed to them; long
streaks of rust stains ran down the face of the damp stones
from these, and the floor seemed to be of hard-packed earth.

"I think we're in a keep, Emmett, probably in the cellar,
but . . . but there're no windows, so it should be dark as pitch
down here. Where is the illumination coming from?"

O'Malley chuckled. "From *us*, Ken, and from the console.
This effect has been noted before. Creatures and objects
brought back by the projector have a glow of varying intensities—how bright and how long it lasts seems to depend upon
the amounts of metal said creatures or objects incorporate.
The console may remain that bright for weeks, our own light-
ing will likely fade in a few days, quicker if we are exposed
to sunlight for a while."

With the tall, broad-shouldered O'Malley in the lead, they
started up the steps, which proved to be steep and slippery
with seepage from the walls. The landing at the corner where
the stairs made a right-angle turn to the left was less than a
meter square and slightly concave, centering a puddle of icy
water. After making the mistake of looking back the way
they had come, Harold negotiated the last half of the second
flight on hands and knees.

At the top was another landing—this one no wider than

the one below but at least twice as long—and at the end of its length was a low, wide door of some dense, dark wood studded with the broad heads of hand-hammered iron spikes. Emmett pushed the door, pushed harder, finally put his shoulder against it and heaved with all his strength, but the portal remained as firm as the very stones of the walls. Stepping back, he checked the power crystal of the heat-stunner, switched the weapon to full heat, and began to play the invisible beam upon the damp, rust-stained wood. Within the blinking of an eye, rotten-smelling steam wreathed about the glowing, cherry-red nailheads and bent-over iron points; then, with a sudden *whoosh*, the face of the door became a single sheet of flame.

Prodded by Emmett, Harold backed gingerly down a few steps and the two men remained, O'Malley standing nonchalantly on the bare foot-width of slimy stone, until the tinkling sound of metal dropping out of burned-through wood told them that the way was clearing.

The two men used the blades of their broadswords to lift the charred beam that had barred the door, then passed under the archway. Before them lay another flight of stone steps; on the right hand was a blank stone wall, on the left, another door, seeming as heavy and solid as the one they had just destroyed. Harold was for climbing the steps, getting as high as possible in order to get a wide view of this countryside, but before he could speak of this to O'Malley, two sounds came from beyond the door—the first a hoarse, guttural scream of agony, the second a chorus of demonical, cackling laughs.

The terrible sounds raised the hackles of the two scientists. Harold drew his belt-model stunner and Emmett checked his larger one carefully before setting hand to the door. Another of the hideous screams came as the door swung slowly open, accompanied this time by a sizzling, frying-pan sound. The air that gushed from the unseen space beyond the door was heavy with a burnt-meat odor, underlaid with stinks of wet wool, hot metal, and long-unwashed flesh.

Although the massive iron hinges of the door squealed shrilly, that sound was lost in yet another horrific scream from the near-nude man hanging by his wrists from a rope looped over one of the beams supporting the next floor.

To Harold, it was as a scene from the works of Dante—black-streaked stone walls and a soot-coated ceiling, a filthy greasy floor littered with odds and ends of smashed furniture, clothing, weapons, broken crockery, gnawed bones, and a couple of dead, well-hacked corpses. The huge bar that had barred another, larger door was broken in two pieces and lay before that door, which hung drunkenly from a single hinge. Snow blew in to melt slowly into puddles, but it blew from out of darkness.

Out of darkness into near-darkness, the large chamber was very dimly illuminated. All light came from a couple of smoky torches thrust into wall sconces and from the roaring fire in a recessed fireplace at least six feet wide. The fire seemed to be fueled exclusively with worked wood, probably from the ruined furniture, and a number of iron bars lay on the hearth, their tips thrust deep into the glowing coals. It was with these bars that the hanging man was being savagely tortured.

The hairy, bearded, black-robed figures grouped about the victim cackled and cavorted insanely, sometimes chanting a singsong rhyme in a language Harold could not understand. Two or three of them had what looked to be a representation of a Celtic cross sewn to the backs of their sleeveless robes; these two or three also seemed to be better dressed and armed, their feet shod in real boots rather than the rawhide brogans of the others.

One of these men tucked an iron bar back into its fiery nest, wrapped a piece of wet hide around the hearth end of another, and pulled it from the fire, its tip glowing and sparking. But when he made to press it into the helpless man, Harold—peace-loving Harold—leveled his stunner and pressed the stud and felt well served when the unconscious man crumpled to the hearth and rolled into the fire.

The stunners made no sound, of course; therefore, Harold and Emmett had dropped most of the original dozen torturers before one of them turned and saw their attackers. It seemed that every greasy hair on the short, stout man's head stood up straight, his bloodshot eyes bulged out from the sockets in a face suddenly gone the color of curds. He screamed once, then spun about and ran out the broken door. The others tried to follow, but were brought down by the stunners.

Harold used his sword to saw through the rope above the bloody, lacerated wrists of the terribly burned victim, while Emmett eased the body to the floor. After only a moment, however, he straightened and stepped back, shaking his head.

"He's dead, Harold. With all that those bastards had done

to him, his eyes and all the rest, death was probably the most merciful thing that could've happened."

Harold heard but could not answer until his stomach had ceased spewing up its contents. Then, weakly, "Oh, my God, Emmett, I . . . I'd thought . . . I'd hoped we'd left this kind of senseless atrocity behind us."

Before Emmett could frame an answer, there was a metallic clanking just beyond the smashed door, then that portal was thrust aside with such force that the last hinge tore loose and the ironbound panel slammed onto the floor. Framed in the opening were two man-shapes; their black, sleeveless surcoats bore the red Celtic cross and partially covered full suits of plate armor. The one on the right gripped the foot-long hilt of a sword that looked to be five feet or more in the blade, while the one on the left carried a weapon that the scientists recognized from their studies as a Lochaber axe.

One of the armored figures shouted something incomprehensible and both rushed toward Harold and Emmett, moving much faster and far more easily than Harold would have thought possible for men burdened by such weights of steel.

"Did you hear him?" crowed Emmett, in delight, seemingly oblivious of the sharp-edged death bearing down upon him. "Did you *hear* him, Ken? That was *Gaelic* he was speaking, Scots Gaelic, and not really archaic, though somewhat slurred."

Harold tried to shout, to tell Emmett to stun the two, but no word would come. Frantically, with palsied fingers, he fumbled out his belt stunner and tried to set it for maximum range. The coming killers were half the length of the room before he aimed and depressed the stud, shifting from one to the other, back and forth, horrified when they did not immediately crumple.

Crumple unconscious, they did not; stop, they did, briefly. A mighty stench of burning again filled the room—burning cloth, burning leather, burning flesh. Dropping their weapons, both men began to scream and tear at, tear off, helmets and portions of their armor. One man's black surcoat smoldered, then burst into flames, flames which singed off his lank, greasy hair, his bushy eyebrows, even the stubble on his pockmarked face. Howling like moonmad hounds, leaving weapons and helmets behind, they raced out into the snowy night.

Harold turned to find Emmett doubled over in laughter, his green eyes streaming. "Oh, Ken! Ohhhho, Ken! You set . . .

Ohohohh, your stunner was set on 'heat'! Those bastards must've thought they were roasting alive, with all that steel super-heating around them."

"Man, what a hotfoot," commented Bass Foster.

"Hotfoot?" queried the Archbishop, raising his thick white eyebrows.

Briefly, not wishing to break the old man's train of thought, Bass explained. Then he asked, "Well, where were you, Hal?"

Smiling, Harold of York shrugged, "Where else, my boy, but Whyffler Hall?"

CHAPTER 10

"Of course, the Whyffler Hall of near two centuries ago was not the Hall in which we now sit, Bass. The old tower sat on a low hillock, most of which was leveled when the present hall was added fifty years later. There was no circuit wall then, only a timber stockade on a stone-and-earth ramp at the base of the hill, fronted by a dry ditch, with a few rude outbuildings between stockade and tower.

"As did you and your friends more recently, Emmett and I had arrived at a critical juncture. The Balderite Heresy was in its full flower and the entire Scots border was aflame."

Now it was Foster's turn to speak and ask, "Balderite Heresy, Hal?"

Harold steepled his fingers. "Your wife tells me you were born and reared a Roman Catholic, Bass. Have you not noticed something singular about the practice of Catholicism here?"

Bass chuckled. "How long a list do you want? A cardinal named Ahmed, knight-crusaders with names like Ibrahim, Riad, Sulimen, Murad and al-Asraf. I could go on forever."

"No, Bass, something more basic. Think! In *our* history, Bass, yours and mine, the practice of Roman Catholicism was bound up inextricably with the Cult of the Virgin—the Earth Mother Cult, really, which had predated Christianity in many parts of Northwestern Europe and had been incorporated in northwestern European Christianity. In our history, the Council of Ephesus declared Mary *theotokos*—'Mother of

God'—over the strong objections of the followers of Nestorius and many others, which fact served to fragment the Church. Here, in this world, that did not happen; the Council supported Nestorius.

"Now, true, the Virgin Mary is venerated, but more as a high-ranking saint than as an outright divinity. The Council of Ephesus took place in the early fifth century; two hundred and fifty years later, the Council of Whitby declared the Roman forms to be the only acceptable forms, and began the long struggle to bring the Cluniacs into line. After a while, it seemed that the Cult of the Virgin and the Cluniacs were both extinct, but then, more than a thousand years after the Council of Ephesus, the Balderites burst upon the world.

"No kingdom wishes to claim the first Balderites, naturally, but it is thought that they originated in western Scotland. A few were ordained priests; most were not, but they were powerful and persuasive orators, preachers, to a man. Their creed was a mixture of Cluniac Christianity, Virgin Cult-Earth Mother paganism, Druidic Naturalism, and, at least in the Scottish Highlands, a strong streak of Celtic nationalism. The Balderites spread out from their place of origin, and in less than three years' time, all Scotland was in chaos and two of the Irish Kingdoms—centuries-old enemies—were marching against the High King, while a third kingdom was racked by civil war.

"The Balderites gained a few converts in parts of Wales and Cornwall, but on the whole they did not fare too well south of Scotland. The English folk were more apt to stone them than to listen to them, and quite a number were burnt by episcopal authorities, here and there. But the realm was then involved in one of the perennial wars with France, so the poor Borderers were on their own, militarily, for a long while. Too long a while, for many of them. Too long a while, at least, for Sir Hubert Whyffler, whose seared body Emmett and I cut down after we'd stunned the Balderites who had been torturing him, hoping that his screams would bring the remaining defenders down from the upper levels of the tower.

"Of course, Emmett and I did not know that there were people in the tower, above us, and we didn't explore, because we were fearful that more opponents would come through that open door and trap us. Emmett did what I could not; he went from stunned body to stunned body, cutting throats. He spared only one of the better-dressed men, but bound him securely with the bloody ropes from off the body of Sir Hubert.

Then he urged me to sleep while he kept watch. I knew I could not, but I did, nonetheless. He wakened me half through the night and I watched while he slept, but no one came near the door. Though the bound man had recovered consciousness, I could not understand a word he said, nor, apparently, could he understand me; moreover, he seemed in dire fear of me—moaning, whining, and weeping whenever I came near to him.

"The reason, of course, was our 'glow,' but in all the excitement, Emmett and I had completely forgotten the radiance we emitted. For that reason, plus what I had unintentionally done to the two leaders—Scots knights, both of them, one, the chief of Clan Grant—we had completely broken the almost victorious besieging force, and although we knew it not, they were all headed back for the Highlands as fast as flesh and bone could bear them.

"As it happened, Whyffler Hall was one of only four border keeps that were not overrun by the Balderites before King Henry came north with his own army reinforced by French and Flemish Crusaders. When all the border keeps were once more in English hands and secure, Henry marched on to relieve the siege of Edinburgh, and went on to help King Robert scour Scotland of Balderites. That accomplished, the French, Flemish, and Burgundian Crusaders, along with six hundred English knights and several hundred Scots, sailed to the assistance of the Irish High King. Emmett sailed with them, but I—sickened almost to the point of insanity by all the carnage I had seen—stayed behind, in England."

Bass said, "Pardon me, Hal, but I don't see how any kind of war could be, could have been, more savage, bloodier, than our recent campaigns against the various Crusaders. You were in the very thick of a lot of it and, if it did bother you, you sure as hell didn't show it."

The Archbishop smiled fleetingly. "Violence no longer bothers me, Bass; I now realize that it is a fact of life. But in those days, when first I came here, I was in effect a forty-odd-year-old child—I had read of violence, heard of it, even, but so sheltered had been my existence that I never had seen a single instance of bloodshed. Possibly, you, Captain Webster, dear Krystal and the rest could not understand, coming as you did from a more primitive and far more violent period than did I, but my emotional trauma was devastating."

Bass thought of the soul-sickness he had felt upon viewing

by daylight what he and his men and the double-charged swivel-guns had wrought on the field near Hexham. "Yes, Hal, yes, I think I can. But, from what you've said, your friend O'Malley seemed unaffected."

"Emmett O'Malley was an atavist, a throwback to your era or even before. He visibly blossomed here, proving as bloodthirsty and as savage as the people we had been projected among. He was knighted on the Field of Badenoch by King Robert himself, and could have returned to Scottish lands and titles, had he not elected to stay in Ireland, at the court of the High King.

"As for me . . . I did not lose my sanity, as you can see. The hypnotape courses had made me a respectable craftsman of jewelry and I had a fairish supply of gold and cut stones, even after Emmett had taken a share, so I established myself in York, which then as now was one of the King's regional seats, and I prospered for a few years. Occasionally, I had letters from Emmett.

"The Irish High Kings had had an ages-old reputation for welcoming to their court at Tara artists and fine artisans of all descriptions and any nationality. With his well-earned Scottish title and his metallurgical abilities, Emmett soon became a favorite of the then High King, Brien VIII, and was even married to one of the multitudinous royal bastards. He was granted lands and the wherewithal to support him and his family, and invested with the title Swordsmith to the High King. It was through him that I came to the notice of King Henry; Hal and Brien VIII were third cousins and old friends."

Foster cleared his throat. "Pardon, but I'd gotten the idea that a more or less permanent state of war existed between the Irish and the English."

The Archbishop chuckled. "Right, Bass, but only up to a point. The High Kings have not formally declared a foreign war in centuries, for all that they have and do now maintain the largest standing army for a country their size in the known world. Ninety percentum of their fighting is internal, and never in all the long years I've been here have there been as many as five consecutive years of peace in Ireland.

"These days, men speak of the Five Kings—which figure does not include the High King, who is less an Arthur-type king than a referee—but there have been times when there were seven, or nine, or even eleven. Most of the borders are hotly contested; those of Meath, the High King's, are the only generally constant and unquestioned ones . . . but only because he happens to be a strong, ruthless man with a large armed force, not because of his rank.

"In those long-ago and yet-to-be days when we were preparing to project out of our own world and time, Emmett used to rant and rave about the long and brutal and illegal occupation of Ireland by the English and later the British, but in the here and now it's easy to see just why they invaded Ireland . . . well, one of the reasons. Whenever the kinglets of Ulaid Araidi and Laigin and Muma aren't busy fighting each other, they like nothing better than raiding England, Scotland, France, Spain, even Scandinavia and Iceland. And it used to be worse before Ailich and Connacht, with their bigger fleets, became involved in their New World settlements to the extent they now are. Perhaps, after the current unpleasantness be done, Arthur will put paid to these old accounts."

As 1501 became 1502, Arthur Tudor, Prince of Wales, lay dying and nothing the physicians could do for or to him seemed effacious—bleeding and purging only seemed to make the sixteen-year-old boy weaker; rare and expensive medicines compounded of unicorn horn, genuine mummy dust and other such esoteric ingredients were promptly vomited up. Arthur's royal father was frantic, for if Arthur should die, there would be only little Henry, and if something should befall him, too . . . the horrifying specter of the vicious and long-drawn-out Wars of the Roses could then bid well to follow the King's death.

In one spate of his perennial brainracking, he thought of Cousin Brien and that monarch's patronage of all sorts of artists and craftsmen.

Perhaps . . . perhaps the current roster might include a physician or two . . .?

Master Harold, the goldsmith, was locked in his private sanctum, carefully completing the wax carving for a bit of jewelry promised to his old friend James Whyffler, when an insistent knocking at the barred door finally brought him, more than a little angry, to throw open the portal and grimly confront the journeyman who had dared to so disturb his master. White with fear, the young man had stuttered that a noble visitor, a foreigner by his dress, had not only refused to return another day, but had solemnly promised to notch the

153

journeyman's nose and ears did he not speedily present his master.

Harold slammed the door, locked it, pocketed the big key, and stalked out to confront this arrogant foreigner. Artisans of precious metals lived and worked under the personal protection of both King and Church and were seldom subjected to such abuse by English nobles. He intended to say a few choice words to this foreign jackanapes, and if the noble fool chose to take offense . . . well, the fine sword Harold had brought with him into this world hung handy on the wall near his desk and he had not forgotten how to use it.

The man who confronted him was as tall as was he, tall indeed for this undernourished time, big and muscular and lithe for all of it. His clothing was all rich silks and dyed doeskins, handsomely tooled leather and gold or silver buckles. The outlines of several large ringstones showed through the soft gray leather of his riding gloves; the hilts of both sword and long dagger were bejeweled gold and so were their cases—and the gold was fine workmanship, the goldsmith Harold noted professionally.

The huge gold-and-amethyst brooch securing the nodding, deep-green ostrich plume to his baggy crushed samite cap was a true work of art, like the several small and single large order pendants hanging from the massy-gold, flat-linked chain round his neck. The man's face was masked, but a pair of sea-green eyes and a brick-red beard forked in the Spanish style were visible.

"Does my lord speak English?" snapped Harold. At the stranger's curt nod, he then demanded, "All right, my lord, what is of such importance that my lord felt compelled to threaten my man with disfigurement did he not fetch me away from my work?"

Chuckling a maddeningly familiar chuckle, the richly garbed man stripped off his gloves, then unfastened his mask. It dropped to reveal the grinning face of Emmett O'Malley. "The importance, Harold, is that I'm damned thirsty and the *bouchal* ne'er even offered me a stoup of ale. Well, man, are ye just going to stand there wi' y'r mouth open fit to catch flies?"

Over dinner, Emmett talked only of his wife, family, work and the numerous small wars in which he had taken part, related current gossip of King Brien's court and listened to Harold talk of his own past few years in York. After the dinner, over pipes of Spanish tobacco and a dark, sweet wine of

154

Malaga—the wine carefully chilled with ice cut from the River Swale in winter and stored in sawdust and straw in the spring-house of Harold's small establishment—O'Malley got down to business.

"Ken, I didna come to England strictly to see you. I be here wi' a delegation of physickers from Tara; the rest be in Coventry at the summer court. I rode up to see ye and to broach on a matter."

Harold thought Emmett had changed greatly over the years. He had not aged perceptibly, of course, but his manner now was that of a wealthy nobleman, accustomed to power and to unquestioned obedience to his commands; also, in addition to a honey-thick brogue, he had acquired a bit of longwindedness.

"Ken, be it true that the longevity boosters incorporate a universal and powerful antibiotic? I seem to recall something of the sort frae lang agone, but it wasnae my field and sae much has happened since . . . but ye helped tae master the process, an' formulated the booster doses we brought wi' us."

Harold nodded. "Yes, your memory is accurate, Emmett. The combination of drugs in the boosters will ward off any known disease except the common cold. Why?"

"Prince Arthur of Wales be dying, Ken, of some wasting fever. Everything has been tried—pilling, purging, bleeding, decoctions of herbs an' God alane knows whatall, not tae mention nonstop masses an' endless chauntings o'er the *bouchal*—but I think me he'll nae last oot the moon. Y'r King Henry sent tae my ain King hoping, I suppose, that a physician of Tara might be more learned, but they all hae told me privily that nane of them can do aught what hasnae already been done."

The Irish nobleman puffed his claypipe back to life, then took a long pull at his wine goblet. "Had I brought any of my ain boosters wi' me, I'd hae tried ane or twa on Arthur me ainsel' but they all be carefully hid in the false bottom of a small casket an' in the care of the good fithers at Fora, so I thought of ye and saddlepounded me poor arse up here. Ye may say all ye wish about the endless wars of Sweet Ireland, but for a' that, our roads at least are good an' well tended. I'd ne'er before heerd of mudholes in the heat of a dry summer, Ken, not till I rid the track frae Coventry tae York, I hadnae!"

Harold left his shop and house in the care of his guild and took the road to Coventry astride his big, smooth-gaited mule, followed by his body servant and a pack animal. As befitted a noble in-law of the High King of Ireland, Emmett's train was much larger—a dozen servants and armed retainers and no less than eight heavy-loaded pack mules. O'Malley's spotted stallion was the first of the famous Irish leopard-horses Harold had ever seen.

The shoulders of the big horse were loaded and straight, the chest was deep and powerful, the quarters broad. Like all the better specimens of its breed, the destrier stood nearly seventeen hands at the withers and weighed a good fifteen hundredweight; the neck was comparatively long and the head comparatively small, a testament to the rich Arab heritage of the breed. Mane and tail were long and show-white and the back was indented as if nature-designed to hold the richly tooled saddle fitted with brass and silver. Though the skin beneath was black, the stallion's base hair color was an off-white and the odd-sized and -shaped spots were a very dark gray. He was high-spirited and Harold's mules were terrified of him.

The old Archbishop sighed and closed his eyes briefly. "Travel was pleasant in those days, Bass; for all that the roads were no better than Emmett had complained, there were no bands of robbers to contend with between here and Coventry and such highwaymen and footpads as may have worked the area were no doubt intimidated by Emmett's well-armed and clearly pugnacious Irishmen.

"When first I saw him who later became King Arthur II, he was all but dead, only sallow skin and bones, his head and body covered with sores from the leeches. I doubted then that even the longevity boosters could save the boy. Nonetheless, I began to dose him with them, ten a day for a couple of weeks, by which time he had recovered sufficiently to begin to eat broth and syllabubs.

"King Henry had been so frantic upon my arrival that he had hardly inquired my name; at that point I think he would have allowed a being with horns and cloven feet to try to cure Arthur, since all the vast assemblage of physicians and surgeons had frankly despaired. Nor were they at all happy that I had succeeded where they had failed; indeed, they had me hailed before an ecclesiastical court on a charge of sorcery and witchcraft.

"There was no possible way that I could have explained the compounding of the longevity boosters to a tribunal consisting of a Renaissance bishop, two abbots, and two monsignors, but that never became necessary, fortunately. King Henry's men surrounded the monastery where I was being held prisoner and solemnly promised to raze the entire complex unless I was delivered—safe, sound, and whole—to them. Once I was free, the cloak of royal protection was cast over me.

"Of course, the clergy appealed to everyone of power from the Roman Pope on down, and the Physicians' Guild made no secret of the fact that they were out for my blood after I had informed their representatives that much as I would have liked to do so, I could not share with them the formula that had cured the Prince.

"The upshot of it all was that sly old Hal, knowing that there was little likelihood of the Church's hounding me were I one of their own, had me whisked off to Canterbury—where the Archbishop then had his seat—ordained a priest, and then advanced to a monsignory. In this world, clergy are allowed, nay even encouraged if they demonstrate a talent, to dabble in alchemy and all matter of arcane pursuits. I then was publicly rewarded for saving the life of the Prince of Wales with the post of Court Alchemist.

"Close as Arthur and I became during his long reign, Hal and I were even closer friends, confidants, by the time he died, nine years later. He was a level-headed and completely practical man, Bass, but open-minded, for all. Though he often put on great shows of piety for public consumption, he actually was an agnostic and he recognized the Church for what it truly is: this world's most powerful and wealthy political force.

"After careful consideration, I told Hal the whole truth about the advent of Emmett and me into this world, and, at his insistence, we journeyed up here, to Whyffler Hall, that he might see the console. And well it was that we came just when we did, too. Both his first two wives having died in childbirth, James Whyffler had wed a young heiress, replaced the stockade with the present stone wall, and was in the process of leveling the hill to lay the foundations of this hall when His Majesty's retinue arrived. It had been his original intention to dismantle the upper levels of the old tower-keep, utilizing those precut stones in the foundation of the hall, while filling the lower level with earth and rubble for a ready-laid stretch of foundation."

"Of course, King Hal forbade any such thing, citing as public reason that the old keep had withstood the Balderites plus God knew how many generations of Scot reavers; he ordered that instead the tower be incorporated into the new hall. And after he had seen the console and I had shown him the operation of one of the hand-stunners, he had the masons wall up the only entrance to the tower cellar, marked the closure with the Royal Seals, then had James Whyffler vow that only I or the King would ever be allowed to break those seals. I'm sure James thought that royal treasure or religious artifacts or both had been deposited in that cellar, and no doubt he was highly flattered by the secret honor thus accorded him and his house.

"In 1508, the first of the so-called Priests' Plague outbreaks occurred. The disease had afflicted portions of Armenia and Turkey as early as the waning years of the fifteenth century and was thought to have died out there, then it burst like a petard in the Balkans during the summer of Arthur's illness. After lying dormant through the winter, it moved north, into Europe proper, the next summer."

"Yes," said Foster, "I've heard talk of this Priests' Plague; it had something to do with the senior archbishopric being moved from Canterbury to York, didn't it?"

The old man shook his head. "No, not this first outbreak, Bass, but the second, which occurred during the reign of Arthur II. There have been other outbreaks since that one, but not in England, thank God."

"Okay," said Foster, "the obvious question, Hal. Why the designation 'Priests' Plague'? Simply because it wiped out the then Archbishop and all his household?"

The white-haired head shook again. "No, Bass, the disease was called Priests' Plague long before it came to these islands. Why? Because eighty percentum of the victims were clergy, nobles or merchants—chiefly in towns, but in the countryside as well, notably in monasteries.

"I theorize, Bass, that the plague is transmitted by way of luxury goods, likely Asian in origin. I've never been able to pinpoint any closer than that general classification. But consider you this: the Court was hard hit, the King and his two sons only lived through my lavish expenditure of my longevity booster capsules; the queen refused to take them and so died. Throughout the rest of this realm, almost nine out of ten town-dwelling clergy were stricken and more than half of those died; in the wealthier monasteries, there frequently was not a single survivor . . . yet very few of the simple, com-

158

paratively poor village clergy were afflicted and the stricter, less luxurious monastic communities survived intact.

"Inside two months, three-fifths of the greater nobles of England were dead, along with their families and even their entire households, like as not. Of the commoner sorts not connected with service of nobles or clergy, most deaths occurred among merchants dealing in commodities from overseas, their households and employees, or those commoner townsmen grown wealthy enough to afford luxuries.

"Even as England was slowly recovering, a fresh outbreak was raging through Italy, southern France, and Catalonia, so there was no objection from Rome when the King took upon himself the old royal right to fill vacant sees and other clerical offices. Right many a humble, middle-aged priest suddenly found himself with the ring of a bishop on his finger. And, if the truth be told, Bass, the anti-Rome sentiment of the English people began at that time, through the preachments of these commoner-priests-cum-prelates against the sloth, indolence, money grubbing and posturings of the Church hierarchy.

"I was invested Archbishop of York, though I saw precious little of my see while Hal remained alive, or during the first few years of Arthur's reign. You'll have heard the tale of Hal's death, I'm certain, of a broken neck while hunting. It's the way he would have preferred, I trow, for he had a very terror of a slow, lingering final illness, God bless his gallant old soul.

"So Arthur II became king at the age of twenty-five; he was then a recent widower with two young sons and an infant daughter, but he quickly rectified that marital situation by taking to wife the Princess Astrid of Denmark, and she bore him two more sons before she died."

"He's beginning to sound," remarked Foster, "a bit like the Henry VIII of my—of our—own world."

"Not so," replied the Archbishop. "That Henry put aside one wife, executed two, and annulled his marriage to another. Arthur's bereavements were none of his deliberate doing; both Catherine and Astrid died in childbirth, and Brigid of Tara, his third wife, died shortly after a birthing, of what I strongly suspect was puerperal fever. On the twentieth anniversary of his coronation, Arthur was once more a widower; so too was his brother, Duke Henry of Aquitaine . . . and that situation spawned the War of the Three Marriages."

159

"That was the war in which Henry was killed, right?" asked Foster.

"Well . . . in a manner of speaking, Bass," answered the old man. "He was badly wounded in one of the last battles and, before he could regain his strength, he died of Priests' Plague . . . but that is all getting ahead of the tale, again.

"François III was then King of France, and a widower, too. He made overtures for the hand of Marie, daughter of the Duke of Burgundy, but Burgundy and France are traditional enemies and the old Duke saw in these French overtures a hidden plot to gain a claim to the duchy by the French king, so he married his daughter to Arthur of England. Only a few months later, Duke Henry of Aquitaine became the son-in-law of his neighbor, the King of Navarre-Aragon, and at almost the same time, a match was arranged between the Grand Duke of Savoy-Corsica and Arthur's once-widowed eldest daughter, Camilla Tudor. Whereupon François III began to feel threatened."

"I can't imagine why he should have felt threatened," chuckled Foster, picturing the situation on a mental map. In this world too, England and France were age-old enemies. Only a couple of centuries before the time of which the Archbishop was speaking, the Kings of England had held more French territory than had the Kings of France and, though they had then lost all save Aquitaine and the bare sliver of territory around Calais, François III must have lived in mortal dread of a fresh English invasion of Normandy and Brittany, especially at a time when his armies might be occupied with difficulties on other borders.

No doubt the unhappy French monarch had suffered waking and sleeping nightmares of English foemen pushing out from Calais, Aquitaine-English and Navarreños marching up from the southwest while Aragonese ships harried and raided the Mediterranean coast, Savoyards coming from the southeast, and Burgundians from the west and north, all intent upon slicing sizable chunks out of the French pie.

"Of course, I cannot speak for the aims of Savoy or Navarre-Aragon or Burgundy or even, really, for Henry—who was always a warhorse champing at the bit—but I assure you that Arthur II had no immediate designs upon France," the old man went on. "For a Tudor, Arthur was a singularly peaceable, unacquisitive man.

"But François chose to anticipate the worst and commenced to levy troops, fortify his borders, and try to foment trouble for everyone involved, especially for England. He first approached the High King, but Arthur's third wife had been the half-sister of Brien IV and he likely would not have joined France in attacking England even had he not had a plentitude of home-grown problems to occupy him and his army.

"Then the Scots were sounded out. Ailpein Stewart, the grandson of that King Robert whom Hal had aided against the Balderites, was then on the throne . . . but just barely. He was a young and a foolish man and a very weak monarch."

Foster nodded. "Sort of like the Alexander who led the invasion, last year?"

The Archbishop frowned. "No, Bass, not at all. Alexander was a strong, a very strong, king. But neither strong kings nor weak last long on the blood-splattered throne of the Kingdom of Scotland; only the shrewd men who know when to display strength and when to bow to the wills of the powerful nobles who are the real rulers of Scotland.

"These Scots be a strange race, Bass—two races, really, two, at least. The Lowlanders share in a full measure of the native pugnacity that seems to mark the Celt, wherever you find them. Over the centuries, they have caused their own kings almost as much trouble as they have caused the English kings, escalating reaving raids into border wars at times most inconvenient to Scotland.

"The Highlanders, on the other hand, while no less bloodthirsty, would much rather fight each other than the English or any other foreigners, and the great lairds of the various confederations of Highland clans reflect these isolationist sentiments at Edinburgh. Ignoring them, in favor of the Lowlander nobles, can be exceedingly dangerous if not fatal, for more than one unwise king has been driven into exile or slain by hordes of aroused clansmen streaming down from their Highlands to march on Edinburgh.

"So it was with the overtures of the emissaries of François: the Lowlander lords were heartily in favor of an invasion of England in support of the French, while the Highlander lairds, tied up as tightly as ever in their own endless feuds, voiced a resounding 'Nay!' Ailpein swayed first one way, then the other, like a willow switch in a windstorm.

"The Frenchmen, mistaking Ailpein's inability to make up his mind for a devious means of haggling, offered more and more inducements—gold, guns, a permanent alliance, even, I understand, a French princess to wife. It all was just too much for Ailpein; forgetting just exactly who and what he was—a mere figurehead puppet of the lords and lairds and great chiefs—he agreed to serve the interests of 'his royal brother,' François, in exchange for gold, guns, a loan of French troops to beat the Highlanders into line, and an investment into the Order of St. Denis. It was his greatest and almost his last mistake, Bass."

CHAPTER 11

"The Highlands began to boil, the Lowlands began to arm, the islanders—as often they have—declared a plague on both houses and a flat refusal to supply troops or wherewithal to either King or rebels. Of the Lowland lords there was a division: those of the south wanted to march immediately upon England, while those of the areas north and east of Edinburgh saw and favored the need to deal first with the savage menace of the Highlanders, wherein Eannruig of MacIntosh was busily assembling the Clan Chattan Confederation at and around Inverness while both the Campbell Confederation and Siol Alpine were gathering about Loch Tay, only a few days' march from Edinburgh itself; and Goiridh of Ross was rumored to be marching down from the far north with the most of the Ulbhaidh Confederation at his back."

Despite the crackling fire before him and the warm tipple spreading its alcoholic heat outwards from his belly, Foster shivered, recalling again that hellish night of droning bagpipes, Gaelic war cries and the demonic chorus of human throats mimicing the howling-roaring-bellowing-snarling of the totem beasts—the wolf of Ulbhaidh, the lion of Campbell, the wild bull of Siol Alpine and the moorcat of Chattan—there on that blood-soaked moor near Durham.

The old man drained his cup, refilled it from the ewer, and heated the fresh liquid with one of the ready loggerheads before going on with his tale.

"With the arrival of the promised French troops—several

thousand Slavic, Croatian and Albanian mercenaries, with a few score French knights and sergeants—the border lords grudgingly agreed to join with the other Lowlanders just long enough to put paid to the account of the Highlanders.

"Like the late and unlamented King Alexander, Ailpein was personally brave but a most intemperate commander. Rather than holding his troops in defense of the area about Edinburgh where his heavy cavalry might have done him some good, he chose to *invade the Highlands,* driving straight for Loch Tay.

"He met the confederations of Campbell and Alpine, who were also on the march, at Earnford and defeated them in a singularly long and sanguineous battle. But his was a Pyrrhic victory, and before his messengers had had time to reach Edinburgh with news of his triumph, his mauled and battered army had been almost extirpated at the hands of Eannruig of MacIntosh and Clan Chattan, who had been marching a few days behind the Campbells and Siol Alpine. Then the Highlanders marched on to Edinburgh.

"The city had been stripped of garrison and many guns to strengthen Ailpein's venture and, on sight of the Highland army, threw open the gates. Ailpein had fallen on the field of the second battle, so Eannruig quickly wedded Ailpein's sister, Catriona Stewart, assumed himself the royal patronymic, and the overawed remnant of the Council of Nobles declared him lawful successor and crowned him.

"That, Bass, is why the Highlanders showed such loyalty to the former and the present King of Scotland—Alexander and James descend not from Lowland Stewarts but from Highland MacIntoshes.

"But back to François of France. He had arranged a wedding and an alliance with the Venetians, who had recently gobbled up Milan and were casting acquisitive eyes upon the Piedmont of Savoy. What Venice lacked in lands and troops, she more than made up in money and her powerful fleets. In the opening contest of the War of the Three Marriages, the Aragonese fleet was decisively defeated by a Venetian fleet commanded by the Doge, François's new father-in-law, Angelo di Pola. Shortly, the Aragonese had been driven from the sea, their very ports and coasts were being raided or threatened, and a growing army of mercenaries was pressing upon the eastern border of Savoy, while the western marches of that state watched the steady buildup of the French.

164

"But before François could send the word to march on Savoy, he was himself invaded by the combined armies of Aragon-Navarre and Aquitaine, all captained by Duke Henry Tudor, so François felt compelled to strip the Savoyard border and apply those troops where he really needed them.

"Meanwhile, the Venetians, flushed with victories and cocksure, had tied up one of their fleets in a siege of Genoa—an ally of Savoy, whose own fleet was busy conquering some islands somewhere in the Aegean—the second to maintain her trade routes, and the third to harry Aragon and either stop or pursue and try to capture any ship bearing the flag of England or Burgundy.

"Inevitably the Venetians fired on one ship too many. Arthur and his father-in-law assembled their own fleet and set sail for the Mediterranean, where they not only soundly defeated the Third Venetian Fleet, but mauled the First so badly that the survivors raised the siege of Genoa and limped home. Upon that note, the Burgundians besieged Marseilles and the English, after annihilating the French Mediterranean Fleet in a great sea battle off the Iles d' Hybres, besieged Toulon.

"On land, however, things were not progressing so well. Duke Henry, though brave as his father, was impetuous, as his father never was. He never in his short life lost a battle, true, but then few of his victories were ever clear-cut and his losses were usually heavy, ruinously heavy. And the Venetians and their mercenaries were finding Savoy a very tough nut to crack, without the other jaw of the pincers—France—to apply pressure; moreover, the Genoese fleet—recalled at the onset of the siege—had broken off its Aegean operations and was harrying Venice's Adriatic ports and sea routes and had seized the island of Corfu.

"The Florentines, who had never made a secret their unease at the Venetian conquest of Milan, were actively aiding, abetting and arming a force of Milanese exiles. King John of Naples took opportunity of the chaotic conditions to wrest the ports of Otranto and Ragusa and the island of Lagosta from Venetian control, whereupon the Genoese ceded Corfu to him, thus freeing ships and men for more and wider privateering against Venetian ships."

"And what," asked Foster, "was Rome doing all this time, Hal?"

The Archbishop smiled. "What Rome always does when these kinds of war flare up, Bass—observing, warning all of the implicit neutrality of the Church, her clergy and her properties. That and making a few fortunes selling sacred powder to everyone with the gold to buy it.

"Henry Tudor found it necessary to retire to Aquitaine to rest, reinforce and refit his army, but François and his French had no rest, for the Burgundian Army, under the old Duke himself, invaded from Old Burgundy, while other units marched down from the Burgundian Low Countries, and François had to hurry north and east to meet the new threats."

Foster said drily, "It would seem the French had their testicles in a crack." Then, "And what was the English army up to, at that point, Hal? The border Scots?"

The old man shook his head. "No, the border war had fizzled out with the death of Ailpein and the subsequent elevation of Eannruig. The Lowlander lords lucky enough to have not died with Ailpein were keeping their armed bands close to home. Some English knights and soldiers had gone with the English fleet; the rest were impatiently awaiting Arthur's word to commence another invasion of France, but King Arthur was biding his time.

"The Venetians, whose greed had started the war, were suffering far more than was France, however. They had lost the best part of all three of their war fleets and many of their merchant-ships; most of their Adriatic Coastal possessions had been seized by various nations, nor was their war against Savoy doing at all well.

"They had hired a huge army of mercenaries, not expecting to need them for long, had paid them half down and agreed to pay the remaining half upon completion of six months' service, but by the time the payday rolled around, not only was the war still grinding on but Venetian income had dried up to a bare trickle, thanks to the Genoese blockade, and the lands from which taxes might have once been ground were by then under other flags, most of them."

"So, what did they do?" inquired Foster.

The old man shrugged. "What could they do? They knew that if the mercenaries were not paid on time they could well cease hostilities with Savoy, if they did not march against Venice herself. Putting up state treasures of art works and jewels for collateral, the Republic borrowed heavily from the Church. That got them enough to pay the balance of the original contract."

"And then they pulled out of the war. Right?" said Foster.

"No, Bass, though a people with more sagacity and less

foolish pride would certainly have so done. Doge Angelo caused a ruinous tax to be levied upon all persons within reach—both the high and the lowly—and had quantities of gold and silver plate and jewelry seized, melted down, and minted into coinage with which he rehired the mercenaries to another contract.

"By that time, he was obliged to reduce operations against Savoy due to a guerrilla war in Milan which was rapidly becoming a full-scale, duchy-wide rebellion and calling for the committal of more and more troops. Also, it was felt necessary to display a show of force on the northeastern border of the Republic, since the King of Hungary had been becoming increasingly cool toward the Venetian envoy.

"Had the Hungarians actually invaded and crushed the Venetian Republic, the war might have had a lasting effect, but the only Hungarians who crossed the border were refugees, fleeing a fierce re-outbreak of Priests' Plague. One of the first Venetians to die was, I understand, old Doge Angelo. Troops returning from the Hungarian border took the Plague into Milan and the Savoyard-Piedmont. It ravaged the Venetian camps all winter and was taken into France by the Savoyards who invaded that country the following spring.

"It was the Plague ended that war, Bass, not conquering armies. France, already marched over and fought over and ravaged by fire and sword, was terribly hit by this fresh outbreak of disease. Not only the rich and the mighty were struck down then, but whole country villages were emptied of living populations and some two-thirds of the folk of Paris died.

"The Burgundian army fled back behind their national borders and closed them, shooting full of arrows any man, or woman, or child who tried to cross from France, but they were not spared.

"Almost all of the Aragon-Navarre-Aquitaine Army died of the Plague, including Duke Henry Tudor. The disease was brought back to England by the Fleet when it returned from the intaking of Toulon. It was taken to Ireland, this time, by certain Irishmen who had been serving as mercenaries with the armies of Burgundy, and for over three years there was no real war in all of that island.

"Arthur II had always been of poor constitution, Bass; only my lavish use of the dwindling supply of longevity boosters had kept him alive on several occasions during his reign. By the time I had made certain he would survive his bout of Plague, I was down to less than two dozen capsules.

"When the Plague had at last run its course in both England and Ireland and matters were again approaching normalcy, Emmett made his only other visit to England. All of his family, save only one grandson, had died of the disease and his grief was clear to read when he once more came to me in York.

"Of course, the manner of our meeting was somewhat different, that time. He still was a wealthy Irish nobleman, true enough, but I was become the most high and most powerful churchman in all of England, with a court large as that of any earl, so it required several days and extensive palm grease to get him an audience; nor had I, in the press of my new duties, any idea he was in England until he was before me.

"Physically, he was unchanged, but woe had carved deep lines in his face, his green eyes were filled with a soul-deep sadness, and seldom did smile or laugh bring up the corners of his mouth.

"Immediately we were alone, he leaned forward and asked in intense tones, 'Ken, hoo mony capsules hae ye left?'

"'About twenty,' I sighed.

"His eyes went a little wild, then, and he grasped my arm so hard that my flesh bore blue fingermarks for a week after. 'Nay, not wi' ye, mon, I mean in all?'

"'That's what I mean, too, Emmett. I have a total of twenty-two capsules left me.'

"The blood drained from his face and the strength from his body; he sank back in his chair, even more woebegone than before. In a hushed whisper, he said, 'Och, God and His Saints help us both, then, auld friend, for we be doomed tae die far afore ooor time. What hoppened tae y'r ain?'

"'I used them, a few here and a few there, to keep old Hal and then King Arthur alive, Emmett; I could have done no less. But what of you? You had nearly three hundred, as did I.'

"He cracked the knuckles of his big, scarred hands, vented a deep sigh, and then told the tale. 'The Plague first took hold in Waterford, but it spread like tae fire through dry heather, and afore ony could prepare or hardly pray, most o' the Court at Tara lay dead or dying. When it's sairtain-sure I was that the Pest was abroad w'in me ain hoosehold, I give o'er me plans tae move me folk tae my lodge in the Wicklow

168

Mountains; instead, I took me tae horse wi' a small small guard and rode tae Fora, straight, for I'd me ain capsules hid in the false botthom o' a treasure casket an' under th' keepin' o' the gude fithers, there.

" 'Early on in the onset o' the Plague, Bishop Padraigh, at Kells, had ordered ony church properties strucken w' the Pest be burnt. And me and me men rode tae Fora ainly tae find roofless an' smoke-blackened walls fu' o' ashes. An' nae any single trace o' me casket, though we sifted ash days on end. It seemed that th' thrice-doomed looters had been there afore us an' fled God alane knew whence.

" 'And when, at last, I rid intae me courtyard at Tara, nane were left tae e'en greet me, the Pest had ta'en them a'—me new, young, bonny thaird wife and a' her bairns, a' me get ain me ither twa wives, an' a' their get an' beyont. Only a few o' the meaner sorts o' sairvants were spared, they an' me grandson, Tim. He had been o'er sea in Great Ireland, wherein the Pest had ne'er took holt.

" 'For a lang year, I prayed daily and nightly for a war, that I might fling mysel' intae the forefront o' battle, in a bear's 'sark an' wi' only a club. But nae ane o' the kindgoms had been spared; land lay open for th' mere takin' an' nane livin' tae fight for it or ony else. So, since I couldnae die in honor an' put me pair soul at peace, I turned back tae the world.

" 'Torcull, a half-brother o' King Brien, had been crowned High King, for a' that he were the bastard spawn o' a dalliance wi' a crofter's dochter, but a gude king he's proved, for a'. Mony a high hoose had been wiped oot, entire, so meself resolved tae win an empty throne for me Tim. I began tae gather men and, when a respectable-size band I had, it's King Torcull I went tae, for we was friends of auld. When he'd hear'd me oot, he was after givin' me his blessings as High King as weel as loanin' me half what was left o' the army.

" 'Noo, Tim's grandmither—me second wife—were a lawful-born half-sister o' King Ahmladh o' Lagan. His ain mither were a dochter o' the hoose o' Ahmladh's cousin an' successor, King Seosaidh, an' the *bouchal*, hisself, chanced tae be foaled in Lagan. So, wi' the most o' the Royal Hoose o' Lagan cauld in the clay, it were clear that me Tim had as guid a claim as ony an' far better nor some tae the throne o' his greatuncle.' He sighed. 'An' that be hoo it were, Ken. Wi' the loan o' Tara troops, me force were near twicet agin the size o' ony ithers, an' as King Ahmladh IV, Tim now be into th' secun' year o' his reign, is wedded a year tae a pretty,

169

little thing oot'n the Hoose o' Muma an' she's a-nursin' a foine, strappin' *bouchal* twa moon, noo.'

" 'And you saved no capsules at all, Emmett?' I asked him.

" 'Anely these twa.' He operated a hidden catch which a cunning master jeweler had worked into his smooth-worn class ring and produced two capsules from within the secret chamber.

"At the recommended dosages, Bass, we had then between us enough to maintain us for no more than sixty years before we began to age. Now this meant far less to me than it did to Emmett, for I had been middle-aged to begin with, but he was a young man and was literally horrified at the thought that he might lose his youth, vigor, looks, and abilities. Though I offered to freely give him all of my remaining capsules, he would not be mollified, and, at length, decided to see if he could use the console to bring into this world that portion of the lab in which were the components and devices for manufacturing a fresh supply of capsules."

"So you two came up here to Whyffler Hall then, eh?" said Foster.

"Not so," answered the Archbishop. "We first needed King Arthur's permission to break his father's seals and have the wall covering the door to the tower cellars dismantled. Too, affairs detained me in York, so there was nothing for it but that Emmett remain there a-fretting for a few months . . . and so he did.

"He and I had intended to journey to London or Oxford or Bath, wherever the King happened to be when I could wrench free, but as it happened, Arthur and his court arrived in York before I found time to leave. Of course, Arthur was privy to my 'secret' as his father had been, and when I had explained the matter to him, he had a document prepared giving me a lifetime right to enter royally sealed buildings and chambers at my discretion. I think he was eager to come up with us and see these marvels, but the poor man was even more harried with affairs of state than was I with ecclesiastical matters, and as many of his court and council had died of the Plague, he need must labor with half-trained replacements.

"The royal party remained for two months in York, then moved on in the then-regular circuit, but still I was unable to break away, so I finally dispatched Emmett—provided with the royal document—as my emissary, to Whyffler Hall that he might examine the console and commence certain needed modifications we had discussed. When at long last I gained a respite from my many duties, I journeyed north and joined Emmett here.

"This hall, built in stages, had but just been finished then, Bass. The present formal gardens had not even yet been sketched, so it was fairly easy for us to pace off the distances, compare them with our two memories of the distances involved on that other world, and make the appropriate settings on the console. Sir James had died of camp fever in the War of the Three Marriages, and Whyffler Hall was then held by his grandson, young John Whyffler, who was Sir Francis' grandfather. Naturally, the young man was terribly curious about all that was going on, but he also was a very proper young man and never intruded, making it a point to mind his own business and to see that his family and household did the same.

"Finally, one night after Emmett had been at work on the console and his calculations for near three months, we sat in this very chamber, talking privily over an ewer of John Whyffler's best ale. He had been in an increasing sweat and fret for weeks, brusque in his speech, and short-tempered on all occasions.

" 'Weel, Ken, we'll be tryin' it an hour arter dawn, on the morrow. By sich calculation as meself can make, an' as me memory serve me, oor time be about six hours ahead o' theirn, so the lab ne'er will iver be missed.'

" 'Never missed?' I said. 'But Emmett, surely when the morning comes, they'll notice a missing building?'

" 'By St. Sola's toenails . . .' he began, peevishly, then stopped and smiled slowly. 'It's sorry I'm bein', Ken, but the strain on me poor mind hae been sommat fierce, these last moons; ye dinna ken, I see. We be here in the past, e'en should we hold yon lab here for years, it'll be as the bare blinkin' o' y'r e'e to the folk in that world.'

" 'No, Emmett,' I disagreed, 'it's you who don't understand. You never really knew much about history—the history of *our* home world—so I don't think you ever have understood just what happened to us, just where we really are. Emmett, this is *not* our world we were projected into, *not* the history of our world we've been living, all these years. Emmett, we can only be on a *parallel world*, so what is projected here from that other world must be here for good and all. Just look how long the console has been here, yet you said that it could be expected to snap back to whence it and we came within hours or at most days after our arrival. Doesn't its continued presence tell you something?"

"The Irishman shrugged, shaking his full head of hair, his stiff moustachios aquiver. 'Y' may be a-havin' the right of 't, Ken . . . y' may be wrong, too. Aye, lang years has it been . . . here, but how are we tae ken the relation of *oor* time tae that of yon world we quitted, sae lang or short a time agone? There, in that sad world, the beam of that bitch's heat-stunner still may be a-cracklin' the air neath those computers, y'know? All what I may say for sairtin sure be that yon console still be a-drawin' poower frae that world . . . or frae somm'eres. An' wi' luck an' the blessin's o' the saints, it's bringin' that lab tae us we will be.'

"And to this very day, Bass," sighed the aged Archbishop, "I know not which of us—me or Emmett—was right in our suppositions. But that night I issued an order that all activity on the north side of the hall be suspended until the nones of the next day.

"As the sun rose like a new penny out of the eastern mists, I was in my place on the battlements atop the tower-keep, whilst Emmett did some last-minute tinkering and calculating in the torch-lit cellar . . . He had my wristwatch—his own having been battered to ruin in some long-done skirmish—so I could only cast glances at the sundial.

"At length, he came panting up the steep stairs to join me upon the donjon roof and peer anxiously betwixt the ancient merlons, snapping glances at the watch on his hairy wrist. Finally, he devoted all his attention to the face of the instrument, then he looked up.

"'It's time, Ken. The console's on automatic, it should switch onnnn . . . *now!*'"

The old man lifted the ewer and poured the last of the ale into his mug. Impatiently, Foster said, "And? Then what, Hal? What happened, dammit?"

The Archbishop smiled, while plunging a loggerhead into the brew. "Patience, Bass, patience. My throat's getting dry." When he had sipped at the steaming ale, he leaned back, wrapping his cold hands about the warm mug, closed his eyes, and went on with the tale.

"What happened, you ask. Nothing, friend Bass, not really. Oh, I thought to see a brief flicker of moving, brown water, flanked by square, blockish buildings, for an eyeblink of time overlying the hall and grounds, but then it was gone—if ever it was in anything or anyplace other than my memory-nudged mind.

"Emmett began to curse then, foul, frightful, blasphemous curses snarled out of a terror-spawned rage. Spinning about, he raced down the several flights of stairs—I following—until he once more stood before the console. He beat at the device with his fists, kicked at it with his booted feet . . . for all the good it did him, or me.

"He kept trying, through every day, two or three or four times each day, for a week and more, before he finally admitted defeat. Then he began to make rapid plans for a quick return to Ireland. At our constrained parting, I gifted him most of the remaining capsules, retaining only a brace of them for myself. I never have seen or heard from him since that long-ago day that he and his retainers rode west from York.

"After a reign very long for this world, Arthur II died after a lengthy illness. Unfortunately, no one of his sons outlived him—Henry, Edwin, Phillip, Edward, Patric, Harold, all died before him from one cause or another. But Henry, who had been the eldest, had had two sons, one of whom had succeeded his father as Prince of Wales, and that Prince, Richard, succeeded his grandsire as Richard IV.

"As I lowered the crown onto Richard's head, I had a presentiment that that act presaged dark days for this realm, Bass, nor was I wrong. Richard was not a good king; though loving and pious, he was weak. His scheming wife and her Roman coterie soon had him and England dancing to their own tunes; the nation's wealth soon was flowing—nay, rushing, torrent-wise—into their greedy hands and, through them, into the insatiable coffers of the Roman Papacy.

"There had been anti-Roman sentiment a-broil in all of England since the very first of the Priests' Plagues, Bass, and, of course, under Richard it grew apace, 'mongst nobles and commons alike. Nor did a rumor that Queen Angela had persuaded her royal spouse to journey to Rome, sign over England to her uncle, the Pope, and then accept it back as a Papal feoff help matters at all. It was only by unremitting luck that we avoided civil war as long as we did.

"When Richard died—and it was not murder, Bass, no matter what you may have heard to the contrary; rather, it was simply a resurgence of the strain of bodily infirmity that had killed Richard's father and almost taken off his grandsire several times—and King Arthur III was crowned, it were safe to state that all the land breathed a collective sigh of relief, for Arthur had never kept a secret of his personal disenchantment with the grasping ways of the Roman Papacy, his utter loathing of his sister-in-law and her clique, or his impatience with his brother's weak will.

"The nation rallied to Arthur unrestrainedly, Bass. The mourning period for Richard was scandalously short, and few paid it more than mere lip service. Arthur was only eighteen, but in most ways he was far more the man and the King than his brother ever had been. He openly scorned the machinations of certain factions to wed him to Angela, his brother's still-scheming widow, remarking in her very presence a distaste for half-eaten apples, before sending her and all her pack from court.

"It was not until Angela dropped her shoat that Arthur decided to wed, choosing the daughter of Lothair, Elke, and announcing to all within earshot that no Italian bastard ever would sit the throne of the Tudors."

Bass nodded. "Yes, I've heard that rumor, too, Hal. Is there any truth in it?"

The eyes of the Archbishop narrowed. "Possibly. Though Angela, of course, made much public show of fealty and devotion to Richard, it was well-known in court circles that she despised him, and several courtiers and foreigners were bruited at one time or another to be her chosen bedmates, most notably Duque Tomaso del Monteleone, Ambassador of the Kingdom of the Two Sicilies.

"Too, the child bears no resemblance at all to the Tudors—being swarthy and black-haired and -eyed, with high cheekbones and a hooked beak of a nose that looks not at all like either his mother or his supposed paternal line, but quite a bit like the House of del Monteleone in general and the late Duque in particular."

While reheating his own ale, Foster asked, "Is that the chap Arthur had tortured to death early in the war and then sent the corpse back to London in a pipe of brandy?"

His old eyes sparkling, the Archbishop rasped a dry chuckle. "A bit of psychological warfare that succeeded too well, that, Bass. A few weeks after poor Arthur learned of the murders of his wife and children, the Duque was captured during a cavalry action, but he was seriously wounded and died just as he reached the King's camp. Arthur had the still-warm body stripped, flogged, burned, racked ferociously, and terribly mutilated. When the corpse gave every indication of having succumbed not to wounds of battle but to protracted torture, he had the thing immersed in brandy and sent it back to Angela along with a letter in which he assured her that he had now proof of his charges of adultery and bastardy.

"The farce was intended only to intimidate the so-called Regent and her folk, but now most of the army and nation believe it and Arthur is fancied a cold, vengeful, implacable man, one not to be trifled with."

Foster suddenly found his throat tight, but asked the question anyway. "Hal, your . . . your friend, Emmett, how old would he look, by now?"

The old man shrugged. "No older than he did when last we parted, late-twentyish . . . unless he lost his capsules, again."

"And if he did lose them?" probed Foster.

"Younger than do I, by far," smiled the Archbishop. "Possibly his appearance would be about your age. But why ask you?"

Foster thrust a hand into his pouch and closed his fingers about the ring he had prized from the clammy hand of the dead Irishman. "You'll see why soon enough, Hal. But, please tell me. What college did Emmett graduate from, and what year? Can you recall?"

The older man frowned in concentration. "M.I.T., I recall that, but the year, hmmm . . . Ninety-seven, or was it ninety-six? No, I think it was ninety-eight, Bass. Yes, that was it, nineteen-ninety-eight."

Slowly, Foster drew the worn, golden ring from his pouch, cupped the bauble in his palm, and extended the hand to his companion. "Could . . . then . . . this be . . . be your friend's ring, Hal?"

CHAPTER 12

The winter had been long and harsh, but at length it ended. The hills round about Whyffler Hall traded their coats of glistening white for verdant mantles of bright-green grass with splashes of bold colors where early-blooming flowerlets burst out among the protrusions of weathered rock. Feathered clouds of birds descended from skies of blue and fleecy-white to perch upon the budding branches of the ancient, huge-boled trees, chirping and trilling avian tales of their long, winter sojourns in Languedoc, Andalusia and Africa. The season of growth had commenced . . . and the season of death.

With the melting of the snows, Foster sent out gallopers, and soon knots of well-armed riders were converging upon the hall, all prepared and provisioned for yet another season of war. But this year they came from both sides of the ill-defined border, those from the north of it completely uninvited and none too welcome by their English cousins . . . at first.

A council among the Archbishop of York, Duke Parlan, Foster, and the leader of the Scots volunteers, Andrew, Laird of Elliot—a scar-faced, broken-nosed man of apparent middle years, whose bushy salt-and-pepper eyebrows overhung deep-blue, predatory eyes; despite a noticeable limp, the tall, lithe Scot moved with the grace of a panther and he sat his fully trained stallion like a centaur, controlling the iron-gray beast solely with knee pressure and voice, since his left arm ended in a brass cap and hook—settled the matter and then Foster met with his officers.

When all the English officers had taken places about the chamber, Captain of Dragoons Squire Guy Dodd posed the question that was on the minds of all his comrades: "M'lord Forster, Bass, when d'we get tae chivvy them black-hairted bastids back tae their kennels?"

"You don't!" Foster snapped. "They're damned good fighters—as you all well know. And when has His Majesty's Army ever had enough horse, eh?"

"But . . ." protested Captain Dodd, "they be *Scots*, thrice-domned Scots!"

"And, as such, they are no longer our enemies, Guy. The full agreements are not yet drawn or signed, but the King and the Kingdom of Scotland now are allied to Arthur and England. There is to be peace and amity between England and Scotland; both Kings and the high nobles all are agreed upon it."

The other captain in the chamber, grizzled old Melvin Hall, snorted. "Y'r pardon, m'lord, in an thousun years an' more they's been nought save war on t' border. An' like it'll e'er be so, kings and great nobles be domned!"

Most of the assembled borderers nodded assent to the verity of Hall's words, and a squinty-eyed lieutenant asked, "M'lord, did thet brother-murderin' Jim Stewart, then, send yon pack o' cur-dogs?"

Foster shook his head. "No, these men were gathered by the man who commands them, Laird Andrew. It seems that the Elliot agrees with Captain Hall, in some respects; therefore, to prevent border trouble this year, he impressed every hothead and fire-eater he could clap hands to, formed them into a troop, and brought them south to fight *for*—not against—King Arthur.

"The Reichsherzog, the Archbishop, the representatives of the King, and I feel his actions are commendable and he and his troop have been accepted by us for our King's service. I shall expect you gentlemen to set a good example for your men in accepting these former enemies among you with good grace."

It was not all that easy, of course, nor had Foster or any of the others thought for one minute that it would be. But, after several floggings and a couple of salutary hangings, the men got the message.

"I hate like hell to leave you here alone, Krystal, without even Nugai to look out for you. But both Hal and Wolf swear you'll be safe. The entrenchments and guns will continue to be garrisoned and manned at least until the negotiations with the Scots are completed, and like as not long afterward. But Wolf says that even should Crusaders land on the coast, march this far inland, and invest and take the hall, you'd have nought to fear, since you're legally Marchioness of Velegrad and, as delicate as are the current relations between Rome and the Empire, the very last thing the Church desires is an incident that would tend to worsen those relations.

"And when I tried to get Hal to promise to send you down to York, he flatly refused me, saying that you and the baby would be better fed and healthier here."

Krystal nodded. "Yes, there was a terrible outbreak of typhoid there last summer, honey, and food still is scarce and dear in York, so Hal is probably right. He usually is, you know. They say that experience is the best teacher, and let's face it, he's had something over two hundred years of experience.

"But I'll be all right, Bass. Of course, I'll miss Nugai. I'll miss him almost as much as I'll miss you." Her soft, slender hand crept into his broad, callused palm. "But I'll have Meg and Polly and Trina here with me, and we'll manage just fine, dear."

Foster was vastly relieved that his wife had burdened him with none of the importunings to accompany him south that she had in the past. He could well imagine the slimy, stinking, hellish pestholes which the camps circling London were certain to be after the wintering of thousands of decidedly unhygienic men in them and he wanted his wife and son nowhere near to them. It was bad enough that he and his horsemen must live in them at least long enough to map out the strategy for the season's campaigning.

Immediately after the gentlemen-officers were all mounted, Freiherr Sebastian Foster, Markgraf of Velegrad, Lord Commander of King Arthur III's Horse and Tendant of the Fort and Estate of Whyffler Hall, called for the stirrup cup. When he had drained off the contents of the ancient silver-mounted horn, he drew his fine Tara-steel blade, brought his leopard-spotted destrier to a sustained rear, and saluted the assembled ladies. All save his wife *oohed* and *aaahed* his courtesy and horsemanship. Krystal gave him back an amused smile, then turned to graciously accept the compliments of the other ladies upon her noble husband's manners, skills and dashing appearance.

Amenities thus discharged, Foster nudged the fettlesome stallion over to where stood old Geoff Musgrave and Henry Turnbull, who would stay behind to see to the estate and the hall proper. Keeping a tight rein on Bruiser—the war-trained charger had become safe enough around the familiar-smelling men of Foster's campaign staff and entourage, but would deign to trust very few other humans and was likely to bite or to kick, as the mood took him—Foster shucked his mailed gauntlet and offered his hand to each of the men.

"Well, Geoff, old friend, I'm off to war again. Pray God, for the last time. I've no instructions to give you—either of you—for you and Henry between you manage Sir Francis' holdings far better than do I."

The Estate Warden, Geoffrey Musgrave, shook his scarred, grizzled head, "Och, nae, Sir Bass, y'r worship shouldnae say sich. Y' need but tae learn a bit more an' y'll be—"

Chuckling, Foster waved his hand. "I thank you for the compliment, Geoff, but I do know the truth of the matter. I can only hope that when, and if, I assume my own holdings at Velegrad, I am so fortunate as to have fine men such as you to so competently handle my affairs as you handle those of Sir Francis."

Musgrave frowned and scratched at his close-cropped iron-gray hair. "Y'r lordship's pardon if I seem tae be speaking' oot o' me place, but y'll gang far e'er y' finds a better, all-round man than y'r war-servant, Noogay—f'r a' he be a cat-footed, slant-eyed heathen."

Foster tried not to show his surprise. He had been completely unaware that Musgrave and the silent, usually solitary Nugai had been as much together as this comment implied.

"Again, I thank you, Geoff," he said, gravely. "I trust Nugai with my life and"—he grinned to lighten the conversation—"he's not failed me . . . yet."

Foster turned to Majordomo Turnbull. "Henry, so long as the Lord Archbishop remains, he—and only he—is master of the house; should any of the other gentlemen issue orders contradicting his, courteously refer them to him. God willing, I'll see you both before the first snows."

Then, because such was expected, he turned his horse and paced slowly across the flagstones to where stood Krystal. Leaning from his saddle, he encircled her waist with the steel-encased right arm, lifted her up, and kissed her, thoroughly, to the lusty cheers of his gentlemen-officers and the assembled folk, one and all, noble and common.

With her arms clasped about his neck and her lips close to his ear, that he might hear her words above the raucous tumult, she said, "I love you, Bass Foster. Oh, God, I love you so very much! So take good care of yourself, for me and for little Joe. Don't be reckless and come back to me, to us . . . *soon*. I need you, Bass, I need you every moment of every day, I . . ." She sniffled. "Oh, dammit, I swore I wouldn't cry, not now, not until later. Put me down and get on your way before . . . before your armored sots swig so much ale they can't sit a horse!"

As he lowered her slowly, a mischievous twinkle came into her swimming eyes. "Those women over there are right, you know, you do cut a handsome figure, Sir Sebastian. The answer to a maiden's prayer. That's what you are, a knight in shining armor. And you'd better be damned glad that that armor is so hard to get off quickly, or I'd rape you in front of all of them."

Foster in the lead, trailed at a few paces distance by his bannerman and squad of bodyguards and, behind them, nearly twoscore gentlemen-officers, the column walked their horses down the gravelled way toward the main gate to the cheers and well-wishes of a heterogeneous throng of hall folk, farm folk from round about, Fort Whyffler commoner officers and other ranks, wild Scots of the treaty party, soldiers and servants of the English treaty negotiators, and a small knot of crippled veterans—the incomplete jetsam of many a hard-fought field who never again would ride out to war and who so eyed Foster's whole, sound, and heavily armed bodyguards enviously.

From the forefront of the platoon of cripples stepped Olly Shaftoe, and Foster reined up at sight of his one-armed sometime orderly. "How many children, now, Olly?"

Fingering his forelock, the man smiled shyly. "Still only the twa, milord. But me Mary be due tae foal soon, by Beltane we figgers. If it be a lad, might we ca' the tyke Sebastian, milord?"

"I would be honored if you named your son after me, Olly. And when your good wife nears her time, be sure to bear her to my house, where my lady-wife can care for her properly."

"As always, milord, I hears ever word an' I'll obey." The

man drew himself up into near-military posture and rendered a hand salute, then extended that hand. Foster again shucked off his gauntlet, reined Bruiser's head around to the other side, and leaned from his saddle to take the proffered clasp.

Tears brimming from his eyes, Olly wrung Foster's hand and said chokedly, "A' oor prayers gae wi' ye, Lord Bass. I beg ye, dinna turn yer back ain them thrice-domned Scots, sir."

Foster found that he must swallow hard to clear the lump from his throat. "Never fear, Olly. The Scot's not yet spawned who can put paid to me. Expect my banner between Blood Moon and Snow Moon."

Beyond the main gate, the column wove its way between and around the entrenchments, palisaded ramparts and batteries. Then, in what had once been the outer park until King Alexander's army had chopped down most of the trees for fuel, drawn up on opposite sides of the road, they came upon the troopers—all mounted, packed and road-ready.

Following a brief inspection by Foster and the other officers, the column was formed up and set out southward.

At nightfall, they camped about the shattered, blackened remains of Heron Hall, and some of the officers and troopers, after killing or driving out the vermin, supped and settled into the littered ruin of the hall itself, but Foster could not feel comfortable in the place as now it was, peopled for him with the ghosts of so many happy evenings, so retired to the fine, new pavilion which his secret hoard of Irish loot had purchased after the defeat of the Crusaders' southern army.

Nugai awaited him. The ugly but highly intelligent little man had, in the winter spent in attendance upon Krystal, learned to speak an English far more comprehensible to Foster than the dialects of many of his own officers and troops. While helping his lord to shed armor and outer clothing in the entry chamber of the pavilion, he said matter-of-factly, "Lord Bahss, two men await you in the next chamber. One say that of old he knows my lord. Nor armed are they neither and truth Nugai thinks they speak with no harm meaning."

Nugai delivered Foster's armor to the trooper who waited outside to clean and oil it, while Foster laved the day's accumulation of dust and dirt from face and hands in a bucket of cold water. Then, closely followed by the oriental—who, for all his protestations of trust in the motives of the visitors, kept his hands near to the cocked pistol and the kindjal knife in his belt—he lifted aside the canvas and entered the second chamber of the luxurious pavilion.

Two men in rough, dirty, ragged clothing confronted him. One was vaguely familiar, looking to be nearly as broad as he was tall, his body all big bones and rolling muscles, his face a single mass of hideous scar tissue, shiny in the lamplight. The other man was taller, flat-muscled, and far slimmer, his hair and eyes coal-black and his complexion a dark olive; his handsome face bore but a single scar, which began somewhere on his scalp and bore downward the full length of his left cheek to the very point of his chin.

The broad man's scarred lips twisted. "Y'r ludship doesnae reckernize me eh? Nae wunner it be, neither. Heh heh! M'lud, I be Dan the Smith. How be the noble Captain Webster?"

Suddenly it all came back to Foster. That last night of cheer at Heron Hall—the fine dinner for which John Heron so vociferously apologized, the shared singing of bawdy songs by high table and low, the endless drinking, the quarterstaff bouts, and Webster's difficult victory in wrestling this very man, Dan Smith.

When the newcomers had had their fill of the jerked beef, campaign biscuit, and ale—and Foster had never before seen one man eat so much of the tasteless fare at one sitting—Dan Smith launched into the promised tale of the fall of Heron Hall. He told of the completely unexpected attack by the screaming horde of savage, Highland irregulars composing part of King Alexander's Scottish army; told of how the folk of the hall had manned the inadequate walls and fired the cannon and swivels until the Scots were upon the walls and into the courtyard at their backs; told of how the hard-pressed men upon the walls had even then managed to turn some of the guns and pour hot death into the blood-mad mob of Highlanders attacking the hall itself.

Picking his teeth with a broken and dirty fingernail, the smith said, "Wha' chanceted then, Lud Forster, I canna say. I'd but turned tae throw a domned Scot frae the wa', when the demiculv'rin blowed up and knockdted down part o' t' wa', an' Dan Smith under it all. Belike t' thrice-domned Scots bastids were o' a mind that not e'en a Dan Smith could live wi' a wa' an' cannon an' a' on him. But live, I did! But when I crawlted oot frae unner it a', the Scots were a' lang awa', the hall were sackted an' burnt oot an' nane save Dan Smith an' ain old tomcat were left alive."

Foster wrinkled his brow. "I was here, last autumn, Smith, on my way north to Whyffler Hall, yet I saw nothing of you."

The lips twisted again. "Belike I were oot arter food, m'lud; far an' awa I've had tae range fer sommat tae fill oor bellies."

The other man spoke in good, if accented, English. "Yes, Lord Forster, I do recall a visit by a troop of horse last autumn, but of course I had no way of knowing who you were or what your intentions, so I remained in hiding until your departure."

"As to that matter," inquired Foster, "just how did an Arabian knight come to be wandering alone about the wilds of Northumberland?"

Sir Ali ibn Hossain smiled languidly. "Lord Foster, like many a younger son, my life has been one of eking out a small, yearly stipend by competing in tournaments and on occasion selling my sword. Early last year, fortune found me in Rome and I hired on as a noble bodyguard in the entourage of Cardinal Mandojana, sailed with him to Edinburgh, and then marched south with that abomination that the Scots called an army.

"I had the misfortune to be wounded in the great battle to the south, and on the retreat I was loaded onto a wagon along with many another wounded gentlemen. The driver of that damned wagon should have been strangled at birth! He managed to hit every bump, boulder, and hole from the battlefield to the place at which he allowed the wagon to slip off a ford and into a stream. Most of the wounded drowned. That I did not can be attributed the Will of God; nor was even a cursory search made for any survivors, and I had died of loss of blood, exposure or both together, had not the good Master Smith here found me and cared for me.

"I can provide you no ransom, Lord Forster. My good horse was slain in battle and all that I now own mine own are my sword, a dirk, these boots, and some bits of poor clothing. Mayhap the Lord Cardinal would ransom me, but I'd not count on his mercy."

Foster shook his head. "Cardinal Mandojana was murdered by the Scots on the same night that they murdered King Alexander. Alexander's brother, James, now is King of Scotland, and his ministers are at this very moment finalizing a treaty of alliance with King Arthur's mediators. Be that as it may, Sir Ali, I have no desire for or need of your ransom;

for my part, you are a free man. But how will you get back to Arabia, or wherever?"

Again the young Arab smiled. "There always are lords and captains in need of seasoned fighters, Lord Forster, in any land, at any time."

Foster was never to regret his next, impulsive words. "If your sword is for hire, Sir Ali, why not rent it to me? I ride to war and am ever in need of good men, noble or common."

"Only if the contract includes Master Smith," said Sir Ali. "I owe him much and he cannot live well or long here, in this ruin."

Foster nodded. "An honorable man always pays his debts. I'm beginning to like you already, Sir Ali, but I'd have taken Dan Smith along, at any rate. Good smiths are hard to come by, and besides, I know him of old. So, what do you ask for your services, sir knight?"

After the usual haggling, they settled on armor, pistols, clothing, and necessary gear as pay for a period of six months or the length of the campaign; in addition, Sir Ali would have the use of a charger until he could either seize one in battle or win enough loot to purchase one. His place would be with Foster's bodyguards for the nonce, while Dan Smith would take his place on the march with the packtrain.

Foster did not lead his force directly south to the marshaling rendezvous at Manchester—rather did he ride southeast, toward York. For one reason, he was running perilously low on shells for his anachronistic sawed-off shotguns-cum-horsepistols; the other reason hinged upon Pete's last letter before the snows had effectively closed communications between Whyffler Hall and points south.

"While Buddy Webster is hobbling around, out on the Archbishop's farm, up to his knees in manure and loving every minute of it, this old boy's been busier than a one-armed paperhanger. After I come back from the King's camp, I put my factory in high gear, twenty-four hours a day—we got enough light to work nights with these reflectors I worked up—and, come spring, not only should we ought to have finished enough worked-over long guns and cylinder sets to give every one of the king's harkay-bussers fourteen quick shots, but I should have at least five dozen pairs of them long-ass pistols altered from slowmatch to flintlock, like you and Buddy and me used to talk about. So you bring your boys down here on your way, next year, and I guarantee you a good half a hundred of them will have them a real edge on any other pistol-toters they run acrost."

So they marched onward, making fair time despite swollen streams and deep, seemingly endless mud. They came across no brigands, nor did the folk to be found working the fields in preparation for planting have much to report of any skulkers, for the winter had been both long and hard and, in a land all but denuded by the Scots' army last year, few if any of the bushwhacker bands had survived it.

The town of Hexham, pillaged and burned by Alexander's Scots just before his army met that of Arthur, was being rebuilt and was a buzzing hive of noise and activity. But with the arrival of the van of Foster's force, construction was abruptly given over to a rousing welcome for royal horse and—when it was established that the leader of this force was not only Lord Commander of King Arthur's Horse, but that very paladin who had smashed the left wing of the late and unlamented King Alexander's army, had turned that wing with only his squadron of cavalry and so, or so said many men, ensured the great victory wrought that night by English arms—the welcome became a tumultuous festival; nor were Foster and his men able to tear themselves away in less than three full days.

South of Hexham, the column's way lay along the range of small hills whereon had sat the Scottish reserves and baggage. Here and there among the heather and other rough growth gleamed a picked-white skull, and rib bones crunched now and again under the hoofs of the horses.

Dan Smith and some of his cronies ranged out in a thin skirmish line, afoot, on either flank of the column, seeking anything of value missed by earlier battlefield looters. With a yelp of triumph, the big man wrenched from the skeletal hand that had held it a long and heavy and very old cross-hilted sword—broken-pointed though it was and with the wood and leather of the grip rotted almost away from beneath the wire wrappings, still was there much good, reusable metal in the rusted blade.

The track wound downward, passing close by that little round flat-topped hill where, amid the heather, Foster had rested the remnants of his battered squadron, while straining to see through the fog-blanketed vale the course of the battle. Today, the sun shone brightly on a party of local men and boys assiduously cutting the peat whereon warhorses had trampled, whereon men had marched and charged and died, last year. The little stream that had run thick and clotting-red with those men's lifeblood now sparkled and gurgled between its banks with the clear water of the melted snows.

Farther on, on that plain where had been King Arthur's camp and the long beleaguered wagon fort, bones lay even more thickly than upon the hills. For a moment that was blessedly brief, Foster could hear again the drone and wail of the bagpipes, the demented shrieks of the charging Highlanders, the roar of the swivel-guns, boomings of muskets and pistols, death cries of men, the nerve-wracking screaming of a wounded horse somewhere nearby in the flameshot hell of fog and wreaths of lung searing powder smoke.

That night, in their camp many miles south of that terrain of peat and death, Nugai ushered Dan Smith into Foster's pavilion. Before the Lord Commander of the King's Horse, the burly blacksmith laid an outsize sheathed broadsword.

"M'lud, ain o' t' Hexham peat-cutters come acrost this unner t' bones o' a horse, in t' bog. Dan Smith thought he'd seen it afore, so he gi't t' man a piecet o' siller he'd won a-gamin', for't. Ain't many as could use a ol' bastid-sword for a broadsword. Be it Cap'n Webster's, m'lud?"

Foster drew the thick, broad, antique blade from its rotting scabbard. Smith had evidently spent some time and effort in cleaning the weapon, for the steel gleamed free of any speck of rust and gave off a smell of tallow.

He nodded. "Yes, Dan, I feel certain that this is Buddy's blade. He had thought the Scots had gotten it, while he lay with his broken leg pinned under his dead horse. I'm sure he'll be very pleased to have it back, for all that he's no longer a soldier."

But Dan Smith flatly refused the offer of a coin to replace the one he had paid a peat-cutter for the big sword. "Och, nae, m'lud. 'Twere foun' money, coom by t' dice. An' t' noble Cap'n Webster be a frind o' old."

Foster nodded again. "Very well, Dan, if that's as you want it. But when we get to York, you'll give it to him."

With his troops encamped on the old royal campgrounds outside York—principally due to the presence of the Scottish contingent, for they could expect no less hostility here than they had suffered under at Whyffler Hall—Foster, his bodyguard and a few selected officers rode into the city and sought out Pete Fairley's manufactory.

Pete, clad in the same rough clothing as his horde of artisans and laborers, said, "Damn! Carey's gonna be mad as a wet hen he missed you. He's on the road down to Lunnun with a dozen new light nine-pounders and four rifled eighteens we worked up this past winter—an' they'll throw further an' straighter an' harder 'n anything thesehere folks is ever seen, too. Time you gets over to Manchester, then down to Lunnun, your own self, he'll probably be here or on the way back, so he won't get to see you, a-tall. Sheeit!"

In the long, wide, high-ceilinged building which once had been the riding hall of the archepiscopal residence complex, Foster stood amazed at the end of row upon row of heavy work tables, before which a hundred or more artisans were fitting Pete's version of the snaphaunce lock to horsepistols. The place was a hubbub of chatter in broad, north-country dialects, the clattering of tools and, from afar down at the other end of the room, the huffs of leather bellows and the clanging ring of hammer on anvil.

Feeling a pull upon his sleeve, Foster turned to confront Dan Smith. "M'lud, d'ye think Master Fairley would lemme make use o' his smithy? An' it be well-fitted, a minit or twa an' Dan Smith could have Cap'n Webster's big sword good as new."

After a few minutes of standing and watching the accomplished metalworker go about the minor repairs needed on the oversized broadsword, Pete said, "Bass, yon's a true master smith; he could serve his king much better here than down south, shoeing horses."

Foster shrugged. "If you want to offer him a job, take it up with him personally; he's no soldier, he no longer has a home, and his liege lord is dead, slain by the Scots' army, last year. I brought him along with my force to keep him from starving in the countryside or turning brigand; he had no other options.

"By the bye, where are these fantastic pistols your letter bragged about? And I need some shells for my own brace, too."

Pete's test-firing was done on a field just beyond the city walls, where there was a low hillock to backstop bullets, balls, and other missiles. On a long table in a low-ceilinged wooden shed lay an assortment of small arms, with all the loading paraphernalia; from the dimness behind the table poked the brazen mouths of several light cannon.

Pete picked out at random a pair of the snaphaunce lock horse-pistols and rapidly charged them with smooth, practiced motions of his stained, work-roughened hands.

"Now, Bass, look, thesehere pistols is sommat shorter an' lighter nor your reg'lar-model hosspistol, for all they about seventy-five caliber. An' looky here, all the ramrods is brass, not wood, an' they all hinged to the barr'l, too, so you caint lose 'em. You jest unscrews 'em out'n the fore ends, like this. See? Then, when you done, you jest screws 'em back in, no more o' this tryin' to poke the rods back in a pouch. Heanh, Bass, you shoot 'em."

Bass Foster took the proffered weapons and hefted them. "Nice balance, Pete." Cocking one of the primed pistols, he extended an arm, aimed at a man-sized wooden effigy some thirty yards distant, and squeezed the trigger.

The wedge of rosy flint clamped betwixt the jaws of the cock was propelled forward against the pan cover, its impact sending a hail of tiny sparks into the pan filled with fine-grained priming powder, and smoke spurted sideways from the pan a split second before the heavy pistol roared and bucked upward, launching its ball on a yard-long flame.

Downrange, splinters flew from the deep-seated target, and the tattered, weather-grayed Highland bonnet atop the "head" of the effigy was knocked askew by the impact of the weighty ball.

Foster's left hand had been forcefully shaking the other pistol of the pair, both right side up and upside down, jarring it against his booted thigh. Now he brought it, too, into his right hand, cocked, and fired. It performed no less well than had its mate. When he had looped the straps of powder flask, priming flask, and bullet bag round his neck, he called for his horse, mounted, and began to trot Bruiser up and down the field, all the while loading and priming the pair of pistols. Then he wheeled about and came in at a full-jarring gallop, reins in his teeth, to come to a rearing halt and discharge one pistol and then the other at the battered target.

After three repeats of this performance, he next reloaded, then hurled both weapons to the ground, hard. Dismounting, he picked them up, cocked, and fired. Both pistols spat, faithfully, despite the mistreatment, though the recoil now was heavier, due to powder fouling in the bores.

When he had turned over Bruiser to Nugai, he strode back to the waiting Pete Fairley, smiling. "If they all perform this well, we're in business. It's the devil to keep slowmatches going, not to mention dangerous as hell to reload with one of them clamped in the cock, and many a man has been killed before he could reload, reprime, span, and cock his wheellock. These pistols seem like just the ticket, Pete; they're quick and easy to reload, seem to be both tough and reliable, and they're hard-hitting without excessive kick. How many pairs have you got?"

"Thirty-one," answered Pete, then added, soberly, "But let's go back to my office and wet our throats. I got some bad news for you, too."

Later, in his cluttered little office, Pete gestured at the pair of flintlock pistols on his desk. "See? I made the barrels of thesehere set zackly the same len'th as your pistols you carried las' year. Better leave them old ones here—I might be able to use the parts like barrels and springs and all, but they ain't gon' be one damn sight of good to you, 'thout no shells for 'em."

Foster shook his head ruefully. "Replacing them with muzzle-loaders isn't going to hurt as much, morale-wise, as is the loss of a good, reliable, multi-shot sidearm, Pete. You can't imagine how reassuring it is to have personal firepower in reserve."

Pete nodded in sympathy. "If it 'uz any damn thang I could do, Bass . . . ? But, hell, it ain't but so miny times you c'n reload even them good, plastic shotshells, you know, they gits sorta frayed on the ends. B'sides, it looked like the mo' loaded ones I sent to you, the less empty ones you sent back."

Foster shrugged. "Pete, you can't understand or appreciate the utter confusion of a battle or a skirmish or a pursuit unless you've ridden one. At such times, usually, hanging on to spent shells was the last thing on my mind, I'm afraid."

"Naw, Bass, I ain't done no fightin' here and now, but I done my own share of't in Nam, so I c'n understan'. Hell, I'd of figgered enybody tol' me to save my brass had to be plumb loco, too.

"But cases ain't the end of it, Bass. I got me a pretty good bunch of boys, metalworkin-wise, and I could prob'ly git tight with 'em and make us some sheet brass and *make* some cases, but I ain't got nuthin' near what it'd take, in know-how or in nuthin' elst, to make no primers . . . and, Bass, I got less'n a hunert an' fifty of them fuckers lef', for the shotshells, none atall what'll fit the cases for thet hawglaig." He gestured at the M1873 Colt Peacemaker holstered at Foster's side. "How miny roun's you got lef'?"

Foster unsnapped a small leather belt pouch and gingerly fingered its contents, then sighed. "Twenty-two—sixteen in the pouch and six in the cylinder."

Pete scratched at his scalp with his cracked, dirty nails, then spread his hands on the crowded desk top and looked up at Foster. "Looky here, Bass, I'll tell you, you hang onta thet superposed pistol, heanh? I got what it takes to make you up 'tween ten and 'leven dozen shells, and then that'll be all she wrote. You keep them and thet superposed till you done run out'n ammo fer the hawglaig, then you jest have thet slant o' yourn fix up your holster to take it stead'n the Colt." His shoulders rose and fell. "Two shots is better'n none."

The next morning being fair and sunny, Pete accompanied Foster and his entourage on the easy three-hour ride southwest to the estate that Harold, Archbishop of York, had turned over to Buddy Webster. He rode beside Foster, red-eyed from lack of sleep—he and Dan Smith and Nugai had labored over the restoration of the huge sword Dan had brought from the peat-cutter far into the night, long after Foster and his bodyguard and staff had returned to the camp outside the city—but bubbling over with enthusiasm at the oriental's skills at intricate metalwork.

"I tell you, Bass, Dan Smith's a master and no mistakin' it. I still wawnts him fer my hashup and I a'ready done offered him a job, but he says he wawnts to tawk some to you and a feller name of Alley fore he gives me a answer. Yeah, ol' Dan's a past-master smith, he is, but thet Newgay, manoman, he suthin' elst!"

Foster smiled. "Nugai appears to be a man of truly endless talents, a Renaissance man *par excellence*."

Pete just stared at him blankly. "Well, I dunno nuthin' bout thet last thing you said, I don' tawk nuthin' but Ainglish and Vietnamese and a lil bit of Tia Wanna Spick, see. But I do reckon thet ol' Newgay could do bout enythin' he set his min' to. You got eny ideer how hard it is to draw wire right, Bass?"

"No, Pete, I can't say that I do," he chuckled. "It's another of those things I guess I never really thought about."

"Wal, Bass, it ain't so bad fer copper or brass—all it takes is a strong man with a steady hand on the pincers, so he don't break or cut it after the firs' lenth done been drawed, and bout the same thin' goes fer sof' iron. But when it comes to steel, buddy, thet's a whole different bawlgame, I tell you! And thet's why everbody here uses leaf springs or none atall and all the grips of the swords and dirks and all is wound with brass wire."

(Nugai, face, bared torso, and arms sweat-shiny from the heat of the forge whereat Dan Smith was handling the strange tools to single out those that chanced to be to his liking for balance and weight, looked askance at the hanging-chairs, dies, and pincers, then remarked to Pete, "Ach, Meister Fairley, most primitive this iss."

"Primitive?" yelped Pete. "Ever dang master smith in the damn Ridin's done come to see it and they done swore it's the bestes' wire-drawing' setup they ever seed."

Nugai just sniffed, his flat, yellow-brown face inscrutable. "Yust so, Engelant a primitive country iss."

"Well, goldurn it, lessee you do better, *Mistuh* Newgay!" Pete had demanded, stung in both personal and racial pride.)

After wetting a dusty throat from Foster's saddle bottle of brandy water, Pete went on with the tale. "Piss-pore thing bout drawin' wire t'way it's done here'bouts, Bass, is cain't no man, no matter how strong he is, git no single drawin' longern a few inches shortern his own arm length, and thet means it's allus some filin' and smoothin' down to do, speshly after the drawer starts on a-gettin' tired.

"Wal, ol' Newgay, he done fixted thet fer good and all, I tell you! Afore I hardly knowed whutall he wuz up to, he'd done took him a piecet of roun' pole and some odds and ends and done made him a windlass-like. After he'd filed down the end of a brass rod, he had drawed hisself near three foot of wire on my ol' setup, wrappted two, three inches of it rount a iron spike he'd done hammered in his pole, then he got on one crank and he got Dan Smith on t'other one and fore you could say 'pee-turkey,' theyed done drawed thet whole, dang rod into the purtiest piecet of wire you ever set eyes to. Now ain't thet suthin', Bass?"

Without waiting for Foster to answer, Pete rushed on, saying, "Nother thang, too. While we all was a-workin' on thet sword, Newgay tolt me how I could set up the workin's of the Archbishop's grist mill for a-drawin' wire. After we was done and a-settin' in my office a-havin' us some ale, him and me got to makin' us up some drawin's on it, and you know,

Bass, I'm rightly sure it's gonna work. And the bestest part is, if I can make up *iron* gears and shafts and all, I'm dang sure thet hashup would draw *steel* wire, eny dang gauge a body wants! And I'm a-gonna do 'er, come nex' winter, too."

CHAPTER 13

One day out of York, the rain commenced, never really hard, but constant, day and night long, more than a week of it, turning roadside fields into shallow lakes and the roads themselves into treacherous quagmires pocked with seemingly bottomless pits of mud and filth, so that the leg of the journey from York to Leeds was one long travail—with both men and horses plastered with mud from top to bottom and end to end, camps cold for dearth of dry fuel, officers and other ranks shivering half sleepless through the dismal nights, while their bellies rumbled and complained at the wolfed-down chunks of hard bread, salt bacon, and sour, slimy cheese.

So woebegone and bedraggled was his command upon arrival in Leeds that Foster felt constrained to do that which he strongly disliked, though many commanders of royal forces had no such compunction and regularly exercised that right—he quartered his men upon the townsfolk and commandeered stables, barns, and vacant structures for his animals. Then, after a week of rest, recuperation, and warm food, he again took the road, anxious to reach the rendezvous near Manchester, marshal his squadrons, and proceed southeast to the siegelines still tight-drawn about London.

He had been pleased that there had been so little grumbling from the much put-upon folk of Leeds, relieved that his high-spirited command had precipitated but little trouble during their week of residence, and most gratified that Andrew Elliot had so well controlled his heterogeneous pack of border thieves and reavers that not one hanging had been necessary and only a bare half-dozen floggings.

Although it still grated hard on his twentieth-century sensibilities to order hangings and floggings, although he still threw up his last meal in the privacy of his tent or quarters each time he returned from his expected supervisory presence while a malefactor's back was publicly shredded to a soggy red pulp under the bite of the nine braided-leather tails of the whip, still his realistic nature forced him to realize that fear of rope and whip and sword and pistol was all that kept the wild, barbaric border Scots under any sort of discipline . . . or, for that matter, many of his own English and Welsh troopers.

At the rendezvous—the old royal campground, southeast of Manchester—Foster found the Midlands English contingents awaiting him, along with a few early, Northern Welsh . . . and a fresh surprise.

Baron Turlogh de Burgh's English was flawless and unaccented, and, for all his relaxed manner, flawless too was his courtesy and deportment. With his blue-black, wavy hair, beard, and mustachios and blue-gray eyes, he bore a striking resemblance to his Norman forebears who had, some four hundred years before, hacked out patents of Irish nobility with dripping swords and axes. Mid-thirtyish, de Burgh was widely traveled and fluent in at least a dozen languages.

Like another Baron—Melchoro Salazar, whose ransom had duly arrived at Whyffler Hall in full, in gold and accompanied by a letter of twenty chatty, friendly pages from the nobleman himself—whom Foster well remembered, de Burgh had interspersed and added to his education at several universities during numerous campaigns in large and small wars. Brief as had been their initial conversation, it had been enough to impress Foster that the Norman-Irishman was a seasoned soldier and a born leader, as thoroughly versed in the niceties of European warfare as he, no doubt, was in the fierce, savage, hit-and-run tactics which characterized most of the endless, internecine Irish conflicts.

When once Foster had read through King Arthur's letter of introduction, as well as the other letter, delivered clandestinely by one of the sovereign's corps of undercover messengers, he had summoned his principal lieutenants to his pavilion. After a long and sometimes heated discussion, he ordered wine and sent for de Burgh to join them.

194

Seated directly across the table from the newcomer and flanked by his officers, Foster tapped the two unfolded letters lying on the board before him.

"Baron de Burgh, one of these is familiar to you, of course, since you yourself bore it here from the royal camp on the Thames; the other came to me by way of a secret courier."

The Irishman smiled lazily. "Kings are the same, *mein Herr Markgraf*. All over the world, secrets are the very delight of the royal, I've found."

"His Highness has detailed, herein, your very commendable qualifications, as he did also in your letter of introduction. However, the King has left up to me the question of if and just how you should be employed. Whether I should allow you to summon and land your squadron, simply add you alone to my staff, or send you packing, which last was my first thought, sir."

There were some assenting grumbles from the Welsh and English officers. None of them had much liking for Irishmen of any description. But the matter had been thoroughly thrashed out; they all respected the Lord Commander of Horse and, barring some untoward happening, would hold their peace.

"You were most sagacious to not try to land your men before my arrival, Baron de Burgh, for all the lands between this place and the sea were ravaged by the Irish so-called Crusaders, not too long a time ago, and you may be assured that your welcomes would have been far from cordial."

De Burgh sighed, shaking his head of thick, shoulder-length hair. "*Mein Herr von Velegrad*, although the Crusade was preached the length and breadth of the country, the High King and most of the others ignored it, having their own fish to fry. The unfortunate circumstance to which you allude was entirely the doing of the late and lamented King Eamonn of Lagan. The venture was well underway before the High King had any inkling of it."

Foster nodded. "And he did not one damned thing to scotch it, either."

De Burgh sighed again. "*Mein Herr*, the relationships between the High King and the other kings in Ireland, it seems, have never been understood by many foreigners. Traditionally, Tara has no real control over the actions of the other kings, who mount raids and make war when and as and upon whom they please. Though right often they are likened to

King Arthur's earls and dukes or to the Emperor's herzogs, the actual situations are not the same, for Irish kings hold their lands by the force of their arms or by inheritance or both, not by way of oathings to Tara. True, the High King may suggest or request, but if he really insists upon having his way, his only means of being sure of getting it is outright war.

"And at the time of the crusading raid upon this coast, the armies of the High King were otherwise embroiled . . . in Munster, to be exact. Himself could do no more than to curse Eamonn of Lagan, at the time, though he did take other action later."

"You mentioned that this King of Lagan is dead," said Foster. "Who slew him, us or the High King?"

"Neither," answered de Burgh. "Though I am given to understand it was a near and damned chancy thing, his escape from these shores, after the defeat of his force. He got away with nought save his sword and the clothes upon his back, all else he owned he left behind—loot, gear, warchest, horse, and panoply. Ships' officers who watched the debacle on that beach through long-glasses say that Eamonn's bodyguard fell to the last man ensuring the escape of their coward king. Even Prince Emmett, who was an infamous warlock of an age beyond human reckoning and the great-great-grandfather of Eamonn, so they say, though he appeared no older than do I, was seen to fall upon that bloody strand.

"At any rate, King Eamonn's kingdom was neither large nor overly rich and neither he nor his father before him had exercised overmuch thrift, so he had been constrained to borrow heavily from certain agents of the Church in order to finance his Crusade, meaning to repay both principal and interest from the loot he had felt sure he'd bring back from England. But when return he did, it was as a royal pauper. With the bulk of even the royal jewels lost with his warchest, his only remaining assets were his lands and castle, and to these agents of the Church laid claim. But he resisted these just claims, attesting that his great-great-grandfather, Prince Emmett—who had actually affixed the royal signature and cipher to the documents—had not had his, Eamonn's, leave to do so, had been acting on his own as it were, and therefore had contracted an illegal loan. Eamonn did not deny receipt of the monies or subsequent use of them, only that he and his kingdom were responsible for repaying said monies."

De Burgh grinned. "Eamonn's defense was a patent fraud,

a fact easily seen by the judges and the High King, who unanimously found in the Church's behalf and ordered Eamonn to surrender his lands and appurtenances to his creditors, forthwith. But this the royal miscreant refused to do; rather did he close his borders, fortify his castle, and easily beat off the small token force which was all that Tara had on hand to send, at that time, the most of the army still being occupied in Munster.

"As a largish sum was involved and the Church likes not to lose even a groat, the Papal Legate in Dublin, Archbishop Mustapha of Kairouan, hired himself some Flemish mercenaries—a hundred lances, two squares of pikes, and an eight-piece siege train."

Which should have been, thought Foster, more than enough to subdue an impoverished pocket principality—five hundred cavalrymen, three thousand infantry and arquebusiers or crossbowmen, eight large bombards, and probably three or four times that number of smaller cannon, plus the inevitable catapults and spearthrowers.

"Upon the approach of the Legate and his *condotta*," continued de Burgh, "Eamonn's closed borders suddenly became open borders, wide open, his bowmen and knights and gallowglasses melting away like late snow. Whereupon the Flemings invested Castle Lagan, pitched tents, dug in and set up their bombards, with the intent of commencing the battering of the walls the next dawn.

"But they all had reckoned without the tenacity of King Eamonn, the loyalty of his retainers, and the pugnacity of the folk of Lagan. Betwixt the midnight and the dawn, Eamonn sallied forth at the head of his picked garrison, and whilst the Flemings were fighting and dying to protect their camp and trains and guns from the one, clear menace, a strong force of knights and mounted gallowglasses, supported by a host of archers and armed peasants, took them in the rear and on the flanks, looted and burned their camp, and made away with vast quantities of equipment, food, gunpowder, wheeled transport, and draft animals, and an assortment of weapons, including a dozen demiculverins and sakers. Out of the eight bombards, five were dismounted and the other three deliberately overcharged and so destroyed.

"With the dawning, the badly mauled *condotta* sagaciously withdrew from Lagan, harried at flanks and rear by King Eamonn's victorious followers. In Lagan, they left seven out of eight bombards and most of the smaller pieces as well,

197

plus everything they could not carry on their backs or behind their saddles, those who still had mounts. It is attested that Archbishop Mustapha rode into Dublin in an embroidered nightshirt and a lancer's travelcloak, all his clothing having been either looted or burned along with his pavilion."

"I would imagine," remarked Foster dryly, "that His Grace was not in the best of moods just then. So what was his next move?"

De Burgh chuckled. "He appealed to Tara, of course, but the war in Munster was continuing to drag on and Tara's only support could be simply moral. The High King sympathized, of course, but . . ." The descendant of Norman reavers spread his hands and shrugged in a typically Gallic gesture.

Foster, too, smiled. "His High Holiness felt for the put-upon cleric, but he couldn't quite reach him, eh?"

De Burgh nodded. "Well and succinctly put, *mein Herr Markgraf*. While men may put their gold on the larger dog to win, still will they cheer the shrewd nip of the smaller, through sheer admiration of courage in the face of odds. Had the High King had troops to spare in the beginning, he would have personally seen to the crushing of King Eamonn and deliverance of his lands and all to the Church, for he then was most wroth at Eamonn. But when Lagan and its king proceeded to accomplish the impossible, to defeat and throw back in utter confusion several times their numbers of seasoned, professional troops, such valor bought for them the admiration of all true Irishmen. The Archbishop, who always has been a proud, arrogant, stiff-necked, and usually difficult man, was rendered a laughingstock, the butt of many a cruel jest or jibe or scurrilous song or ribald rhyme. Such was his disgrace that he saw fit to leave Ireland within a bare month of his military debacle in Lagan."

De Burgh paused in his narrative to take a long pull from his jack of Rhenish wine, sighed gustily, then went on. "And all Ireland thought we'd seen and heard the last of that particular squabble and affairs returned to about normal.

"Eamonn had two of the captured great bombards mounted at previously vulnerable points on his castle walls and sold the other three, their carriages and accessories to King Colm XVI of Ailech—which went a long way toward covering his debts for that abortive Crusade. However, the agents of the Church, in Dublin, upon accepting the gold he proffered them, noted that when once the original loan was paid off and its interests and penalties, he still would owe the costs of hiring the Flemings, the cost of their transport, bloodprices for all mercenaries slain or wounded, the full values of all weapons and equipment burned or looted under his walls or anywhere within the lands of Lagan . . . and so on; the list was long.

"King Eamonn had as much pride as any other gentleman, and the agents of the Church were supercilious and openly insulting to him. Moreover, it is unheard of in Ireland for a defeated party to try to dictate terms of reparation, and with the sure knowledge that public opinion already weighed heavily in his favor, Eamonn made certain that attested copies of the demands of the Church were widely circulated.

"I, myself, was near to the High King when first His Majesty read his own copy and I can here state that his comments were of a most colorful nature, nor calculated to endear him to Their Holinesses of Rome, Constantinople and New Alexandria. Nor did what lately followed from Rome especially endear the Church to His Majesty of Tara.

"Which last, *mein Herr Markgraf von* Velegrad, gentlemen, is what has precipitated the dispatch of me, my officers and squadron to England; hopefully, if current negotiations betwixt Tara and King Arthur proceed as my monarch desires, my horsemen will constitute only the vanguard of Irish troops serving here in support of the just cause of England."

Foster hoped that his face did not mirror his inner dismay and confusion at the Irish nobleman's words, for King Arthur's correspondences had hinted at nothing concerning any alliance with the High King. Though, if such did come to pass, this little affray—which had begun as a purely English dynastic dispute and would have been speedily resolved, had the Church not seen fit to poke her long, greedy, meddlesome fingers into it—could bid fair to shake wide expanses of the world and singe the Church and her interests severely.

Feigning application to his jack of wine, Foster made the time to marshal his thoughts before saying, "Please elucidate, my lord Baron, what are the Roman busybodies up to now? How did they manage to alienate your sovereign?"

De Burgh again showed every strong, yellow tooth in another wolfish grin. "As *mein Herr* doubtless knows, His present Holiness of Rome is of Tunisian antecedents, as so too is Archbishop Mustapha, and they two have been close friends for many years, so that His Holiness took his Legate's humiliation at the hands of Eamonn as it were his own. Immediately after the esteemed archbishop arrived in Rome and had audience with His Holiness, a deputation was dispatched to Tara.

"The gist of their demand was that the High King should cease any other military activities, throw all his force against Lagan, turn the conquered lands over to the Church agents in Dublin, and forward King Eamonn, himself—or his head—to Rome.

"Obviously, neither His Holiness nor the deputation took overmuch trouble in studying the High King, his attitudes and reputation, for they took the worst possible tack in dealing with him—attempting to dictate his actions.

"His Majesty's reply was, however, the very soul of diplomacy. He pointed out that his own law court had found for the Church in the dispute with King Eamonn and that he had even loaned Archbishop Mustapha a few royal troops in that worthy's first attempt on Lagan, their expenses coming out of his own, royal purse, slim as it was. He added that his personal sympathies certainly lay with His Holiness and the cruelly humiliated archbishop, but that to withdraw his armies at this critical juncture from Munster would be to sacrifice all that his arms had earlier gained in the protracted struggle.

"That deputation departed, but in a bare month, another had arrived, bearing an awesome document from His Holiness's own hand. *Mein Herr,* His Holiness must be a very stupid man—or ruinously stubborn—because his folly here, in England, has taught him nothing, it would seem. The ultimatum of His Holiness stated this: Either the High King did all he had been bid by the first deputation or all Ireland would be placed under interdict and all Irish royalty and nobility excommunicated until said work was accomplished to the satisfaction of His Holiness! Also, the strong possibility of a Crusade against Ireland was implied toward the end of that horrendous letter."

"*God's death!*" swore Earl Howell ap Owain, overall commander of the North Welsh horse. "The Holy Ass must be mad. His unwarranted and officious intrusions in the strictly internal affairs of *this* realm, alone, have already cost Rome Christ knows how much gold, a thousand pipes or more of blood, and a loss of prestige that may be irretrievable. At this very minute are the royal churchmen of England and Wales loyal to King Arthur—God keep him, that is—seriously exploring the institution of a purely insular Church, possibly along the lines of that Celtic Church displaced by Rome, long ago, and the Scotch clergy are corresponding with them in a most civil manner, as too are certain bishops of the Empire, I understand."

Foster felt himself reeling. This all was news to him. If Archbishop Hal had known aught of it, he had breathed not a word in Foster's hearing.

But Earl Howell went on. "With all England and Wales in the King's hands, as it doubtless will be ere this summer be done, with King James of Scotland allied to His Majesty and with Emperor Egon giving tacit if not open support, a blind man could see that Rome is in real trouble, that the Church stands in dire need of every loyal ally.

"That His Holiness then, under such conditions, sees fit to callously alienate those folk who crouch at England's very back, so that they can but seek to make common cause with King Arthur, does but prove out His Majesty's contention that Rome, that the Church herself, is become a senile and fast-fading power in the world, depending more and evermore upon the blind faith of the credulous to enforce a bankrupt political policy in areas wherein the Church really has no business."

De Burgh inclined his dark head. "My lord Earl, the High King and his council are in complete agreement with those sentiments. When first the council heard the insulting words and threatening nature of that letter, they raged for hours. One of the 'suggestions' was to have off the head of the leader of the deputation, stuff the letter into his mouth, sew up the lips, and thus return it to Rome. And, when the word filtered out to the court, it was all that the High King could do to get those churchmen and their folk out of the capital alive and unharmed.

"My sovereign lost no time in sending copies of the letter to all the kings and greater nobles of Ireland, since all were threatened equally by the terms of it. That was last autumn. Now, for the first time in the memory of any living man, all Ireland is at peace; moreover, all the kings have journeyed to Tara and there sworn most solemn oaths to support the High King in all his ventures against the Church or any other enemies of Ireland, to place their armies at his disposal, to abide by his decisions and to submit all disputes of any nature between kingdoms to his judgment."

Foster whistled soundlessly. The stubborn independence

and pugnacious factionality of the multitudinous Irish kinglets was proverbial in this world.

"As was to be expected," said de Burgh, "the Church, throughout Ireland, began to refuse to sell priests' poudre, but the High King scotched that quickly enough. At his order, every Church poudre manufactory and warehouse was seized, as were a number of already-laden ships at various ports which were to bear available supplies of hallowed poudre out of Ireland.

"And," his dark eyes sparkled with mirth, "my sovereign also has published an edict forbidding the exportation of any more than two pounds of silver, a half pound of gold, or any gems other than personal adornments until further notice, nor is any vessel other than smaller fishing boats to leave any port without an inspection by royal officers. Emulated by all the other kings, the High King has seized all the treasures and plate of the cathedral in Tara for *safekeeping*"—the wolfish grin flitted across his face—"until his differences with Rome be resolved.

"Too, a goodly number of erstwhile churchmen have publicly announced their devotion and have given their oaths to the High King, and certain of them already are manufacturing poudre at Tara and other places."

"*Alia iacta est*," said Earl Howell slowly and solemnly. "Robbery and defiance the Church might have forgiven if not forgotten, but unhallowed powder, never. I wonder which nation will next break the chains of Rome, now your king and ours have proved those fetters so fragile, for all their seeming strength."

When first Foster clapped eyes upon de Burgh's vaunted Royal Tara Gallowglasses, as that squadron trotted into the camp near Manchester, followed by the long line of wagons and creaking wains burdened with their camp gear and supplies, he thought them to easily be the most villainous-looking crew of mounted troops he ever had seen for all their burnished armor, shining leatherware, and showy, colorful clothing and equipage.

Not one single face he spied but was scarred at least in two or three places, and the scar-faced men were armed to the very teeth, the broad-bladed, black-hafted axes cased on the off side of their horses being only a beginning. The hilts of their heavy, cursive swords jutted from under the near-side thighs, braces of big-bore wheellock pistols were holstered on pommels, and many of the men also carried pistols in their belts or in bootleg holsters; depending from the belts were shortswords and at least one dirk or dagger. Those who did not have a round targe strapped on their backs were carrying a one- or two-barreled wheellock fusil slung there. All save the officers carried either lances or wide-bladed, knife-edged hunting spears, the shafts of the weapons gruesomely decorated with fluttering fringes of human scalps.

After a fortnight in camp with them, Foster hoped he never would have to put civilized troops up against the gallowglasses. Sober, the Irishmen were irascible, hotheaded, and unfailingly pugnacious—in other words, murderous, since they never could be found without at least a shortsword and dirk; drunk, they were a nightmare personified, for at the one minute they would be singing mournful songs of lost battles and errant loves whilst tears rolled down their seamed and stubbly cheeks and, in the blinking of an eye, they would be well about the carving up of any man in sight. That Elliot's wild Scots were terrified of the gallowglasses was, in Foster's mind, testament enough to their ferocity. And, belatedly, he knew just why King Arthur had left the decision of their employment to him.

When summoned by Foster, de Burgh's attitude was nonchalant. "Ah, *mein Herr* Sebastian, the *bouchals* need but a few good fights to calm them down, an honest sack, a little rapine. True, they're a little rough round the edges, but they're good soldiers, none in all the world better, I trow."

Foster grimaced. "*I'd* better not hear of them sacking or looting or raping, my lord Baron! The only occupied city left in this realm is London, and if I know the King, there'll assuredly be no sack whenever it does fall to us. But if it's fighting your barbarians need . . ."

At his nod, two of his officers unrolled a map of the southern counties rendered upon thick parchment. Using the point of his dirk, Foster indicated the towns of Chard and Axminister and the port of Lyme. "I had thought that we had run to ground all the invaders, last year, but it would appear from reports forwarded to me that several troops-worth of Spaniards, traitorous Englishmen, and assorted foreign riffraff evaded my patrols. They're operating northeast from Chard, using it as an advance base for their predations, while being supplied from Spain via Lyme-port.

"They recently were reinforced and are now numbering something over five hundred heavy horse and perhaps twice that number of light cavalry, and they *must* be dislodged, exterminated; there cannot be harassment of the siege lines around London. Do you think a thousand or so Spaniards would be sufficient to scratch the itch of your gallowglasses, Baron de Burgh?"

CHAPTER 14

What came to be called the Battle of Bloody Rye was unquestionably the most sanguineous cavalry action in which Foster had ever had a part. Deliberately avoiding any save fleeting contact, he had swung his hard-riding squadrons well west, to the rear of the eastward-faring Spanish force, to fall upon Chard—unsuspecting and ill-prepared for any defense—like the wrath of God; with that town and the adjacent camps blazing nicely, a forced, cross-country march brought his brigade onto Axminister far sooner than any had expected them, then it was on to Lyme.

With the smoke of burning ships and buildings darkening the sky to their rear, Foster's horsemen met the vengeful Spaniards in planted fields, whose crops the traitors of Lyme would never again need.

Predictably, the enemy center was composed of the Spanish heavy-armed horse, and also predictably, they lost the battle at its very inception through charging before the wings were prepared. Foster's six little field guns, which had accompanied his lightning operations on muleback, did yeoman service that day, wreaking gory lanes through the compressed mass of horse- and man-flesh until, when he felt the time was ripe, he ordered in de Burgh and Viscount Sir Henry Powys, commanding the Royal Tara Gallowglasses and the Cumberland Heavy Dragoons, respectively. His reserve, the North Wales Dragoons and the Lincolnshire Lancers, were then moved forward to fill the center of the English line.

And, on that grim day, the Spanish hunger for infighting was fully sated. With a soul-chilling, wolflike howling and yelping that made fair to drown out all other sounds, de Burgh and his gallowglasses smote the oncoming Spaniards like a thunderclap, and a general melee ensued. Like the Spaniards themselves, the Irish seemed to prefer to make use of lance or spear, ax and sword, saving fusils, carbines, and pistols for emergencies, and the blacksmith symphony was deafening even at a distance.

Foster, lacking any really high ground from which he could view the battle at large, kept moving up and down the English line, trailed by his staff and bodyguards, which was how his personal involvement in the bloody fracas came about.

When he spied several hundred of the light cavalry composing the enemy's left wing trotting forward, certainly bound to support the embattled center, he sent the Buckingham Legion to oppose and occupy these reinforcements. However, as that farthest-right unit moved out, the Scots, to the Buckinghams' immediate left, surged forward, bearing their livid, furiously shouting commanders—Foster had been in in-saddle conference with Eliot, at the time—on the crest of their intemperate charge. Loyally, the bodyguards and staff followed the Lord Commander of Royal Horse into the murderous maelstrom of whetted steel which lay ahead.

Seeing nothing for it, Foster drew his broadsword, let the blade dangle by the knot, and unbuckled the holsters on his pommel and the one on his belt, then he barely had time to lower his visor before he was confronted with an opponent. Ducking the first swing of the opposing sword, he managed to catch three or four jarring buffets on his own blade before he and the Spaniard were swept apart.

As he traded blows with a broad, stocky, armored Spaniard astride a nimble, dancing roan mare, Foster sensed menace from his left a moment before a shrill scream of equine agony from that very quarter all but deafened him. At that same moment, his shrewd thrust penetrated between the bars of the Spanish helmet and, clapping his bridlehand to his face, the stocky man pitched from off the roan.

The mare's reins dangled loose but a split second, then they were within the grasp of an armored figure Foster recognized as Sir Ali, and seconds later the Arabian was in the mare's saddle. The dead Spaniard's mount made as if to rear once and twice snapped yellow teeth at Sir Ali's steel-sheathed legs. Then Foster was faced with another fight and had no more time to watch Sir Ali.

Furious that, lacking control, the battle might well be on the way to being lost, Foster put that fury into his sword arm and fought aggressively rather than defensively as had been his wont, spurring forward to seek out opponents when they seemed lacking in his vicinity. Abruptly, the supply of Spaniards seemed to run out and those few he saw through the visor slits were either lying dead or had their backs to him. Roaring, he spurred after a foeman and, when he saw that the Spaniard's mount was faster than Bruiser, reined up, drew his belt pistol, and shot the man out of his saddle.

He sat panting for a time, the smoking pistol hanging from the numb fingers of his suddenly world-weary arm with the fine Tara-steel swordblade—now blood-cloudy from tip to quillions, though still knife keen on every edge—dangling on the swordknot beside it. He became aware that sweat was pouring down his face, that his nose was itchily dribbling blood, and that he harbored a raging thirst. As it was comparatively quiet about him and as no fresh foeman had come into his somewhat limited view since he had pistoled that last man, he holstered the pistol, then raised his visor before wrapping Bruiser's reins about his pommel and going about the removal of the stifling helmet.

He first rinsed his mouth, spit out the pinkish fluid, then threw back his head and avidly guzzled at least half the quart of tepid brandy-water, and it was only then that he became fully aware of his surroundings. The familiar terrain of the carefully chosen battlefield was nowhere in sight! And though the smoke of burning Lyme-port still sullied the horizon to his left rear, either the fires had died far faster than was normal or the shattered town was many miles farther away. At least a half mile in front of him, five or six armored riders, with men on foot clinging to the stirrup leathers of two of them, were making over the crest of a low-crowned hill at a slow trot, but aside from these and a scattering of still forms here and there no man stood in his sight, only a wounded horse—dragging great, ballooning coils of fly-crawling guts, moving in slow, erratic circles on shaking legs and screaming piteously.

The stricken beast was within easy range, but when Foster made to shoot it, he discovered that although he could recall firing but the single recent shot, all five of his pistols were empty and thickly fouled and his hands were too tremulous to recharge one.

Very slowly, jerkily, his big stallion turned to his signal, his speckled hide streaked with foam, his proud, fearsome head hung low in utter exhaustion, his thick barrel working like a bellows as he gasped for air. Fifteen yards behind Foster, Sir Ali drooped in the saddle of his captured mare, both man and mount looking as utterly spent as Foster felt. The Arabian nobleman's unsheathed sword was as gore-clotted as was Foster's own, his armor was blood-splashed from crown to spurs, and the plume had been raggedly shorn from off his helmet. Beyond him, at irregular intervals, were six or seven men that the Markgraf of Velegrad could barely recognize as members of his bodyguard, and, beyond them, some battered gallowglasses and a sprinkling of Scots.

As the stumbling Bruiser neared, Sir Ali grinned crookedly at Foster around his knocked-askew visor, his entire lower face crusted with blood from a nose canted and obviously broken. "My Lord hides his talents well. So mild is his daily manner that I had not realized just how formidable a paladin he truly is." Slowly, the clearly injured man came erect in his saddle and brought up his hacked and crusty blade to render his commander an intricate, formal salute. "It is my great good fortune to fight behind the banner of Your Worship."

Sir Ali's solemn salute was the first, but far from the last, for every man or group that Foster passed as he allowed the leopard-stallion to pick his own slow way rendered him such evidences of honors as their conditions made possible—officers and other ranks, English, Welsh, Scots, and even the Irish. Foster had never before been accorded such, nor had he seen any other commander so treated with such awed respect by drooping, exhausted, wounded men.

Along a slow two miles of human and equine dead and wounded, wherein riderless mounts wandered here and there and the ground lay increasingly thickly littered with swords, pistols, carbines, broken lance shafts, axes, powder flasks, and other oddments of equipment, Foster made his way, trailed by Sir Ali and such others of his force as were capable of the journey. Then he came onto the true battlefield.

On that stricken field, the dead and dying lay so thickly that a man could have walked from end to end or side to side without once setting foot to the hoof-churned blood-mud beneath them. The phalanxes of circling carrion birds all but blotted out the sun, and flies rose up in a noisome black-and-metallic cloud around the intruders who disturbed their feastings.

It proved too much. Foster leaned from his saddle and retched until his emptied stomach could yield no more, but still his body heaved and shuddered with his sickness and horror. As he woodenly searched for a bit of rag to wipe his lips, the tears came, cascading, cutting lighter trails down his sweaty, soot-blackened cheeks, and his armored body shook to his wrenching sobs; nor did he care who saw or heard him, as he sat there on an all but foundered charger, with flies gorging on his bloodstained armor, trying to avoid gazing again upon that rye field whereon over two thousand men had fallen.

That night, in his headquarters in an unburned cottage on the outskirts of Lyme, Earl Howell, who had taken command of the uncommitted forces when Foster was swept into battle on the Scots' unordered charge, rendered his accounting.

In preface, the grizzled old soldier said sternly, "The Lord Commander of Horse is not expected to lead cavalry charges any more than the King is; both are too valuable to the kingdom to risk in a melee, and if the Lord Commander does elect to take a personal part in a battle, the very least he should do is to notify his principal lieutenants in advance, not just go galloping off with his bodyguard on the spur of the moment."

Then he softened his rebuke with a smile. "But your sudden charge, Bass, was what won us the day, both sooner and at much less cost than anyone had expected. Those Irish ruffians met their match in the Spanish heavy horse, they had lost their impetus, the rear ranks of the Spanish center were rapidly reforming, and the countercharge would surely have driven our center back with a heavy loss.

"Yours was a shrewd blow and delivered at just the proper place and time, Bass. Of course, your position there on the right gave you a perspective which mine own denied me, but I am here to state that you accomplished what was undoubtedly your purpose, accomplished it with a vengeance, I might add, and gallopers were dispatched to the King with news of your victory ere you and your retinue had returned to our lines."

"But what of the Spanish right?" croaked Foster hoarsely. Two jacks of honeymead trickled down his throat still had not restored his voice, for some reason.

209

The old Earl's shaggy salt-and-pepper brows raised into arches. "Why, your charge rolled the center right back into their right, of course. As I said, Bass, 'twas a well-planned and shrewdly delivered stroke. You must tell me someday just who were your mentors, in your salad days; they've produced in you a rare combination of priceless qualities.

"Who else would have thought of disassembling those little falconets and their carriages and packing the lot on mule-back? Yet they gave our squadrons a hefty edge over the damned Spaniards. I have soldiered the most of my fifty years, Bass, from England to Persia and from Suomy's frozen lakes to the heathenish jungles southwards of Timbouqtu, yet each day I serve under you I learn a new and better way to do something, militarily speaking.

"Perhaps you were not aware of it, Bass, but Earl Lucius and I were set with you by the King's express command, to watch you and to take over if the post seemed too much for your then-unknown talents as a great captain. Although you did great deeds last year, only the smaller actions of late summer and autumn saw you in an unsupervised, independent command. But this glorious day has proved you in all capacities; this is Earl Lucius' opinion as well, and our gallopers are carrying those very words and more to the King, you may be sure.

"Bass, Sir Bass, my lord Marquess of Velegrad, please allow me to humbly state that it has been, is and will ever be a signal honor to your servant, Howell ap Owain, to have the privilege of serving under so accomplished and puissant a captain, and this honor will be duly noted in the records that all my descendants may share my justifiable pride."

There were tears sparkling in the old soldier's faded blue eyes and his voice shook with sincerity. Stiffly, he fell to one knee and, taking Foster's hand, pressed it to his lips.

When Earl Howell had finally departed into the night, Foster was on the point of arising from his chair and wondering if he could make it the short distance to the bed in the adjoining tiny room when Nugai padded in, wobbling slightly, his head and a large part of his flat, yellow-brown face swathed in bandages.

"Now, dammitall, Nugai," Foster croaked angrily. "I ordered you to stay flat on your back until morning. You're certain to have at least a concussion, though the way your helmet was sundered, you're lucky as sin to be alive. If you won't think of yourself, man, at least think of me; the Lady

Krystal will never forgive me if I don't bring you back alive."

The oriental just grinned at the reprimand. *"Drei Irischer Herren* to see My Lord visch. Vill they to admitted be?"

Foster nodded tiredly. "Might as well see them now as later. Show them in, Nugai, then you get your yellow ass to bed or I'll have you put in it forcibly and tied down."

The thick-bodied little man answered only with a bob of the head and another grin, before slowly stumbling out the door, to usher in the Irish officers.

Foster could recall having either met or seen all three, but he could not just then begin to cudgel his weary brain into expelling their guttural, almost unpronounceable Gaelic names and patronymics.

After nodding welcome and raising a hand to acknowledge their salutes, he croaked, "Please make your business brief, gentlemen. Tomorrow will come early and end late, I am very weary, and, as you can tell, my voice is almost gone."

The spokesman for the trio bore his right arm in a sling and a dirty-bloody rag was lapped about his left hand. He moved with a decided limp, and the brogue-imbued English that lisped through the gap of new-lost teeth proved indecipherable unless Foster devoted to the speaker his undivided attention.

"M'lord Markgraf, thith delegathion be reprethenting every living offither and axeman o' Thquadron o' Royal Tara Gallowglaththeth. Pained it wath to poor Baron de Burgh that he could nae lead uth in thith, but wi' hith kneecap thmathed by a domned Thpanither'th mathe, he cannae e'en rithe frae hith blanketth, but he bid uth thpeak in hith name ath well.

"Ath nane o' uth had e'er theen m'lord thwing thteel, we a' had thought him but anither, cauld-bred Thaththenach, but nae more. M'Lord, if ath the domned, bludey churgeonth thay, Baron de Burgh can ne'er agin lead intae battle, t' thquadron would hae y'r worthip for oor chief. Where'er m'lord may go, whome'er he may war on, t'will be our ane rare honor tae ride at hith back."

"But . . . but aren't you all pledged to the service of the High King?" Foster asked.

"Nae." the spokesman shook his head, but gently, for it hurt. "Nae, m'lord. Pledged we a' were tae Baron de Burgh, anely he wath pledged tae Tara." Then, his voice dropping to conspiratorial tones and his hazel eyes gleaming, he added, "An' it'th I be thinkin' a far better king would m'lord be makin' than mony who thtyle themthelveth thuch in Ireland.

When onthe they thaw m'lord fight at t' head o' hith gallowglaththeth, it's ivery mon o' any mettle would be after followin' y'r worthipth banner."

Foster could not resist a chuckle. "Sir Liam, my lands lie far to the east, in the Carpathian Mountains; I harbor no designs on any Irish kingdom."

The wounded knight nodded. "Then it'th eathward we'll be ridin' . . . an' m'lord will hae uth."

"I am pledged to King Arthur, Sir Liam, until his kingdom be cleansed of his enemies within, and unthreatened from oversea. Only then could I think of seeking my Empire lands."

"Och, aye, m'lord," the Irishman nodded, smiling jaggedly, "nae doot will gi' uth time tae thee if Baron de Burgh e'er can lead agin, ath well ath tae thend for more gude men frae oot o' Ireland tae fill thothe thaddleth emptied thith day."

CHAPTER 15

The royal camp under the walls of besieged London was every bit as noisome and stinking as Foster had imagined it would be; not even the incenses and perfumes with which the interiors of the King's pavilion rooms had been infused could mask the intruding reeks of ordure and corruption from the camp streets outside. Fat flies swarmed everywhere, pigs rooted in the rubbish heaps and wallowed in the fecal-stinking mud, and Foster once more thanked his stars that he had had the foresight to send his seriously wounded either to their homes or to the cavalry-camp at Manchester to recover, for precious few of them would have lived long in this royal pesthole.

He himself had been afforded no opportunity to return to Manchester, the King's summons having reached him a bare week after the battle in the ryefields, while still the survivors of his brigade were being reorganized after burying the plundered corpses of their enemies, rounding up stray warhorses and the like.

The captain of the resplendent horseguards sent to escort him back to the royal siege camp proved to be none other than that officer of heavy horse who had proved so good a friend on that long-ago day when Foster and Webster had had their near-fatal tiff with William Collier. Captain Sir Richard Cromwell looked no older than Foster recalled him, though his face showed a couple of unremembered scars.

After Cromwell had formally delivered the summons, he

cheerfully accepted Foster's invitation to share some of the bounty of food and wine provided by the Spanish.

Under the direction of Sir Ali, Nugai and his new gallowglass assistant had butchered and dressed a kid, stuffed it with a mixture of walnuts, almonds, spices, and its own chopped lights, then roasted it to crackly perfection on a spit over coals, liberally basting it with oil and wine. Preceded by Sir Ali—who had appointed himself majordomo of Foster's field establishment—Nugai and the hulking Samhradh Monaghan bore in the huge platters containing the kid and a quartet of large stuffed and roasted fowls, while trooper-servitors followed behind with crusty loaves of fresh-baked bread, cheeses, bowls heaped high with exotic fruits, spiced bean pasties, sweetmeats, and confections.

Sir Richard appeared vastly impressed by the lavish board and even more so by the score of rare vintages offered in accompaniment. "Winter in the King's camp was hard, Lord Forster," he admitted. "Almost as hard for us under the walls, I trow, as for those within them, with both food and fuel at a premium and fodder for our beasts all but nonexistent. Too, there was much illness—camp fever, rheums, fluxes and the like, such as always afflict sieglines. This will be the first decent meal I've set tooth to since Christmas, when our good Lord Admiral drove off the escorts of a Papal fleet and captured the victualing vessels intended to succor London."

Then the stocky captain laughed and slapped his thigh. "On the day after the feast, King Arthur had twoscore earthen pots of dung catapulted over the city walls, noting that he was certain his sister-in-law would not mind if hungry men passed her provisions through their bowels before sending them on to her. The camps chuckled for weeks over that rare jest!"

"Speaking of the Lord Admiral," Foster injected, "I have a present for him in the form of three fine Spanish caravels, of which we shortly shall enjoy part of the cargos. He needs but to send crews to man them, since their previous complements are either dead or occupying a prisoner pen down near the waterfront."

Cromwell stopped with a joint of kid halfway to his mouth and he fixed Foster with widened, ice-blue eyes. "Now, dammit, Lord Forster, I'll be first to grant you the new model Alexander, but just how does a brigade of horse go about naval operations?"

It had been absurdly simple, to Foster's way of thinking.

Three days after the battle, the morning sun had glinted upon the three suits of sail beating up from the south and, later that morning, the Spanish victualers had sailed into the harbor, bold as brass. The plan had actually been hatched by Sir Ali and Sir Ruaidhri de Lacey, both of whom had had wide-ranging careers as mercenaries and both of whom spoke flawless Spanish.

Rowed out to the flagship of the minuscule convoy, the two knights had spoken at length of the disastrous fire that had leveled much of Lyme, engulfing even the wharves, the ships tied to them, and eke the beached smaller craft and fishing boats—that their own rowboat had been charred here and there bore out their tale. Then they had launched into a story concerning the capture by the Spanish force of a London-bound English siege train, including a score or more of huge, infinitely precious bombards, which guns would be entrusted to the ship captains for transport to and sale in Spain, if only a way might be contrived to get such large, heavy, and bulky monsters on board the ships. Naturally, as cavalrymen, none of the land force knew anything of such labor.

Just as naturally, as the two knights had well known in advance, the ship captains and their crews were old hands at loading and off-loading all manner of bulky and weighty objects, and, fully appreciating the immense value of the booty, their shrewd minds were no doubt hard at work calculating the very maximum percentage of the sale prices they could hope to squeeze out for their services, even as they smilingly assured the two emissaries that the task could not only be accomplished but would be a great honor to them.

When the last boatload of supplies had been piled upon the beach, the two larger ships had eased up to either side of a hastily repaired wharf. The third, smaller ship rolled at anchor, all save two of its crew members having been sent to beef up the working parties of the two larger vessels. Just landward of the wharf, the muzzles of three cannon gaped seaward—not bombards, any of them, but large enough, nonetheless; each a full cannon, capable of throwing a ball of at least a half-hundredweight . . . or its equivalent.

And that equivalent was just what the unsuspecting seamen received, to their horror, but not until the ships were firmly tied up and decks and wharf thick with men rigging heavy tackle under the supervision of officers and mates. Then, suddenly, all three of the waiting cannon roared, at pointblank range, like monstrous puntguns at a flock of unsuspecting

215

waterfowl. Packed nearly to the muzzles with canister and langrage—the former bore-sized cylinders of thin wood filled with arquebus balls and the latter bags packed with odds and ends of iron, brass, and lead—the effect of the close-range volley upon the ships' companies was terrible. So shocked and devastated were the stumbling survivors that most surrendered meekly to the troopers and gallowglasses who rushed them with pistols, axes, and broadswords at the ready.

Sir Richard Cromwell had sent gallopers off for both the royal camp and the fleet headquarters base on the Isle of Sheppey with news of the fantastic victory of cavalry over ships, and by the time he, his charge, and their respective retinues had made the long, muddy journey ahorse, the three newest royal prizes were already riding at anchor in the waters of the Thames, just downstream of the siegelines.

But King Arthur was not to be found in his pavilion and Sir Richard's party was redirected to Greenwich, and so great was Foster's relief at being able to quit so soon the nauseating stenches and generally pestilent surroundings of the siege camp that he could not put any real feeling into his part of the chorus of curses that the road-wearied men trailed after them on this last and unexpected leg of the journey.

The officer of the day for the pavilion guards had been summoned from a game of draughts and was curt to the point of surliness, but that spry, ancient little factotum Sir Corwin Shirley had been his usual effusive self. Foster had not seen the wrinkled but highly energetic little man since the day of William Collier's downfall, but for all the brevity of that one meeting, Sir Corwin recognized him at once.

"Oh, my, yes," he had chirped, wringing his blue-veined hands, smiling and bobbing a bow all at once, all the while shifting from one foot to another as if performing a dance. "I do believe that it's the Lord Commander of the Royal Horse, Sir Sebastian Forster. Oh, yes, young man, His Majesty is most anxious to see you, most anxious, indeed.

"But you do all things so fast, Sir Sebastian, you were not expected for the best part of another week, no, and His Majesty is at Greenwich, yes. There's so much sickness in the camps, yes, and His Majesty has need to entertain some high-ranking gentlemen from Scotland, Ireland, Burgundy, and the Empire. They all went down this morning on one of those fine Spanish ships, you know, yes.

"My nephew, young Sir Paul Bigod, is pleased as punch, yes indeed. Says the ships are well-found, most manageable, yes, and with all those fine, long-barreled bronze guns, yes. And His Majesty would not but sail down to Greenwich on one of them, yes, His Majesty and His Grace of York and the Reichsherzog and all the foreign gentlemen, yes. And His Majesty strutting and crowing that nowhere else in the wide world could any of them sail on a ship prized by a brigade of horse, yes.

"His Majesty is most pleased with you, just now, Sir Sebastian, yes indeed. My goodness gracious, yes; why this morning, I think me he'd have gifted you half his kingdom, young sir!"

Then a frown had further wrinkled the oldster's seamed countenance. "But I must send a messenger ahead of your party, yes, indeed I must, for the castle there is not all that large, no. And with all the fine, foreign gentlemen and their folk and their retinues and with His Majesty and all his nobles, yes. And His Majesty would assuredly be most wroth were his greatly esteemed Lord Commander of the Royal Horse obliged to camp out in some muddy field, yes, or bide in a stable.

"So, Sir Richard, escort you the Lord Commander down to Greenwich but, please, do not hurry too fast. I doubt me the King will have time to see Sir Sebastian today or even tomorrow, anyway, no."

Nor was old Sir Corwin's estimate of the royal schedule too far off, Foster discovered. It was a good two hours after sunset of his second night at Greenwich before a brace of Yeomen of the Guard—brave in their scarlet finery, but handling their polearms in a very professional manner—arrived to escort him to his initial audience with King Arthur.

The cramped little suite that had been found for him was not only smaller than his field pavilion, but draftier, and with room only for himself, Sir Ali, and Nugai. He really envied the remainder of his and Sir Richard's party their tents in the park surrounding the castle.

Formal as had been his summons, there was nothing formal about his greeting in what seemed a small, private dining chamber. With the King were many familiar faces—Reichsherzog Wolfgang, Harold, Archbishop of York, Sir Francis Whyffler, new-made Duke of Northumberland, Parlan Stewart, Duke of Lennox, and Sir Paul Bigod, Lord Admiral of King Arthur's small but pugnacious war fleet.

Arthur allowed only the most perfunctory of courtesies from Foster before waving him to a chair at the table. When

217

his ale jack was filled and the usual toast to their imminent victory had been downed, the King got directly to the point.

"Sir Sebastian, Bass Foster, Hal, here, has but recently told me many things, things which I confess I found hard to credit, but I cannot doubt his word, so I can but believe. Nonetheless, I still also believe that some guardian angel must have had a hand in guiding you and Master Fairley to me and to England in our time of need, for which I nightly thank the good God on high.

"The brilliant innovations wrought by Fairley in multi-shooting arquebuses, cannon, stronger gunpowder, transport, vehicles, and this new, simple, inexpensive ignition system have rendered my army well-nigh invincible. And he will soon be rewarded as well as lies within my power."

It took Foster a moment to realize that Arthur had used his actual name, had not called him "Forster" as on previous occasions.

"Much as I love my dear cousins, Emperor Egon and Wolf, here, fool I'd be to allow such a jewel as you've proven yourself to be to slip through my fingers and go off to serve the Empire, and, as Hal can tell you, we Tudors are anything but fools."

He grinned at the Archbishop, who smiled and nodded, between sips of wine.

"Now, I had meant to appoint you Warden of the Scottish Marches this day, for if any man does or can, you have and do hold the respect of our northern neighbors, both as a warrior of some note, a captain, and a man of honor, and that office still may come to you in future years, are we granted true peace.

"But as matters now stand, that tiresome, meddlesome man who pleases to style himself Pope of the West is unlikely to allow England any long term of true peace, not whilst I rule in place of that half Moor-half Dago bitch, Angela—some pure, saintly angel, eh, gentlemen? 'Tis said that her current light o' love is some black, heathenish Ghanaian mercenary. Which, I suppose, demonstrates the utter depths of that pagan bastard's depravity, for all know that her own depravity needs no proof."

Red-faced with anger, breathing heavily, the monarch stood for a brief moment, silent but for the loud pops of his crackling knuckles, then he raised his wine to his lips and sipped several times. When he replaced it upon the table, his calm had returned.

"Therefore, my good Sir Sebastian, in these parlous times, I may well need my Lord Commander of Horse nearer to my capital than the Scottish border, and I have decided to not wait for the surrender of London to see you invested in that office I have chosen for you, lest Cousin Wolf find a way to smuggle you out of the realm.

"Although the actual, formal, necessarily public investiture will not take place until tomorrow morn, out in the audience-chamber, there"— Arthur waved a beringed but strong and callused hand vaguely in the direction of a tapestried wall—"I am urged by Hal and others to apprise you of what will take place, that you not be—in your well-known modesty—dumbstruck and require embarrassing prompting to fulfill your part of the ceremony.

"Since I still mean to have you as March Warden—if we can come to a reasonable agreement with Rome; and such will never be until the present Pope's bloated corpse in underground and his black soul has gone to his master, Satan— you'll receive of me Whyffler Hall and its environs as a barony; it and the County of Rutland you'll be able to pass on to your son, along with the title of earl. But Rutland still is a bit farther away than I'd like, so—although neither title nor lands will be hereditary, they'll return to the Crown upon your demise, Sir Sebastian—you'll also be receiving Norfolk as a duchy."

In a state of shock, Foster could never have found his way back to his quarters without the guidance of the brace of Yeomen of the Guard. Arrived before the door to his suite, he simply stood dumbly until one of the big men opened that portal and gently nudged him in, where Nugai and Sir Ali took over, seating him and pressing a jack of brandied wine into his hands.

Nugai's flat face showed no emotion, as usual, but Sir Ali's more mobile features and more emotional nature expressed a mixture of anger and pity.

"My lord Bass," he began, "the fickle nature and disgratitude of monarchs is proverbial, but—and please believe me; I know whereof I speak—there he many another kingdom than England and many another king to serve than Arthur. I am your man, as is Nugai, nor should you forget those fearsome Irishmen, they would gladly follow you to the very Gates of Gehenna and back and will make you a fine *condotta*. You are a born leader of men, a gifted cavalry commander and one of the personally bravest men beside whom it ever has been my honor to swing sword.

"Now if you are in danger of close arrest, I can fetch some of our men from the camp and—"

He broke off when Foster began to laugh, uncontrollably, the full jack of liquor slipping from his fingers unnoticed, finally, tears of mirth and release rolling down his cheeks. Before he had told the two men more than half the tale, there was a sharp rapping upon the door, then it was opened to reveal two different pikemen, six or seven servingmen who immediately invaded the suite and began to gather up the personal effects of its occupants, and the same upper-servant type who had originally shuffled Foster brusquely into these tiny, gloomy rooms.

Bowing far lower than it seemed his bulging belly should allow, the man almost tearfully begged "Your esteemed lordship's" pardon for the "terrible misunderstanding" which had seen him and his gentlemen assigned to such poor quarters.

"News travels fast hereabouts," remarked Sir Ali wryly. Nugai said nothing, but kept his keen eyes upon the servingmen, lest one try to steal something, scowling fiercely and fingering the worn hilt of his kindjal. The men appeared duly impressed, impressed to the point of near terror.

CHAPTER 16

Dear Krys,

Please sit down before you read any further. I know that you've hardly gotten used to the title Markgrafin, but you're going to have to start getting used to another, honey: Duchess. I'm still Markgrafin von Velegrad, Wolf has made that clear, but Arthur has also made me Duke of Norfolk, Earl of Rutland, and Baron of that portion of the central marches that contains Whyffler Hall. Since the siege drags on and there is little of anything for my cavalry to do, I took a few weeks to ride up to Norwich and then over to Rutland, and of the two, I think you'll like Rutland best. Therefore, start packing and, in a few weeks, I'll send up Nugai and a couple of troops of my personal squadron to escort you and Little Joe and anyone else you want to bring down to your new home.

Don't be afraid of these Irishmen, Krys. They look downright Satanic and fight like the legions of hell, but they're intensely loyal to me, swear that that loyalty extends to any member of my family, and while they'll fight at the drop of a hat, drink anything they can lay hands to, cheerfully rape or murder, steal, plunder, and burn, they never lie.

No matter how I rack my poor brain, I cannot think what I've done to deserve all these rewards. For all his faults, Bill Collier really did much more for Arthur and England than have I—he was the true architect of Arthur's earliest victories, you know, with his deep knowledge of strategy, formation of the Royal Army into manageable units, standardization of ranks and instruction in the proper use of artillery.

Pete Fairley's contributions will soon reach to every corner of the kingdom, if not the world. His latest martial innovation is a battery of six thirty-pounder breech-loading rifled cannon. Breech-loading cannon are nothing new here, of course—the port-pieces, sling-pieces and murderer-pieces are common on ships and fortifications, but they are damned near as dangerous to men behind as to the men in front, much of the time. Pete's cannon are, however, not only much heavier than usual breechloaders, they are safer to fire, lighter in weight than any other gun of their bore, have a greater range than anything anyone here has ever seen, and have unbelievable penetrating power, thanks of course to pointed, cylindrical shells and rifling. Three of them, served by Fairley-trained crews, are on three of our ships on Fairley-designed and -installed swivel mounts that allow them to be used as chasers in pursuit or as a most effective addition to the broadside battery in close actions. The King has been amusing himself with the other three guns, firing time-fused, explosive shells over London's walls into various parts of the city as a terror tactic, and pleased as punch at the extreme range and close accuracy of the new cannon.

As I mentioned in my last letter, Webster too has done tremendous things with his stock-breeding enterprises on one of Hal's estates. At Hal's request, Wolf had several aurochs calves shipped in from Bohemia, Slovakia, or Poland—I still cannot get the maps of this world's Europe straight in my mind—and Buddy is trying to breed so as to combine the size, strength, and vitality of the wild ox with the tractability and milk-producing qualities of the various domestic breeds; furthermore, he seems to be having a fair measure of success, for when I was at the estate with Pete in the spring, Buddy had a pair of gigantic—almost six feet at the withers!—young half-aurochs bulls that trailed him about like hounds and would even have followed him into the hall, if he'd let them.

Now he is talking about domesticating deer, since they can thrive in areas wherein even a goat would starve to death. King James of Scotland seems very interested in Buddy's experiments and has sent down an observer, Sir Lachlan Mac-Queen, with whom Buddy gets along famously, or so Pete says.

I, on the other hand, have done nothing for this world except kill good men and horses, give the orders that caused the deaths or maimings or disfigurements of God knows how many more, burn manors and villages, and condone—if not actually performed—rape, torture, murder, and pillage. And I can't help but feel that I am unjustly enjoying the honors and rewards that should rightly go to men whose deeds are and have been more worthwhile than have been those of the red-handed professional killer I am become.

This letter will come to you by the hand of Sir Ali ibn Hossain, a younger-son mercenary type who seems tickled to death to style himself "Herald to His Grace, Sir Sebastian, Duke of Norfolk, Earl of Rutland, Markgraf von Velegrad, Baron of Strathtyne, Knight of the Garter, and Noble Fellow of the Order of the Red Eagle." I would have sent Nugai, but Sir Ali can perform a mission for me that Nugai cannot: he will knight Geoff Musgrave in my name, and it will be well that those two get to know each other, as I mean to take Sir Ali's oaths of fealty for Heron Hall and its lands—since poor Squire Heron's heirs died with him in defense of his hall from King Alexander's army and those lands are too rich to leave long fallow.

You see, I'm even beginning to think like a feudal lord . . . which is, I suppose, just as well, since Hal has assured me that there exists no possible way for me or any of us to reverse the process, to get back to our own time and world.

I love you, Krys. I love Little Joe, the son I thought I'd never have, would never have had on that other world. I miss you both and I pray for winter to hurry with all the fervor that Arthur prays for the capitulation of London with.

For all the fact that they're my enemies, I cannot but pity the poor folk inside that doomed city. The refugees who have managed to escape for one reason or another paint a grim picture—not one horse, mule, ass, cow, or goat is left within London, and even rats are becoming rare as gold hen's teeth, their supplies of both gunpowder and fuel are scant, and . . .

Well, Krys, Sir Ali is ready to leave for the north and I have still to sign this and some other letters, sand them, seal them, and pack them in a waterproof tube. Hug Little Joe for me and be ready to move to Rutland as soon as the gallowglasses arrive to escort you.

I do hate to ask you to leave the creature comforts of my little house, honey, but Fort Whyffler is just situated too far north for me to establish it as my principal seat.

All my love always,
Bass

Krystal Kent Foster refolded the letter and looked again at the elaborate beribboned seal of dark-blue wax. Her husband had obviously wasted no time in acquiring a coat of arms, for the largest blob of wax bore the deep imprint of those arms, but the detail was too tiny for her to make it out in the poor, fading light of the westering sun.

She had been living in Whyffler Hall for most of the summer. The central-air-conditioning unit in Bass's house had worked in a fair manner for about a week after she first turned it on, but then had begun to blow only hot air. Her limited knowledge of the mechanics of the unit led her to believe that quite probably the device needed a fresh injection of coolant gas—neon or xeon or freon or some such name. She had no idea of whether or not Bass had any stored in his workshop and would not know how to put it in if she could find any. Without air conditioning, the trilevel was an oven, stifling from top to bottom.

Whyffler Hall, on the other hand, with its high ceilings behind thick stone walls, was divinely cool. Gradually, over a couple of weeks, Krystal moved most of the contents of Bass' house into the hall, returning to the trilevel only to use the tub or shower.

She judged Sir Ali to be somewhere around twenty-five. He was dark of hair and eyes, with deep-olive coloring, and handsome despite the numerous scars on his face and the jutting beak of a nose that seemed almost too large for the head on which it was mounted; urbane, charming, and very courtly of manner, the Arab moved with the grace of a leopard.

He had arrived at Whyffler Hall a bit before noon, by way of the York Road, at the head of the most villainous-looking pack of mounted cutthroats Krystal had ever seen. Apparently Lieutenant Smythe, who commanded the small royal garrison still manning the Fort Whyffler defenses, had been similarly impressed, since the party had been trailed at a discreet distance by a dozen pikemen and half that number of men armed with the seven-shot arquebuses, their matches smoking.

"Saints preserve us a'," old Geoffrey Musgrave had muttered, as he had stood beside but a little behind her on the broad veranda. "I c'd swear those pack o' twa-legged wolves be o' t' domned Irish breed, none save t' Irish gallowglasses bear an ax and *twa* swords, tae boot. W' sich as them aboot, m'lady, t'would be well tae arm t' serving men and bury t' plate."

But the troopers at the Arabian knight's back had proven themselves, if not exactly models of civilized decorum, at least manageable.

When Sir Ali had made his formal obeisance and had been ushered into the hall, he had announced to all those assembled, "I, Sir Ali ibn Hossain, appear here in my function as herald to our most puissant lord, Sebastian Foster, Duke of Norfolk, Markgraf von Velegrad, Earl of Rutland, Baron of Strathtyne, Knight of the Garter, Noble Fellow of the Red Eagle of Brandenburg, Lord Commander of the Royal Horse of England, and good and faithful servant of His Majesty Arthur III, God bless and preserve him."

He had gone on, at great length and in the same, stilted manner, to announce that Sir Francis Whyffler, now Duke of Northumberland, had ceded his ancestral lands to the Crown, at Arthur's personal request; that Bass Foster had received those same lands in feoff from Arthur in a formal ceremony at Greenwich Castle and so he was, consequently, now their overlord.

"However, our lord, burdened as he is with his military duties, attendance upon our King and the affairs of his duchy and earldom, will likely be unable to return to this barony for some time; therefore, I am to place its affairs in the charge of his lady-wife, Her Grace the Duchess of Norfolk, and the present intendant, Captain Geoffrey Musgrave.

"Captain Musgrave, please step forward."

Then, in a simple and businesslike manner, the Arabian had knighted a bemused Geoff Musgrave in Bass' name, had himself knelt to buckle the gilded prick spurs onto the old reaver's scuffed jackboots. Then, still in Bass' name, Sir Ali had presented the new knight with a fine Spanish sword, a dagger of the reknowned Tara steel, and a brace of the new flintlock horsepistols, as well as a thick, wax-sealed letter from Duke Sebastian.

Due to all the excitement and ceremony, dinner had not been served until after two in the afternoon. Throughout the long meal, the normally voluble Sir Geoffrey Musgrave had said hardly a word, and from time to time Krystal had noticed him fingering the heavy, golden thumbring and the golden pendant of his office as a duke's intendant on its gilded chain as if he expected them to imminently disappear in a wisp of smoke. Krystal supposed that the items had been within the folds of the letter or inside the pistol case.

Finally, Krystal had said, "Sir Geoffrey, Geoff, you can't

live on ale alone; eat something. The good Master Millán is the finest parting gift that the Archbishop could have given us; he is an outstanding chef and has really done his usual genius on these fine pork-and-herb pasties. Try one."

A pained expression came over the grizzled warrior's countenance. "Och, y'r ladyship, His Grace, y'r noble husband, Duke Bass . . . er, Sebastian, meant well and a' I ken me, but he should nae ha' done sich. Och, aye, the Musgraves—semets o' 'em—beo' the auld nobility, but I be but a common wight, y' ken? I be a younger son, younger grandson, and eke younger great-grandson and precious little noble blude flows in me. I be but a plain, bluff sojer, no true knicht, nor wi' His Grace's generosity or the noble Sir Ali's buffet make o' me elst."

Krystal shook her head. "What's all that got to do with the price of bagels, Geoff?"

"My lady . . . ?"

She shoved a brass platter toward him. "Have some of the goose, Geoff. Common or noble, you need food."

The scarred and wrinkled face screwed up and Sir Geoffrey Musgrave hung his head and said in a low voice. "I . . . fear . . . I fear to disgust my lady. I be a base, common mon and I hae not the high-table skills and manners and a' . . ."

Sir Ali leaned back in his armchair and roared with laughter then. Leaning forward and speaking around Krystal, he said, "You'll never learn them, Sir Geoffrey, by starving yourself to death. Not that they be all that important to any save soft pampered courtiers, anyway. Draw your belt knife and have at that goose, I'll tell you all you need to know.

"Now, firstly, when dining at high table, a gentleman should use but his right thumb and two fingers to convey his victuals to his mouth, never allowing grease or sauces to come into contact with his palm." Grinning, he displayed a hand greasy to the wrist.

"Secondly, he should be careful to never spit back small bones or gristle into a common dish."

"I'd ne'er do sich, high table or low, my lord!" said Musgrave indignantly.

"You see," nodded Sir Ali, with mock seriousness, "you're more inherently noble than you thought. And I am not your lord, Sir Geoffrey, not any longer. You may address me as Sir Ali or preferably, as just Ali, since I'd be your friend.

"But, back to the lesson. You may throw table offal beneath the table only if your host does so first, and if sharing a cup with a dining partner, be certain that your beard and moustachios be free of crumbs before drinking; but beware, never wipe your mouth and beard with your sleeve or the back of your hand." In illustration, Sir Ali did just that, then added, parenthetically, "Although if a host is not sufficiently modern and civilized to have provided a *footah* or *panolino*"—he touched the large square of cloth tied around his neck and covering his front—"or if the improvident guest has not brought one with him, I have often wondered just how he is expected to remove stains from lips and face without making use of Nature's *footah*.

"You see, Geoffrey, high-table manners are, I feel, the invention of those who take but little joy in their victuals and so would selfishly make the act of eating as difficult as possible for those who do."

CHAPTER 17

On the morning after Sir Ali's arrival, the two knights rode out with their respective retinues—Sir Ali's gallowglasses and Sir Geoffrey's lancers—to formally post and announce the change of overlords to the villages, hamlets, and the small halls and yeoman farms to the barony. Krystal, once she had broken her fast, seen to Little Joe, performed the most immediate duties of a chatelaine, and informed Master Millán, the chef, that the day's meal would be even later than on the previous day, since the two knights could not be expected back much before sunset, collected her three serving women and left the hall to walk down through the formal garden fronting it to the brick-and-frame trilevel house squatting incongruously among the yews and boxwoods. If she did not have a hot bath at least every third day she felt so grubby that she could not stand herself.

When the house had been so mysteriously transported into this world, Bass had not been the only living creature to come with it. His three house cats, four or five flying squirrels, and two or three mice had come along for the ride. One of the cats had been sterile, but the other two had lost no time in joyously fighting and fraternizing with the half-wild stable and barn cats of the hall, so that now the environs of Whyffler Hall abounded with all manner of feline mixtures and mutations, nor had the flying squirrels had any apparent qualms about bringing forth fresh generations, finding the formal gardens and the small park within the perimeter walls much to their liking.

When she made her way through the empty, echoing house to the large bath off the master bedroom, it was to discover that a young queen had, sometime within the last two days, decided to produce her litter in the bathtub and was currently in the full throes of labor—her legs twitching, her long, pink tongue drooping out from between her fangs as she panted in agony.

With a sigh, Krystal gave up the idea of a long, slow, leisurely tub bath and turned instead to the tiled shower stall. As she dropped her robe and stepped under the hot spray, she could hear the three serving women—Trina, Meg, and Bella—giggling and jabbering in their north-country patois as they added ice cubes from the refrigerator to a big pewter ewer of honey mead brought from the hall and then placed it in the unit to chill more thoroughly. Usually while the mead chilled the women would troop down to the bathroom on the lower level and take turns under the shower, which they never failed to find fascinating.

While she was showering, Krystal decided to shampoo as well, and as she fumbled blindly on the shelf just outside the shower stall, the lights flickered briefly, then went out.

"Oh, dammit," she breathed to herself, trying to think of where there still might be an unneeded bulb. The spares were long since used up and another winter here would see any occupants of this house existing by light of lamps or candles.

Finally out of the shower, she toweled her long hair briefly, then formed of the towel a turban and shrugged into her terry-cloth robe, slipped her feet into the soft, beautifully decorated pair of "shoon" that the dextrous Bella had crafted for her mistress from the hide of a fallow doe taken during the great Christmas hunt of last winter. Then she checked on the cat in the bathtub.

While she had showered, two tiny kittens had been born and cleaned, and now were both nursing, their minuscule forepaws treading at the straining belly of their mother. Having cleaned her offspring, bitten through the umbilicals, and eaten the afterbirths, consumption of which stimulated her lactation, the brownish tabby now was in a third bout of labor.

Kneeling by the tub, Krystal gently stroked the head and back of the queen. "Good girl. That's a good little girl. And your kittens are just as beautiful as you are." Then, standing, she called, "Meg, Bella, is the mead cold yet?"

When she received no answer, she opened the door to the master bedroom and repeated the question, raising her voice a bit louder. Still not being answered, she shook her head and proceeded out into the third-level hallway. Her mouth open to shout once more, she reeled instead against the doorframe, her eyes wide in horror.

The living room and entrance foyer on the second level were filled to within a foot or less of the very ceiling with muddy brown water! Capped with grayish-yellow scum, the water was lapping perceptibly higher on the stairs; even in the brief moment she watched, yet another tread went under the dirty, opaque water, leaving only two steps between her and the water.

Snapping out of her momentary paralysis, Krystal stepped across the hallway and opened the door to what had been Bass' office, strode across the bare room, and raised the venetian blind, then the window. Only then could she clearly hear the terrified screaming of her maidservants.

The three women, two of them stark naked, their wet hair flopping about their backs and shoulders, were racing through the formal garden and up toward the front of the hall, screaming their lungs out the while. Already, their wailings had attracted the attention of some of the hall servants and a couple of off-duty artillerymen from the remaining garrison, but not one of these was making any move to meet the running women; rather did they, one and all, seem to be staring down at the trilevel house.

Abruptly, the sun-dappled hall facade, garden, running women, gawking servants, and soldiers, everything, seemed to waver before Krystal's eyes, to go out of focus. She blinked, hard, once or twice, and when she again opened her eyes, the scene that lay before them set her heart to pounding in sudden terror.

Gone was Whyffler Hall and all its grounds; before her lay a seemingly endless expanse of tossing, swirling, gray-brown water, rushing from her left to her right, its surface dotted with uprooted trees and other assorted flotsam, including the roof of what had been a smallish house or largish shed. Then, in another eyeblink, there again was Whyffler Hall, up at the head of the garden, with the group on the stairs grown by a dozen or more, their shouts and shrieks drowning out those of her maidservants.

"Oh, my dear, sweet God," she thought, recalling suddenly Bass' recountals of his last few hours in this house before he awakened here, in this world. "The . . . the house is going back! Back to . . . to that *other* world, to the same time, the same place, in the middle of a *flood!*"

Turning from the window, Krystal went out into the hall. The stairs and the hardwood floors below were visible and dry with no trace of water anywhere. But before she was half down the steps, the cold, filthy water again was covering them, swirling about her legs at mid-thigh level. Whimpering, she retreated back to the upper hallway.

After a moment or two of blind, sobbing terror, she pulled herself together. She must get out of the house before it ceased to flicker back and forth between worlds/times and returned to a watery doom in the world it had once escaped. But how? In the moments when it was in that other world, the house was her only safe abode, although the creakings and groanings as it shifted on its foundation gave ample warning that it would soon collapse, be ripped apart by the surging waters.

"Think, Krystal, *think!*" That was what her papa used to say; he had been the only member of her family who ever had addressed her by her self-chosen name, rather than by the name Rebecca, which appeared on her birth certificate. "You are a woman, yes, Krystal, but nowhere I know does any law say that a woman must not use the brain God gave her. Emotions are fine, as long as you don't let them rule you. You have a fine mind, girl, use it."

All right then, Papa, she thought. The intervals in this world seemed to be becoming shorter, those in that other, longer. There would not be time for her to make the dash from the upper hallway, through the living room and foyer, and out the front door and then across the stretch of lawn before the flood was once more filling the spaces. So, okay, she would have to be at or at least near to the front door when next the house shifted back to the dry world. If ever it did . . . ? But, furiously, she drove that seed of doubt from her mind.

Shedding her robe and kicking off the shoon, she grasped the handrail and stepped deliberately down into the icy, muddy waters, now only six inches or so below the floor of the upper hallway. She continued down the unseen steps until she was waist-deep, then, crouching slightly, she kicked herself toward the door. She dog-paddled and scissors-kicked, for the ceiling was too close to the water surface for her best swimming strokes.

Halfway across the room, she realized that the whole of the picture window had been smashed in and debated remaining there to make her frantic egress, then remembered that that window would be whole, unbroken, and impassable in the world of Whyffler Hall.

For a long, frightening moment, her seeking hands could not find the door. With an irrepressible sob of frustration and fear, she took a deep breath and dove beneath the surface, feeling blindly before her, for her eyes could see not even inches in the dark water. Down she drove her body, deeper into the swirling currents. Then, just as one outstretched hand touched the floor . . .

She found herself falling headfirst toward that hard, dry, sun-dappled hardwood floor!

Gasping in the welcome air, she caught almost all her weight on her hands and, completely disregarding a slightly skinned knee, dashed through the open door. The weed-grown patch of lawn lay ahead, and it seemed to stretch on to the ends of the earth. Momentarily, she expected to be engulfed in the raging, flood-level Potomac River. Suddenly she sped, full-tilt, into a thick-grown boxwood. Then Krystal surrendered to her repressed emotions. Sobbing with relief, she collapsed onto one of the graveled paths of the formal gardens of Whyffler Hall.

For almost a minute before it was forever gone, the awe-struck servants and soldiers saw the always strange brick-and-board house half submerged in a rushing torrent of brownish water. Then it was gone, as if it never had been, and the shrubs and hedges in the space it had occupied—or had it ever?—stood as green and perfect as the rest of the garden expanse.

Many of the folk assembled moaned and cried out, many more crossed themselves, fumbling for crosses or relics of saints, some of the men and all of the soldiers grasped steel buckles or sword- or knife-hilts, muttering the ancient benison to ward off the Old Evil, *"Cauld iron!"*

EPILOGUE

State Trooper Jerry Erbach dashed the sweat from his forehead with the back of a big skinned and dirty hand, then lowered his beefy body through the hatch of the obsolete armored personnel carrier that the National Guard had contributed to the emergency. Placing the cumbersome headset over his head, he mouthed, "Thishere's Troopuh Erbach, get me th'ough to Lootenunt Gear, raht away, too. Y'heanh?"

Turning to the NG driver of the track, a pink-cheeked Spec-4 from the western part of the state, Erbach grinned. "Gotta keep awn them gals' tails. Leave it t' them, they'd spend awl their time a-jawin' to each othuh 'bout guys they's laid or guys they's gonna lay or—"

The set crackled and Erbach answered, "Yessir. Yessir, I'uz tryin' to get Lootenant Gear. Yessir, Lootenant Martin Gear. Right. Yessir."

Then, after a pause, "Marty? Thishere's Jerry Erbach. We fin'ly done foun' the roof awf Foster's house, whut's left of 'er, leastways. Huh? Clear down to Quantico, almos', thet's where. Naw, no trace of Foster, the dumb-ass bastid, jest a ol' cat an' the fucker tried to bite me, too, wild as hell.

"Well, looky here, Marty, thishere driver says we needs POL, bad, so we jest comin' awn in. Heanh? It'll be gittin' awn dark, soon enyhow.

"He still may turn up, y'know, Marty, what's lef' of him, enyways. But I got thishere gut feelin', Marty, thet Mr. Foster ain' no more in thishere world."

ABOUT THE AUTHOR

ROBERT ADAMS lives in Altamonte Springs, Florida. Like the characters in his books, he is partial to fencing and fancy swordplay, hunting and riding, good food and drink. And when he is not hard at work on his next science-fiction novel, Robert may be found slaving over a hot forge to make a new sword or busily reconstructing a historically accurate military costume.